THE
QUEEN'S
DOLLMAKER

THE QUEEN'S DOLLMAKER

CHRISTINE TRENT

KENSINGTON BOOKS
www.kensingtonbooks.com

KENSINGTON BOOKS are published by

Kensington Publishing Corp.
119 West 40th Street
New York, NY 10018

All Kensington titles, imprints, and distributed lines are available at special quantity discounts for bulk purchases for sales promotion, premiums, fund-raising, educational, or institutional use.

Special book excerpts or customized printings can also be created to fit specific needs. For details, write or phone the office of the Kensington Special Sales Manager: Kensington Publishing Corp., 119 West 40th Street, New York, NY 10018. Attn. Special Sales Department. Phone: 1-800-221-2647.

Kensington and the K logo Reg. U.S. Pat. & TM Off.

ISBN-13: 978-0-7582-3857-3
ISBN-10: 0-7582-3857-6

First Kensington Trade Paperback Printing: January 2010
10   9   8   7   6   5   4   3   2   1

Printed in the United States of America

For my husband, Jon,
for loving, coaching, and encouraging me
through this book
. . . but most of all for believing in me

ACKNOWLEDGMENTS

No book is written in solitary, and I think I needed more than my share of help. First, I'd like to express my gratitude to the team at Kensington Publishing: from Audrey LaFehr, editor extraordinaire, who decided to take a chance on a fledgling writer; to her wonderfully helpful assistant, Martin Biro; and to my copy editor, Tory Groshong, who has an eagle eye for mistakes and really shaped up my prose. I'm very lucky to be in such professional company.

The pundits say you should never let your mother edit your work. Those folks never had my mother cheerfully poring over their manuscripts night and day. Thanks, Mom! My thanks also to Diane Townsend and Carolyn McHugh for graciously reading and correcting my manuscript many more times than I deserved. All three of these wonderful women were my champions throughout my entire journey to publication.

I have the best husband in the entire world. Jon's unflagging enthusiasm for my efforts is nearly beyond this writer's ability to describe. He helped me think through plotlines, built me a small writing nook in our home, and let me purchase as many research books as would fit in our library. I'm pretty sure I don't deserve him.

I also extend my appreciation to British historical romance author Rosalind Laker, who gave me the first inspiration to write my own book. Rosalind, you taught me that to write about historical events is truly "to dance with kings."

Finally, I would like to give humble thanks to my Lord and King. We creatures may nourish, develop, and hone our talents, but we are blessed with them to begin with from our Creator. I am astonished every day that He chose to bless me in this way.

THE
QUEEN'S
DOLLMAKER

PROLOGUE

Paris, 1765. Five-year-old Claudette Laurent raced down the street from her father's doll shop to knock on the door of Charles and Michelle Renaud.

"Madame Renaud!" she exclaimed when the door was opened. "Is Jean-Philippe here? Papa is taking us to see the Dauphine. Can Jean-Philippe go along?"

Claudette's best friend, barely a year older than she at age six, popped his dark head around his mother's skirt.

"Claudette?"

Claudette reached out to grab his hand. "Come, Jean-Philippe, we're going to see the Dauphine!"

"What's a Dauphine?"

"Papa says she's a princesse who is coming from a faraway land to marry the king's grandson. One day, when the king dies, they will become the king and queen."

Jean-Philippe's eyes were round. "Is the king going to die soon?"

Claudette frowned. "Papa didn't say. But come, Mama and Papa are waiting."

Étienne and Adélaide Laurent, along with their young daughter and her friend, lined the dusty street of St. Denis along with hundreds of other French citizens. The day was unseasonably hot, but the expectant crowd was in high spirits. Some of the crowd was also in high smell, from both the heat and being unwashed, and combined with the odor of various animals roaming the streets it bordered on noxious. Standing in close confinement with so many other people gave the inquisitive Claudette an opportunity to listen to plenty of gossip and hearsay, most of which she couldn't understand. She overheard two women talking nearby about the new Dauphine.

"I hear one of the king's four daughters entered the Carmelite nunnery here, and that's why they're visiting here on their way to Versailles."

The other woman nodded. "Poor thing will have a time of it.

She's but a child, and undoubtedly old Louis will send her Austrian entourage back right away. She won't have a soul for a friend."

The first woman elbowed her friend. "Better a peasant than a princesse, eh?"

"Hah! Better to drink imported bourbon than to be in the House of Bourbon."

The women laughed uproariously at their own jokes.

Claudette was still puzzled by part of their conversation. She pulled on her father's sleeve. "Papa, what is the Dauphine's entourage?"

"Eh? Oh, an entourage is a group of other people that surround the Dauphine, either as advisors or servants. Some of them will be French, and some from her native land."

"Does she have friends in her entourage?"

"Well, the people that have come with her from Austria might be her friends, particularly her personal maids. Most members of the entourage, though, have either their own motives, or are under strict orders of the king to watch the Dauphine's every move."

Claudette was puzzled. "What is a motive, Papa?"

Étienne patted his daughter's head. "Never mind. Keep watch for the Dauphine."

Many children, Claudette and Jean-Philippe included, held flowers at the ready for strewing in front of the Dauphine's carriage. After several hours of waiting, the crowd could see the stirring-up of dust in the distance, a sure sign that the troupe was on its way. The dust cloud got larger and the sound of hoofbeats louder as the carriages approached. The cavalcade slowed near the town, as the Dauphine's procession prepared to make a stop to greet its residents.

Claudette clutched a handful of wilting posies in her hand. She tried to peer around her parents to see the oncoming carriages, but the crowd was too thick. Jean-Philippe took up her free hand and whispered, "Let's try to get closer."

With the young boy in the lead, the two children pushed their way through the throngs of people. A woman swatted at them, chastising them to get out of the way. Jean-Philippe looked up at the woman with a winsome smile.

"Madame, if you do not let me pass, the Dauphine will miss seeing me."

The woman shook her head in exasperation, but smiled and let the children through. Jean-Philippe used his youthful charm to get them past the burly fishwives and their husbands. Finally Claudette burst in front of the crowd. Her flowers were now mostly mangled. Jean-Philippe, still clutching her hand, continued pulling her away from the squeeze of eager spectators.

"Claudette, let's go meet the Dauphine!"

"No, Jean-Philippe, Papa will be mad if we leave."

"Follow me!"

Claudette was swept down the street toward the carriage procession. In the background she heard her mother shrieking, "Claudette, no! Come back this instant! Étienne, she will be injured." Her father was also shouting to her, but Jean-Philippe's grip was secure and their destination exciting. She willingly ran with him, closer to the approaching mass of horses and carriages.

The man riding the first horse in the procession was dressed in a fancy uniform of white. He was wildly waving at the children to get out of the way, but they stood there, dumbfounded by his finery.

"Brats! Out of the way! I shall run you through myself!" He put his hand menacingly on the sword belted to his side. From far behind them the children could hear a collective gasp from the crowd, and the faint calling of Claudette's parents floated distantly through the air.

Claudette and Jean-Philippe reacted to his movement and stepped quickly aside. However, by this time the entire entourage had slowed down. As horses and their conveyances were brought to a walk, the children got a good look at the riders and the carriage occupants.

They gaped at the gentlemen and ladies who rode by in an endless pageant of silks, satins, feathers, bejeweled throats and wrists, and ribbons fluttering in the breeze. Near the center of the pageant was the largest and most spectacular carriage of them all. The closed white carriage, shaped like an inverted teardrop, was decorated with gilded wheel spokes and gilded moldings along the top edge. Paintings depicting themes of love decorated all sides of the carriage.

From spires on the four top corners of the carriage flew a hodge-podge of colored ribbon streamers, still flapping gaily even though the conveyance was moving at an unhurried pace. It came to a complete halt next to Claudette and Jean-Philippe. A man who had been riding horseback just behind the carriage leapt down, ran to the door and unfurled a small folding stair next to it. Opening the door, the snowy-liveried servant proffered his arm to the occupant.

Out stepped a young girl only about ten years older than the children on the ground. She was petite and delicate, her fresh features marred only by a lower lip that protruded unpleasantly from her face. She was dressed even more elegantly than anyone the children had seen yet in the procession. Her robin's-egg-blue gown was stitched with lace and many sizes of pearls, and her tiny feet were adorned with heeled shoes encrusted with a matching pattern of pearls. The sumptuous gown was dusty all along the edges from road travel, and her shoes had splotches of mud on them, but she bespoke elegance, style, and sophistication. In her hand she held a small box tied with a bright white ribbon, a white lily tucked in the loops.

The beautiful girl called out in very rough French, "Come to me, little *enfants*, I have a treat for you."

Claudette and Jean-Philippe approached cautiously, their earlier bravado having fled completely in the face of this graceful creature.

She leaned over, holding out the box with one hand, untying it with the other. "Would you like some marzipan candies? Everyone loves sweets. I know I do."

They reached into the box and each took a sweetmeat, chewing slowly. The girl giggled delightedly.

"Do you know who I am?" They both nodded dumbly. "I am the new Dauphine of France, and I have recently met my new husband and now I am being taken to the Palace of Versailles. Do you know where that is?" They shook their heads no, still silent.

"Well, I am a bit frightened, first of the king, second of the Dauphin, but mostly of this strange new country that is now my home. So next time you are frightened by someone on his big horse waving a silly sword, remember me. Remember that even a princess has moments of terror."

The children's mouths hung open, showing the Dauphine chewed-up candy. She giggled again and looked expectantly at Claudette. When Claudette did not move, the princess asked, "Are those for me?"

Claudette looked down at the drooping flowers in her hand. "Yes, Mama told me I should throw them in front of your carriage. I did not do it. I was too afraid. I am sorry, Princesse." A tear rolled down Claudette's cheek. She struggled not to burst into a sobbing bawl and shame herself before this very nice lady who was not even mad at her for interrupting her travel.

"There is nothing to be sorry for. If you will give them to me now, I shall take them with me as a souvenir of my stop in St. Denis."

Claudette handed over the flowers, many of which were matted in her tiny, grubby hand. The princess acted as though she were receiving a gift of great value.

"And what is your name, little one?"

"I am Claudette Laurent," she said shyly.

Jean-Philippe stepped forward. "And I am Jean-Philippe Renaud. Claudette is still only a baby. I made sure she got down here to see you."

"I am not a baby! I'm almost as old as you."

"You're just a noisy little girl. I'm nearly a man—my father says so."

The Dauphine broke into their disagreement. "Well, Jean-Philippe, you are indeed brave. I am pleased to make your acquaintance." With that, the princess reentered the carriage, and waved to the children as the procession embarked again on its journey through St. Denis.

❧ 1 ❧

Paris, September 1781. After a busy day in her father's shop, Claudette was deep in a sleep of pleasant dreams.

"Claudette! Claudette! Up, my child." Her beloved papa's grimy face appeared above hers. Why was it so black? "Quickly, *il y a le feu.* A fire is burning down the street and will be here soon. Get dressed, then join your mother outside. I must go back and help." As quickly as he had appeared, her father was gone, clattering down the stairs.

She lay still for several moments, still half asleep, and then she heard the shop door slam shut. The sound brought her more fully awake. Papa never hurried unless he was upset.

Had she just dreamed that her father, covered in black streaks, had told her there was a fire outside? Surely not. Surely that was part of her dream. She rolled onto her side, resting her cheek comfortably on her long, curly golden hair. The faint aroma of burning wood tickled her nose. Sniffing the air cautiously, she realized it was no dream. Reluctant to leave her cozy bedcovers, Claudette slowly sat up and stretched. She never slept with her hair tied up at night, and a curl from her perpetually unmanageable blond tresses fell forward into her eyes. She brushed it away impatiently. She could hear men shouting in the distance. Throwing back the blankets with a resigned finality, she walked to her bedroom window.

Pushing up the sash, she could see the glow of a fire less than a mile away. Other neighbors were in the street, carrying lanterns, and discussing the severity of the fire.

"What do you think, Michel? Is it coming this way?" the butcher across the street said to his friend.

Squinting his eyes and looking into the fire's distant glow, Michel responded, "No, I think it's far away and will burn itself out before it gets here." The two moved on down the street.

A merchant talked with his wife. "Well, here we are again. The king does nothing to protect the streets of Paris, and now we have another fire. I promise you there will be no help from old Louis for those poor people losing their homes." The two walked hastily up the street in the direction of the glow, as though to get a closer look.

The owner of the Hôtel de Garamond, however, hurried his guests out of the building and into the street. Grumbling and demanding a refund, one portly guest threatened to burn down the inn himself if he was not permitted to reenter and gather his things.

The crowd in the street grew larger and more unpleasant as neighbors began arguing with each other, then took wagers as to which direction the fire would eventually go. No one seemed to perceive any immediate danger.

From her second story vantage point, Claudette was aware of a sudden wind shift that the people on the street could not sense. Waving out the window, she called out, "*Mes amis,* the wind is shifting. Listen to me! The fire might be turning this way." She was completely drowned out by the noise of the street.

Turning back into her room, Claudette realized her father was right. She needed to get dressed and leave the house immediately. She carefully made the bed, and hurriedly dressed in a plain dress made specially for her tall, willowy figure, and sensible shoes, which she thought suitable for what might amount to a temporary flight out of the city. She pulled her unruly hair back into a knot and ensured Jean-Philippe's ring was still hidden on the chain around her neck. Claudette found her reticule and packed it with her treasured possessions. She stuffed it with her letters from Jean-Philippe, a comb, a mirror, and a miniature of her parents. Lifting her head, she noticed that the smell of smoke was becoming more intense. She crossed quickly back to the window. The glow was much higher now, and she could hear distant creaking and booming, as though buildings in the fire's path had protested all they could, and were now succumbing to their fate.

She also saw that her neighbors were now realizing that the fire was more dangerous than they had thought. Claudette's mother was across the street, talking frantically with another neighbor. The neighbor looked puzzled. Claudette knew that her mother was probably babbling in a mixture of French and English, as she did whenever she was agitated. Born of an English mother and French father, Adélaide learned both languages growing up, but could not concentrate enough to use one or the other when upset. She had insisted that young Claudette also be taught English, and the girl was fluent in both tongues.

"Mama! I'm coming down! Wait for me," Claudette shouted through cupped hands. Adélaide did not notice her through the din on the streets. Claudette turned once more into her room, grabbed her reticule, and headed into the hallway and down the stairs.

She paused at the entry to the workshop, then shook her head against the thought of taking along any dolls. More than likely, the fire would be put out before too much damage was done. She passed through the doorway of the workshop into the showroom, looked with regret at the latest *grandes Pandores* she and her father had created, then opened the door onto the street to join her mother.

Her mother was no longer with the neighbor. In fact, the street was now thronged with people hauling carts behind them laden with furniture, clothing, and all of the other household wares that could be carried away in a frantic rush of fear. Crying, barefoot children were dragged along by harried parents. An unkempt man, staggering and carrying a bottle of some sort of intoxicant, came lurching by and stepped across Claudette's toes.

"Ow, monsieur. Please watch your step."

"Eh, you'll be burning in hell soon, mademoiselle. My, but you are a pretty one. How about a last-minute romp with old Pepin before the devil takes us all?" He leered at her with bloodshot eyes, then put his face near hers. The stench of alcohol was overwhelming.

"Get away from me!" Claudette pushed her way past him and moved into the crowds. When she turned around to look moments later, the drunkard was moving up the street in the opposite direction. The crush of people trying to leave the area was becoming oppressive. She could not see where her mother may have gone.

"Mademoiselle Claudette!" She heard a voice above the commotion. Old Jacques, who was their neighbor and a wine importer, was calling to her from nearby. "Mademoiselle Claudette, your mother is looking for you." Claudette made her way back through the crowds to the shop near her father's. "Come inside, my dear, or you will be trampled to death."

Stepping into the wine merchant's shop, she saw her mother get up dazedly from a chair. "Oh, Claudette, I was not sure where you were."

"Mama, I was sleeping of course. Where is Papa?"

"He has gone to help a family named Bertrand save their home."

"But what about our shop?"

Giving a helpless shrug she said, "You know your papa. Someone came asking for help, so he went."

"Mama, we need to leave the area right away. The fire will likely come through here."

"Yes, my dear, you're right."

"Thank you, Jacques, for keeping Mama safe. Will you come with us?"

"No, I'm staying here. The fire may not come this far, and you know my shop will be the first one ruffians will break into when they think no one is looking."

With Claudette guiding her mother out, the two women stepped back into the clamor of the street, and Claudette began walking quickly in the opposite direction of the spreading glow of the fire. Adélaide tugged on Claudette's arm. "Claudette, we should go and find your papa."

"No, Mama, we need to leave."

"I cannot leave without knowing where your father is."

"Mama, please, we have to get out of here. Papa will find us, I'm sure. Besides, we will never find him if he is helping others put out the fire."

Adélaide stood still and refused to budge, much like some of the braying donkeys now crowding the street, refusing to move for their masters out of sheer stubbornness. Claudette, exasperated, said, "Very well, we'll go and look for Papa."

Turning toward the fire instead of away from it, Claudette grabbed her mother's hand so they would not be separated.

The closer they got to the edge of the burning area, the more difficult their journey became. More and more people were streaming away from the fire, and the smoke became denser, choking them and stinging their eyes. "What are you doing, walking into that kingdom of hell?" shouted a woman carrying what was apparently an infant securely wrapped in several dirty rags. A toddler was crying at her feet. "Best you turn back now. You'll never get out of there alive."

Claudette looked at her mother. "Mama, we should not do this."

"I want to find your papa." Adélaide was resolute.

The mother and daughter continued their uphill battle against humanity, smoke, and the occasional burning embers floating around them. A piece of ash landed in Adélaide's hair, but she seemed unaware of it until Claudette saw it and tamped out the cinders with her hands.

They finally reached the outer perimeter of the firestorm. The heat was intense. Claudette worried that she and her mother would suffer burns to their skin simply from the heat. She stopped the nearest man she saw and asked, "Have you seen my father, Étienne Laurent?"

"No, I don't know him."

She moved on with her mother, asking everyone who would stop for her whether they had seen Étienne Laurent. Finally, a young man lugging two pails of water was able to help them. "*Oui,* your father is over on the Rue d'Henri." He pointed off in the distance. "Go through that alley and turn right. You'll find him there for sure."

"*Merci.*"

Claudette and her mother hurried in the direction the young man had pointed. In the alley, dark now that the buildings obscured the fire's glow, they obtained some relief from the overpowering heat of the inferno, but did not stop for respite. At the end of the alley, they turned right as instructed, and came upon a line of men passing buckets of water to quell the furious burning of a parquetrist's warehouse, where the combination of wood flooring and stains was threatening to make the fire even more incendiary. Searching through the sweating, breathless, straining assembly of men, Claudette spied her father near the front of the line, grunting under the weight of each bucket passing through his hands.

"Mama, wait here. Papa!" She hurried over to the line.

"Ah, Claudette. What are you doing here?"

"Mama is with me. She wanted to find you."

"I told her to go with you out of the city." A yielding sigh. "Very well, where is she?"

"I'll bring her to you."

Claudette ran back to her mother to let her know that she had found Papa. Together they went to where he was accepting yet another heavy wooden pail. His face was beet red, but it was unclear if this was from the heat or the exertion. Claudette's mother rushed forward. "Étienne, I'm so scared without you. Come with Claudette and me now."

"Adélaide, I told you to take care of Claudette. I'll find you later." He hastily kissed the top of her head and continued passing buckets.

"No, Étienne, I want to be with you."

"Come, my love." He signaled for the other men to continue while he attended to his wife, and steered her away from the frenetic work with the water buckets. Claudette joined her parents as her father walked her mother about twenty feet away. He sat her down against an overturned barrel in the street. "Now, you must promise to stay here until I am finished; then we will all leave together. Will you promise?"

"Yes, Étienne." She had a desperate look in her eyes, and she seemed unable to release her hold on her husband.

Claudette approached the two of them. "Papa, I'll stay here with Mama. Mama, let go of Papa's arm and hold on to me."

Adélaide took this instruction literally and gripped her daughter's arm fiercely. "I'm so afraid."

"It will be fine, Mama."

With a deeply concerned look, Claudette's father turned to resume his work, while his wife and daughter watched from afar. The band of fire was approaching closer to the long line of makeshift firefighters, devouring everything in its path and threatening to encircle them. Claudette felt an unease she could not explain. "I think that perhaps—"

Her father dropped the pail he was holding and crouched down with his hands on his knees. His chest was rising and falling rapidly. He closed his eyes and began swaying. He crumpled to the ground in a curled position, his eyes staring sightlessly at his wife and daughter. The worker to his left simply continued the fight, handing buckets of water over his prone figure. No time to help a fallen worker.

Claudette's mother made a strangled noise in her throat. "No, no, no, no, no." The words stuck in her throat and she gave a long, low moan. She stood up from the barrel and staggered to where her husband was lying on the ground. "Oh, Étienne, my love, no." She dropped on her knees next to him, and threw herself on his chest. "No, no, no, it cannot be." Her sobbing caused her chest to rapidly pulse in a mock parody of the way her husband's had only moments ago.

Claudette's eyes opened in horror at what was happening before her. A hand over her mouth to stifle a scream, she watched her mother's agony. Yet even through her anguish, Claudette sensed that something else was wrong. Another noise was rising above the din of men shouting, fire crackling, and women screaming for their children. Out of her peripheral vision she caught a flash of the source of the noise. Crashing through the middle of the already chaotic melee was a horse pulling a driverless carriage. The frightened animal galloped wildly through the streets. The firefighters began to disperse, some of them trying in vain to seize the horse's reins whipping behind its head. One managed briefly to grab the side of the carriage, but slipped on the wet pavement and released his hold.

The commotion was now out of control. No one was able to pay much attention to the loose horse. In an instant, all of the fire's madness—the noise, the heat, the smell—receded into the background, as Claudette watched the horse carelessly gallop straight toward her parents and leap over them, leaving the carriage to drag itself full force over the prone figures.

Claudette succumbed to shock and smoke, collapsing in the street.

❧ 2 ❧

Her lungs were gasping for air. She was drowning. No, water was dripping on her face. It was raining. Pain and soreness were making themselves uncomfortable companions throughout her body.

"Mademoiselle Claudette?" A face loomed over her. Papa? "You are awake, no?" It did not sound like her papa. "Mademoiselle, let me help you sit up." Masculine arms pulled her unwillingly into a sitting position. She gradually opened her eyes. She appeared to be in a park. What was she doing here?

Focusing her eyes, she looked up into the face of Old Jacques. His kindly, wrinkled, unshaven face peered with concern into hers. It all clicked into place. Old Jacques had reunited her with her mother, then she and Mama had gone to look for Papa, then the rampaging carriage—

"Can you walk?"

She choked out an answer. "I believe so. I need to stand and walk, to clear my head." He helped her struggle to her feet, handed her her reticule, and began guiding her through the pathways of the park. The early dawn revealed hundreds of homeless Parisians, some under makeshift tents of clothing and linens, some simply sitting in the elements. There was an eerie quiet to it all, as though her fellow city dwellers were stunned into silence that their worlds had collapsed around them so quickly.

"Jacques, how did I get here?"

"I was worried when you and your mother left the shop and I saw you turn in the direction of the fire. Étienne would have never forgiven me if I allowed his wife and daughter to wander about in that confusion, so I decided to follow you to make sure you were both safe. I did not catch up to you until you turned the corner and found your father working to put out the fire at the Bertrands'. I had just decided to turn back, when I saw Étienne fall, then your mother go to him—" He stopped this line of thought. "Well, then I saw you fall to the ground, and knew that you might end up trampled yourself. So I picked you up and carried you myself to this park. You have been unconscious for hours."

"I must return and find my parents."

He looked at her pityingly. "Claudette, there will be nothing to find, little one. The fire spread from there down to our block."

"Someone may have found them and taken them to a hospital."

"*Cherie*, no," Jacques shook his head. "No one will have found them."

Claudette blinked rapidly at him. She felt tears burning her eyes, but was unable to stop them. In a rush, she threw herself at her family friend, sobbing against his shoulder. He patted her head awkwardly while she grieved.

Raising her head eventually she declared, "But I must give them a proper burial."

He shook his head again. "No, Claudette, it is best that you not return there, for you will find nothing but sorrow and wreckage. You will find nothing of the doll shop, either, as passersby have told me that our street is almost completely destroyed. I assume my wine shop is gone, but to fire, not vandals, as I had originally feared. I have a cousin in the town of Versailles, and I will head out there to stay. Why don't you come with me?"

"No, no, I must return home."

"But there is nothing left. We are all homeless."

"I must see for myself."

"Mademoiselle, where will you go from there?"

"I cannot think of that now. No, wait, I will find Jean-Philippe and his family, and they will take me in."

"Jean-Philippe? The Renauds? Why would they take you in?"

"Because I—because Jean-Philippe is my—oh, because our parents know each other." Claudette could see a mixture of skepticism and sympathy in his eyes for this girl who he obviously thought was out of her head from grief. She offered her hand, which he took and kissed.

"Farewell, Jacques. Thank you for saving my life. I shall never forget you."

"Farewell, little Claudette. Remember, my cousin is Bertrand Jonceaux, and he lives just two blocks from the palace. You will always have a friend there."

She looked up, saw the Notre Dame spire in the distance, and used it as her compass needle to find her way back home.

As she trudged her way back to whatever might be left of her home, she noticed that the farther she walked, the fewer people she encountered. An occasional dog or cat wandered by, but of course what Parisians would be wandering around in the rain through burnt-out ruins? At a street corner she saw a discarded bucket that was filling with rainwater. She knelt and peered down into the water, into a filmy reflection that shocked her. Her cobalt-blue eyes, normally sparkling and inquisitive, were overcome by the heavy dark circles under them. The rest of her face was thin and pale, and she had lost the band that had held back her disorderly golden hair, which now cascaded in a tangle midway down her back. She scooped water up to rub grime from her face, neck, and arms, and used her slightly clean hand to run a finger across her even front teeth. Her dress was still sooty, and now stained by wet grass, but the wash made a small improvement in her appearance.

Rising from the bucket, she felt distinct aches in her back and legs that not even youth would heal rapidly. She felt much older than her tender years. She continued her journey through the wreckage until she came to her father's doll shop. She had called the E. Laurent Fashion Dolls shop home for sixteen years, and had been her father's assistant for most of that time, spending her early years sweeping up sawdust and scraping wax drippings from the floor, and later helping her father carve doll figures and take care of customers. Looking around on the street, she saw that the fire had not been quite as devastating to their home as it had been to Old Jacques's wine shop. Probably their stone storefront had kept the fire somewhat at bay. Claudette stepped through the remaining doorway.

The second story was gone, having mostly burned or fallen onto the first floor. The fashion dolls that were her father's greatest pride, next to his wife and daughter, had all but disappeared in a heap of cinders. His newly acquired "baby" houses and their furnishings were nearly destroyed. The few remaining *grandes Pandores*, the mannequins that were Claudette's favorite addition to the shop, were bizarre caricatures of themselves. The iron frames, mangled and probably fragile to the touch, still stood in the same arrangement they were in when Claudette left the shop the previous day. However, their wigs, gowns, and padding were completely gone. It was as though she were looking at a collection of empty birdcages, whose occupants had flown away from an irritating disturbance.

She stepped gingerly over scattered debris until she reached the workshop. The fire did not appear to have destroyed everything in here. Perhaps there was something to salvage? Rooting through the fragments of doll molds, scorched body parts, and tools, she attempted to find salvageable pieces, reminders of the father and life she loved. An hour of searching in the rain, which had now become a light mist, produced some carving tools, fabric scraps, some paints, and one of her father's old wooden toolboxes, into which she put the remaining items. With this small box and her reticule, she left the shop.

In the street, she turned around one more time to look at the shop. Just twelve hours ago she was comfortably ensconced in her bed, secure in the affections of two doting parents and Jean-Philippe, whom she had loved as long as she could remember. Now she was alone, penniless, and beginning to notice a small gnawing of hunger in her stomach. What was she to do now? Her only hope was to find Jean-Philippe. Surely he was looking for her as well. But what if something happened and he had not survived? How could she find out what had happened to him and his family?

* * *

Even at the young age of twelve, Claudette could not remember a time that she and Jean-Philippe had not been the best of friends, preferring his company always above that of the girls she knew.

Jean-Philippe was unhappily apprenticed to a locksmith named Gamain. Jean-Philippe hated being trapped all day in a workshop, hammering away at metal and firing it in ovens that produced unbearable heat. He also found the detailed work of assembling lock mechanisms to be mind-numbing. However, the locksmith would sometimes drink, and drinking made him garrulous. During those times, he allowed Jean-Philippe to sit and listen while he aired his views on the French and Indian wars, on the rising cost of bread, on the evils of the aristocracy (no matter that they provided him with healthy commissions for work), and on the extravagances of the royal family. The boy did not understand much about what he was being told, but Gamain seemed very worldly, and Jean-Philippe was rapt when he had the opportunity to get away from his apprenticeship duties.

When Claudette arrived at the Renaud home, they always went for a long walk through nearby streets and parks, except when the days were cool and short. Then they simply stayed at his home huddled around the fireplace until twilight, and Claudette would then run back home to her parents. During the brutally cold days and long nights of the deepest part of winter, they sometimes went weeks without seeing each other, only to reemerge in the spring, each in wonder at how much the other had grown and matured in just a short time.

Jean-Philippe frequently shared Gamain's stories and theories with Claudette, but he did not understand them well himself and so usually relayed them in a muddled way. Claudette found it impossible to comprehend Gamain's personal philosophies, or Jean-Philippe's translation of them, but listened politely. Conversely, Claudette would rattle off to Jean-Philippe exacting details about the latest carving or sewing technique she had learned, and Jean-Philippe would try to be interested.

After the first flush of chattering, the two would delve into what idle gossip they had heard, then settle into companionable silence, walking along quietly. Jean-Philippe would often stop to boldly pluck flowers from overflowing containers in front of windows, and Claudette would wind them together and trail the floral rope through her curly locks of hair. Sometimes they held hands on their return home, swinging them through the air as they sang silly songs they made up together.

Once they were scampering through the garden of a nearby convent, seeking out the largest tomato they could find. Jean-Philippe, streaked with stains and juice, shouted from where he was crouched, "Look! Here is the biggest tomato in all of France!"

Getting no response from Claudette, he looked up and saw her worrying over something near the west corner of the convent building. Forgetting his very important fruit harvest, he hurried to her side. "What have you there?"

"Shh," she commanded. Her hands were cupped together, and she pulled them slightly apart to show him a bedraggled mass of white feathers punctuated by two blinking eyes. "It's a little bird. I think it fell from the second story ledge. Do you think we should ask one of the *nonnes* if she will pray for it?"

"It's a dove. Papa says they bring good luck. We could nurse it ourselves, then we will have luck."

Always ready for an adventure with Jean-Philippe, Claudette agreed, and the two young teenagers created a nest that evening for the fledgling bird, with twigs, leaves, and material scraps, all loosely arranged in a doll box Étienne had discarded. They dug happily for worms, grubs, and other crawling creatures, experimenting until they figured out what the young bird would and would not eat, Claudette completely forgetting her sophisticated work in doll-making. Two weeks later, they watched as the dove, now named Jean-Claudette, after hours of bickering about whether the bird was a boy to be named after Jean-Philippe or a girl to be named for Claudette, took wing from the box hidden in the convent's garden, never having been detected by the residents.

To ensure what they were certain would be a very good run of luck, they tried for several weeks to find another dove in need of help, but little Jean-Claudette seemed to be the only injured bird they could find. Jean-Philippe suggested just finding another dove and capturing it, pretending it needed their help, but Claudette refused. Soon their attention moved on to other distractions as can be found when wandering just a few blocks from home in a large city.

Their strolls and explorations took them onto the beautiful Jardin du Luxembourg, located in the shadow of the century-old Palais du Luxembourg. They would sit next to the Fontaine de Médicis, enjoying the mist from its vast sprays and dipping their feet into the surrounding water. They also listened in on the conversations of the passersby, many of whom grumbled and fretted about the anxieties of daily life.

"How will we make it through another winter with so little for our bellies?" they heard.

Other people complained bitterly about the royal family, an enduring practice in monarchist societies. They listened to a man who promenaded regularly through the park selling newspapers. The man had a brother in prison for failing to pay a gambling debt. "The queen convinces fat Louis to give 12,000 francs to debtors in prison, but oh, not to just any debtors," he groused to no one in particular. "She only wants to save those who failed to pay their wet nurses. Why? Because soon she will be plump with a child herself and she thinks France now forgives her all her own wasteful spending now that she will produce an heir. *Mon Dieu*, why would any woman need a 400,000-livre diamond bracelet? That could have bought every household in France a loaf of bread."

The children looked at each other and shrugged. They only remembered the queen as a beautiful girl who gave them sweets by the side of the road. And wasn't it exciting that she would be giving France its much-needed heir?

But now Claudette had no food at all, much less a luxury like candy.

She wandered about the four city blocks between her and Jean-Philippe's home, searching for a familiar face that could help her. The streets were mostly deserted, except for a few shop owners who had dared venture back to examine damage to their livelihoods.

Approaching a man she knew only as Félix, a baker, she asked, "*Pardon*, but I am Étienne Laurent's daughter. Do you know what has happened to the Renaud family?"

"Eh? Who? What do I care about anyone else? Do you see what has happened to my shop? My precious oven! My sacks of grains! I am ruined!" He was clutching the side of his head and grasping handfuls of hair.

"Pardon me, monsieur, my parents were lost in the fire, and I am trying to find my friends who will help me."

"My father and my father's father ran this shop. And now it is over. Over!" He had a wild look in his eyes. "And who will help me rebuild? You? Is that what you want? To take over my business? Get away from me, you filthy *morue*."

Claudette stood transfixed. Had this man actually just called her that? She was from a respectable family, and certainly no common woman of the streets. She moved on.

She drifted for hours before returning to the park where many of the homeless were encamped. Perhaps someone there would remember seeing Jean-Philippe and his parents. She descended a small set of steps into the park, and was taken aback by how the area had grown in population since she had left it that morning. It was as though all of Paris had moved into a square city block. She asked passersby randomly, "*Pardon*, do you know the whereabouts of the Renaud family?" No one seemed able, or willing, to help her. Finally, someone directed her to the local commissariat, located three blocks away. She asked a policeman sitting at a desk near the door of the station, "Please, I am trying to find friends. Can you help me?"

The policeman, tall, lanky, and with an air of utter boredom, responded, "Name?"

With relief, Claudette gushed, "Renaud. Charles and Michelle Renaud, and their son, Jean-Philippe."

"Relation to you?"

Swallowing, Claudette uttered words that she had never voiced before outside of her beloved's presence. "Jean-Philippe is my betrothed."

He yawned in indifference to the pleadings of a dirty, bedraggled young girl. He picked up a grimy stack of papers and began casually looking through them. The longer she waited, the more a sense of dread came over her. The silence in the room created a deafening pounding in her ears. He looked up. "Sorry, mademoiselle, we have no listing for such a family. Try the docks. Many families have left Paris that way." Dismissively he added, "If we see him, we'll tell him you were here."

Before giving in to the desire to break down in tears, Claudette turned and marched out of the commissariat. Far from the overnight soaking rain that had finally put out the fire, the day was now unseasonably hot. Pushing a fallen, disheveled lock of golden curl away from her face, she moved on to the docks.

The dock on the River Seine was again teeming with wandering subjects of the realm. How would she ever find Jean-Philippe's whereabouts here? Approaching a man in a captain's uniform, she once again inquired as to information regarding the Renaud family. The man's uniform was ill-fitting on his thin frame, and his brown eyes were large and luminous in his gaunt face.

"No such family passing through here. Are you without family, mademoiselle?" He spoke awkward French; clearly he was English.

Bending her head to hide the lip she was chewing, she whispered, "Yes, monsieur, I am."

He put a hand under her chin and said, "There, there, I cannot bear to see such a beautiful young lady in distress. My name is Simon Briggs, and I can help you. Do you see that group of young ladies such as yourself over there?" He pointed to a cluster of chattering young women, all seemingly from various stations of life. "They have answered my notice for domestic help over in England. Fancy ladies over there need hardworking girls as governesses, house servants, and so on. Just think, you could be nanny to an important family."

"But I'm the daughter of a dollmaker. What do I know about such things?"

"You will learn. There's plenty of training. Once we get to London, that is. Why don't you join the fortunate ones over there? We'll be putting up in an hour or so, and then we'll be having a big meal. You're hungry, aren't you?"

She was famished. But to get on a ship headed to such a far-off land just for a meal seemed absurd.

Briggs saw her indecision. He said gently, "Mademoiselle, are you by any chance a victim of yesterday's fire? Hmm, I thought so. Many of the women boarding today are in your same predicament. Surely you will find a friend here."

Was this a perfect opportunity for her? Her home and family were gone, and Jean-Philippe was nowhere to be found. Both her stomach and her purse were achingly empty.

Claudette made her choice. She numbly walked toward the other waiting passengers, still stunned that her warm, sheltered life had been so abruptly destroyed.

❧ 3 ❧

Versailles. The marriage between the fifteen-year-old Dauphin Louis and fourteen-year-old Marie Antoinette was companionable, if not entirely successful. Louis, slow and dim-witted, did not have the apparent courage to pursue an intimate life with his young new wife. The court, initially twittering amusedly about this, became concerned about the lack of an heir when this state of affairs stretched into years. Was there something wrong with the Austrian woman that she could not entice her husband? The people of France soon sniffed the troubles, and expressed their concern in the streets and in newspapers. Letters flew back and forth between Austria's Empress Maria Theresa and Marie Antoinette, the mother giving explicit, embarrassing direction as to how to lure a husband; the daughter hurriedly replying, shamefaced, assuring her mother that she was doing everything possible.

The Dauphine enjoyed life, even if she could not enjoy the attentions of her husband. She attended suppers and parties, and focused on her instinctive flair for fashion by having dozens of bejeweled gowns made, along with matching hosiery, shoes, fans, and hats. Soon she had rooms full of trunks overflowing with brocades in every shade of blue imaginable, pale gold and crimson silks, Belgian laces, and enough velvet to make gowns for all the women living in the town of Versailles. Decorated and embroidered extravagantly, shoes that would never be seen from underneath the wearer's skirts lined rows and rows of shelves. The entire court was prone to extravagance, and the Dauphine made the most of it, to cover her personal unhappiness.

On an icy January night, Marie Antoinette attended an opera ball at which Louis was not present, he always preferring to stay behind to work on his locks and mechanical devices rather than suffer through social intercourse. The champagne flowed freely, and the fresh young princesse laughed delightedly at her own exuberance and those of her court attendants, while forgetting about the cold weather and the frigid state of her marriage. The wide panniers of her gown bounced happily as she twirled around the dance floor with one partner, then the next, in one of the Viennese dances she had made popular. The musicians all wore powdered wigs and matching costumes in the Dauphine's favorite shade of pale blue, which most courtiers were also now adopting in their own dress. She was pleased to see how the reflection of hundreds of candles resting in crystal chandeliers made the diamonds in her hair sparkle and reflect brilliantly against mirrors that she whirled past in time with the melody. Attendants at the ball who were not actually dancing themselves stood to the side, clapping and cheering as she rotated past them.

It was so lovely to be loved by others, even if perhaps your husband was less than amorous.

During a break in the music, she cooled herself with a pearl-encrusted fan while she sipped champagne proffered by an aloof waiter, wrinkling her nose at the stars dancing up her nose. From the corner of one eye, she saw a gentleman leaning against one of the ballroom's many support columns, staring at her intently. She winked playfully yet innocently, as she did at all court admirers. The man walked nearer.

Up close, she could see that he was strikingly handsome, with huge, dark, almond-shaped eyes beneath thick dark brows, and hair fashionably pulled back in a queue, but left unpowdered. His clothing was impeccable and he carried himself like the hero of one of the new romantic novels that had become vastly popular. His gaze upon her was intense, and left her slightly breathless.

"I am your devoted servant," he said, giving an elegant courtly bow and snapping his heels together.

She put the fan up before her, partially hiding her face. "Why, monsieur, how forward of you. I do not know who you are. You have me at a disadvantage."

"Permit me to introduce myself. I am Count Axel Fersen of Sweden." He dipped his head again in a slight bow.

Marie Antoinette handed the glass to another bored waiter standing respectfully nearby and offered Count Fersen her hand to kiss, which he did with flourish. The feel of his lips and soft breath on the back of her hand created a strange sensation in her stomach she had not felt through thousands of subjects paying homage to her.

"I am certain you have not been presented at court before," she said, thinking that she would have remembered the feel of her hand in his.

"Alas, Your Highness, I have been on the grand tour and have just recently made my way to France. But I am here now, and had been hoping for an opportunity to meet you." His large eyes darkened as he fixed his gaze on her again. Marie Antoinette could feel the room receding away from her. Was she about to embarrass herself by fainting?

"La, monsieur." She laughed in recovery. "It seems that the music has started again and I have no dance partner."

He offered his arm. "Please allow me to escort you and be your partner."

The pair twirled around the floor together in the *contredanse allemande* and other large group dances. Whenever she was passed through the line back into the count's arms, he would subtly rub her back or stare down intently at her. She pretended to ignore him, but she was barely able to concentrate on her steps. She was dimly aware of courtiers whispering behind cupped hands whenever she was partnered with the count. Marie Antoinette remained at the ball until nearly dawn, departing only with a commitment from her new friend Axel Fersen to attend her next salon. She returned to the palace in a state of excited tension she had never before known.

Soon, though, the tension would lose its excitement, as King

Louis XV died May 10, 1774, and she and Louis became king and queen of France.

The couple was terrified of taking the throne, falling on their knees and praying together upon hearing of the king's death: "Dear God, guide and protect us. We are too young to reign."

The long reign of Louis XV—who was once called "Well Beloved"—had begun in admiration of the splendor of the monarchy, and ended in contempt and near-bankruptcy mingled with bitterness due to the crushing taxation that fell heaviest on those least able to bear it—the poor. This was the France that these two young, ill-equipped people had inherited and were hardly prepared to guide.

❧ 4 ❧

Walking toward the vessel, which was sloshing gently in the Seine, Claudette approached a group of three women who appeared to be slightly older than she. "Are you bound for England, as well?"

The tallest of the group nodded condescendingly to Claudette. The second member of the group did not stop talking long enough to notice Claudette, but the third woman turned aside to address the bedraggled teenager, who was already starting to look much older than her adolescent years.

"I'm Elizabeth Preston." The woman, whom Claudette guessed to be about twenty, stuck out her gloved hand in a gesture of friendship. She was in a traveling outfit of pink trimmed in fur, with a matching hat jauntily resting on a mass of upswept ebony hair, and her wrist-length gloves had embroidered flowers on them. She was one of the most fashionably dressed women Claudette had ever seen. Claudette looked down at her own sorry state of attire, and apologized for her own appearance.

"Never you mind," said Mademoiselle Preston. She leaned over to Claudette and whispered confidentially, "They tell me sable is all the rage, but do you know I think I'm getting a case of fleas?" Claudette laughed despite her misery and introduced herself.

"Well, Miss Laurent, it is my pleasure to make your acquaintance. Have a safe journey." She turned back to listen to what the other women were saying.

Claudette saw another young woman on the dock, standing alone except for a small girl clutching her legs. Realizing that they looked even more pitiable than she did, she walked up and initiated another conversation. The young woman seemed eager for companionship, but was trembling. Her eyes were red-rimmed from some unshared grief.

"I am Béatrice du Georges. This is my daughter, Marguerite." The woman urged forward a child of no more than four years. The child looked Claudette boldly in the eye and said, "I am Marguerite. My mama is going to buy me a new dress in England."

Claudette was impressed by the little girl's bravery, but wondered how she had developed such a forward personality. Surely not from her mother. Noticing the gold band on Béatrice's left hand, she inquired, "Is your husband joining you?"

Béatrice's face became suffused with red, and her lower lip quivered. At the same time her cheeks, already noticeable because of their high color, began an odd twitching. "My husband is gone. Gone these last three months from a case of stones. I've been living on the bounty of different relatives, both my and my husband's, but no one wants the responsibility of a widowed mother and her daughter permanently. Our recent keeper was my husband's brother and his wife. After two weeks there, I came home yesterday from shopping to find the notice of this ship's departure on my bed." Tears were welling in her eyes. "What choice did I have? Clearly, our relatives do not want us. I need a better life for my daughter and myself. The English are supposed to be drunken pigs, but surely they will treat me better than my own relations."

Before Claudette could comment, Captain Briggs began blowing a whistle and calling, "Ladies! Get yourselves aboard ship. We push off within the hour." Briggs moved through the crowd, shouting for all passengers to climb aboard quickly. The groups of women hurriedly dispersed. Keeping one arm around her small cache of possessions, Claudette tucked her other arm into Béatrice's, and with Marguerite clutching her mother's skirt, the three marched grimly onto the ship.

*   *   *

During a light meal with the rest of their shipmates, Béatrice filled Claudette in on her entire history. Born to French merchants of some wealth, she grew up in an affluent, if emotionally austere, lifestyle. Her parents had arranged a marriage for her to a very minor member of nobility, but Béatrice had met and fallen in love with a theology student attending the Collège de Sorbonne, whom she had met at an art exhibition. She thought she could convince her parents to break the marriage contract to enable her to marry for love, but she had not counted on her mother's determination that Béatrice marry up and improve the family's fortunes. Several beatings, imprisonment in a closet for a day, and four days without food, finally broke Béatrice, and, weeping at her mother's feet, she agreed to marry her parents' choice. However, early the next morning, she stole out of the house carrying just a small valise of personal belongings, and walked to Alexandre's tiny apartment in the Rue Soufflot near the university. Together they eloped to the countryside, he working random jobs, and returned to Paris a year later with their infant daughter, Marguerite.

Although her husband continued working odd jobs and earning little, the three of them were very happy together. Béatrice used some of her family connections to help establish a small school for teaching young pupils how to play the harpsichord, but when her parents found out about it, they ensured that business dried up completely. Realizing that earning money on her own would be futile, she stayed home and tried to economize wherever possible. Four months ago, her husband had begun complaining of pains in his stomach. At first they assumed it was just indigestion, but as the pain wore on and grew worse, they summoned a doctor, using the last of their savings. He assessed at once that Alexandre was suffering from a serious case of gall stones and required surgery to remove them. Terrified not only of a potentially barbaric surgical procedure, but his ability to pay for it, Béatrice's husband insisted he would recover on his own. He died in bed a month later, delirious.

After a pauper's burial, Béatrice solicited her husband's family for help. Most of them felt she should return to her own wealthy family, and were reluctant to help her. Those who would help would only do so for a short time, and made it quickly apparent that they were not interested in sponsoring a poor wretch and her daughter. At one desperate point, she even went back to her parents' home, but when her mother opened the door her eyes narrowed into little points, and she slammed the door loudly in her only daughter's face. The glimpse she got of little Marguerite was her first meeting with her granddaughter. Defeated, Béatrice returned to her lodgings with her brother-in-law, and then yesterday received the not-too-subtle hint on her bed.

Claudette told Béatrice of her family's doll shop in Paris, now just a hull of debris. Béatrice expressed surprise that dollmaking was a profitable enterprise, assuming, as many people did, that dolls were typically crude, homemade items hastily thrown together by servants for their children.

Claudette's grief tumbled out as she explained how her father's business had evolved from his humble beginnings as a carpenter's apprentice to his uncle, to a highly respected dollmaker who had customers among members of the nobility. She had shared her father's love for wood and wax, and in time became his apprentice and heir, since her parents had no other children. Her papa had always told her that she herself would be a formidable dollmaker one day. Claudette's voice cracked as she thought about her father's dreams for herself and the doll shop, now just a rain-soaked heap of ashes.

With her heart sunk into the deepest recesses of her chest, Claudette also shared her love for Jean-Philippe with her new friend, and held out the chain that still firmly possessed her betrothal ring.

In May 1779, a month after Claudette turned fourteen, she and Jean-Philippe met again after not seeing each other for nearly twelve weeks during the winter. Claudette was startled by how broad Jean-Philippe's shoulders had become. She could even see slight stubble where perhaps he had started shaving. His coltish gait even had a bit of swagger to it. What, she wondered, did he think of her?

They strolled together as they always had, hand in hand as they started their trip back to the Renaud home. Jean-Philippe reached down and pulled a clump of wild irises for Claudette. Instead of directly depositing them into her hand as usual, he pulled one out of the bunch and playfully batted her across the nose with it.

"Jean-Philippe, stop!" she protested, laughing.

"Do you remember, Claudette, when we saw the Dauphine out at St. Denis?"

"Of course. We were little children. You nearly got me into unspeakable trouble. Fortunately we met the new Dauphine, which distracted my parents from our reckless behavior. I also remember"—she scrunched her nose at him—"that you referred to me as a baby!"

"What I remember most about that day was the matted mass of posies you were holding. Not a single stem with a decent flower on it left by the time you offered it to the Dauphine. And most of it stayed behind in your hand."

"I was very young."

"You were very pretty. You are still . . . still . . ."

"I am still what, Jean-Philippe?"

The two teenagers had by this time turned down an alleyway behind a cluster of shops. It was quieter here, and their discussion became more serious. Jean-Philippe stopped Claudette under a stone arch that divided two sets of buildings.

He trailed a bloom along her jawline, the other stems now shoved into his pocket. His face was a breath away from hers. His dark eyes stared intently into her blue ones. "You are still . . . no . . . you have become . . . very beautiful, Claudette. You remind me of the sweet white dove we once saved." He dropped the flower, and pushed a tendril of her hair back, tucking it behind her ear. He kept his face close to hers.

Why did she feel like she could not breathe? Her heart was pounding inexplicably. Was this what Mama meant when she said that the world seemed to stop when she was falling in love with Papa? *Am I in love?* she wondered.

Jean-Philippe brought his lips to her ear and whispered, "Claudette, I am almost a man now. My apprenticeship will end in a few years, and then I will be free. You are my best friend in all the world, and I would have you for my wife when that day comes."

Claudette was paralyzed, torn between joy and the uncertainty of what would come next. Mama had not explained much about being in love, beyond the fact that the stars in the sky would cease movement in order to shine down heavenly approval on lovers. Claudette remained silent.

"Claudette, do you hear me? I love you." Jean-Philippe gently kissed her ear, then her cheek, and briefly pressed his lips to hers. For all of his mature talk, he was as inexperienced as she. He was also unsure what came next.

A prostitute and her customer came laughing down the alley-way, the customer clearly drunk, the prostitute pretending to be. She laughed uproariously at something slurred and unintelligible the customer said. He had his arm around her shoulder, trying to reach her breast, at the same time applying sloppy kisses to the side of her face. The prostitute was supporting the customer and keeping him from falling. As they neared the teenage couple, the customer made an offhand comment about the young boy also being in the market for a good time. The prostitute's ringing laughter and teasing remonstrations diverted the man's attention back to her.

Jean-Philippe hid Claudette's head against his shoulder until they had passed. He tilted her face back up to him and said, "Claudette, you have my heart. I will forever cherish and adore you."

He brought his lips back down to hers, this time more inquiringly. Claudette responded by putting her arms around his neck.

Mama had forgotten to tell her that not only did the earth stop moving, the sun and moon directed their rays down only on those in love.

But had both celestial orbs completely abandoned her?

As Claudette concluded, Béatrice reached her hand across the table and gripped Claudette's in silent sympathy. Claudette noticed a peculiar reddening of her new friend's face. It engulfed her entire forehead and cheeks, cheeks which seemed to have their own emotions as they pulsated nervously under the redness.

"Oh, Claudette, *tu es ma meilleure amie.* I have no one else in the world now but you and Marguerite. Let us promise to stay together once we reach England. If we do not, what shall I do? I'm just a poor widow with a child and no resources."

Attracted to the girl because of her open and honest manner, Claudette was nevertheless concerned about Béatrice's agitated and nervous state. Realizing, though, that she had no one else as well, she smiled at Béatrice and replied, "Friends unto death, right?"

Béatrice's cheeks immediately stopped their erratic movement, and a beam of sunshine spread across her face. "Yes, friends unto death!"

"Get your filthy, rotten, son-of-a-whore hands off of me, you common little turd!" Claudette whipped around in time to see Elizabeth Preston bring her fist across Simon Briggs's face. "Touch me again and you'll find yourself hanging from your tiny little jewels. If I can even find them, that is." Laughter and scattered applause erupted in the room.

Briggs pulled his lanky frame up to be as towering as possible, his face nearly black with rage. "How dare you strike your better?"

"Hah! You're nothing but a snuffling pig. I paid good coin for passage on this ship. I do not recall putting up with crude hands and stinking breath to be part of the fee for passage."

Briggs's mouth opened once to retort, then he clamped it shut and stalked out of the room.

"May I join you?" Elizabeth inquired, although she was already sitting down on the bench across from Claudette.

"Certainly. Are you hurt?"

"No. That horse's arse is a coward. I saw him pinch a passenger's derriere on the dock before we sailed. I knew I was going to set him straight if he got anywhere near me."

Béatrice was staring at Elizabeth with clear admiration. What a bold, brave woman!

"Miss Preston, what is your purpose in going to England? You are clearly a native of that country," Claudette asked.

"I'm actually returning home. I have an aunt who moved to Paris years ago. I am her heiress, so I make sure to visit at least once a year to keep my eye on my inheritance. Once I have it, then I can find a suitable husband." She winked conspiratorially at Marguerite. Béatrice's mouth was now a fully formed O.

"Where do you live in England?"

"In Sussex. And please, do call me Elizabeth. I would like to call you Claudette, if I may. After all, people sharing an adventure such as this should be friends, should they not? And who is this blinking little puffer fish?"

"Elizabeth, this is my friend, Béatrice, and her daughter, Marguerite."

Béatrice recovered enough to nudge Marguerite. "Marguerite, please give your greeting to Mademoiselle Elizabeth."

"*Bonjour,* Mademoiselle Lizabut . . . Mademoiselle Bizalit . . . Zibeth . . . Lizbit? *Bonjour,* Mademoiselle Lizbit!"

The three women laughed congenially at the child's mispronunciation of Elizabeth's name. The newly christened shipmate declared, "Well, if this young lady says I am to be Lizbit, then so shall it be!"

Briggs's performance now forgotten, the three women continued chatting and sharing stories until a deckhand came down to announce that Captain Briggs wanted all women aboard ship planning to seek employment in England to come topside for instructions.

"Well, my friends, I suppose we depart from each other here. It has been a pleasure to meet you. May we meet again." Elizabeth, now Lizbit, stood and made an exaggerated curtsy to Claudette and Béatrice, who had stood up to go to the upper deck.

"Now, when we dock, you ladies look your best. The rich folk will come to the dock to see you and decide if they want to take you home." Briggs was speaking, and periodically poking his tongue in his cheek, as though playing with something loose.

"Monsieur, what will our wages be?" a tiny blond girl piped up.

"Well, now, that just depends on how much your employer thinks you are worth. And you'll be giving me part of the take, since I'll be helping you in getting your situations arranged. No more questions. Here are contracts for you to sign."

Briggs had two younger women sitting near him distribute the contract sheets to the group of women seeking employment, which Claudette estimated to number about forty-five. Most women were quickly scribbling their signatures on the contracts. When she received hers, she glanced down at it, and saw immediately that it was written in English. Surely most of these Frenchwomen could only read French, even if they could speak some English. What were they signing? She peered closely at the paper. Béatrice was about to sign her own contract, but Claudette stopped her. "Wait," she whispered. "We don't know what this is."

Claudette raised a hand to be noticed over the laughter and excitement of the other girls. "Monsieur Briggs! Monsieur Briggs, please, I have a question."

Captain Briggs looked up from where he was collecting signed contracts. Squinting in Claudette's direction he replied, "What do you want?"

"What does it mean about a commission of fifty percent?"

The captain shifted uncomfortably. "You can read? Well, well. The commission is what you give me for helping you find employment."

Claudette pursed her lips and approached him. "You will take fifty percent of my wages for as long as I am employed?"

"Yes, yes, I'm giving you free passage to England, am I not? What, are you one of those learned girls? You think knowing a bit of English makes you better than the rest of the girls here?"

"No, but fifty percent, monsieur, it seems a little high."

"Then you can just go back to France for all I care. But not on this ship! Find your own passage. I don't take with ingratitude."

"Monsieur, I am grateful for your help, but just trying to understand my position. What kind of positions exactly will we have? And we should know what our wages might be."

Briggs laughed and called over one of his mates. "Hey, Jemmy, get your lazy, barnacled arse over here and listen to this. This chippy thinks she deserves special privileges for her free passage on my ship!" Both men dissolved into laughter.

"What's yer name?"

Confused by their laughter but not wanting to be played a fool, Claudette drew herself up as tall as she could. "I am Claudette Renée Laurent."

"Well, Mistress Laurent, you might be playing a great lady, but it's dead serious work. Now sign here."

At that moment, a commotion caused by two women vomiting

overboard, victims of seasickness, or perhaps the several-day-old fish served at dinner, sent Briggs away, shouting to the other women to move off. He threw the contracts down onto a nearby barrel, and Claudette inserted hers in the middle of the pile without signing it. She signaled to Béatrice to bring her contract over, and placed Béatrice's unsigned contract in the center of the sheaf as well. With Marguerite in tow, the two women retreated into the ship to seek Lizbit's counsel. Lizbit was outraged, but refused to say why, merely advising Claudette and Béatrice to leave the ship as soon as possible.

Having been in France a full nine years, Marie Antoinette had learned that royal popularity was easily soured, and, once lost, not easily regained. The public was initially wild about the young archduchess, with her pleasing manner and elegant grace, and delighted to read in the local newspapers about her salons, dinners, and influence on fashion. But when no heir was produced, whispering started that would not stop. A daughter, Marie-Thérèse, later known as Princesse Royale, had finally been born in December 1778, but a son, the long-sought heir in the Bourbon line, was nowhere in sight.

The queen despaired of fulfilling the sole purpose of her life in France. Everyone at court whispered behind closed doors, speculating about her ability to produce a boy. Was it the king or the queen who was infertile? Or was the queen unable to, er, *inspire* the king to his duties?

Her mother, the empress, continued writing letters regarding her intimate life with the king, inquiring about such personal details as the frequency of their bed-sharing, and also the regularity of "Generale Krottendorf's" appearance. "For if the Generale arrives with regularity each month, daughter, you are certain to get with child soon."

In reaction to the constant probing and prying about such a delicate situation, the queen developed—in an eloquent fashion—a cultivated private life. Only a very few trusted souls were brought into her inner circle to share in her new private life, the Princesse de Lamballe and Axel Fersen being primary members of this group.

The queen organized, and participated in, theatricals of her own devising as a means of escaping the oppressiveness of everyday court life. These plays were fanciful and silly, but harmless, and she loved escaping her daily life by performing. The king approved and welcomed his wife's changes, which also included the abandonment of heavy makeup and the adoption of plainer clothes in place of ostentatious court dress. Marie Antoinette could frequently be seen strolling about the sculptured gardens of Versailles without any jewels adorning her neck, fingers, hair, or clothing, and wearing the simplest of muslin gowns with not so much as a stitch of embroidery on them. Many of the senior women of the French court were severely disapproving of this escape from court tradition, and vengefully gossiped that she was guilty of the sin of pride.

Another victim of her new lifestyle was Rose Bertin, the queen's couturier.

"Majesty." The Duchesse de Cosse, mistress of the robes, entered the queen's chamber clutching the wardrobe book and a pincushion. "Would you like to select your outfits for today?"

The queen was expected to select several clothing changes each day. One dress might be for breakfast and taking a short walk afterward. Another might be a horse-riding habit, should she choose to follow the king on the hunt. Yet another change of apparel was required for receiving visitors later in the day, and perhaps a fourth change for a supper party. The queen sat up in her canopied bed topped with ostrich feathers and turned the pages of the well-worn book, each page cataloging a separate outfit with swatches of fabric, lace, and other trims attached. It was her privilege each morning to mark the pages containing selections she wished to see by inserting a sharp pin into the appropriate pages. The mistress of the robes then had the porters bring in taffeta-covered baskets containing the apparel for the queen's final approval.

The queen flipped past the pages of Flemish laces and East Indian silks, and arrived at the back of the book, which contained newer creations. She marked three pages with pins, and handed the book and pincushion back to the duchesse, thinking that her choices created an ensemble Count Fersen might find flattering on his planned visit that day. The duchesse curtsied appropriately and backed out of the room, her face in a scowl over the queen's distasteful selection. She knew exactly whom to see before giving the book to the porters.

Twenty minutes later, the queen heard a soft scratching at the door. One of her ladies entered, apologizing for the intrusion, but before she could state her mission, a loud voice behind her drowned the woman out.

"Madame! This is outrageous!" A large, overbearing woman stalked into the chamber, waving the queen's selections in her hand. The other woman quickly fled the room.

The queen sighed good-naturedly. "What ails you today, Madame Bertin?"

"This." She held the wardrobe book pages out to the queen. "Surely you wish to wear something more suitable, instead of a peasant's costume?"

Rose Bertin was one of few people with such familiar access to the queen, who relied on the dressmaker heavily for the creation of extravagant court outfits. Such was Rose's influence with the queen, and subsequently with all the court ladies, that she was referred to as the Minister of Fashion.

Marie Antoinette ignored the proffered pages. "I have no court business today, so what I have chosen pleases me very much."

Bertin tamped down her impatience. Really, this simplicity phase of the queen's was intolerable. Rose Bertin had built her considerable reputation largely on the queen's patronage. The more extravagant a gown she wore, the more profitable her business, as ladies of the court flocked to her shop to imitate what the queen was wearing. However, no one wanted to wear a commoner's garb. And there was little profit in outfitting someone who did.

"But it is unseemly for the most important woman in Europe to be dressed so, so . . . shamefully."

The queen laughed lightly. "Unseemly for the monarchy, or unseemly for Madame Bertin?"

The couturier reddened, but pressed her case. "Your Majesty," she cajoled. "The people love to see their queen dressed regally so they can admire her."

The famous Hapsburg lower lip jutted out, a sure sign of impending stubbornness.

"The last thing the people care for is to see me strolling about in finery. I am pleased with the light blue muslin and straw hat I selected. In fact, I think I should like a pink sash for my waist. Please tell the duchesse this."

Bertin made no move to leave, her mind still furiously working to concoct a way to convince the queen to abandon her love affair with common garb.

Marie Antoinette prompted her. "You will need to tell the duchesse right away, before the porters have finished gathering my clothing."

Madame Bertin huffed, but realized she could push the queen no further. She departed with the wardrobe book pages still in her hand, tossing them to the lady-in-waiting posted outside the door. "Tell the Duchesse de Cosse that the Antoinette wants a pink sash to go with the splendid milkmaid's dress she is wearing today," she said imperiously, hardly glancing at the woman. The woman gaped at Bertin's coarseness in referring to the queen just outside her bedchamber. After all, most people talked badly about the queen out of earshot, and in whispers.

As for Marie Antoinette, she could not please the people of her country, no matter how she dressed. Only the birth of a Dauphin could soothe them and return her to a favored place in their affections.

❧ 5 ❧

London pier was teeming with every species of life imaginable. The confusion of dock workers, stray animals, and travelers was disorienting, and was comparable to the chaos Claudette had experienced during the fire, less the acrid smell of burning wood. However, the odor of rotting offal that seemed to be everywhere gagged her similarly, and brought her tamped-down memories to life again. Had she just lost Mama and Papa forty-eight hours ago? Did Jean-Philippe and his parents know that her parents were gone? Were they looking for her? She fought back a sob. The sound of Simon Briggs's voice brought her out of her daze.

"You ladies gather round here," he directed once they had disembarked. "We've got some customers coming up now. Smile, show them how agreeable you are."

Most of the women, barely out of their teens, had no idea how to demonstrate that they were "agreeable," and so just smiled and called out inane things like, "Here, sir!" "Pick me, sir!" and "I'm a hard worker!" Their voices were a cacophony of French voices sprinkled with occasional English. Several finely dressed men approached the group, and looked the women over as though appraising thoroughbreds.

Lizbit appeared behind Claudette and Béatrice. "I think it is time to make your exit from this fine company of associates. Follow me." The three women and Marguerite joined hands and started walking casually away from the congregation, slipping away as the customers began making their selections among the newcomers.

They were about to step into the dusty street at the end of the dock when they heard a shout behind them. "You nasty little sluts get back here! I'll beat each of your arses until they bleed." Simon Briggs and Jemmy were running toward them, the other women and customers staring after them. Seeing the trio of women and the small child running away, with their ship's captain in hot pursuit, the other women began chattering among themselves frantically. Lizbit stopped and turned around. "Run, ladies! They want to soil your virtue!"

Panic ensued among the remaining women, as they attempted to move away from the prospective "employers." Some of the women ran back onto the ship, while others scattered in other directions off the landing pier. Realizing his situation was completely out of control, Briggs scurried back to reassure his customers, shouting at Jemmy to "Round up them whores or I'll have your hide as well."

Béatrice had swung Marguerite up in her arms as the three women continued their escape. Lizbit led them down several roughly cobbled streets and narrow alleyways, until she felt reasonably certain that Briggs was no longer going to pursue them.

"Well! That was simply exhilarating, was it not?" Lizbit's hair was tumbling out from her hat, and part of the heel had snapped off one of her shoes. She removed the broken mule and held it up. "What a fine remembrance of our escapade. I shall treasure it always." She laughed, clenching her footwear and shaking it.

Claudette was damp with perspiration and fright. Béatrice was red-faced and panting heavily, with her daughter sniffling miserably at her side. Lizbit said, "My goodness! Did our little adventure knock the wind out of you? I know, let's stop somewhere for tea and plan what to do with you."

Lizbit treated the women to a light meal at a nearby coffee house so they could regain their composure, and offered a suggestion.

"You want honest work here in London, right? My aunt would be of no help at all—she keeps her fortune locked up tightly and cannot bear to see a farthing go to anyone other than her precious architect—but I think there's a better way. Let's find a church parish that would take you in and help you to find work. They would feed you and provide you with a reference, I'm sure."

Getting no response from Béatrice other than a pathetic, pleading look for help, Claudette accepted for them both. They trudged through Southwark until they found a fruit vendor who pointed them to St. George the Martyr's. Amid kisses and embraces of professed friendship at the steps of the church, the three vowed to reunite in the future, after Lizbit became a Woman of Substance and Claudette a Woman of Independence. Privately, Claudette thanked Lizbit profusely.

"Lizbit, I will be ever grateful to you. I will never be fooled by a man like Simon Briggs again."

"My dear, don't ever let any man make a fool of you."

"I promise." She looked over to where the curate's wife was chatting gaily to Béatrice and Marguerite about her herb garden. Béatrice understood minimal English but gave the woman her devoted attention. "I have too much responsibility now to allow myself to be deceived by anyone."

Lizbit followed her gaze. "I fear you will grow up very quickly."

Versailles, March 1781. Marie Antoinette had been in mourning since November of the previous year, when a messenger reported that her mother, Empress Maria Theresa, had died following a protracted illness. However, now she hugged herself with a secret: she was certain she was *enceinte*. This time it simply must be a boy. *Perhaps*, she thought, *I should have the new art tutor for the king's sister, Madame Elisabeth, paint a picture of the country's queen in glowing health from carrying the nation's heir.*

Such a portrait would require a new gown, one that flattered her emerging condition. And perhaps she should be painted next to the royal cradle. A new one should be purchased in anticipation of the heir, who should not sleep anywhere that another mortal had, even his sister. The cradle should be gilded, as befitting a future king.

She would speak to Louis about the purchases as soon as she shared her secret with him. She wondered fleetingly if a gold-leafed cradle cost a significant amount of money.

Oh bother, Marie Antoinette thought. *I have no head for money, and the people see how simply I try to live. Monsieur the king will decide.*

❧ 6 ❧

London, October 1781. Claudette's stomach was gnawing away irritatingly as she stood at the imposing front door of the Ashby family's two-story brick residence. Behind her, Béatrice cowered, while her unflappable daughter kept up a steady stream of conversation. "Whose house is this? Why are we visiting? Do you know them, Mama?" Claudette hushed her, then lifted the bronze knocker, a lion's head with bared teeth and narrowed eyes.

The door was opened by a middle-aged woman, severely dressed in black. Her eyes were tiny pinpoints of gray, devoid of warmth and mostly obscured by a large hook nose. Her hair was pulled so tightly into a bun at the back of her head that the woman's hairline was white from the pulling. Claudette was certain that stray hairs would not dare to escape without the permission of their owner.

"Yes?" the woman asked.

"I am Claudette Laurent. Reverend Daniels has given me reference to work for Monsieur Ashby and his family."

The woman held out a great paw of a hand, and Claudette handed over the reference. She glanced down at it, and Claudette thought the woman was unable to read it.

"Seems to be a reference all right. Who are those two?" she asked, pointing her head toward Béatrice and Marguerite.

"This is my friend, Béatrice du Georges. We have recently arrived in England and are seeking employment together." Claudette nudged Béatrice forward.

"And the brat?"

"This is Béatrice's daughter, Marguerite. She is a very well-mannered child and can even help with duties. She is no trouble at all and is very quiet."

"Mrs. Ashby won't like you bringing a worthless mouth to feed. You'd better be off." She began to close the door, but Claudette stepped forward and held it open.

"Madame, we are very tired and, quite frankly, very hungry, since we have eaten little beyond pottage and warm ale since arriving here. I was assured that this reference would grant us an interview for work in this home, and I intend to have my interview."

The servant stood and stared at Claudette for several long seconds, deciding whether to establish her position and dominance in the household over this sassy young woman, or risk the legendary Maude Ashby anger for not admitting two referenced servants into the house. Slowly she stepped back to let the two women and the accompanying energetic child in.

"I am Mrs. Lundy. I am the housekeeper and therefore all other servants are in my charge. You'll wait here and I'll see if Mrs. Ashby wants to talk to you." She held the reference out in front of her with distaste, and left the room.

Béatrice let out a great moan of despair. "Oh, Claudette, that woman does not want us here. It's Marguerite, isn't it? She doesn't like my child. If we don't find positions here, what will we do?"

"Stop it, Béatrice. We will find employment here. If we don't, we'll knock on every door in London until we do."

Marguerite, who was momentarily cowed into silence by Mrs. Lundy, found her voice again. "Mama, Mama, is this our new house? Who lives here? Are they your friends? Mama, I'm hungry." Béatrice absentmindedly patted her daughter's head. "Yes, *chérie*, these are our new friends."

After a short wait, Mrs. Ashby arrived. She had clearly been an attractive woman in her youth, and still retained that beauty in a cold, statuesque sort of way, with the help of bold hair dyes, subtle cosmetics, and skin softening lotions. She held the reference in her hand.

"So Reverend Daniels sent you to me. Don't I line the church's offering box well enough without him sending me charity cases on top of it all? Surely he knows that I cannot afford . . . that I don't require any more servants here at Ash House." She stared at the threesome for several long moments, tapping the document against the front of her fancy, if slightly ill-fitting, dress. Claudette envisioned nipping the waist in just slightly to emphasize Mrs. Ashby's slender frame a bit, and adding some lace to the bottom of her three-quarter length sleeves. A doll would have never left Papa's shop in such poor condition as what she saw here on this wealthy lady.

A dramatic sigh emanated from Maude Ashby. "I don't suppose either of you have ever done domestic work, have you? Let me see your hands. Humph. As I thought, coddled and pampered your whole lives."

Béatrice shrank at the accurate description, but Claudette took a step forward. "Madame, I am the daughter of one of Paris's finest dollmakers. I am well-accustomed to serving customers, cleaning a shop, and all aspects of fine dollmaking. It is my father's death that brings me to reduced circumstances, but, assuredly, I am used to hard work." She pulled Béatrice in closer. "As is my friend."

Mrs. Ashby rolled her eyes. "I suppose I don't have much choice, or else next Sunday we'll be getting a sermon on 'Helping the Poor' or 'Loving Your Neighbor.' Worse yet, the good reverend may ask us to give up the Ashby pew at the front of the church, and I have worked entirely too hard and long to get that location to have it taken from me now. How the Harrisons would love to see us lose it so that they could buy it." Another sigh. "Very well, I'll take you on, *temporarily,* but any trouble from you and I'll toss you back to Reverend Daniels and tell him you are unmanageable. And try not to be so *French*. You're in England, for heaven's sake, not that godless country of iniquity."

Mrs. Lundy showed them to their living quarters—narrow rooms in the attic painted pale green, smelling strongly of rancid oil, each with a cot and small washstand—and were immediately put to work.

Claudette was placed in the kitchen as a serving maid, and Béatrice requested assignment in the laundry. By serving in the laundry, Béatrice could keep out of sight and have Marguerite close to her. But Béatrice's work was hot and grimy, and utterly ill-suited to her stamina. Her hands quickly became chapped, then swollen, and even sometimes bled from the breaking of her dry skin. She cried often in private, clenching and rubbing together her painful fingers. How did one family create so much dirty linen?

The Ashby family was comprised of James Ashby, his wife Maude, and two twin children, Nathaniel and Nicholas, age twelve. Mr. Ashby was abnormally pot-bellied, with a receding hairline that seemed to belong to a man much older. Years of iron-fisted rule by his wife had resulted in a small stoop, and with his extended abdomen, gave him the appearance of a wispy-haired, hard-boiled egg.

Maude Ashby had come from a modest family whose star had begun to ascend when one of her aunts became the mistress of George II earlier in the century. Maude's aunt was one in a series of mistresses the king enjoyed following the death of his stoic wife, Queen Caroline. George had presented his lovely mistress with fine gifts of jewels, wine, and silken fabrics, and she in turn presented him with an illegitimate son. At that moment, the king decided he was through with the lovely Matilda Carter, and settled upon her a Yorkshire estate and £500 a year from the privy purse, considering himself especially generous since he had not yet decided to publicly claim the child as his own.

Maude's mother had drilled into her repeatedly that it was her duty to learn from her aunt Matilda and reject a mistress situation: marry well, and bring prestige—but more importantly, additional wealth—into the Carter family. James Ashby had seemed a good match: a £20,000 inheritance from a recently deceased distant relative, shares in a new shipping company trading with the American colonies, and a family with a spotless reputation. But the colonists had gone to war against Britain, and the shipping company was dissolved. James had spent most of his inheritance—what was left after the purchase of their large town house in St. Marylebone—trying to keep the company buoyed, but when two ships were captured and stripped of all their goods by the rebellious British subjects in New York harbor, the last of James's fortune was washed away.

Maude, who now had two boys for whom she also wanted to make advantageous marriages, did not meet his unfortunate run of luck with sympathy. *Who wanted to marry a man whose father had lost his money in a failed business venture?* Maude would periodically snort to herself and wonder how she could have married such a dolt. And now it was up to her to maintain the illusion of a family fortune, while scrimping and saving behind the scenes, going through her own inheritance from her aunt, until one day a suitable investment could be found that would once again raise her to her deserved social status. At least she had her boys—dear Nathaniel!—to comfort her.

Nathaniel Ashby resembled his father in shape, but was his mother in temperament. And as he desired nothing more than the top position in his mother's affections, his own vitriolic disposition was most frequently turned onto his twin, Nicholas. Nathaniel would devise plots to get Nicholas, a quiet and pensive boy, into trouble and undeserved beatings by his mother and schoolmaster. His latest scheme involved the capture and hiding of a snake and his brother's schoolbooks in a stack of folded bed linens. That stupid ass of a new maid, Béatrice, found them, and the shrieking and braying that commenced would have been enough to waken the entire block. Nathaniel was able to truthfully report to his mother that the books were clearly Nicholas's, and Nicholas did obviously spend quite a bit of time wandering down to the laundry. And so once again Nicholas received a beating and was sent to bed without supper, no questions asked. Sometimes Nathaniel felt a twinge of guilt, particularly when Nicholas would turn his large, quiet eyes toward him, unblinking yet knowing in his thin pale face; but he was always able to push the feeling aside as soon as his mother popped a sweetmeat in his mouth.

Nicholas should have been his mother's favorite, since he was most likely of the Ashby males to eventually recover the family fortune, but instead he was largely ignored. He realized his brother's intent toward him, and even at some level understood it, but the continual torment forced him to recede into himself, to walk hallways quietly and unnoticed, to speak only when spoken to directly. Nicholas would spend hours alone with books, or sitting outside under the trees, contemplating leaves and earth and sky. A passerby would say to himself, "Now there's a fine and serious boy!"

The arrival of Claudette and Béatrice was of interest to Nicholas. Their French accents and mannerisms were unlike anything he had seen before in his quiet existence. They carried themselves in a way that the other servants did not, and they even seemed to take some small notice of him. He took to following them around, quietly of course, sometimes creeping up to doorways without announcing himself and watching them work. He had to be careful, though, that Nathaniel did not catch him.

Of the two servants—or ladies, as Nicholas thought of them— Béatrice was evolving as his favorite. She exuded a fragile nature, and was in such contrast to his mother that he was inescapably drawn to her, like the hummingbird to the flower, beating his wings with a childish desperation. Of Marguerite he paid no mind. She was just a little girl, immaterial and unworthy of his adoration.

Béatrice, instinctively recognizing the boy's awkwardness, would invite him to talk with her sometimes while she was washing, or folding, or mending.

"What subjects do you learn in school, Monsieur Nicholas?" she asked once in her improving English, on her knees shaking her dripping, reddened hands over the wash bucket.

Blushing furiously he replied, "Oh, just grammar and sums. And history."

"And just what history did you learn today?"

"We are memorizing the names of all the English kings and queens, the greatest monarchs ever to rule in the world."

"Ah, yes, I suppose that may be construed to be so. Did you know that your Queen Elizabeth once made sport of France's Duc d'Anjou, pretending she would marry him, but never doing so? All to maintain friendly relations between England and France."

"She did? We have not learned that. At least, not yet."

Béatrice picked up another bundle of clothing and began sorting it. "So I suppose that if the greatest queen of England thought she should be friendly with the French, then we must be friends as well, *oui?*" With a wink, she turned around to find the soap, massaging her raw hands together discreetly out of his sight.

Claudette, meanwhile, was trying to survive the battlefield of the kitchen. In this part of the house, the servants jockeyed for position and recognition under Mrs. Lundy. The staff members were perpetually spying on each other, in order to have an opportunity to report a fellow employee's bad behavior. In this way, the competitor might be unceremoniously fired, opening up a new position for the spy. Or at the very least one might be rewarded for informing Mrs. Lundy about goings-on in the house, and proving loyalty to the Ashby family.

Quickly Claudette learned to stay out of everyone's way, associating with no one but Béatrice, and concentrating solely on carrying out her daily orders from Mrs. Lundy, which usually consisted of the worst of kitchen duties, in addition to whatever else the other servants did not want to do. Her long days, which turned into long months, were frequently spent cleaning pots and pans or scurrying up and down the stairs on spiteful missions initiated by the housekeeper. Unfortunately, the other servants decided they did not like the new French interlopers even more than they disliked each other, no matter that these foreigners were taking over the most undesirable tasks in the household. Jealousy of the educated and well-mannered newcomers created an odd sort of alliance among the remaining staff, and Claudette would frequently hear their whisperings and laughter.

The worst of the servants was Jassy Brickford, a thin teenage girl whose parentage was in some doubt, although she insisted proudly that she was distantly related to Charles II. What young woman of suspect heritage couldn't claim that relationship? Claudette wondered.

Jassy despised Claudette's French manners, which she recognized as elegant and cultured, and completely unlike her own. She spent many days talking to the other female servants. "Frenchy is very uppity, ain't she? Why, just th' other day I heard Mrs. Lundy give her an order to collect up all the dead flowers in the house and replace them with new ones from the garden. Of course, Frenchy doesn't know anything 'bout proper English flower arranging, and Mrs. Lundy made her do it all over again. Little Frenchy Fifi sassed Mrs. Lundy, told her it was impossible to do any better with what was available. I thought Frenchy's teeth would come out, Mrs. Lundy slapped her across the mouth so hard." Jassy giggled at the recollection, and the two maids she was talking to snickered with her. "What airs she gives herself! Why, even though I can claim a certain *distinguished* background, I don't get impertinent with my betters. And especially not with Mrs. Lundy. Who needs their ears boxed all day by that old horn-nosed tyrant?" The other servants loved hearing Jassy tell a story, and were only too willing to agree with her that the two French servants, Claudette in particular, were filthy laze-abouts.

Besides Nicholas, the only friend they had in the household was an undersized youth of about eighteen named Jack Smythe. His big personality more than made up for his lack of stature, and he openly welcomed the two French women. Jack did not appear to have any one specific job, although much of his time was spent running errands and delivering messages, since he was small and quick and could move about town swiftly. Jack lived in the basement with the other male servants, but Claudette had witnessed him more than one night creeping out the window at one end of the attic and sliding down the ivy-covered side of the house, off on some adventure. He always made an appearance each morning when he was supposed to, and never seemed to lack for sleep. It was a relief to know there was one servant in the household who wouldn't happily see them thrown into the Thames.

Each evening, regardless of how exhausted they were, Claudette and Béatrice met in one of their rooms after Marguerite had been put to bed in a trundle on the floor of Béatrice's room, to talk over their day and give each other comfort. When possible, Claudette would bring up leftover desserts and other scraps to supplement their regular meager meals, taken with the other servants after the family had eaten. Claudette pretended not to notice Béatrice's raw and scaly hands and flushed face, and Béatrice deliberately ignored Claudette's noticeable weight loss. They even tried to make light about their existence, each expressing envy over the other's lot.

"Béatrice, if only I were you and could hide in the laundry, far from the prying eyes of Mrs. Lundy and that horrible little Jassy Brickford, I would just iron all day and make the crispest bed-sheets anyone had ever seen. In fact, I would happily *wear* a bed-sheet to get out of this apron and cap."

"Don't be silly! You have the opportunity to see all of the Ashbys' interesting friends and guests. Just think, soon you might get to meet some of them. Not only that, you have access to all of the dishes, and therefore pose a much better chance of tossing one of those infernal English teacups at Jassy than I do."

The two women could laugh and cry happily during these moments, returning to their separate beds to fall into a weary sleep until waking up the following dawn to begin again. Usually dreamless, Claudette's sleep was sometimes punctuated with sharp, dramatic images of Jean-Philippe, whom she had now not seen in nearly a year. In her dreams he appeared in boldly colored clothing in hues of red or turquoise or violet, always reaching out to her with something in his hand. Sometimes a rose, or a book, sometimes the locket she had given him. Always he was whispering her name over and over. Claudette woke from these dreams shaking and damp with sweat. To calm herself, she would pull up the chain from her neck, kiss her betrothal ring, then slide it around so that it rested under her cheek. The discomfort of it distracted her from her troubled thoughts. Usually her mind drifted back to the day Jean-Philippe gave it to her.

Jean-Philippe had become more and more animated on a single topic during their walks together, always talking about what Gamain had to say about the world.

"Do you know, Claudette, Monsieur Gamain says that the American colonists had the right idea. That we in France suffer under the same oppressions as they did. He thinks it is the fault of the king and queen, that they are taxing us outrageously and spending the money frivolously on themselves. He says we should be throwing off the yoke of monarchy."

"Jean-Philippe, hush. You cannot say that about our sovereigns. It's, why . . . it's treason!"

"Maybe. Is it treason to want justice?"

The two walked more often in silence now, breaking their stride only for surreptitious embraces, or for more exposition on the extraordinary wisdom of Monsieur Gamain. Claudette delighted in having Jean-Philippe's arms—now growing stronger because of his demanding daily work tasks and even sprouting dark, curly hairs between wrist and elbow—encircling her small waist as they leaned against a tree to nuzzle each other. Even more breathtaking were his professions of love, and his plans for their future together once he was released from his apprenticeship. Claudette's singular bliss was spoiled only by Jean-Philippe's periodic return to the subject of the exceptional Monsieur Gamain.

"Did you know that the queen hosts supper parties and loses thousands of francs a night playing cards? Monsieur Gamain says the queen spends money all day long on clothes, jewelry, and gifts for her friends. Also, they say that the queen commits unnatural acts with her friends. She has orgies in the shrubbery at Versailles."

Laughter bubbled up uncontrollably in Claudette's throat. "Jean-Philippe, what a ridiculous story. The queen of France, whom we have both met and found to be a picture of innocence, dallying immorally inside some hydrangea bushes! I could no more believe that than if you said she had sprouted wings and was now flying about Paris and landing on trees. I think your employer is toying with you."

"Monsieur Gamain says the queen has over five hundred servants, and that she even has someone whose special job it is to hand her a glass of water whenever she is thirsty. It's a crushing burden to those of us in the bourgeoisie—and the peasants—to pay for them. Why do we need to bear the burden for it, Claudette?"

But Jean-Philippe forgot about the people's burden whenever he held Claudette, and she forgot about the ubiquitous Monsieur Gamain during those moments of tender embraces and soft whisperings of affection.

On a cloudless day in June, the two were on their usual walk and had wandered into the Jardin des Plantes, spending time in its intricate maze. Afterward, instead of seeking a bench ideally positioned to observe the populace, as they typically enjoyed doing, Jean-Philippe guided Claudette farther into the center of the park and spread a blanket under a centuries-old oak tree with a canopy nearly thirty feet across. Once seated, Jean-Philippe awkwardly rambled about his feelings for Claudette. When he became nearly incoherent, she interrupted him. "I know that you love me, and that when we are of age we will be married. Are you trying to tell me something else?"

He paused to gather his thoughts again. "Claudette, I have been saving what little I earn, and I have something for you. It is a poor gift for you, but I hope you will accept it until I can afford one that is more worthy of you." He fumbled in his pocket and brought out a tiny package wrapped in string.

Claudette opened it. Inside was a small pewter ring. The band was simple, topped with an intricately formed knot. She stared at it for several moments, not quite understanding. Jean-Philippe lifted the ring from her palm and turned her hand over to put it on her third finger.

"Little dove, this ring is my promise of marriage when we are eighteen and I can leave the yoke of my apprenticeship. Will you marry me in two years?"

She stared down at the ring in disbelief that this was happening. She managed to whisper, "Of course." She reached up and removed her locket—the only piece of jewelry she had owned until now—from her neck, and gave it to Jean-Philippe as a symbol of her return promise. They sealed the betrothal with a kiss and a pledge to keep the engagement a secret until his apprenticeship was finished.

They rose together from the ground, ignoring the blanket. Jean-Philippe took Claudette's arm in his, patting her hand with his opposite hand as they walked. He whistled happily as they strolled through the park as though it were any other day together, and she blushed furiously, sure that this was what it felt like to be a grown woman out with her devoted husband.

Claudette kept her betrothal secret from her parents, and Jean-Philippe did likewise, knowing that his parents would be furious to know that he was jeopardizing his apprenticeship. Both sets of parents assumed the two were still just childhood playmates, and allowed them to see each other as frequently as ever.

Because Jean-Philippe had a small income now from Monsieur Gamain, their times together consisted of more than just walks and stolen kisses. In addition to picnics in parks, they attended plays and sat in coffee houses. Claudette felt very grown-up to have her first cup of coffee, a bitter brew that she downed anyway because it made her feel sophisticated. Jean-Philippe laughed and praised her brave attempt at liking the popular beverage. Often, though, he remained serious.

"Gamain tells me that the middle class—that's us, Claudette— is completely shut out of politics. The aristocracy and the priests have all the say in the running of France. We make up most of the population, yet we have no influence. The American colonists are fighting to get control of the government. We should do the same."

"But Jean-Philippe," Claudette protested, walking alongside him on the cobblestones down a narrow street of tightly fitted houses with pink and red flowers exploding from window boxes. "Aren't the colonists trying to establish a separate country, since they are so far away from England? We live right here with our government."

Jean-Philippe was confused, but only for a moment. "It doesn't matter; the French people must have a voice. Now, little dove, I have just been paid and must treat you to a custard."

He took her hand in his arm and lovingly stroked it again. Claudette forgot all about Gamain, the colonists, and the troubles of France. A girl in love has no memory beyond what her beloved has last done for her.

As she lay in her narrow bed now, her memories were blotted out by the dull ache of loneliness and misery that had taken permanent residence in her heart.

ॐ 7 ॐ

As part of Maude Ashby's ongoing efforts to elevate her family
back to the status to which she deemed was her due, she frequently staged parties. At first, she invited neighbors and business
associates of James's, not those who were her true intended target,
but a good stepping-stone until her reputation improved. By offering surprise entertainments, such as the time she had a trained
monkey performing at one of her social gatherings, she ensured
her reputation as a remarkable hostess. Slowly, she was building
what she considered her "clientele" at her parties. With each party,
she discarded a few people from her invitation list whom she now
considered herself having passed by socially, and invited a few
new representatives of the elite, whose ranks she desperately
wanted to join. Even though she could hardly say that her parties
were exclusive and her invitations in great demand, still she kept a
restricted invitation list as a way to generate a sense of exclusivity
for her events. For several days she had been mulling over an idea
for further social advancement, rolling it back and forth in her
mind, finally deciding it would be to her advantage, and arranging
in her usual fashion to set things in motion.

She went to James in his study, smoothing her skirt and practicing her best smile. "Mr. Ashby, I think it's time to have another
dinner party. Don't you agree?"

James Ashby looked up from his book in surprise. When had

Maude ever consulted him about one of her parties? For that matter, when had she last spoken to him civilly, without the veiled reference to his inadequacies as a husband, father, and provider?

"W-why, yes, my dear, if it makes you happy."

She sighed, exasperated. "James, it does not make me *happy*,
but it does provide me—I mean, you—with an opportunity to min-
gle with the right sort of people. Not only that, I have an idea that
will set us apart as unique members of society."

As Maude Ashby proceeded to tell her husband of her original
idea, certain to gain the respect and admiration of everyone in attendance, James Ashby gazed past his wife at a painting on the
wall, already drifting off to thoughts of going to the club the following day with one of his friends, to drink brandy and smoke cig-
ars away from the infernal carping at home.

"She wants you to do *what?*" Béatrice was incredulous. "But
Claudette, Mrs. Ashby does not like either of us. Why does she
want you to do this after all of these months here?"

"I don't know, Béatrice. But I suppose I am to do as I am commanded, no matter how ridiculous I will appear. I imagine I will
have the opportunity to meet all of those interesting people you
are hoping the Ashbys know."

"If only you could meet someone who could help us get out of
here. How I would love to miss just a day of cleaning Nathaniel's
filthy breeches. I believe he purposely wipes bugs and mud on
them to make my work especially hard."

Claudette hugged her friend. "Well, I don't know that anyone the
Ashbys know would be a friend to us, but I do know that Mrs. Ashby
is giving me several new dresses in payment for my role, and I plan
to share them with you."

Jassy was furious. How could that little French bitch be getting
elevated to the position of lady's maid? Why, Mrs. Ashby ain't
never had a lady's maid, and if she was all of a sudden getting that
high in society, well then it might as well be Jassy in that position.
After all, she thought, *I been here almost four years, and I know how to
dress hair, I do indeed. Didn't I always do my aunt Mary's hair all them*

*years before she passed? If it wasn't for that French la-di-da and her
mousy little friend, I'd now be lady's maid, and a lady's maid can catch a
better man than a kitchen wench.* Jassy's eyes narrowed. It weren't fair,
and that stuck-up, high-and-mighty kitchen slut was going to have
to reckon with Jassy Brickford before long.

Preparations for the Ashbys' latest party, now publicized on invitations as "Soirée à la Français," went on day and night for weeks,
sending the entire household into a frenzy. Carpets were beaten,
linens aired, and silver polished. James frequently took to staying
out at Brooks's Gentlemen's Club until late hours to avoid his
wife's incessant grumbling about how these parties are just so *difficult,* but it is all part of her sacrifice to save the family name and
fortune, which was just so *unfortunately* lost.

Nicholas and Nathaniel watched with interest all of the goings-
on. Nicholas volunteered to carry things down to the laundry, and
would mysteriously take an hour at a time to do so. Most of the servants and other family members were too preoccupied to notice.
When Nathaniel wasn't scavenging leftovers from Cook's trial pastries, he occupied himself with considering what kind of practical
joke he could play on one of the guests. A spider in a wine glass?
No, too silly—he was getting too old for such baby tricks. Perhaps
he could set a small fire outside and panic all of the partygoers. No,
his father didn't get mad often, but a trick like that would ensure
the perpetrator would be the recipient of a beating, and he probably couldn't pass it off as Nicholas's idea. No, it would have to be
simple, yet untraceable.

In her new, temporary designation as lady's maid, Claudette was
given hours of instruction as to how she was to position herself behind Mrs. Ashby ("Always behind my left shoulder, close enough
that I do not have to raise my voice to issue you an instruction, but
far enough away that I shan't have you tripping on me. I don't want
to actually sense you are behind me, I just want to know that if I
reach behind me to drop my napkin, you will of course be there to
catch it"). The lessons went on interminably. When to say something to guests (only when Mrs. Ashby was showing her off), when
to smile, when to look serious, when to leave the room, when to

say something glowing about her mistress, how to serve wine to her mistress in a humble yet adoring manner, determining the right moment to say something solicitous to her mistress.

The deportment lessons were punctuated with lessons on how to do Mrs. Ashby's hair ("What if something falls out of place? People will simply *expect* you to take care of me immediately."). She also received instruction on how to subtly apply rouge and powder to Mrs. Ashby's face in the event it wore off ("So that I always look my best. It is so important that I look *magnificent* all evening.")

Mrs. Ashby's final admonition after weeks of this training was, "Just think—if you do well, I might actually keep you as my lady's maid. What a splendid promotion for you. And how envious of me the other ladies will be."

Claudette choked back her internal desire to scream by smiling dumbly at her employer. She comforted herself with the knowledge that she would be getting a small, but new, wardrobe that she could share with Béatrice. During fittings she requested that the garments be made a little more loosely so that Béatrice's slightly larger frame would fit them. Mrs. Ashby certainly did not allow Claudette to have any fine fabrics, but compared to the uniform she had been trapped in, the clothing—including one actual gown—was heaven-sent. The seamstress had attempted to imitate a French fashion that unfortunately was about ten years out of date. Marie Antoinette was keeping a busy fashion industry even more hectic with drastic changes in acceptable colors and styles every season. The fabrics, though, were more than serviceable and of good quality. They reminded Claudette of the fabrics her father used to dress dolls for customers, and she found herself longing for Paris and its comfortable smells and noisy streets, for her parents and their cozy doll shop, and most of all, for Jean-Philippe. Perhaps dead, perhaps alive. Could she one day get back to France to find him?

The morning of the party was glorious, nature not daring to disobey Mrs. Ashby's command for perfect sunshine with a slight breeze. The frenzy of the past weeks culminated in one final push of polishing, dusting, and cleaning. A cache of genuine beeswax candles, normally kept stored away, were brought out and placed in the freshly buffed silver candelabra and sconces all over the ground floor. The intoxicating smell of artfully arranged fresh flowers permeated the house as they stood at attention in vases on tables and sideboards. The boys did not escape the household improvements. They were scrubbed until raw, then fitted into matching breeches and jackets, even though they were firmly instructed that they would be spending less than an hour with the guests before being sent to their rooms. Mr. Ashby was dressed in his finest waistcoat as well.

Mrs. Ashby stayed hidden for hours, attended only by Claudette. The other maids were angered by Claudette's rise in stature, but none so infuriated as Jassy. She vented her spitting rage before any other servant who would listen to her. Something would have to be done about Miss High and Mighty Frenchy, she thought, viciously attacking the brass doorknocker with paste and a rubbing cloth.

Mrs. Ashby spent an hour practicing her entrance down the main staircase with Claudette trailing behind her, not too closely but not too far away. A little to one side, so guests could see her new French lady's maid, but not so far out that she took the attention away from Mrs. Ashby's décolletage in her new ballgown, a new design imported directly from Paris. Claudette thought the pea-green color trimmed in silver threads to be particularly ill-suited to Mrs. Ashby's dark features, but wisely refrained from making any helpful suggestions.

Mrs. Ashby's entrance before her guests went off flawlessly, and Claudette must have obeyed the impossible instructions sufficiently, for she was not chastised when they reached the ground floor and the hostess began mingling with her guests.

Periodically Mrs. Ashby sought out her husband, ostensibly to mildly flirt with whomever his companion of the moment was, but really just to make sure he wasn't saying anything too ridiculous or inane. Truly, the man could be so *laughable* as a host.

Once Mrs. Ashby was satisfied that she had approached all of her early-arrival guests at least once, she took up a post in the drawing room, angling herself so that she could see any further guests coming through the door, yet remaining far enough in the room that arrivals would be forced to seek her out to pay court to her.

As Claudette stood just behind Mrs. Ashby, she saw a large, purposeful, perspiring woman striding through the door, barking at someone behind her. Another poor hapless lady's maid, Claudette thought. Mrs. Ashby turned back and hissed to her, "I knew she would show up. Claudette, pretend you do not know English. Respond to her only in French—it will drive her simply *mad*."

Turning back to the woman who had now reached her, Maude waved her fan ostentatiously in front of her face and exclaimed loudly, "Why, Mrs. Harrison, I am *so* delighted that you are here. I was just telling James this morning how very *disappointed* I would be if you could not make it. Mrs. Harrison, have you heard about my new lady's maid, Claudette?" She pulled Claudette forward, and Claudette dipped lightly into a curtsy. "She's French, you know. I had her brought over from Paris just to serve me. I've always said to James that it is so *important* that the boys have some Continental influence. He agrees with me, of course." Maude sighed deeply, bringing the fan into slow motion, overcome at the thought that her boys were becoming so cultured because of her foresight. "The poor thing doesn't speak a *word* of English, but I am *quite* skilled at demonstrating what I want, so things have been working very smoothly. Alas, I don't know if you would be able to do the same, Mrs. Harrison. A shame, really, because it is *incredibly* delightful having a French lady's maid in the house."

Claudette picked up her cue. Emily Harrison peered into Claudette's eyes as though inspecting a new pair of gloves for purchase, then snapped, "I can certainly make my point to anyone I choose. Claudette, fetch me a glass of wine." She pantomimed taking a glass from a tray and tipping it back into her mouth. It was quite clear, and only an idiot would not have understood her action. Claudette screwed up her eyes slightly, pursed her lips, and shook her head. She began talking to the woman in French, saying whatever popped into her head. "Yes, madam, you do look like a garishly made-up elephant, but I would gladly ride out of here on top of you to get away from my deranged employer."

Emily Harrison presumed Claudette was expressing her inability to understand what the lady wanted, so she began pantomiming more intensely. Now she was throwing her head back over and over for the drink, her hand clutching tightly at the imaginary glass. Claudette shrugged and looked at Maude, who was positively beside herself with joy. Emily stamped one thick-legged foot, muttered something about the French not having any sense whatsoever, and lumbered back to the front door, shouting for her lady's maid to call for the carriage.

"Ha! I knew I could get rid of that old harridan if I simply put my good *sense* to the task. Now I can remove her from my invitation list, and the Denbys will come if she won't be here. If I can get the Denbys, then I am just a few invitations away from an earl or duke from their social set." Maude was very close to clapping her hands with glee.

These kinds of absurd interactions went on for about an hour, until dinner was ready and Maude went to find James to have him accompany her into the dining room. Claudette used the opportunity to retreat to the library, to sit alone for a while. She felt utterly robbed of breath and dignity. Settled in a chair whose red velvet fabric was worn but whose padding was blessedly plush, Claudette leaned back with her eyes closed in the dark room, gathering strength for the remainder of the evening.

She did not hear the door open again. The flaring of a match startled her to alertness, and she saw a man lighting a lamp picked up from the candle stand next to the door. His face was partially hidden, coming into full view as he picked up the lamp and moved into the room. He was tall, and carried himself like an aristocrat, which, Claudette realized with an inwardly disgusted sigh, he probably was if Maude Ashby had asked him here.

He moved to a bookcase, raising his lamp to examine titles on the shelves. The light illuminated his profile, which showed a tall, solid man, his light hair curling about his collar. Claudette shrank against the chair, instinctively not wanting to be noticed. The man picked a volume from the shelf and hefted it in his hand. He turned to leave the room and his light brought Claudette into view.

"What the devil? Who's there?" He held the lamp aloft. In perfect French he said, "Why, you're Mrs. Ashby's lady's maid. What in heaven's name are you doing in here?"

Claudette arched an eyebrow and replied in English, "I suppose a lady's maid could not possibly be educated enough to read?"

"I said nothing of the sort. But I would have supposed that a young woman who could not speak a word of English just an hour ago could not possibly have learned to speak it proficiently by sitting in a darkened room full of books for such a short time."

"You don't understand, I—"

"I am certain I see well enough. You have some deep, dark secret you want no one to know of. Let us see if we can solve the mystery. Perhaps you are Mrs. Ashby's long-lost secret daughter."

"Never! How horrid you are!" Claudette slapped the arms of her chair and stood up.

"No? Hmm, well then maybe you are a spy for the French royal house, seeking to determine whether England can be conquered by infiltrating her citizens' dinner parties."

She stamped her foot, hands on her hips. "I am no such thing. How dare you? I am Claudette Laurent, an émigré in the employ of the Ashbys, no matter how humiliating that may be. My father was Étienne Laurent, one of the greatest dollmakers in France. But I am certain, monsieur, you would not understand the meaning of hard work, and greatness achieved through talent."

The man threw his head back and laughed. "Why, Miss Laurent, I am honored to make the acquaintance of the daughter of so great an entrepreneur. The next time I enter your presence, I shall ensure that I am adequately humbled and deferential."

Claudette dropped back into her chair, arranging her skirts. She felt her cheeks burning. "Monsieur, you are not a gentleman, and I shall not listen to another word. I cannot understand why Mr. and Mrs. Ashby would have someone so boorish as a guest in their home."

"Oh, I suspect my family name and connections quite overcome any objections Mrs. Ashby may have to my considerable personal faults." He tucked his selected book under his arm, and put the lamp back down in its place. "Well, I leave you to your slumber."

"I am *not* slumbering—" But the door had already clicked behind him.

Claudette blew a loose tendril away from her eyes. An infuriating man. What absolute nerve to speak to her so. He was certainly not a gentleman nor an intellectual like Jean-Philippe, despite whatever disparity there might be in their social strata. She twisted her betrothal ring, now worn on her right hand, with the thumb and forefinger of her opposite hand, trying to remember Jean-Philippe's passionate discourses on politics. Yet her mind drifted.

Who *was* that man?

The tinkling of a bell startled Claudette out of the chair. It was another of Maude Ashby's endless prearranged signals for Claudette to attend to her. She hurried out from the library to the dining room. Mrs. Ashby motioned for Claudette to pull up a chair behind her. The man from the library was sitting directly across from his hostess, a wine glass in his hand. He leaned back, a hint of a smile about his lips.

"My dear Mrs. Ashby, where have you been hiding your new lady's maid? She is French, is she not? Given how superior they believe they are over the English, it seems that we should show them otherwise. I speak freely since, of course"—he leaned forward conspiratorially—"she knows no English whatsoever." A small titter of female laughter emanated from somewhere at the other end of the table. For the first time during the evening, Mrs. Ashby seemed a bit unsure of herself.

"Why, Mr. Greycliffe, she naturally knows how to interpret her mistress's commands. I am quite good at making my wishes known."

"Yes. Undoubtedly you are. Does your lady's maid know how to dance the minuet? It would be charming to see it danced by a genuine Frenchwoman. In fact, I would be happy to lead her and our entire assembly."

Mrs. Ashby snapped open her fan and fluttered it furiously. This was a highly inappropriate suggestion, but should she risk offending a member of the Greycliffe family, who had recently come to royal notice for some particularly effective trade negotiations in the Caribbean? Royal appreciation usually led to a title.

"I was just about to suggest that it was time to retire from din-

ner and join together in dancing. James,"—she held out a hand—
"would you please escort me to the gallery?"

The man called Mr. Greycliffe walked over to Claudette, made
a small bow, and extended an arm to her. "Mademoiselle?"

She stood and took his arm, but refused to look at him. As they
led the Ashbys and the rest of the company into the gallery,
Claudette hissed under her breath, "Monsieur, I know nothing of
dancing. I am but a dollmaker's daughter."

"Oho! How far you have tumbled in so short a time, mademoiselle. Were you not the heir to a great merchant when I last saw
you?" When she did not respond, he leaned down. "Never fear, I
will guide you."

When the guests began entering the long room bordered on each
side by chairs, the musicians immediately struck up the polonaise.
Mr. Greycliffe led Claudette to the front of the room and slid a sur-
prisingly strong arm around her. He whirled her gently through the
S-patterns of the dance, showing her silently how to remain on the
balls of her feet, with heels rarely touching the floor.

"You are a quick study, Miss Laurent."

Claudette did not respond. She was thinking of Jean-Philippe.
The last time she had been in a man's arms it was to say good-bye
after a walk through a park, not knowing it was to be their last meeting. She felt for her betrothal ring. Still there. This man was taller
than Jean-Philippe, and blond, not with the dark hair and eyes she
had come to love. He did have a fierce and protective hold on her
waist, though. How many women had fallen under the spell of his
tightly comforting grip? He smelled clean, with a faint trace of
leather behind soap. She inhaled deeply. Jean-Philippe always
smelt of soap, but it was a more delicate scent than what this man
possessed. She shook off her reverie. Mr. Greycliffe was one of
them, a conceited, arrogant Gentleman of Rank. She had no interest in him, and certainly he would have none in a French maiden
in reduced circumstances.

The dance ended, and Claudette quickly disengaged herself,
still burning where his arms had been. William Greycliffe leaned
over her hand and said softly, "*Enchanté*, Mademoiselle Laurent.

Let us hope we can repeat this experience." His green eyes sparkled at her.

Fearing that he was once again making light of her, she fled the room quickly, feeling his eyes attached to her retreating figure.

Béatrice was not in her room, so Claudette went straight to her own bed, ignoring the knocks of other servants searching for her on Mrs. Ashby's behalf. Her friend showed up hours later, flush with excitement.

"Where have you been? You will not believe what happened."

Claudette sat up on her creaky bed, listening.

"I witnessed Nathaniel pulling a despicable prank and ruining Mrs. Ashby's party. He slipped a snake—some harmless, garden variety—into the gallery. It slid into where the guests were dancing together. It crawled across a guest's foot as she was waiting her turn in the *contredanse.* She began screeching and flapping around and wouldn't calm herself until she knew the snake was captured. The lady's husband took care of the snake, but everyone was outraged and demanded that something be done about Nathaniel, since it was clear he was the only one who could be responsible. You know Mrs. Ashby—she hugged her precious little boy to her and insisted that he couldn't possibly have done it, even though everyone knows what a monster he is."

"So Nathaniel was naughty. What is so unusual about that?"

"You haven't heard what happened next. One of the guests knelt before Nathaniel and gave him such a sermon about duty and honor that the little brute actually broke down in tears and fled the room crying. I've never before witnessed Mrs. Ashby so speechless."

Claudette almost regretted having left the party, not only because she was surely in for a lecture from Mrs. Ashby for leaving without permission, but for having missed this.

"Which guest was it?"

"A tall man with light curling hair. Quite handsome, really. He did not accompany anyone. I didn't ask who he was."

"Hmm," was all Claudette responded.

❧ 8 ❧

Versailles, October 1781. It was unbelievable. Finally, the queen's dream had come true, and she was safely delivered of a baby boy, the heir to the throne of France. If the streets of Paris were wild with joy and pealing bells, the scene inside the delivery chamber was no less chaotic. Attending the queen's delivery were no less than eight people, not including her *accoucheur*. The king was not present, but came later to tell her that she had provided the kingdom with a Dauphin, as everyone else in the room had forgotten to do so in the pandemonium following the birth. In the aftermath of delivering France with the longed-for heir, Marie Antoinette was, for a short while, portrayed in newspapers almost spiritually as a perfect mother and wife. It was mild compensation for the years of libel and slander, but she basked in it.

❧ 9 ❧

Marguerite's forehead was scorching to the touch, and she had been in and out of consciousness for hours. Béatrice turned to Claudette, her eyes red and weepy. "I am so worried. She has never been ill before. My dear Alexandre died of gall stones. Do you think she could have them as well?"

"She doesn't appear to have internal pain. Let's hope it is just a passing fever. Did you bring more cloths from the laundry?"

The two women took turns at Marguerite's side, applying cold compresses and washing the rags in a basin to refresh and cool them again. After seeing Béatrice secretively bundle up rags in the laundry, Nicholas had quietly followed her upstairs, and saw that the daughter was abed, her eyes glazed with obvious sickness. He periodically crept up to see how the girl was faring, and wondered what he could do to aid Béatrice, the object of his worship.

After a day of slipping upstairs to watch the women caring for the girl, he summoned the nerve to make his presence known when Claudette was not there. "Miss Béatrice?" He cleared his throat.

Béatrice jumped, accidentally kicking the water basin and sloshing water on the floor. "Nicholas! How you frightened me. Whatever are you doing on the servants' floor?"

He looked down at his shoes and mumbled, "Just seeing what is keeping you up here all the time."

"My daughter is sick. But please, you mustn't tell your mother. She would turn us out for certain, and we would have nowhere to go."

Nicholas glowed inwardly at the opportunity to keep a secret for Béatrice. "No, miss, I would never do that. You can rely on me. You see, I—"

To his chagrin, Claudette showed up.

"Why, Nicholas, why are you up here in the attic? Your mother would cane you if she knew you were dawdling about in the attic with the servants."

"Yes, ma'am." His eyes never moved from Béatrice.

Moments passed; Claudette grew impatient. "Nicholas, what can we do for you?"

He pointed to the bed. "Does she need medicine? I can get it for you."

Béatrice asked, "You can? From where?"

He hedged. "I just can. What do you need?"

Béatrice ticked off on her fingers a decoction of tamarind, ice chips, and also some marshmallow roots so she could make her own soothing drink for her daughter. Claudette chimed in to request more blankets and another pillow, since Marguerite's had been soaked through with sweat. Nicholas returned in less than an hour with everything, presenting the bundle to Béatrice as though he had slain a dragon and was presenting the trophy to his queen.

Claudette held up the bottle of medicine made from tamarind. "How were you able to get this?"

He did not reply, but gazed at Béatrice, who praised his efforts. "We are indeed indebted to you, Nicholas. How can we ever repay you?"

The boy blushed scarlet and fled the room. However, he returned each evening to check on the women and see what they needed.

On the third day, the child's fever broke. As she regained strength, she complained of boredom. Béatrice conferred with Claudette. "Do you think Mrs. Ashby would let us ask Nicholas for some of his toys for Marguerite to play with?"

"Never. Besides, his interests are too old for her. We'll have to think of something to make to entertain her."

Claudette was able to find some primer books from the Ashby library, which she stealthily took upstairs for Marguerite, but the girl's concentration was still low, and she insisted that reading hurt her eyes. Claudette returned the books to the library, pausing to sit in the chair where she had been intruded upon by that dreadful Mr. Greycliffe. The aristocrats were as pompous and self-serving in England as they were in France. To think how hard her papa had worked to build a name for himself, and never a conceited bone in his body, and this Greycliffe fellow with his fine clothing and firm hands just dismisses Papa's famous creations as nothing. Why, the man never laid his eyes on one of Papa's justifiably popular *grandes Pandores*, his baby houses, or his miniature dolls, or his . . . oh! Of course!

Claudette jumped out of the chair and ran to the attic, nearly toppling over Mrs. Lundy in her haste. Mrs. Lundy yelled at her, but Claudette had no time to stop. She dashed up the narrow back stairs, skirts in hand, until she reached her tiny room. Reaching under the bed, she pulled out her forgotten trunk of dollmaking supplies. Perhaps now she could bring back the spark to Marguerite's eyes.

With Béatrice's help, Claudette worked far into the night to fashion two crude dolls for Marguerite, both roughly carved from scraps of stored firewood. One wore black breeches made from a discarded leather glove and the other a muslin dress whose fabric had been snipped from Béatrice's apron. They crushed bruised strawberries to dye the fabric.

Marguerite was enchanted. "Mama! For me?" She petted the dolls and put them to her face. "These are my new *bébés*."

The next evening, after a particularly trying day with Jassy, Claudette checked in on Marguerite. Béatrice was sitting on the side of the bed, listening to her daughter play-act with the dolls.

"Now, Mrs. Ashby, I say you must not be so rude to your servants, especially Madame du Georges, who is *much* smarter and nicer than you. I shall have to take a switch to you if you cannot behave properly. And you, Mr. Ashby, I expect you would like to be at Brooks's right now, wouldn't you?" Marguerite covered Mr. Ashby with her pillow and continued admonishing the Mrs. Ashby doll. Béatrice clapped lightly and hugged her daughter. A soft knock on Béatrice's door interrupted them.

Their fellow servant, Jack Smythe, entered, delivering a summons for Claudette to attend to her mistress after dinner before she and Mr. Ashby went calling on some friends. Claudette turned away from Jack and rolled her eyes.

The young man saw Marguerite playing with the Mrs. Ashby doll on the bed and asked about it. Marguerite immediately brought Mr. Ashby out from his hiding place to show them both to Jack. "Mademoiselle Laurent and Mama made them for me," she enthused. "They are my new *bébés*, although when I grow up I shall have ten real babies of my own."

Jack touched the dolls speculatively. He looked at Claudette. "Do you have more of these?"

"No, I just put those together to comfort Marguerite. Why?"

"I could sell them at Surrey Street Market. Can you make more by next week?"

"I suppose I could. Does Mrs. Ashby send you to the market regularly?"

"No, that's my own business on my own time. I'll split the money we make in half with you."

"In half! But I have to purchase materials for making the dolls. Wood, paints, fabrics, needles, scissors, that sort of thing. I'll agree to half, but you have to gather up all of the supplies I need."

"Agreed."

So the bargain was struck, and, with Béatrice's assistance, Claudette got to work on creating a dozen crude dolls for the following week, working far into each night, and wondering exhaustedly each morning how Jack managed to spend his nighttime hours prowling the streets.

Claudette's work reminded her of her apprenticeship under her father. She knew how to measure and cut small planks of appropriate width, using all available wood as efficiently as possible, and how to sand them to a smooth finish and then bring out the deep grain and color of the wood by wiping the boards with wet cloths. As she practiced her skills she experienced many a cut thumb and splintered palm, until she once again developed the finesse necessary for handling the wood parts. She then spent many nights bent over the tiny individual finished pieces of incomplete dolls, rag and wax in hand, buffing furiously to bring each piece to a final, shiny gloss. What little money she had was rapidly expended on tallow candles to illuminate her midnight work.

But it was truly the carving that required the most concentration. Claudette spent hours carving the rudimentary dolls. From a roughly-hewn block of wood, she used one of the few paring tools available from her father's box to first shape a round head, followed by long, shaped arms with rounded knobs for hands, a straight trunk with slots in the top and bottom to accommodate limbs, and legs and knobbed feet. She joined the limbs to the torso using twine, to give them range of motion.

She then fashioned wigs out of yarn or narrow strips of cloth, gained from discarded rags she took from the trash bin when Mrs. Lundy was not watching. The paints Jack was able to find were poor quality and looked faded almost as soon as they were applied, but she had Béatrice apply coat after coat of eyes, lips, and cheeks until she was pleased with their appearance.

Each evening, Jack would quietly scratch at Claudette's door to see what her progress was, almost as excited by the project as the two women were.

The most difficult part of creating the dolls was keeping it secret from the other servants, particularly Jassy, who seemed to have instinctive talent for ferreting out the activities of the entire domestic staff. The girl's ruthless spying and reporting to Mrs. Lundy had cowed most of the servants, but Claudette refused to succumb to her intimidation.

"So, Miss Frenchy Laurent," Jassy said as she sidled up to Claudette unexpectedly one day while she was chopping vegetables, part of her normal routine when she was not being elevated to lady's maid. "I notice you've been spending time with Jack Smythe." Her voice was low and sly. "Would you be needin' someone to guard your door for you at night? I could make sure no one bothers you."

Claudette slammed down her knife. "You nasty little chuff. Have you nothing better to do than buzz about tormenting every-

one around you like a wasp? For someone of such *royal* blood, you
have no more class than the tomcats I throw scraps to in the side
yard. And your temperament is far worse."

Jassy was momentarily stunned into silence but recovered herself. "So there *is* something between you and Jack. I'll find out
what it is, and then I'll make sure Mrs. Lundy knows. Of course,"—
she began sauntering away—"if I don't find out the truth, I'll just
make something up. You should have learned by now not to cross
me."

Claudette returned to her work, chopping and slicing furiously
for her employer's evening meal. Between Mrs. Ashby's sly servants and her arrogant male guests, Claudette could not find a moment's peace.

Jack was true to his word, and sold the first three dolls Claudette
had given him in less than a week. She now had four shillings in
profit, and tried to give half of it to Béatrice, but the other woman
insisted that Claudette keep it. "I have no head for money," she
said. "You keep it and use it to help us find a way out of this
wretched house."

Claudette jingled the coins in her hands, elated to have a tiny
bit of money that Mrs. Ashby knew nothing about, then tumbled
the coins into an envelope stored in her small chest of doll supplies. The chest was kept hidden under her bed.

As Jack found more and more outlets for selling the dolls,
Claudette and Béatrice spent many more sleepless nights producing them. They were exhausted, but Jack kept requesting more,
and the shillings were piling up in the chest. He never discussed
what he was doing with his share of the profits, and the women instinctively knew not to ask. After all, they shared nothing with
him, either.

Jassy could frequently be seen lurking outside their doors, eyes
opening innocently when caught. She always offered an excuse for
her presence—"Mrs. Lundy needs you to go with her to the
butcher's," or "The mistress needs a button sewn"—but was obviously swept away with curiosity as to why Claudette and Béatrice
were retreating to their tiny rooms as often as possible.

When she had saved a little money, Claudette gave some to Jack to go out and purchase an additional set of carving and painting tools, so that she and Béatrice could work on two dolls at once. Claudette usually had to help Béatrice through each step. What Béatrice lacked in experience, she more than made up for in enthusiasm and a desire to help. Her chatter while they worked usually centered on saving enough to get their own place. Claudette's thoughts, kept to herself, stayed firmly focused on saving enough money to return to France and find Jean-Philippe.

Each year at Easter, Maude Ashby brought both her family and servants to St. George the Martyr's for services. After assisting the Ashby family to their seats, the servants were sent back to a rear pew to bask in Mrs. Ashby's generosity. The current year was no exception to the routine.

The Ashby household arrived just before services were to start, and all of the servants, Claudette and Béatrice included, walked to the front of the church and waited stoically while the Ashbys settled themselves. At the last moment, Maude signaled to Claudette that she should sit in the high-backed, carved oak pew with the family.

Claudette attempted to settle her trepidation over what was happening. Why wasn't she released with the other servants? Was this some interesting new form of punishment?

She watched as the other servants retreated to the back under the staring eyes of the good reverend and the congregation. Jassy Brickford, her eyes slitted and stormy, hissed at Claudette as she walked by, "Well ain't you just the duchess!"

Mrs. Lundy discreetly pinched the girl to move her along, but also shot Claudette a look of derision.

Across from Claudette, Maude leaned over to her husband and whispered, "Did you see, James? Everyone is awestruck by how many servants we have now."

"My dear, everyone is stricken, but probably because they are appalled that we paraded—"

"And Reverend Daniels must be overly impressed, to see his

little orphan girl being treated so specially by us. We must be sure to tell him afterward that she has been elevated to lady's maid."

"I hardly think he cares if—"

"I wonder if we should place him on the invitation list for our next garden tea. It would lend an air of holy approval, don't you think?"

"Well, I—"

Their conversation was interrupted by the start of the service. As Reverend Daniels asked everyone to bow their heads in prayer, Claudette kept one eye on Mrs. Ashby, whose lips moved in earnest supplication for divine approval on her plans for an upcoming festivity.

Claudette shut that eye, and concentrated on her own request for intervention on her dismal and unpromising circumstances. So intent was she on her own prayers that she only felt the faintest movement of someone moving up the aisle to sit in the pew across from the Ashbys'.

As Reverend Daniels intoned his sermon, she lifted her eyes to take note of the newcomer, who was seated with his profile to her. Obviously a gentleman if sitting in a front pew, tall, blond hair curling at the nape of his neck . . . why, it was that Mr. Greycliffe. He looked over at Claudette and greeted her with the slightest wink in his otherwise very serious face.

How dare he, she thought. What was he doing at the Ashbys' church? Was he a member of this congregation? Or was he simply here to torment her?

Or was the Almighty simply taking an opportunity to mock her?

Claudette nodded civilly to Mr. Greycliffe and then focused on Reverend Daniels, her hands folded together in her lap to keep them from trembling. Maude Ashby was visibly quivering with excitement, and trying—quite unsuccessfully—to discreetly nudge her husband while rolling her eyes toward Mr. Greycliffe. Next to Claudette, Nathaniel was scuffing his feet on the floor and wriggling impatiently, while his brother sat serenely, the only member of the pew actually paying attention to the sermon.

At the conclusion of the service, Claudette stood quickly to leave, but Mrs. Ashby was quicker. She also stood, which was the cue for the rest of her family to stand, thus blocking Claudette's easy exit from the pew.

"Why, Mr. Greycliffe, what a delight to see you again so soon. I had nearly forgotten that your family attends this church when in London. I'd like to be in more frequent attendance, of course, but my duties as a wife, mother, and society hostess are simply so *demanding*, making it difficult to get away each Sunday. Of course, we always like to make sure we grant the servants at least one visit each year, which is only the charitable Christian thing to do."

Still behind the pulpit, Reverend Daniels was frowning upon the oblivious Maude Ashby as she worked on ingratiating herself with a respected member of the congregation without bothering to step outside St. George's sanctuary.

"Yes," William replied. "Charity begins at home, as the Good Book says. Perhaps I can escort you to the confectioner's for some iced creams. And let's continue being charitable and invite along everyone in your party. Your husband and I have some business details to discuss anyway, don't we, Ashby?"

"Ah, so you've decided to move forward on my proposal. Excellent. Why don't we—"

"Mr. Greycliffe, it certainly is not necessary to invite the servants, as they have had their outing for the day. In fact, I was planning to give them the rest of the day off. Claudette, you may have the rest of the day to yourself, and we won't expect you back until this evening. Let the others know, will you?"

Humiliated at being condescended to in front of Mr. Greycliffe, she struggled past the family and into the aisle without responding, not caring about the lecture she would receive later for her disrespect.

After passing on Mrs. Ashby's message to the other household staff—for which even Jassy was willing to part with a small smile toward the detested Frenchy Fifi—Claudette asked Béatrice to spend the afternoon off without her, as she just wanted to be alone. She ignored the questioning look in her friend's eyes, and fled outside the church to escape what would surely be another painful interaction with the Ashbys and Mr. Greycliffe when they made their way to the door of the church.

She looked around wildly for a place of refuge, somewhere to catch her breath and her nerves while her employers and her tormentor gave their respects to the reverend and prepared to depart. A small cemetery adjoining the church contained a few dozen graves, and in the center of it a large oak tree provided a brand new canopy, its spring leaves bright green from their first unfurling. Under the tree were two benches, one facing the church and the other facing an ivy-covered brick wall that separated the churchyard from the busy street beyond. She had spent time there grieving upon her initial arrival in London. Reaching this bench, Claudette sank down heavily, her chin in both palms and her elbows on her knees as she despaired over her situation.

Was this to be her life until she died? She fit nowhere inside the Ashby household, being considered uppity by the other servants and barely tolerable by Mrs. Ashby. *I have no designs on being a lady, I just want to go back to creating fashion dolls.* She'd never be able to escape her wretched position and get back to France. If only she could—

"Aren't you worried people might think you're daft, sitting there muttering to yourself?"

Startled, Claudette turned to find William Greycliffe behind her, one foot up on the other bench, his now customary smirk focused on her. How positively aggravating he was!

"Why are you here, Mr. Greycliffe? Shouldn't you be stuffing my employers full of sweets and talking about the latest estate you've purchased or whatever it is people of quality discuss? Or did you feel a pressing need to plague me before you could enjoy yourself properly?"

He swung his leg back down from the bench and approached Claudette, sitting uninvited and unsettlingly close to her.

"Does your domestic situation trouble you, Miss Laurent?"

"How could it not? You've seen for yourself how Mrs. Ashby regards me. If she knew that my father owned one of the finest doll shops in France, patronized by the Bourbon nobility, perhaps she might have been a tad bit kinder. But she would never believe me even if I told her. Of course, to someone like you it probably seems a trifle that I would be distressed."

"It's not a trifle to me at all. You see, I understand what it means to be trapped by circumstances."

"You? You're an up-and-coming country gentleman without a care. Society ladies probably fall in l . . . probably fall for your easy charms, which of course I would never do—"

"I would never expect it of you, Miss Laurent."

"And you're probably surrounded by others like me that you can order about and treat like mongrel curs."

"Do you think so ill of me that you assume I am a cruel master? Do you think my limited association with the Ashbys makes me one of them? Miss Laurent, you have many things to learn about me, and we continue to lose time. Soon it will be too late."

"What do you mean?"

"Never mind." He shook his head as if clearing his own muddled thoughts.

He shifted his gaze toward the churchyard and Claudette turned hers to follow. The congregation was gone except for the Ashby family, now lingering on the steps in front of the church. Catching William's glance, Mrs. Ashby waved tentatively to him. But her pained expression told Claudette everything she needed to know about her employer's opinion of William Greycliffe cavorting about with her among the gravestones.

"Miss Laurent, what do you wish to do most in this world?"

"Become the finest dollmaker in England." *What? Why didn't I say that I wanted to return to France?*

He gently lifted one of her hands from her lap. "Then that is what you should do."

He brushed her ungloved fingers with his lips for just an instant, but the gasp escaping Mrs. Ashby caused sparrows in the oak tree to fly off in fright. Claudette herself was alarmed by the tiny seed of warmth that began to grow in her by his move, which had to be due to his proper manners and nothing else. Definitely nothing else.

William stood and bowed courteously to her. "Until we meet

again." He moved off to fulfill his promise to the Ashby family for iced creams.

When Claudette returned that evening, Mrs. Ashby's shock had transformed into complete denial. She made no mention of Mr. Greycliffe's display of affection for a mere servant, and as usual none of the other servants were talking to her much at all. Life for Claudette was as it had always been, and soon she began to wonder whether the incident under the oak tree had ever happened at all.

And so the Ashbys began preparing for yet another of their interminable dinner parties. Claudette, who had slipped permanently into her role of lady's maid—without any of the prestige and grandeur Mrs. Ashby seemed to think would attach to her for it—received a new round of deportment instructions.

While Mrs. Ashby chattered on endlessly, Claudette dreamed of escape. What could she do to free herself from the shackles of this employment? *All of the servants hate me, and my employer thinks I am honored to serve her. I have to consider Béatrice and Marguerite. They could not survive without me. If only I could save enough money to buy passage for the three of us back to France.*

Paris was safe and familiar. London was full of atrocious employers, vile fellow servants, and handsome men by whom she was paradoxically repelled and obsessed. No, it was far too senseless to remain in England. She must return to France. But there was little money between the two women. For the privilege of being housed in their domestic positions, they were paid meager wages. A pair of shoes might cost a week's pay. Damaged household items always resulted in docked pay, and it was not always the guilty party who was docked. They had saved a little money from Jack's secret entrepreneurial schemes, but how would they have income if they left the Ashby residence?

She wondered for the thousandth time if Jean-Philippe was still alive in France. Was he looking for her? If he was alive, surely he was still searching. Perhaps she could send a letter. But to whom? Where? Her entire block had been engulfed in flames and its inhabitants scattered. With a resigned sigh, Claudette turned her attention back to her long-winded employer.

* * *

The day of this latest dinner party was dreary. Rain slid down the Ashby home in great sheets. Outraged that nature had not complied with her express wishes, Maude Ashby was at her most difficult, terrorizing family and servants alike. Only Claudette seemed impervious to Mrs. Ashby's temper, calmly replying to the woman's relentless demands for the impossible. Finally, Mrs. Ashby exhausted herself with finding fault in everything she cast an eye on, and became the Hostess of Good Quality she knew she was destined to be.

Maude positioned herself in the drawing room with Claudette behind her as usual, and the tedious round of guest-greeting began. Claudette stifled a yawn. How tiresome it must be to be a member of English society, she thought. All of these popinjays strutting about, perpetually in a game of rivalry. A small gasp from Mrs. Ashby focused her attentions back to the party.

Mr. Greycliffe had entered, holding an umbrella over a young woman who was clearly a Lady of Quality. Underneath the woman's dark cape, Claudette saw that she was wearing an emerald satin gown sprinkled generously with embroidered flowers and vines. The dress had a scooped neck designed to display perfect cleavage, a waistline that came down in a point to emphasize her tiny frame, and layers of fine lace dripping from her elbows. She wore her lustrous brown hair swept up and topped with a hat accented with pale green ribbons and dyed ostrich feathers, all tied together with lace that matched her sleeves. As Mr. Greycliffe removed the woman's cape, a lining of fur momentarily dazzled the room. She looked up at him as he handed the cape and umbrella to Jack, flashing him her brilliant, even teeth. Mr. Greycliffe leaned over to whisper to her, then offered his arm. The Lady of Quality glided across the floor, her hand touching his arm with exactly the right pressure. She looked right and left, murmuring appropriate greetings to faces she recognized, and inclining her head in acknowledgment of anyone else who made eye contact with her.

Claudette hated her instantly.

She was overpowered with an inexplicable combination of jealousy, disdain, and panic. Here was another woman who had never experienced a difficult day in her life. But Claudette should feel sorry for the poor girl, as she was obviously besotted with the inscrutable Mr. Greycliffe. Yet Claudette did not feel sorry for her. To her own bewilderment, she wished she *was* her.

Mr. Greycliffe and the woman were approaching Maude and James Ashby. Claudette plastered on her best smile, for once glad that she could hide behind her role as a servant who spoke only French.

Mrs. Ashby drew an audible breath and brought her fan to her face. She whispered, "He's brought Lenora Radley with him! I heard from Mrs. Dailey, whose kitchen maid has a sister in Lady Radley's household, that a gentleman of some means was courting Lenora, and that she was hoping for a match. I had no idea it was William Greycliffe."

She began waving her fan furiously. "I wonder if he plans to announce his intention soon. We simply must be the first to extend our congratulations by hosting a party for them."

Claudette froze inwardly, hoping her smile was still visible. A party for that arrogant man and his perfect little milksop. *Of course her hair is glossy and her fingernails exquisitely rounded. She probably has her own lady's maid to toil away as I do.* All to make herself attractive and desirable for *him.* He paled in comparison to Jean-Philippe anyway. Who could possibly find him a good marital match? His family name might be rising, but he was certainly no gentleman. Really, sympathy is in order for her. Imagine having to suffer his embrace, his lips on your neck, his arms caressing your back, his—

As the couple approached, William's eyes briefly met Claudette's, and she saw a darkening in his pupils, which vanished almost at once.

"Mr. Greycliffe, what a delight to see you," Mrs. Ashby fluttered. "And I see you have brought the lovely Miss Radley with you. Our household is graced by your presence, isn't it, James?"

The elbow nudge in his side alerted Mr. Ashby. "Er, yes, graced. Lovely. Happy to have you." Seeming to see William for the first time, he perked up. "Ah, Greycliffe, you must come by soon. I have another investment proposition for you."

William nodded his assent to Mr. Ashby, murmured greetings to the fan-waving Mrs. Ashby, and guided Miss Radley away. As he did so, he leaned his head toward Miss Radley, and twice patted the hand she had placed back on his arm. Claudette's frozen heart now rooted her fully in place. The movement was identical to the way Jean-Philippe used to touch her when he wanted to guide their walks together. She suddenly felt suffocated. Maude Ashby was now engaged in conversation with another guest. *I need air,* Claudette thought. Mrs. Ashby and her guest did not seem likely to end their conversation soon. Whispering, "Madame, *pardon*," she walked quickly out of the room, not caring if anyone noticed her hasty exit from her mistress's side. Once out of the room, she fled down the hall to the library, and through that room escaped onto the veranda and down into the garden at the back of the house. Too late she realized it was still raining, and now it was dark, the only light coming from the windows of the house, the party continuing on gaily within.

Her dress was damp and her hair was plastered down the sides of her face. She stumbled her way to the pergola located in the center of the sculptured garden, two small fountains on either side of it spending futile energy spitting water up against the downpour from the heavens. Inside the relative shelter of the pergola, she sat on a bench, brought her head to her lap and her arms around her knees, and wept. Wept for the loss of her parents, and for the loss of her beloved Jean-Philippe, whose face she was ashamed to admit was becoming blurry in her dreams. She wept for her trapped circumstances in the Ashby household, and for her failure to save herself and Béatrice from their fate. She wept to know that she was only eighteen years old, and already committed to a life of drudgery. She wept especially to know that her father's legacy was dead. Never again would the world know about Étienne Laurent's marvelous dolls. People like that William Greycliffe and his precious Lenora Radley would always look down their noses at artists like Étienne Laurent and his daughter. Especially when that daughter becomes reduced to penury. *Oh, Papa, am I the only one in all of Europe who remembers your talent and genius for carving? Who could ever replace you? The English could understand nothing about your unusual artistic gifts. For them, everything is portraiture.* She mimicked previous houseguests to herself: "Johsua Reynolds did such a real likeness of my Welsh terrier, Pompey," and "Of course, with my connections I was able to secure Thomas Gainsborough for my daughter's coming out painting." Tears now fully spent, she laughed quietly to herself. Imagine the obsessive craze the English aristocracy would be sent into if she produced just one of Papa's *grandes Pandores*. After all, aristocracy is aristocracy, and the dolls had been the rage of the Parisian rich, hadn't they?

Suddenly a shadow blocked the light from the house that had been shining through the cascading rain. Stepping into view was none other than the object of Claudette's spite, William Greycliffe, shaking off an umbrella, probably the same one he had carried over Miss Radley's head.

"I saw you run from the house. Whatever are you doing down here in the rain? Don't tell me you're taking a nap again. Are these parties that exhausting for you?"

Claudette's muddled emotions bubbled over and gave vent to anger. She stood to confront him. "How dare you! You know nothing of me!"

"Nor will you seem to let me."

"Sir, every time I am in your presence, I get the distinct impression that you are being pointedly cruel toward me and making light of my reduced circumstances. I will respectfully insist that you refrain from conversing with me."

Ignoring her remark, he said, "You do look quite a fright with your hair in your eyes, which I recall that, when not swallowed up in the dark, are the most astonishing shade of blue." He dropped the umbrella and approached her, pulling a handkerchief from a pocket. "Miss Laurent." He cupped a warm hand around the side of her face and tenderly mopped her soaked face. "Truly you misunderstand me."

Claudette closed her eyes and let him continue, momentarily taken in by his gentle touch. "What could I possibly misunderstand about you?"

He still blotted her face with the handkerchief, even though she was now dry. His hand slid around to the back of her neck and pulled it gently back. She could feel his breath warm against her neck and knew even in the dark his eyes were staring at her intently.

"You think I'm vain and shallow because I have money, because I'm a rising member of the aristocracy, because I look down upon you as working class. On the contrary, it is you, Miss Laurent, who looks down upon me. You cannot imagine the burden I bear, being the successor to the Greycliffe name and legacy. How I have to give up those things that I want, for that which I do not want. In fact, I have to—"

"Mr. Greycliffe, sir?" A voice floated over the darkness and rain.

Claudette's eyes flew open at the intrusion. William swore impatiently under his breath. "Yes, what is it?"

"Mrs. Ashby is calling for all of her guests. She says she has an important announcement to make." Having found his quarry, the servant slithered back to the house to escape the pelting rain.

William removed his hand from Claudette's neck, pausing only to move a strand of hair over her right ear. "I must go inside, but I have much to say to you." He bent for his umbrella and strode to the house before she could respond.

She stayed in the pergola long after that.

When Claudette returned to the house, the rain had stopped and the guests were gone. She helped the other servants with cleanup, then retired to the attic, where Béatrice was waiting.

"Claudette, wherever have you been? The most exciting thing happened. That Mr. Greycliffe that you detest so much became engaged to a Miss Radley last week. You may have seen her with him tonight. They are to be married in six months' time, and Mrs. Ashby announced tonight that she would be throwing an engagement party for the two of them. Miss Radley seemed ecstatic. She is very elegant, don't you think? I don't know if Mr. Greycliffe's family will want an engagement party here, but, oh, can you imagine being so wealthy and important that people actually want to host a party on your behalf?" Béatrice was chattering pointlessly now. "I could never replace my Alexandre, but if I ever did, I should love to have three engagement parties, each with a different theme. And everyone from all of the parties would be invited to my wedding. My veil would be trimmed with real flowers, I should think . . . Claudette, where are you going?"

Claudette shut the door behind her and slipped into her own room, collapsing on the bed, dry-eyed. William Greycliffe was infuriating. He teased her, taunted her, and just when she thought he was sincere in his manner toward her, he announces to the world that he is engaged to a young lady of society! Not that his engagement mattered. Who cared if he was marrying that spindle-shanked woman? No, she told herself firmly, she was angry only because he treated her as though she were a fool.

Claudette knew then that it was time to leave the Ashby residence, no matter what was required. Being present for—and serving at—William Greycliffe's engagement party was something she positively would not do. Her parents were gone, Jean-Philippe was lost to her, and Béatrice and Marguerite depended on her. She would put aside dreams of any happiness, and concentrate on making herself independent, bring her father's marvelous vision back to life, and transform herself into the heir to his dollmaking world.

Claudette tried valiantly to ignore the preparations for the Greycliffe engagement party. Béatrice prattled about it endlessly, but Claudette retreated into her own mind, dreaming of setting up her own doll workshop and working out plans in her mind. Her first need was money, more than she was earning with Jack's occasional doll sales at Surrey Street Market, which sold more meat and vegetables than household goods.

She discussed with him how they could sell more dolls.

"I'm not sure, Miss Claudette." Jack scratched his short, bristly hair. "Sounds almost like you'd need to export 'em, and I don't know how you could go about a big venture like that without Mrs. Ashby finding out what you're doing. Unless you could find your own shop."

"A shop!" Claudette laughed without mirth. "Impossible. I barely have enough to keep us in warm stockings. And you're right, Jassy would ferret out anything like an export business going on. Besides, even if I could hide it all, how could I afford to stock enough fabric and trimmings to create enough dolls to open a shop? There must be another way."

It was Béatrice who finally came up with the solution. "Didn't you tell me once that your father sold dolls to some dressmakers to show off their latest designs? Maybe we could do the same thing, in exchange for some of their discarded pieces of cloth."

Claudette hugged her friend impulsively. "Béatrice! You are brilliant. That is exactly what we'll do."

The two women worked even more furiously to put together a tray of dolls. With Jack along as a guide, Claudette slipped away on one of her rare afternoons off, granted while the Ashbys were out visiting, to visit various dressmaking shops and offer to give the proprietors dolls as barter for fabric. The rejection stung. "What? I don't have enough work to keep me busy, now I have to sew tiny little dresses at night for silly little dolls?" spat one sour-faced crone. "Are my eyes not dim enough without you bringing me this? And you want payment of my fine fabrics for them, as well!" Another door slammed.

Dejected, she sent Jack home and walked into the next alley-way along the street, sat down against the side of a building with her box, and stared at it. How could she get some fabrics right away? She could not resort to stealing. On the other hand, she could not face an interminable existence inside the Ashby household. She sat lost in thought, even dozing awhile, when all of a sudden she bolted upright. Of course! How stupid. She was approaching the wrong people for fabrics.

Claudette picked up her box, and proceeded two streets over to Gifford's Draper Shop. Inside, a man and his wife were totaling receipts for the day. They looked up in unison as Claudette walked in with her box of wares.

"Sorry, we are not interested in your kittens," said the wife, a short, portly woman with faded brown hair and a resigned air about her.

"No, madam, I do not have kittens. I have a proposition for you that will help both of our businesses."

Raising an eyebrow, the man, who was as short and portly as his spouse, asked, "What is this proposition?"

Claudette told the couple that she was a dollmaker in immediate need of fine fabrics to complete a commission for a set of dolls. It was impossible to wait for a shipment to arrive from the Continent. She showed them her box of samples, which they examined, picking up dolls, moving their jointed limbs and running fingers over their painted faces. She offered to give them dolls dressed in their fabrics, if they would give her extra fabric for her own use. She would then have the fabric she needed at no cost, and they would have a way to show off the fine quality of their cloth other than it sitting on a bolt.

"Eh," said the woman, shrugging her shoulders, unimpressed.

In desperation, Claudette took several dolls to the shop window and showed them how the dolls could be displayed to best advantage to passersby. The couple exchanged a look Claudette could not interpret.

"Hmm, what do you think, Diane?" asked the man of his wife.

"Eh, why not? Give her a few of the bolts that are soiled. She can cut around the stains to get her patterns cut, and we can get use out of bolts that are otherwise of no use to us." Looking at Claudette critically she asked, "Miss, you seem very young. You say you are already an established dollmaker in London?"

Murmuring quickly that her dolls were known as far away as France, Claudette took her leave, promising to return in two weeks with the finished dolls.

She had Jack find some current fashion plates from local dress shops so that she could copy the latest clothing designs for the dolls. She took up the detailed stitching again as though she had never left her father's shop. Béatrice preferred the less detailed work of painting faces. Soon they had more than a dozen dolls ready for Jack to deliver to the Giffords, since his absence from the Ashby house would be less noticeable than Claudette's. He came back to the two women keyed up and animated.

"They took them all, and praised them to the heavens. I probably could have sold them all, and for twice the price I'd get at the market." He produced a heavy package tied with twine. Inside were generously cut lengths of fabric, plus embroidered ribbons and sequins in a small pouch. Claudette pawed eagerly through her new acquisitions, then had Jack and Béatrice help her unfold the fabrics and roll them up together to avoid their becoming wrinkled beyond repair.

The two women learned to operate on just five hours of sleep each night, working long after the rest of the household was asleep to construct dolls for the London fashion industry. The chest now began to swell with coins, and Claudette began to think that in another year they might be able to leave the Ashby employ. They could sail back to France, and Claudette would finally find Jean-Philippe. And she would finally rid herself of Mr. William Greycliffe's presence.

Claudette was organizing Mrs. Ashby's toilette tray one morning when Jassy entered, as sly and secretive as Claudette had ever seen her.

"Mistress wants to see you in the dining room," she said, a smirk on her face.

Claudette replaced the silver hand mirror she had been polishing and stood up to join Jassy, but the girl had already slipped out of the room.

In the dining room, she found Mrs. Ashby and Mrs. Lundy together. Mrs. Lundy was standing next to the sideboard, her hands clasped tightly in front of her and her mouth turned down disapprovingly. Maude Ashby sat erect at the head of the table, drumming her fingers on the smooth mahogany top.

What now?

At Claudette's entrance, Mrs. Ashby rose imperiously. "Have you an idea why I have summoned you here?"

"No, madam, I was arranging your toilette tray when Jassy—"

"Never mind what you were doing just now. It is what you have been doing under my nose these past months with which I am concerned."

"Madam? I do not understand." Dear God, did she know about the dolls?

"Don't use your Parisian deceit on me! After all we have done for you, taking you and that half-wit and her chattering brat in, feeding and caring for you like one of the family. All against my better judgment, of course."

Mrs. Lundy sniffed agreement, while her employer continued her tirade.

"When I think of how I so *generously* elevated you beyond your station, putting you in a position of trust as my lady's maid, and you repay me this way. I am simply outraged—no, I am in disbelief—" Maude ranted on, while Claudette stood still, not sure yet of what she was being accused.

"I am so fortunate that Jassy is a *proper* servant, and has her employer's best interests in mind. What in heaven's name might have happened had she not reported this to me? You might have gotten in trouble and embarrassed me."

"In trouble? How so?" Claudette's fists were clenched at her side.

"Ha! I know of your late-night peccadilloes with Jack Smythe, who was a good and honest boy until he got into your clutches."

"My clutches?" Claudette was still uncertain as to which way this was headed. Had Jassy discovered her doll box? Claudette had not checked on it yet today. Or was she following through on her threat of fabrication?

"Yes, your greedy, grasping clutches. How dare you ensnare him into your bed—the bed I gave you!—to conduct an illicit affair. You know that is strictly against household rules. For all I know you are with child right now."

Ah, so that was how Jassy had played it.

"Or do you know someone in Haymarket who can take care of any trouble you might get into? What have you to say for yourself, girl?"

Claudette breathed deeply. At least Mrs. Ashby did not know about Jack's midnight errands to Surrey Street. But these accusations were intolerable.

Should I grovel for forgiveness and save our jobs? The moments passed, Mrs. Ashby waiting impatiently, Mrs. Lundy's nose quivering with displeasure. Out of the corner of one eye, Claudette saw Jassy pass through the butler's pantry and look in, her eyes fairly glowing with anticipation and malice.

"Mrs. Ashby," Claudette began, "I have tolerated much from you. Poor wages, condescension, and the hatred of your other servants. However, what you accuse me of is not only untrue, it is insulting. I have neither the time nor the inclination for any of these so-called peccadilloes with any of the other household staff. That you would listen to an insipid, lying little six-penny wit like Jassy simply shows how astoundingly stupid and self-absorbed you are."

Mrs. Ashby's face was mottled with rage and she spoke in her most dangerous tone, the one that typically sent servants and family alike scattering. "You are nothing but a lowly street creature. You have no prospects beyond employment in my home. Do you realize I hold your entire future in my hands and could ruin you in an instant?" She snapped the fingers on one hand in front of her face to emphasize her power.

Claudette's mouth curved into a smile. "Madam, you may add 'foolish' to my description of you. And you may consider my employment with you terminated."

Flecks of foam appeared in the corner of Maude's mouth. "You . . . dare to say . . . that *you* terminate . . . *me?*"

"Indeed, madam, I say *au revoir* to you, your wimpy husband, your obnoxious son Nathaniel, and every vicious servant in your household." Claudette cut a look over to Mrs. Lundy, so the woman would know that she was included in the list of offenders.

"Nicholas is the youngest and only decent living person in this home, besides Jack."

Without waiting for her mistress's leave, Claudette turned on her heel and stalked out of the room through the butler's pantry, Mrs. Ashby's threats ringing in her ears. "My connections are prestigious. You will not find domestic employment anywhere else in London. In all of England. I'll see to it."

Claudette did not bother to turn around, instead colliding with Jassy, who had returned to spy on the conversation. The other servant scuttled out of the way, fearful of Claudette's unexpected boldness. From the butler's pantry, Claudette strode hurriedly upstairs, not noticing Nicholas watching her from the second-story landing. She went to the attic, grabbed her doll supplies and scrawled out a note to leave for Jack, then rushed back down two flights to the laundry.

In the basement, Claudette said simply, "We're leaving this house. Now."

Béatrice, not really needing an explanation for a command to leave her post, instantly dropped the sheet she was folding to the floor and picked up Marguerite, hugging the child close as she followed Claudette back up the stairs and out of the house. Nicholas was still observing them from his second-floor vantage point.

❧ 10 ❧

London, April 1783. As she surveyed her cramped shop, marveling over its existence, Claudette could not believe her run of good fortune. From their flight from the Ashby home, she and Béatrice found their way back to Reverend Daniels's house. Although he and his wife half-heartedly chastised Claudette for her rash behavior, in private they agreed that Maude Ashby was perhaps not the most charitable of the Lord's kingdom, and perhaps the Harrisons were a bit more deserving of that front pew.

Jack Smythe visited one evening the following week after the rest of the Ashby household had gone to bed, bringing with him whatever of the women's personal belongings he could find in their rooms. Claudette's haughty departure was the source of endless chatter and gossip. Mrs. Ashby had announced that she had turned Claudette, Béatrice, and "the sniveling brat" out on their ears. Mrs. Lundy was silent on the matter, but Jassy had elevated herself to mythical status among the staff, bragging of her role in discovering the duplicitous behavior of Miss Frenchy Fifi. Miraculously, Jack had escaped punishment, primarily because he was cast in the role of a seduced young lad. Jassy avoided him entirely, cutting short her bragging when he entered a room.

"So all of my nighttime business activities still go unnoticed," he said, giving the women a quirky grin.

Claudette was relieved that he had escaped Mrs. Ashby's volatile temper. In the succeeding days, Jack helped the women find this space, and within a month they were able to bid thanks and farewell to the reverend and his wife. It was small and dark, but it was located in the thriving trade area of Cheapside. Claudette had to give up nearly half of their meager savings to secure it for six months. The three of them shared a bed in a corner of the one-room shop, connected on either side by a chandler and a bookseller. She bartered with the chandler for enough tapers to make the inside of the shop somewhat inviting. The two women and Marguerite would wake each morning, hastily cover the bed, and the child would amuse herself on top of it with her own dolls and some other toys they had procured for her. Claudette and Béatrice would carve and dress modest dolls together on a rough wooden table, then take turns standing outside the shop to sell them to passersby.

"Dollies! Little babies! Who will buy my little babies? Only a ha'penny for a dolly!"

Claudette felt humiliated by this kind of selling after the refinement of her father's shop in Paris, but it seemed to be a common approach here in London for vendors too poor for a proper shop. Sellers of meat pies, brooms, ribbons, flower bunches, and all other manner of goods would walk the streets with baskets or carts, hawking their wares in a singsong voice.

Jack continued coming by every few weeks to pick up the fancier fashion dolls to pass on to the Giffords and other draper shops in exchange for materials. One day, he entered the shop breathlessly, excited by his latest accomplishment. He had convinced several millinery shops to purchase dolls that would be dressed according to their own specifications. They were exacting in their fashion concepts, and demanded that the dollmaker herself visit them so they could discuss designs.

Thus Claudette began venturing out to dress shops to personally collect orders and review fashion sketches for the miniature models. The milliners provided the fabrics and trims that they wanted used for their dolls, and Claudette used the scraps from these consignments for dressing the dolls that now Marguerite sold on the street under Béatrice's supervision.

Seven-year-old Marguerite was a natural charmer, and knew instinctively how to wink and cajole her way into a sale. Patrons loved the little girl's fresh boldness, which was just a step from appreciating Claudette's craftsmanship when Marguerite convinced them to make a purchase.

Claudette became known locally as the "French Dollmaker in Cheapside's Lane," and realized that she needed to formally name her shop. She hand-painted a sign for the window that read:

C. LAURENT FASHION DOLLS
FRENCH AND ENGLISH
C. LAURENT, PROPRIETRESS

Each morning she put a new doll in the window to interest passersby, but rarely did it interest anyone enough to come into the shop. Her trade was primarily with those who used them as tools for selling their own fabrics and clothing, and secondarily through Marguerite's efforts in hawking outside the shop.

One interested visitor was Nicholas Ashby, who had convinced Jack of his genuine concern for the trio and elicited their location from him. When he arrived, Claudette met him outside, having just returned to the shop after delivering a basket of newly-made dolls to a shop specializing in hats and gloves.

"Nicholas! What a delight to see you. How did you find us? No matter, come inside. Béatrice and Marguerite will be glad to see you."

Inside the shop, they encountered Béatrice in a coughing fit over a heap of wood shavings, an unfinished doll torso and knife next to the shavings.

Claudette rushed to her side. "Béatrice, the wood dust must be filling your lungs."

Her friend was covering her mouth with her hand. "No, no, I'm fine. But I think I'll rest for a while." She dabbed her lips with a handkerchief from her pocket. "Why, is that Nicholas come to see us?"

Nicholas bent his head down. "Yes, Miss Béatrice. Jack told me where you were. I just wanted to see for myself."

Béatrice reached out to hug him briefly, and he inhaled the combined scent of burnt wood and glues, with a faint background of lavender. Embarrassed, he quickly disengaged himself.

"Where is your daughter?" he asked.

"That little scamp can't seem to leave the bookseller next door alone. She is forever borrowing and returning books from him. One day I expect he will have barred her from his shop, but so far she seems to win over any heart she encounters. Except your mother's, of course. Oh, I am so sorry, Nicholas, I didn't mean to say that."

He kept his eyes downcast. "I know, ma'am, what my mother is. She was pretty angry when you left."

He told them that Maude Ashby had gone fairly apoplectic after their departure, and even now was loathe to hear Claudette's name mentioned in her presence. Nicholas thought his mother's primary difficulty was the wounding to her pride when two servants—who should have been completely indebted to her—stalked out of her house. For months she scanned the newspaper each morning at the breakfast table, hoping for news of Claudette's and Béatrice's imprisonment in debtor's prison, "which would only serve those two ungrateful wenches right." It would have also proved her point that they could not survive without her generosity. James and Nicholas took the brunt of her wrath over the situation, while Jack Smythe had indeed avoided penalty. Nicholas speculated that Jack's worth as a clever servant led Maude Ashby to affix blame on Claudette, rather than consider that he may have done anything wrong.

"Jassy Brickford is gone now, too," he added.

Claudette stiffened. "Where is she?"

"Don't know. She and Mrs. Lundy had a big row, something about a new household position Jassy wanted. Mum wouldn't hear of giving it to her, and Jassy, well, she sort of lost her mind. Threatened to burn the place down. So Mrs. Lundy fired her, and she ran off with some of our silver plate. Mum was furious at first, but not nearly so mad about Jassy as she was when both of you left."

Marguerite returned to the shop, taking little interest in Nicholas's presence, and the four sat together at the worktable to a light meal consisting of small slivers of meat pie and weak ale. Earlier in the day, Béatrice had picked up a small basket of fresh strawberries from a street vendor, and they all shared them. Nicholas's adoration of Béatrice was blatant to everyone but Marguerite, who gave a lengthy discourse on Mr. Addleston's latest tome in the front window, *The Life and Opinions of Tristam Shandy, Gentleman.*

"And did you read this all by yourself at your age?" asked her mother.

"Well, no, but Mr. Addleston told me about it, so I didn't need to read it," replied Marguerite, utterly unabashed.

Nicholas soon had to leave, before his mother noticed his lengthy absence. He had claimed he was going to see his school-master for some tutoring, but by now she would be wondering where he was. He promised to return soon, but they all knew it would be impossible to conceal his visits from the all-knowing Maude Ashby for long.

As he was leaving, Béatrice pressed a small woolen-clad doll into his hand. "Save this for your first sweetheart," she said.

"But—" He tried to hand it back to her, words failing him.

She pushed it back again. "You will one day find an eligible young woman your own age, and you might like to give her a token of your affection. Good-bye, Nicholas."

He looked crestfallen, but pocketed the doll. He left the shop, looking back at them as he went into the busy street.

Claudette's heart fairly surged to bursting the day she walked to the Giffords' shop and Diane told her, "We've had an inquiry about your dolls, eh?"

"An inquiry?"

"Yes, one of my customers came in with her daughter and the family dressmaker, seeking fabric for a dress for the girl's natal day celebration. The rich get so carried away with showing off and impressing others. Imagine, that much silk for a ten-year-old to prance around in for a day. Eh, well, it keeps us from starving, so—"

"Madam," Claudette interrupted. "About the inquiry?"

"Eh, oh yes, the mother asked if the dolls in the window were for sale. I told her they were made especially for the shop. She gave me her calling card and asked that the dollmaker present herself at her house to arrange a commission."

Claudette felt the earth beginning to shift beneath her, and she suddenly needed great gulps of air to maintain composure. "Someone of wealth wants to see me? To commission one of my dolls?"

"Don't look so foolish. Does the world come to a standstill because one of these rich snobs deigns to speak to you? Here is her card."

Claudette mulled over her approach to this new customer for the rest of the day. How could she guarantee a sale for herself? She told Béatrice about her potential customer.

"Have you gone to see her yet?"

"Well, no," she said sheepishly. "I wanted to tell you first."

"Claudette! You must go as soon as possible. What a wonderful opportunity for you."

"Any success I may have would have been impossible without you and Jack."

They discussed what samples she would take with her to Lady Helen Parshall. Should she take fabric samples as well? Or just fully-dressed dolls? How could she turn this into a regular commission from Lady Parshall and her friends? How do you impress English society?

They turned over various ideas and finally Claudette had an inspiration.

"Béatrice, I know what to do. It would be unique, and would show off the dolls to their best advantage."

"What?"

"I want you to come with me, dressed as one of the dolls."

"As *what?*"

"It's perfect. I'll fashion gowns for both you and the doll, and we'll present the doll together. These dolls are half your creation, anyway. Here, I'll need a bit of your hair for a wig." She opened a drawer and took out a pair of scissors.

"Claudette! What are you doing?"

"Just a little from the underside, like this." She lifted the hair from the back of Béatrice's neck. "A little snip and I will have plenty. There. You cannot tell a single strand is missing."

Béatrice laughed. "I do hope you are able to make a sale before my head is completely thatched."

The women worked harder than ever before. Five days later, they walked to the address noted on Lady Parshall's card. Claudette's thoughts tumbled together incoherently; she knew she was on the brink of total success or dismal failure. Had Papa ever had a moment like this when he began selling dolls?

"Oh, Claudette, I'm so nervous. I want this to be perfect for you." Béatrice was wearing a confection of golden silk and lace. A matching hat was dipped low across her forehead, and a large peacock feather was attached jauntily to one side of it. In Claudette's arms was a wooden box containing the sample doll, now wearing a wig made from Béatrice's hair, its eyes painted green, and adorned with a miniature outfit that was an exact replica of what she was wearing, even down to the stylish hat.

Walking nervously up to Lady Parshall's door, they knocked lightly. A maid opened it almost immediately. Obtaining their names, she bade them wait in a receiving room, then went to get the lady of the house. Lady Parshall came sweeping into the room, clearly used to being in charge and having her presence respected. She was tall and thin, and dressed in a sunflower yellow gown of embroidered silk, with fine lace dripping from her elbows and protruding profusely from her bosom. Trailing behind her was a small African boy, dressed in the same bright silk, an elaborate turban on his head. The boy did not acknowledge the presence of his mistress's guests, but gazed up adoringly at her. He carried with him a small fan of snowy white ostrich feathers. It reminded Claudette distinctly of her forced role with Mrs. Ashby. Only at least this poor boy presumably didn't have to contend with the aristocracy in the same way.

"So which of you is the dollmaker?"

"I am," said Claudette. "I am Claudette Laurent, and this is my assistant, Béatrice du Georges."

"They say you are French," the woman said flatly.

The women did not respond, unsure if they were being accused of something.

Lady Parshall stared at them impatiently, and tapped one of her satin-clad feet on the large wool carpet covering the floor.

"Sit down, sit down," she commanded, pointing to chairs covered in embroidery. She took one opposite the women, and the small African boy moved to stand next to her chair. He raised the fan and began to slowly wave it on his mistress. Lady Parshall patted his head absentmindedly, much as one would show affection to a dog.

"Marcel, would you like a treat? Go and see Cook. Tell her I said you are to have a sweet. But just one, Marcel. That's a good boy."

Marcel put the fan on a nearby table, bowed elegantly to his mistress, and scampered out. Lady Parshall looked after him briefly, then turned back to her guests, who had been surreptitiously examining the room. It was dominated on one side by a wall of mirrors, and windows on the opposite wall. The sunlight filtering in through the windows reflected off the mirrors and created a dazzling effect in the room. Claudette knew that King Louis XIV had built an enormous Hall of Mirrors at Versailles. Was this Lady Parshall's attempt to imitate French style? Two tapestries depicting pastoral scenes dominated a third wall. The numerous pieces of furniture crowding the room were ostentatious, but Claudette could see the quality in every piece, particularly in the carved legs of the chairs. Claudette was emotionally transported back to her father's workshop, where each day she would be greeted by his booming laugh, the fragrance of freshly hewn wood combined with the exhilarating scents of the *parfumerie* two doors down, filling her childish mind with happiness. She had learned to distinguish varying kinds of wood just by smelling her father's calloused hands.

Seeing her eyes on a gilded writing desk, her hopefully soon-to-be patron said, "You appreciate my furniture, I see."

"Yes, my lady. My father was once a cabinetmaker and taught me much about wood. These are fine examples."

Lady Parshall was pleased with the praise. "All of the best furniture makers in England want to receive commissions from me. Anyone I patronize becomes well-known and prosperous. In fact, I rarely have to pay for anything because of the prestige I can bring to a business."

Claudette felt a prickle on the back of her neck. Was this going to be an unpaid commission with some vague promise of other commissions from Lady Parshall's friends?

"Would my lady like to see a sample created especially for this day?" Receiving a curt nod, Claudette whispered to Béatrice, "Pull the doll from the bag and show it to Lady Parshall, holding it close to your face as I told you."

Béatrice slowly reached into the bag and drew out the tissue-wrapped doll, as though she were unearthing a great treasure. She spent even more time unwrapping the doll in her lap, as though the treasure was so delicate and valuable it might break at the slightest pressure. The moment it was free of paper, she whisked the doll up next to her cheek, facing out toward Lady Parshall, tilting toward it with a heart-melting smile.

"Amazing!" exclaimed Lady Parshall. "She has been prepared to look just like your assistant. Her clothing is identical. Give it to me." She took the doll from Béatrice.

"This hair. It is identical to yours, soft and fine."

"Yes, my lady," replied Claudette. "I cut a small lock of my assistant's hair to create the wig, to give it authenticity. Most dollmakers use coarse fibers for a wig, but I am particular with commissions from important patrons. I believe it makes the doll far more superior; would you agree?"

Lady Parshall ignored Claudette as she began working the doll's joints, scrutinizing the worth of the clothing, unfastening and refastening hooks, examining underclothing, and running her fingers over the painted face. "It is fantastic quality," she muttered quietly. She was absorbed several minutes in her task, and seemed to forget that Claudette and Béatrice were still present.

Finally, she looked up and seemed surprised that they were there. She recovered her brisk attitude and said, "Well, how many will you give me?"

"*Give* you, Lady Parshall?" Claudette was now seriously worried.

"Yes. I wish to have four dolls made, one dressed as myself, and one representing each of my three daughters. I will tell you where to purchase fabric to match particular dresses I am having made for each of us. We will each carry these dolls to an affair being given by the Earl of Boxshire at Cobham Hill, his country house in Surrey, next month. You will *give* them to me, and I will see that everyone attending knows who made them." Lady Parshall stood imperiously. Clearly the interview was at an end, and Claudette was to do exactly as instructed.

Marcel reentered the room, telltale chocolate stains on his ruffled sleeves.

"Marcel, look." Lady Parshall handed the boy the doll. He took it tentatively, staring at it as though it were an object dropped from the heavens. He looked up at his mistress for guidance as to how to react.

"It is a doll. We are going to get several that look like me and the Misses Camilla, Caroline, and Cecily. They will make us the talk of the town, if poor Miss Laurent here is fortunate."

Marcel stared back down at the doll, then handed it to Lady Parshall. She turned back to Claudette once more.

"When will you have the dolls to me?"

"Madame . . ." She hesitated. "It requires great sums to create such high quality dolls, and I have already invested much in my doll business. Would you not consider a small sum in return for the dolls?"

"Deliver the dolls to the back entrance in two weeks. I do not wish tradespeople to be seen at the front entryway." She swept away from the room, completely ignoring Claudette's request.

Giving each other long looks, Claudette and Béatrice knew they had no choice but to comply.

Claudette and Béatrice worked feverishly on the four dolls for Lady Parshall. They made two trips to their new benefactress's home, via the back entrance, so that they could quickly sketch the three girls' faces and hairstyles, and inspect the gowns they would be wearing to the earl's party. Fortunately, all of the fabric for the dresses was to be found at the shop of Gerard and Diane Gifford, who warmly welcomed the young dollmaker back. Diane bustled about, helping Claudette.

"Yes, yes, Lady Parshall is a trial, eh? She constantly wants fabric given to her, always with a promise that we will see more business than we can handle because of her remarkable connections. I suppose we have seen more customers—careful, eh, this silk is new and delicate—although no one of the stature of the Earl of Boxshire." She piled bolts of fabric into Claudette's arms.

Gerard, meanwhile, was poring through drawers of threads and laces with Béatrice. He said over his shoulder to Claudette, whose head was barely visible behind the tower of material, "My girl, you must not worry about payment until after the dolls are delivered. My wife and I both will help you with Lady Parshall, not because we think she will be of help to you, but because we think your dolls will speak for themselves, and will bring the new customers to our shop for fabric."

Claudette impulsively threw the bolts onto a table, put her arms around the proprietor's neck, and planted a kiss on his cheek. Gerard, embarrassed, harrumphed and patted her head awkwardly, before removing her arms and returning to work.

The dolls were delivered carefully wrapped in tissue and tied with bows in colors to match each doll's gown. Lady Parshall's three daughters squealed with delight as Claudette presented the dolls, swathed in colorful silks and laces, to their mother.

"I shall be the most sought-after girl there!" gushed Camilla, a dark-eyed girl who would be quite beautiful except for an alarming case of pimples.

"You will not! My doll looks more like me and I shall be asked to dance by every gentleman there." Her sister, Cecily, a plump blonde, challenged her.

"Mama, please, can I have my doll now? I want to practice holding her for my entrance at Cobham Hill." Caroline was the most solemn of the three girls, if any of them could be termed solemn.

Lady Parshall ushered the girls out of the room with their dolls and turned to instruct Claudette and Béatrice. "I shall expect that you will not make such dolls for anyone else until after I visit the earl's home next week. If I hear that you are making dolls like this for anyone else in London—and I do mean anyone—I will find out about it, and I will destroy you. I will not have our special night ruined by lowly tradespeople who think they have a right to interfere with the social activities of their betters."

The woman clapped her hands, and almost instantly a maid appeared. Lady Parshall informed her that Claudette and Béatrice were not to be permitted back in the house unless they had been summoned. With that, she turned with great purpose and swept out of the back hallway, which was as far as the two women had been allowed to go. The maid escorted them out, and they stood at the back door for several moments, each wondering if they had made the biggest mistake of their lives in agreeing to this folly.

But it was not folly. Three weeks later, at wit's end because she felt too terrified to produce any dolls whatsoever, much less any that might fall into the hands of Lady Parshall's friends, Claudette stopped by the Giffords' fabric shop, and was greeted with delighted laughter. "Eh, Miss Claudette, we've been worried because we haven't seen you. Look at these fabric orders we have from dressmakers all over London." Diane held up a sheaf of papers. "And many of them have instructions for dolls in matching fabrics!"

Claudette could not believe her ears. Were there actually this many orders coming in? Why such a large quantity?

Diane explained that a special entertainment was being held by the royal family at Queen's House, and everyone now wanted to copy the fashion set by Lady Parshall.

"You have much work ahead of you, my dear, but you may have helped us all make our mark in London. Imagine if we could obtain trade with the king!"

King George III was not known for extravagance, but he did have a bevy of children. Would his daughters like dolls? Could the Laurent name be one day associated with the king of England?

❧ 11 ❧

By October of that year, Claudette realized that they would have to move to bigger quarters. The odors of paint, gesso, hemp, and other materials were a noxious blend. Béatrice was coughing more frequently behind her hand, but refusing to take any rest. Not only that, they were producing more and more dolls for selling to the upper class, and their one-room dwelling was becoming intolerably crowded.

Claudette turned to her one ally, Jack Smythe, to discuss the problem.

"How much do you have saved?" he asked.

"About ten pounds."

"Don't know if anyone will rent a decent place to a woman. You may need a backer."

"I will not need a backer. I shall either do this on my own or not at all. My coppers are as good as anyone's."

Jack, who already saw his financial future tied up in Claudette's, was more than willing to seek new quarters for her if it meant more profits. He found them in the form of a three-room building on Old Bond Street, on the edge of the fashionable district of Mayfair. The structure contained a front shop twenty feet long with a wide brick fireplace on one end and soot covering much of the ceiling, backed by two rooms of ten feet square each. The women could use one room as a bedroom, and the other as a workshop. The workshop had a narrow set of steps leading to a small, unused attic. The bedroom contained a window that overlooked an overgrown garden, which Béatrice promised to put to rights immediately. She ticked off the varieties of medicinal herbs and flowers she would plant to ensure Marguerite would always have a ready treatment should she fall ill again. A shared brick oven was set off to one side of the garden, used by the occupants in four buildings surrounding the courtyard.

The exterior of the building showed that it was at least two centuries old, with its steeply-pitched thatched roof and half-timber construction. All in all, it was old, and would require a great deal of effort to make it habitable, and Claudette loved it.

After Claudette signed the lease—the building had been sitting empty for a year and the landlord would have signed it over to a cart donkey if it had had the ability to pay—the trio moved in with Jack's help. He found them a cart, which they heaped with what few personal belongings they had and their mountain of dollmaking supplies, and walked the twenty blocks to their new address.

Leaving the cleanup of both the garden and the interior of the building to Béatrice, Claudette worked at setting up the workshop efficiently and arranging the shop's window to attract customers. Her strategy in her new location was to pack the window view with as many dolls as possible, both the fashion type and little baby dolls. She longed to be able to hire a blacksmith to create a frame for a *grande Pandore*, but she had once again depleted her entire savings relocating. The metal work and extensive fabrics needed for the mannequin doll were financially impossible for the moment. The workshop was also too small to accommodate construction of more than one at a time, and a *grande Pandore* crowding the workshop would preclude any other doll work. Claudette put it out of her mind and instead focused on a new commission for one of Lady Parshall's friends.

This particular assignment required a doll dressed in a bridal trousseau. Several weeks of work produced one of the finest dolls Claudette had ever made, one she thought would have made her papa proud. She showed it to Béatrice. The doll's dress of ice-blue satin had a layered collar and gathered waist. A small frill of lace peeped out from under the collar and at the bottom of both long sleeves. The pulled-in waist gave the lower skirt a bell shape. Complementing the doll's dress was a reticule made of cream-colored brocade dangling from one arm, and a veil made of the same brocade with lace edging.

"Truly, Claudette," Béatrice gasped. "You are a superb artisan."

Lady Parshall's friend apparently agreed, and soon even more orders were pouring in. By the beginning of the following year, Claudette had doll parts, wigs, fabric bolts, and other supplies stacked tall on every available floor and table space.

A new dream was beginning to emerge: that of finding nicer housing accommodations separate from the shop, where she and Béatrice could have their own private rooms. But Claudette tamped down that particularly traitorous dream. How could she possibly think of wasting her savings on establishing permanence in England, when her real dream was to return to France and find Jean-Philippe?

Except Jean-Philippe's face was getting fuzzy in her recollections, and the memory of his strong arms around her did not comfort her as in the past, now that she had a growing trade to occupy her every waking moment. And there was that intriguing, infuriating William Greycliffe who, despite his engagement—or was he married now?—had taken permanent residence in a small corner of her mind.

Oh, Papa, what should I do?

❧ 12 ❧

Versailles, 1783. The long-awaited Dauphin was now nearly two years old. The child was beautiful, but very fragile from the moment of his arrival on the world stage. His destiny was to be hunch-backed and plagued with persistent fevers and illnesses, worrying his parents constantly.

For now, however, the birth of Louis Joseph recovered Marie Antoinette's reputation, though she would never regain the wor-shipful adulation she had experienced when she first crossed from Austria into France.

With her position as wife and mother secure, Marie Antoinette turned her energies to a project she had been contemplating for some time. Summoning the architect Richard Mique, she commis-sioned an extraordinary building project: that of a pastoral village on the grounds of Versailles. The village contained twelve thatched-roof houses, including a dairy, a fishery, a barn, dovecote, and water mill. The centerpiece of the village was to be the Queen's House, consisting of two rustic buildings connected by a wooden gallery, ornamented with blue and white earthenware flowerpots with the queen's initials on them. The house was to contain a dining room, a backgammon room, Chinese room, and both a small and large salon. Later she would add a farm, where she would install a farm-ing couple to supply the queen with eggs, butter, cream, and cheese. The entire village would become known as Marie Antoinette's beloved Hameau, or Hamlet, and from here she would play the part of a simple shepherdess or farmer's wife, dressed simply in a white muslin dress and straw hat. Court members learned quickly that while she was at the Hameau, the strict court etiquette that was so firmly a part of life at Versailles was to be abandoned in favor of a more relaxed atmosphere in keeping with the village.

Most of the court hated this, as the severe court etiquette helped establish pecking orders and dominance of status, and it galled many to have someone of lower rank treated equally. Marie Antoinette was firm, though. Life at the Hameau was to be casual and peaceable, and a place where she could retreat with Alex Fersen.

Claudette continued to save money in the little supply box she had rescued from her father's shop. Even with her new rent and the percentage given to Jack, which was reduced now that she was purchasing her own supplies, she found that by being thrifty she could save even more than she had when living at the Ashbys'. The box began bulging with notes, and she had to secure it with twine to keep it from exploding forth its contents. She casually mentioned to Jack that she might be interested in finding a banker. He introduced her to his banker, a Mr. Benjamin. Claudette was astounded that a servant, particularly one in the Ashby household, should have his own banker, but then, Jack seemed very resourceful about making money. When she asked him about it, he just winked and said, "A man has to look toward the future. I won't always be a household servant."

Mr. Benjamin helped her open an account, and also guided her on some investments, proposing that she purchase shares in an American tobacco plantation. Claudette later thanked Jack profusely, for all of Mr. Benjamin's recommendations became profitable investments, and she was able to reinvest in the shop, and also maintain a decent standard of living for herself, Béatrice, and Marguerite. She even had some new clothing made for the three of them, including pairs of mules dyed to match each of their favorite dresses. The gowns from Mrs. Ashby were sent to a charity box.

That Christmastide they had stuffed capon and roasted vegetables that Béatrice had seasoned with herbs from the garden and cooked in the courtyard oven. They sopped up leftover juices with hot, crusty bread fresh from a nearby baker's shop. Claudette gave them each gifts: a bottle of rose-scented perfume for Béatrice, and a leather-bound copy of Samuel Johnson's *Dictionary of the English Language* for Marguerite. The young girl squealed in delight and ran next door to show it to Mr. Addleston, the bookseller, while her mother and Claudette cleaned up from their small feast.

"What do you imagine the Ashbys are eating this evening? Sugared fruits? Pigeon pie? Custard tarts?" asked Béatrice.

"No matter what they are having, it could not be more delicious than what we shared together this evening."

"To think that two years ago we began toiling for that woman and that awful son of hers. Nathaniel, I mean. Oh, Claudette, what if we had not had your artistic abilities to rescue us?"

"We would have survived. Somehow."

Claudette had spent the morning in the workshop untangling rolls of wool to be shaped into wigs. So intent was she on the masses of fibers that she did not hear the shop's bell tinkle. Béatrice ran into the workshop, breathless.

"Claudette, you have a visitor."

"Who is it?"

"I think you should see for yourself." She fled the room before she could be questioned further.

Claudette dropped the ball she had been working on and stood up, brushing strands from the front of her skirt before meeting her visitor.

Entering the front of the shop, she froze in shock, and inwardly cursed Béatrice for not warning her.

"Good afternoon, Miss Laurent. I was hoping you could help me select a gift for my mother, who celebrates her fiftieth birthday in a few weeks." William Greycliffe stood before her, his cynical smile in place as always.

She swallowed a knot of anxiety and offered him a prim smile. "Does your mother currently own any fashion dolls, Mr. Greycliffe?

You can select one from our shelves, or we can always make something to her—or your—exact specifications." She kept her hands clasped together in front of her.

William moved to stand very close to her. She could smell his soap again and she involuntarily breathed deeply. He seemed intent on inhaling her scent as well, and momentarily forgot why he was there.

"Er, yes, yes, I would like to have something special made for my mother."

"Then please," she said as she waved him over to a desk with two chairs in the corner of the shop near the fireplace, "let's discuss the commission."

Once seated, Claudette picked up a quill pen and slid a sheaf of paper toward her. "Please tell me about your mother's tastes. For example, would she like a baby doll or an adult doll?"

"Miss Laurent, you are making quite a success of yourself here. You were right when you said you were heir to a great dollmaker." William's voice was filled with admiration.

"Yes, Mr. Greycliffe, *I* do not deceive others with my thoughts and intentions." She felt a protective cold wall building around her.

"Miss Laurent, may I have a private word with you?"

A private word? That could only mean trouble, and she did not intend to have any trouble with this man. She raised her voice slightly.

"Why, sir, a doll commission has never before required a private meeting. I am certain that we may conclude our business right here."

His voice dropped to a whisper. *"Please,"* he said through clenched teeth.

Claudette was defiant. "Have you married Miss Radley?"

"I have."

"So you are now her devoted husband?"

"I must be. I have to uphold her honor."

"Oho! So you have sullied her good name by your advances, and now you think to play the gallant. I will not be fooled by you,

Mr. Greycliffe, and I most certainly will not become your mistress, as you so obviously intend."

He looked at her sadly.

She continued in a loud voice, "Now, as you were saying about your mother's tastes . . . ?"

William stared at her for several moments, then broke eye contact, defeated. He halfheartedly gave her suggestions for a doll his mother might like, and Claudette concluded the transaction by giving him a price to which he immediately agreed.

"Very well, sir, your doll will be ready for you in three weeks' time. Your mother will be enchanted, I promise you."

"In three weeks, then, I will return to see you." He looked at her meaningfully and left the shop.

Béatrice's eyes were full of questions, but Claudette merely threw her a wry glance and shut herself in the workshop for the remainder of the day.

Claudette worked personally on the commission for Mrs. Greycliffe, not allowing anyone else to see it. She created a doll with curly blond locks and shockingly deep blue eyes. Holding the unfinished body at arm's length she realized, *Claudette, you silly fool, you have created a miniature of yourself to give that arrogant man.* It gave her an idea.

She dressed the doll in deep blue brocade with wide panniers and a lacy bodice. A wide-brimmed hat adorned with a matching band of brocade and trails of lace sat atop the doll's hair.

There, Mr. Greycliffe! That's what I would look like if I moved in your circle. But I don't; I'm a tradeswoman, and I will never look like this.

As an added spite, she carved a very tiny doll, only a few inches tall with a simple cotton sack dress, but wearing more of Claudette's hair. She glued this second doll into the main doll's hand.

As she wrapped the finished doll in tissue paper to await its pickup she said aloud to the walls, "In case you should forget my rank, Mr. Greycliffe."

On the appointed day, Claudette avoided being in the shop at all, telling Béatrice she had some shopping to do. The other woman pursed her lips, but said nothing. When she returned later that evening, Béatrice handed her a folded note.

"It's from Mr. Greycliffe. He seemed quite distressed that you were not in the shop when he arrived."

Claudette took the note and threw it into the fireplace before succumbing to the temptation to read it. "Please do not mention him to me again."

Béatrice shook her head and went to bed with her daughter without saying good night.

❧ 13 ❧

London, June 1784. Claudette, Béatrice, and Marguerite finished up a particularly busy week in the doll shop and walked several blocks to a coffee house to treat themselves to a raisin pudding. They had just finished eating at an outdoor table and were listening to the latest news being spread in and out of the coffee house by London's busiest gossips. Of particular interest was the recent parliamentary election contest between Pitt and Fox. The king, George III, endorsed Pitt, whereas his son the Prince of Wales was a Fox supporter. As if this was not scurrilous tattle enough, the Duchess of Devonshire had been touring the streets and kissing voters to induce them to vote for Fox. Every man in the coffee shop claimed to have been bussed by the beautiful duchess. The Whig Fox was declared the winner, but Pitt's Tory party was opening an investigation into the election proceedings.

Claudette and Béatrice listened attentively to the political gossip, as they rarely heard any news while buried in the doll shop day after day. Claudette was about to ask one of the other patrons a question about parliamentary procedure when they heard a commotion. A familiar female voice shot across the busy street to them.

"I will *not* be civil, sir. This little cretin purposely threw horse dung at me. If you won't, I will take him to Newgate myself. He can sit there and think about apologizing to me. And I hope he will be beaten every day and fed moldy biscuits." Laughter erupted from the crowd gathering around the fuss.

The two friends craned their necks to see around the throng. A woman in an enormous feathered hat held a young boy by the ear. Béatrice said, "Claudette, look! It's Lizbit. Whatever is she doing?"

"I'd say she's having a battle with a ten-year-old child."

The crowd began dispersing, and the urchin in question used the opportunity to slip out of Lizbet's grasp and scurry out of sight. Béatrice waved wildly and caught Lizbit's attention. Their friend grabbed her skirts in one hand, held her hat with the other, and darted over. The three were reunited at the coffee house table in a great round of hugs and kisses. Lizbit knelt down to Marguerite. "How you have grown! How old are you now?"

"I'm eight years old." She held up only six fingers.

"Why, soon I'm going to have to look for husbands for both of us."

"You haven't found a duke or prince of the blood yet to marry you?" asked Claudette.

"Alas, there are many of them who would marry me, but would I have them is the pertinent question." A wink at Marguerite. "I simply cannot decide if I like English or French men better. One likes to be loyal to one's mother country, but the French men are so passionate and fiery. What I could tell you about them . . ." She looked again at Marguerite. "Perhaps later. But now I insist that I treat everyone to a Punch and Judy show. Would you like that, little one?"

They spent the afternoon together, their lighthearted chatter quickly traversing the years apart. Lizbit had finally inherited her aunt's fortune, and was splitting her time between Paris and London, redecorating homes she now owned in each city, and immersing herself in the frenetic social whirls of both places.

Claudette asked eager questions about Paris, soaking in Lizbit's reports of that vital and pulsating city. She wondered if perhaps she could enlist Lizbit's help in discovering what may have ever happened to Jean-Philippe and his family. But what information did she really have to go on?

The group returned to the doll shop together so that Claudette could show Lizbit her growing venture into dollmaking. As they rode toward Cheapside, the warm sunshine beamed cheerfully on them while their driver spurred his horse on. Sleepy from their happy day together, the warm air, and the rhythmic clip-clop of the horse's hooves, Claudette was lulled into a light doze.

They came to a halt at a busy intersection so that cross traffic could pass. The horse's snuffle of impatience brought Claudette out of her nap.

"Have I bored you already?" Lizbit said. "Is my company less preferable to you than your wee wooden babies?"

"Hardly! I was just enjoying—"

Claudette stopped in mid-sentence. Moving through the intersection was a dark red landau with red spoked wheels, far larger than the hackney transporting the four of them. Two sleek black horses pulled it along effortlessly. Its occupants were seated opposite one another, and each stared out to one side of the carriage.

William Greycliffe again.

Claudette's universe went white and silent as their carriage went by. Mr. Greycliffe was out for a jaunt with his wife, Lenora. Claudette was alarmed by her appearance. The elegant lady who swept into the Ashby home in her fastidiously brushed fur complementing her glossy hair and perfect teeth was now slatternly and unkempt. Her hair was loose, and its tangles and snarls were not even concealed by a hat. Her eyes darted back and forth from her husband to unseen points outside her side of the carriage. Mysteriously, Lenora barked a short laugh at nothing in particular and looked to her husband for approval. He stared straight ahead and did not give it to her. She continued her random visual fixations.

Why did Mr. Greycliffe's wife look so . . . neglected? Like an unfortunate just released from Bedlam. Had her husband been mistreating her? Was that likely? Claudette shivered despite the balmy day. Although she refused to care a fig for the haughty Mr. Greycliffe, the possibility that he was behaving harshly toward his wife both angered and distressed her. He couldn't be guilty of cruelty, he just couldn't. Something else must be wrong.

She held her breath as Mr. Greycliffe caught her eye. His stare was serious and piercing and she felt that her soul was an opaque window through which he was radiating his own shaft of light. He dipped his head in a fleeting nod to her before his carriage rumbled out of view.

In all, ten seconds must have passed, but to Claudette it felt like she had endured a day's worth of waking nightmare. Why? Why did that man rattle her so?

"Enjoying what?" Lizbit cut into her reverie.

"What? Oh, yes, of course, I was just enjoying the lovely day we were having together. Look, we're moving again. I guess our driver found an open spot. It will be wonderful to finally show you the doll shop. There's so much to show you. The shop has such a variety of doll sizes and styles. I'll have to give you—"

"Claudette, what in the name of kingdom come is the matter with you? You're babbling like you've gone completely mutton-headed."

Claudette laughed despite her anxiety. How good it was to see Lizbit again!

Arriving at the shop, the three women walked around while Marguerite scampered off to the bookseller's. Lizbit was more impressed than Claudette thought she would be.

"These are lovely. You are becoming the independent woman we talked about."

"Well, we are not quite successful as of yet. Our living accommodations are barely big enough for the three of us to sleep in. And when Marguerite tosses and turns in her trundle while dreaming, there's no sleeping for anyone. But we're managing."

"I'd say you've advanced drastically since the day I met a trio of waifs on board that ship bound for England. Now we need to figure out how to marry you well, even though you are in a trade. Has anyone offered for you yet?" Lizbit's mind never seemed to stray far from the topic of marriage.

Claudette was silent. She had had little time to think of marriage. In three years, she had lost her parents, her home, and Jean-Philippe, her only love. Definitely her only love. She was only nineteen herself but had endured humiliating servitude, and was now struggling to survive as well as caring for Béatrice and Marguerite. What about Jack Smythe? Jack was near her age, and amusing, but too enveloped in his own secrecies. How could she ever trust a husband like that? The only other man she had had any close contact with was William Greycliffe, and he was galling. Too conceited. Too arrogant. And anyway, he was married to the delightful Lenora Radley now, who was not the woman she was before marrying him. Not that it mattered. It truly didn't.

"Come now, Claudette, where are you again?" Lizbit's merry voice brought her back to the present. "Do you have so many suitors that you cannot name them all?" Her laughter tinkled through the shop.

"Not at all. I've been too busy to even think of it. But what of you? Gentlemen from both England and the Continent pursuing you—it must be thrilling."

Béatrice interrupted to plead a headache that required a rest in the bedroom. Once they were alone, Lizbit replied, "La, my travels give me so many opportunities to meet eligible young men. However, a woman in my position cannot be too careful with whom she associates. I would not want to fall into the hands of a fortune-seeker. And they exist both here and in France."

Claudette smiled at her brash friend. "I can hardly imagine you allowing a young man to take advantage of you. I do, after all, remember how you put Simon Briggs in his place."

"I did, didn't I? He deserved much more than the slap I gave him." Lizbit's cheerful face turned serious. "But d'you know, I do have to watch out for my person in France these days. Despite its culture and vibrancy we talked of earlier, Paris has changed in the last two years, and not for the better. When I go, I dress shabbily and carry my gowns in trunks that I ship separately. People on the street look askance at others they think might be hoarding wealth."

"Why is this?" Claudette asked.

"They are furious with King Louis and Marie Antoinette. They think the king and queen are responsible for all of the bad crops and inflation in the country. Their fury extends to anyone they think might be wealthy enough to associate with the royal couple."

"I had heard this before while still in France. But it's ridiculous. How can the monarch be to blame for deficient rains and soil conditions?"

Lizbit shrugged. "All I know is the people are unhappy and they grumble loudly. It will get worse if the king does not do something. Their complaints are not entirely without foundation. I hear tell the queen spends extraordinary sums on jewelry and clothing and gifts for her favorites."

"I have heard this as well," Claudette said impatiently. "I recall my father telling me that all members of the nobility in Europe do the same thing. Why, even Prinny showers his favorite women with extravagant gifts of land and jewels right here in England. Why is so much abuse heaped upon Marie Antoinette?"

Another shrug. "Perhaps they think the queen simply goes too far. Perhaps she does."

"I do not believe it."

"If I were the queen, I would use my fortune to my own ends for certain, but not be so blatant with it. La, let us not argue. We are friends, are we not? What do we care what's going on hundreds of miles away? It's getting late. I'll return tomorrow, and let's go to Leadenhall Market. They have a man there with the most amazing birds from South America. They talk and perform tricks. Sometimes they even curse in other languages."

The women agreed to meet the next day and go to see the famous birds together.

Béatrice begged off with illness again the next day. She looked a little flushed and was coughing. "It's just a touch of the gripe, I'm certain. Enjoy the market."

Claudette, Lizbit, and Marguerite set off in a hired carriage and were dropped off outside the gate to Leadenhall. The area was teeming with people, and the cacophony from street peddlers and their customers was deafening. Carts and tables were piled high with wares ranging from fruits, vegetables, and fresh slain rabbits, to exotic imports from the Far East. These purveyors of carpets, perfume oils, and cosmetic creams and salves from faraway lands cajoled and flattered passersby into examining their wares. Small wood fires were set in various places where vendors were cooking all manner of meat on sticks for sale. All of the aromas mingled together into one overpowering spicy scent. Claudette had never been to such a large market before and was impressed with all London had to offer. Marguerite was thoroughly dazzled, and the two women each had to hold one of her hands to keep her from wandering off.

"Miss Lizbit! Miss Claudette! Look, it's the birds." Marguerite was practically hopping up and down.

A small circle of people had gathered for the performance about to begin. About twenty cages were stacked up in five rows. Each cage held a different brightly-plumed bird. In front of the cages stood their owner and a variety of stands and perches. The man, introducing himself to the audience as Mr. Spively, announced that the people of London were about to observe the most amazing wild animal feats ever witnessed.

He opened one cage and pulled out a gorgeous white bird, with a thick, full, almost fluffy coat, an ebony beak, and an orange crest on his head that the bird lifted for the audience, as though introducing himself.

"Good friends, meet Peaches." Mr. Spively placed it on a perch and went through a repertoire of words that the sizable bird repeated after him. Peaches clearly enunciated, "God save the king," "Pour us a pint, love," and "The rotten napper took your hat!" and received encouraging noises from some of the onlookers. Mr. Spively spied Marguerite edging her way to the front.

"What's your name, little sprite?" he asked.

"Marguerite du Georges," she replied, for once shy.

Mr. Spively gave Peaches a quick hand signal, and all of a sudden the bird began rocking back and forth on the perch, shouting, "Marguerite! Marguerite! Marguerite! Du Georges! Du Georges! Du Georges! I want a treat! Give me a sweet! I don't like meat!"

The small crowd was enchanted with the bird. Lizbit dropped some coins into Mr. Spively's basket. To Marguerite's dismay, Peaches was put away, and two more birds brought out and placed on perches. These two were even larger than Peaches, and had long tails. One was a scarlet color, the other was bright blue. They were presented as Ruby and Sapphire. Each bird bowed its head as its name was mentioned.

Mr. Spively whispered a command in Ruby's ear, and the bird

took off, disappearing far into the sky. In a few moments, Mr. Spively gave a long whistle, and soon Ruby came back from seemingly nowhere and landed back on his perch. People cheered and laughed.

Sapphire was now given his own whispered instruction. This bird lifted its wings gently, majestically, and began making low sweeping arcs right over the crowd's heads. Marguerite clapped delightedly. While Sapphire made his third circle over the astonished gathering, a loose mongrel sniffing around for meat scraps caught sight of him. Agitated by the unusual bird, the dog ran through the crowd and into the open area where the perches were, barking excitedly. Ruby flapped his wings and screeched in protest in his struggle to remain upright as the dog bumped into his stand. Ruby's unexpected screech and the dog's insistent barking startled Sapphire in mid-flight, and in a panic he dove into the assembled crowd.

Claudette, still distracted by the appearance of the keyed-up dog, did not see Sapphire falling toward her. The bird landed hard against her shoulder, knocking her down in a tumble of skirts and plumage. Still frightened, Sapphire began beating his enormous wings against her and nipping at her with his large white beak. She cried out and attempted to push him away while keeping her eyes tightly shut to prevent his pecking or clawing at them, but it only agitated the bird further. The crowd and Sapphire's owner seemed helpless, and Claudette was suffocating under the bird's attack.

Suddenly she heard a great "whoosh" and Sapphire was gone in a piercing squawk. She didn't resist as she felt someone pick her up and sharply order others out of the way.

"Look at me," a man's voice said. Claudette opened her eyes. She was staring straight into William Greycliffe's face. She began struggling out of his grasp, but he held her closer.

"Don't be an idiot," he said in a low voice. "I'm trying to help you."

"Lizbit—" she began.

"We're here with you, Claudette." She could hear Lizbit's voice and footsteps behind them. She closed her eyes again. Presently she heard a door open, and looked to see that she was being placed in a large elegant carriage, different than the one she had previously seen him in with Lenora Radley. William climbed in next to Claudette after Lizbit and Marguerite placed themselves across from her. William gave directions to the driver.

"Are you all right?" William asked her.

Lizbit silently handed her a handkerchief, and pointed to her neck. A swipe of the cloth showed Claudette that she was messy with dirt and blood from the bird's scratches. He had also nipped her hard in the shoulder, and that was beginning to throb.

"I am well enough." She crossed her arms in front of her in an attempt to seem aloof, but she knew she must look a fright from the bird's attack. Marguerite's big eyes confirmed it.

"Good Lord, Claudette," exclaimed Lizbit. "This gentleman— and I do not believe we have been properly introduced—just rescued you from a savage wild beast with one thrust of his arm that sent it tumbling back to its owner, and all you say is 'I am well enough'?"

"You don't understand," she mumbled. Forcing herself to look at William, she said, "Mr. Greycliffe, I am grateful for your assistance in my distress."

"It is my pleasure, Miss Laurent, to be of some service to you." His eyes were indecipherable, but his voice was light. Drat the man and his sardonic responses.

"So"—Lizbit was brightening considerably—"you know each other. Pray tell how. Claudette has not mentioned you to me. I am Elizabeth Preston, one of her dearest friends." She held out her gloved hand.

William greeted her politely. "Miss Preston, you have my warmest regards as a friend of Miss Laurent's. But you say she has not mentioned me before? I am disappointed. I knew that I had made a less than favorable impression upon her, but I had not realized how poorly she considered me, although I hold her in the highest regard."

Lizbit looked around the carriage, which was fitted with brass trimmings and green velvet seats. "I can see that my friend does not have her own best interests at heart." Her glance then took in William's wedding band.

"Ah, there is perhaps one quality you lack." She said it as a question. William caught the trail of her glance.

"I came to the market with my manservant, Dobry, to purchase a pet finch for my wife. She has a collection of them, but is never pleased with what any of her maids pick out for her. I thought if I came to do it for her she might be satisfied."

Lizbit cocked her head to one side. "And instead of a finch, you have snared the beautiful swan, haven't you?"

Claudette flushed, and felt the heat creeping up to her face.

"Alas," William said. "I never had an opportunity to snare the beautiful swan, and she will always remain out of my reach."

The carriage pulled up to the shop, and he escorted them to the door. Marguerite burst in and went shouting for her mother to hear of their great adventure. Lizbit followed her in, but William held Claudette back to speak with her outside.

"Miss Laurent, may I send a doctor to attend to you?"

"No, I am perfectly fine."

"You may have been more badly injured than you imagine. It would set my mind at ease to know that a physician has declared you well."

Why did it seem as though Mr. Greycliffe always vacillated between sarcasm and kindness? He was really quite awful, but she did now have an aching head, so perhaps a doctor's visit would be advisable.

"I suppose it would not hurt to see a doctor," she agreed.

"Splendid. I will ask our family physician, Dr. Crowley, to come round. I will check in on you myself in a fortnight."

"No! I mean, that will not be necessary. I appreciate your thoughtfulness, Mr. Greycliffe. I must go now, and I am certain your wife wonders why you have not yet returned with her new finch." She offered him her hand, which he pressed between both of his own, as though trying to prevent her from leaving.

"Miss Laurent, I never had an opportunity to tell you how beautiful the doll was that you created for my mother. She talked of nothing else for weeks after her birthday."

"We take all of our commissions very seriously, Mr. Greycliffe. I gave it the same attention that I do all of our custom work."

"Well, yes, I expect that is true. Nevertheless, the quality of the work spoke greatly about the craftswoman behind it. I was particularly impressed with the doll's blue eyes, so sharp in color that they reminded me of, of—"

He pulled her closer, so that the fabric of their clothing nearly touched. He brought her hand up and kissed the top of it, then turned her palm over to place a feathery kiss on her wrist.

No, Claudette, no, she thought. *He is a married gentleman, he does not love you. He deceives you! But his lips make me tremble and I cannot help being drawn to him no matter how dreadful he is. Someone please help me.*

When William received no resistance, he bent down and kissed her scratched and bruised forehead twice, once over each eye.

"They reminded me of you, Miss Laurent, and your infernal sass. Why I am in lo— Why I continue to help you I cannot understand."

He reluctantly dropped her hand. "Until we meet again." He stepped back into his carriage and rapped on the ceiling for the driver to move on, offering her a nod as he rode past.

Claudette waited until she recaptured her senses before entering the shop to find both of her friends waiting to pepper her with questions.

"Why didn't you tell me of this Mr. Greycliffe when we talked yesterday?"

"Did you really get attacked by a bird?" Béatrice was a bit glassy-eyed, but looked much better than she had that morning.

"How did you let such a fine gentleman slip through your fingers?"

Claudette threw up both hands. "I will not discuss the faultless Mr. Greycliffe, and the condition of my face should indicate that I did indeed have a tussle with a wild creature that apparently got the better of me." She moved past them to the bedroom. "If someone were to bring me a cup of tea, I would be most grateful, but I warn you that I will not discuss anything."

She left them to gossip together, with Béatrice telling Lizbit all she knew about Mr. Greycliffe.

Dr. Crowley pronounced Claudette healthy, despite some lingering bumps and scratch marks. He brought with him a note from

Mr. Greycliffe, which instead of immediately burning she put away in a drawer to read once she could be alone.

After supper, Claudette retreated to the bedroom with the letter while Béatrice sat Marguerite at a table next to the fireplace to teach her how to thread a needle.

She turned the envelope over and pried apart the red wax seal.

June 25, 1784
Hevington
Kent

Dear Miss Laurent,
    I pray this letter finds you well and in good spirits after
your recent distressing accident. It was my own good
fortune to have been able to provide some assistance to
you. You have only to ask should you require anything
further. I cannot impress upon you enough my regret that
circumstances beyond my control prevented me from
furthering our acquaintance when the outcome of such
acquaintance might have resulted in the greatest happiness.
However, I shall ever remain,
    Your servant,
    William Greycliffe

Claudette folded the letter again, and this time decided to place it in her supply box, instead of consigning it to the fire. What circumstances were these? Was the mighty Mr. Greycliffe implying a genuine interest in her?

❧ 14 ❧

Paris, 1785. This year would prove to be the one that sealed Marie Antoinette's reputation with the people forever, and all because of a glittering diamond necklace.

Jeanne de Saint-Rémy was born in 1756, the daughter of an impoverished aristocrat who could claim illegitimate descent from Henri II, the last Valois king of France. The Baron de Saint-Rémy taught his children to beg in the streets, saying, "Take pity on a little child who descends from one of our country's greatest kings." Jeanne later developed talents as an actress in amateur theatricals, and through them she met an army officer, Nicholas de la Motte.

The couple married quickly, Monsieur de la Motte resigned his commission, and the two began signing themselves as the Comte and Comtesse de la Motte; or, when they wanted extended credit, de la Motte-Valois.

Jeanne became acquainted with Cardinal de Rohan, a good-looking, conceited social climber, who was also a prince. His one desire was to follow in the footsteps of Cardinals Richelieu and Mazarin. Such a position would enable him to direct the very destiny of France. Unfortunately for the cardinal, the queen detested him for a very unwise letter he had written to Louis XV's mistress, Madame du Barry, in which he made fun of Marie Antoinette's mother. Madame du Barry read the letter aloud at a dinner party, and news of it traveled quickly to the queen's ears. With a stroke of his own pen, he had erased any possibility of advancement.

Jeanne was well aware of this situation as she developed her relationship with the cardinal. First, she enlisted de Rohan to secure a position for her husband at Versailles, intimating that with her husband gone, she and de Rohan could become lovers. Instead, she joined her husband at Versailles in an effort to put herself in the queen's path. When the queen refused, or perhaps just failed, to recognize or receive Jeanne, the ambitious young woman invented other means of achieving her aims, the primary one to have her royal ancestry recognized, which might then lead to a pension.

The "comtesse" employed such antics as fainting in the hallways of Versailles as Marie Antoinette approached. The queen merely stepped around her, fully recognizing a ploy when she saw one. Jeanne would also tell her friends about conversations, all imaginary, that she was having with the queen. Soon she developed a reputation as someone in Marie Antoinette's inner circle. Meanwhile, the queen did not even know her name.

This was all irrelevant to Jeanne, as she and de la Motte had now devised a perfect plan for securing the currency they needed to establish themselves back into aristocracy. They needed the help of Cardinal de Rohan, who, aware of Jeanne's "position" with the queen, was willing to help in order to forge his own relationship with Marie Antoinette.

Jeanne had discovered that the crown jewelers, Boehmer and Bassenge, had spent several years creating for Louis XV's mistress, Madame du Barry, the most magnificent necklace ever seen in Europe, a brilliantly shining array of 647 perfect diamonds. In the purchase of these gems, the jewelers had expended far more than their own fortunes, and the king died before the transaction could be completed, leaving the jewelers in financial straits. They had earlier made lesser masterpieces for Marie Antoinette, and now assumed that she would be enthralled with a piece that could only be described as spectacular. Unfortunately, they did not know that she had lost her fondness for such costly treasures, and was now contenting herself in the novelty of wearing the utmost simplicity in attire and spending time in the pastoral setting of her seemingly simple—but extravagantly expensive—Hameau on the grounds of Versailles.

Boehmer and Bassenge had presented the necklace to Marie Antoinette, but she refused it, considering it too garish for her new lifestyle and also realizing that such a purchase would make her even more unpopular in the country. Desperate to recover their investment, the jewelers were now shopping the necklace with many of the Continent's wealthiest women.

Using several accomplices, Jeanne approached Boehmer and told him the queen was reconsidering the necklace, but needed to make the purchase a secret, due to her unpopularity with the people. A price of one million six hundred thousand francs was negotiated, a sum lower than the cost of the stones. In his haste to sell the necklace, the jeweler did not question who Jeanne was.

Jeanne then approached de Rohan, telling him that the queen very much desired to purchase this necklace for herself, and would be willing to bring the cardinal back into her inner circle if he would advance the money for the necklace and allow her to pay him back in installments. Anxious to get back into the queen's good graces, he did not question the plan.

Jeanne and her husband took de Rohan's money, took the necklace from Boehmer (leaving him a promissory note supposedly in the queen's own writing), then immediately broke up the exquisite piece of art and sold off individual diamonds.

Soon, though, both the jeweler and the cardinal were asking for their money. In particular, de Rohan was confused because the queen's attitude toward him did not seem to change after his very generous gesture toward her, and she never wore the necklace in public. When Jeanne was unable to come up with more excuses for the jewelers and de Rohan regarding the payment delay, the duplicity became obvious to both parties. A scandal ensued, and all parties were arrested and tried, with the exception of Nicholas de la Motte, who fled the country at the first sign of trouble. All of the conspirators except Jeanne were released with little or no punishment. The Comtesse de la Motte was sentenced to be publicly flogged, branded above her left breast, and imprisoned.

None of this episode was of Marie Antoinette's device or desire, but the press and the public laid it squarely at her door. Her already tarnished reputation as a frivolous spendthrift was blackened further, and the French people hated her even more. Her delivery of the royal heir was forgotten in the flood of public ill will.

"Why?" she cried to Axel late at night. "Why do the subjects I love despise me so much?"

He had no answer.

London, October 1785. Jack was in the shop to pick up an order of dolls for a newly opened millinery shop.

"Did you hear the latest gossip about the Greycliffes?"

Claudette stiffened. "No, why should I hear anything about them?" She busied herself with an eye that had fallen out of a doll's eye socket for the third time.

He tilted his head quizzically at her. "Aren't you friendly with Mr. Greycliffe? Didn't he save you from the market birds?"

Claudette did not reply, and continued fiddling with the uncooperative doll's head.

Jack shook his head. "The poor man, to have such a slut for a wife. She left him in the middle of the night, with his own servant, no less. A footman. She's pregnant now, going to have the servant's baby. They're living with his family, who are none too happy about it. Mr. Greycliffe hired their boy and had been a good employer. Funny enough, they say Mr. Greycliffe doesn't seem to mind that his wife left. I suppose even a lowly cur like me could one day hope to marry up, if Mrs. Greycliffe is any indication."

The glass eye fell to the floor again, and this time she did not bother to pick it up. She held the doll tightly so that Jack would not see her trembling.

❧ 15 ❧

London, March 1786. The crowded workroom was pulsating with activity. Claudette was supervising three workers, one a seamstress, the other two carvers. One carver, simply known as Carpenter Tom, was an ex–cabinetmaker who once swung axes and hammers equally with ease, but was now too aged and stooped for harsh carpentry work. The work of carving dolls suited him, since he could sit comfortably all day at a worktable to do so, and Claudette would let him periodically take home a finished product to a granddaughter or great-niece celebrating a natal day.

The second carver she had hired was Roger Hatfield, an enormous, barrel-chested man, whose voice could be heard resounding through the workshop even when he was whispering. He was the hairiest human being Claudette had ever seen, with not only long black hair curling down the back of his neck and a matching beard down the front, but also long tendrils of hair that dangled from his arms like a heavy growth of twining vines. Really, he seemed quite ferocious at first, with his bushy, wiggling eyebrows and massive arms, but he quickly proved to be Claudette's and Béatrice's fiercest protector from unruly customers. He became expert at getting the most doll limbs and parts out of a single block.

Each evening, Claudette would sort out the day's orders, identifying hair, eye, and lip color for each doll, and sketching out the fashion to be made for it. She snipped scraps of fabric and pinned them to the order, with instructions as to what articles of clothing should be made from each fabric. She then arranged the pile of orders by importance of the customer, and left it on the carving table. Carpenter Tom or Roger, whoever arrived first to the shop, knew to begin work first on whatever order was on top.

After the carvers had spent a day or two on a doll, the carved body was wrapped in paper, along with the order, and handed over to Agnes Smoot, the seamstress, who was distantly related to Roger and whom Claudette had hired at his urging.

Agnes would also work with each doll in the order received, fingering the fabric palette that Claudette had selected and going up to the storage attic to pick out the corresponding bolts of fabric. Much to Claudette's pleasure, Agnes would frequently add a lace trim or bow or frill to a doll's costume that Claudette had not thought of, adding immeasurably to the creation's aesthetic value.

Claudette's shop hummed busily six days each week, between patrons shopping in front and workers carving, sewing, and assembling in the rear. She had even taken on a young helper, a thin, bedraggled-looking boy named Joseph Cummings who had come in begging for work.

While profits were not substantial, Claudette realized that she needed larger quarters, particularly if she wanted to begin constructing the *grandes Pandores* her father had made popular in Paris. Claudette knew that England's elite would love the *grandes Pandores*, too; not old dour Queen Charlotte, of course, who only spent her time in bearing children and stitching embroidery, but the rest of the court, which was tired of the stilted and boring lifestyle King George and his wife had instituted.

In earlier times, the English court glittered with political intrigues, elaborate balls, and the continual jockeying for position that made being a courtier worthwhile. But in the House of Hanover, George III in particular, court had been reduced to boring games of backgammon, conversations about farming, and the attendance of endless christenings as the monarch and his wife's only expression of zeal seemed to be in the bedroom.

Claudette's *grandes Pandores* were what the aristocracy needed to restore enthusiasm again.

The small bedroom that she shared with Béatrice and Marguerite was now heaped with materials and supplies spilling over from the workroom. They had already blocked off a small area of the display room with a screen to hide small crates of doll parts. The attic was full of fabric bolts wrapped in tissue and corresponding laces and trims.

"I believe I've found the perfect place!" Béatrice was breathless from her hurried journey back to the shop. Claudette had sent her and Joseph out each day for the last two weeks on scouting missions for a new location. Until now, Béatrice had gone half-heartedly into the streets of London on these missions, returning each evening dejected.

"It's a wonderful shop, Claudette. It has large windows at the front for display, and a huge workroom with a locking door upstairs. The shop is twice as large as this one, and very bright and cheerful. The walls have just been whitewashed and the floors polished, as well."

The proposed location did not have sleeping quarters with it, which would force the women to seek separate accommodations. However, at first glance Claudette fell in love with the property, located on fashionable Oxford Street in Mayfair proper, and decided that the extra expenses generated would be more than made up by increased sales. She and Béatrice quickly found small but clean quarters. They were adjoining flats in a nearby building, giving each woman some privacy, which Claudette relished. Béatrice was grateful that they would not truly be apart, for she still found London to be a fearful place.

But with this move, Claudette had made an irrevocable decision to take root in England. She still thought of Jean-Philippe, but it was no longer with the intense longing of the past. She relegated him and her parents to a special corner of her mind, and periodically reached in to mentally visit them, to assure herself that they would never be forgotten.

To her own personal fury, Mr. Greycliffe had crept out of the small recess in her mind when she wasn't paying attention, and managed to lodge himself in a vacancy in her heart she didn't want to fill. She resolved to evict him the very moment she had time from her frantically busy days. How ridiculous to maintain even a slight affection for a married gentleman! Was she a simpleton?

Their new landlady was a widow, and more than happy to keep an eye on Marguerite when necessary, plying her with sweets, toys, and cast-off clothing from her grandchildren who now lived in far-off Yorkshire. Marguerite flourished under Mrs. Jenkins's kindness and the more spacious quarters she occupied with her mother. Perhaps England was not so bad for a young girl, after all.

Within a month of finding their new living arrangements, the lease had been signed for the new storefront, all workshop supplies had been moved, and sample dolls were set up prettily in the window. The final touch was the hanging of the new "C. Laurent Fashion Dolls" sign, made professionally by a local sign-maker in dark green with white letters and a small doll's head painted on it.

Almost immediately, curious onlookers were crowded about the shop, always interested when a new purveyor of goods arrived. They quickly lost interest when it turned out to be a seller of inferior items, or the same bits of laces, cosmetics or quill pens that could be found anywhere.

Claudette needed to keep the interest of the passersby, and posted a notice in the window.

ON MAY THE TWELFTH
IN THE YEAR OF OUR LORD, 1786
COME TO SEE A MARVELOUS NEW CREATION!
DIRECT FROM FRANCE!
UNIQUE AND UNHEARD OF IN ALL ENGLAND
A LIMITED NUMBER OF ORDERS
WILL BE ACCEPTED AT THAT TIME

Although the English detested the French, they were intoxicated by French fashion and style. Her trials as Mrs. Ashby's lady's maid and her initial sales to Lady Parshall were reflections of English envy of the modes set by the Parisians.

Béatrice tilted her head to one side in front of the sign, frowning. "Whatever is it that we are going to be offering?"

"I believe the time has come for England to be introduced to the *grandes Pandores*. We are going to build two of them; one for display on May twelfth, the other that we will offer to the highest bidder to take home that day. All other buyers will have to wait a month for delivery of their creations. I want these dolls to be very much in demand."

Béatrice's eyes grew large. "Oh, Claudette, do you really think this will work? We've never made them before. What if customers don't take to the dolls? All of the money invested will—"

Claudette smiled confidently. "It will work. We are going to set London on its ear."

Although most of Claudette's apprenticeship had involved working with fashion dolls, her father had dabbled in the *grandes Pandores* that had become the rage of fashionable Paris. These life-sized dolls, built on metal frames, were an extremely effective method for displaying wealth, even among those who were fabulously rich and already jaded by the luxuries of grand estate homes, gardens, jewels, and liveried servants. The dolls were difficult to create, though, and her father had soon abandoned them to return to the fashion dolls that he knew so well.

Claudette set the new workshop to an even more furious level of activity. The spacious quarters meant that the workshop could be set up in a more organized fashion. A long, wide table was in the middle of the room, and the floors were required to be swept clean after each day's work. Around the perimeter of the room, wooden crates were affixed to the walls at angles, each containing supplies in the order in which they would be worked. Candles in sconces were affixed in many places to the walls to ensure the workers had as much light as possible for their detailed work. Several woven rugs were scattered about the wooden floor, to help maintain warmth during the winter.

She stopped all other projects in the shop to have her workers learn how to build *grandes Pandores*. She first sketched out a few simple designs for this new doll, and then hired a blacksmith to build the doll's frame. The metal grid frame was shaped like a bell to represent a woman's flared skirt and forged onto a center pole. Another smaller bell shape was inverted and placed on top of the "skirt" to represent the torso. Now nearly five feet tall, the doll frame balanced itself on the ground. From there, the shop employees padded the frame, then went to work making stuffed arms and large wax molds for the head.

Creating these molds was the most painstaking part of the creation, and utterly unlike the woodcarving to which her employees had become expert. Claudette was surprised when Roger Hatfield quickly became most adept at knowing how hot to make the wax, and exactly how long to let it cool in the wooden mold before breaking the two halves of it apart and letting the doll head drop gently into his lap. The enormous man would coddle the mold in his hands as though it were a puppy, talking to it and coaxing it apart. His expertise came at a price, as he frequently spattered the hot, melted liquid on himself and the worktable, and Claudette and Béatrice could hear him swearing and muttering under his breath. After removing the mold from the cooled wax and smoothing down any rough parts of the head, he would gently pass it on to someone else to paint on facial features.

The final step to affix the wax heads required several tries, as they had difficulty securing them onto the enormous frames. Either Roger or Claudette would arrive at the shop in the morning to find a wax head split apart on the floor next to the frame. Eventually they hit upon pouring hot wax into a mold with two pieces of three-foot-long twine in it. When the mold was removed and the head painted and bewigged, they would place the wax head on the frame, and run the twine through the middle of the frame, securing it on opposite sides of the lower metal skirt.

While Roger and the other workers finished up the actual doll construction, Claudette took measurements for the doll's trousseau. She designed the clothing and gave it to Agnes for sewing. Béatrice assisted Agnes later with the detail work of sewing on lace and embroidering designs on it. They gave the doll a *robe à la française*, a popular style characterized by a skirt completely open in front and draped on both sides, under which a woman wore a petticoat and other complementary garments. Agnes and Béatrice embroidered a pattern of bright butterflies in reds and oranges and pinks running down either side of the pale blue robe's opening. They embroidered one small butterfly on the cream petticoat peeping out from underneath, to look as though the insect had somehow jumped from the robe to the undergarment.

Even young Joseph, whose work consisted mostly of cleaning and sorting supplies, understood and appreciated the magnificence of the embroidery work, and came in eagerly each morning to view the previous day's progress before tending to his own tasks.

The two women created a very small headdress of feathers attached to a dark blue muslin cap and perched it on the side of the doll's head, enough to complete the outfit but not enough to distract from the artistic work of the doll's head and wig, which was pulled up high off the forehead and swept into a large pouf on top of the head, with tendrils hanging down the sides.

When the doll was completely finished, all of the shop workers stood admiring it. This was truly a new facet in their dollmaking business, one they knew would bring in yet more customers and make the shop famous. Béatrice hugged Claudette close.

"*Mon amie*, look at what you have done for us. For all of us."

All of this work kept Claudette and her employees busy for weeks. As she saw all of the dolls take shape and become more and more human-sized, especially as their wax heads and limbs were removed from molds and set in place, she nearly clapped with happiness. What would Papa say if he were here now? She sighed. He would be proud of her. He would laugh at her boldness. And perhaps he would tell her that the eyes on one of the dolls were not evenly spaced. Hmm, that would have to be fixed.

Claudette was gratified to see a small band of onlookers already crowding the window of the shop when she arrived the morning of the presentation. The previous evening she had covered the windows with curtains, to heighten curiosity and prevent anyone having an advance look at the *grandes Pandores*. She greeted the small throng, and asked them to be patient just a few more moments while she prepared.

Inside the shop, Béatrice and Roger were just finishing last-minute preparations and readying the shop for customers. Joseph was positioned on the floor next to a round wooden platform by the shop window, both hands on a turning crank attached to the platform. The most fabulous of the creations was on this platform. It took him four cranks to turn the doll one complete revolution, and he was puffing furiously with the exertion.

Together, Claudette and Béatrice pulled open the curtains to a gasp of admiration outside the windows. Patrons began spilling into the store with a ferocious excitement, peppering Claudette and Béatrice with questions about the dolls. Wherever did you find these dolls? Are they really from France? Does anyone else in London have them?

One intrepid woman attempted to lift the skirt of the revolving doll. Seeing this, Roger barged over and hoisted the crouched woman forcibly under both arms and removed her from the store, lecturing her on the improprieties of lifting a lady's dress. The woman scurried away shamefaced, but returned later in the day with a friend, pointing excitedly through the window at the shop's amazing offerings.

Throughout the day, they were visited by new customers and old friends. Lizbit Preston, Gerard and Diane Gifford, Jack Smythe, and Nicholas Ashby all arrived at various points to hail the shop's success.

The introduction of the *grandes Pandores* was an immediate success. The workshop was now receiving commissions from minor nobility, and various liveried servants began rushing in and out of the shop each day, placing orders for their employers. Fashionable women realized that they could be gossiped about quite thrillingly by having at least one of these gorgeous creations in their homes.

Claudette gave the second doll away by lottery, and the gentleman who won it for his wife acted as though he was the recipient of an unexpected fortune.

Orders did not diminish over the following weeks. It seemed that all of London was talking about the "doll companions." Rumor was brought to Claudette by one of her customers that even Queen Charlotte had heard of them, and looked up interestedly enough from reading to inquire as to how one could possess a doll so large and not have to give it a room of its own.

But even the interest of England's queen did not move Claudette as much as a note from William Greycliffe, congratulating her success as "heir to the finest dollmaker in all of France."

She read and reread his letter in private, away from Béatrice's questioning eyes, and could not resist bringing the thick, cream-colored paper to her face to try to catch his scent on it. She inhaled deeply and was rewarded with the faintest whiff of leather and his strong male fragrance.

Claudette, she thought. *You are the idiot that Mr. Greycliffe calls you. This can never be. He is a married man, and a gentleman besides. He is not in a position to do more than sport with your affections. Stop this now before he destroys you.*

She reluctantly folded the letter again into its small rectangle, noticing the return address in Kent. Word of her growing doll shop had traveled far if he knew about it from there.

Or maybe he was interested enough that he was avidly seeking news of her?

Cease this once and for all, she told herself sternly.

She dug out the old tool chest she had rescued from her father's doll shop and used it as a hiding place for the letter. The chest was full of trinkets: broken doll parts, a few coins left over from her manic saving days at the Ashbys, brightly-hued threads, rusty scissors, and a small jar of gesso, among other heaped belongings. She also had Mr. Greycliffe's previous letter to her from just after her accident with the show birds. Holding both letters in her hands, she made a foolishly sentimental decision. Claudette dashed off to the workshop and returned with a spool of pink ribbon. Removing a long length, she tied the two notes together and buried them at the bottom of the chest. Her hand slid over another ribbon-wrapped stack and she pulled it out. It was her small stack of love letters from Jean-Philippe. She had nearly forgotten them. She sank to the floor on both knees to read them.

His teenage bravado dominated the letters, and she allowed the bittersweet rush of memories of her foolish youth, his headstrong opinions, and their innocent and pure romance to wash over her.

Ah, Jean-Philippe, who knows what might have been had we not been torn apart?

But the pain did not knife through her as it once did. She folded his letters and retied them to return them to the chest. For reasons she dared not think about, she moved Jean-Philippe's letters to the bottom of the chest, and put Mr. Greycliffe's at the top where she could more easily find them.

One last time she admonished herself. *Claudette, thoughts of that man will only bring you to ruin!*

❧ 16 ❧

London, June 1786. The shop seemed busier than ever, especially since Miss Claudette, as she was now affectionately known to her customers and employees, was offering the *grandes Pandores* to an approving public. The English aristocrats were wild for them, some even going as far as "inviting" their doll companions to tea, or having them accompany them in their landaus when they went calling on their friends. Agnes found this type of doll easier to work with, as her patterns for clothing were of the same dimensions as when she had once worked as a *déshabillé* maker, creating underclothing and loose gowns for women.

Around noon one day, Claudette stepped into the workroom, sighing and pushing a loose tendril into her hair band. She poked aimlessly at the dolls in various stages of completion on the work-table, examining them for flaws. Stepping away from the table, she moved over to the row of *grandes Pandores* in various stages of dress. Agnes asked, "Miss Claudette, can I help you? Is anything wrong?"

"No, I just needed a rest from the customers. It has been a particularly trying day so far with Béatrice sick at home."

The bell tinkled in the outer room. Claudette straightened, arranged her skirt, patted her hair, and turned to welcome another customer.

Entering the C. Laurent Fashion Doll Shop was an exquisitely dressed gentleman and what could only be described as his entourage. He was the sun around which several people danced, including two women who appeared to be competing for a nod or acknowledgment from him. Claudette took her position behind the counter while the group examined the sample dolls in the shop. From her vantage point she could observe the customer without appearing obvious. He was a handsome man—no, not just handsome, he was actually quite *beautiful*. He was dressed in the French fashion, as were the members of his party. He turned his profile toward Claudette, and she could see his rounded eyes with their long lashes, his aquiline nose, his high-set cheekbones above a strong jaw. Claudette actually felt herself gasp inwardly as the Adonis made his way to her counter. He stopped, imperceptibly snapping to in military fashion, and gracefully made a small bow to her.

"Mademoiselle, I am Count Fersen of Sweden, and a very close friend of the king and queen of France. I should like to requisition several of your creations. They seem to be the talk of London since I have arrived." He spoke in French! He saw Claudette's startled look. "Everyone says, 'You must visit the little French doll-seller on Oxford Street.' So I assumed that French would be welcome here, although it is not in many circles of England." His voice was gently teasing. He played with some loose wool on the counter. "I do not see any of these lifelike dolls I hear of, *grandes Pandores* I believe they are called?"

"I am so sorry, but we have none on display. They have been very popular and sell quickly. All we have are partially made samples in the workroom."

"Then I insist that you allow me to escort you to this workroom immediately." He held out an arm, and Claudette found herself swept under his spell. Agnes, too, was agog at the handsome count who gallantly swept her a bow upon entering the workroom.

The count spent the better part of an hour appraising the large dolls under construction, examining their birdcage construction and realistic features. He also went back into the display room and looked over various doll styles. His entourage waited to one side, the women shooting daggers at Claudette, unsure what his intentions were with her. Finally he placed an order for three small fashion dolls, to be made in the latest English styles, which he said were a pale imitation of French fashion. He directed that the dolls be delivered to Marie Antoinette, the Queen of France. "She will be utterly amused by them. She is a great enthusiast of dolls, and she will no doubt be delighted in seeing how far behind the English are in their fashions. And you should know that the queen enjoys being a patron of talented artists. You may find that she becomes your benefactor if she likes your designs."

A small alarm bell sounded in Claudette's head. She remembered her first benefactress in London, who insisted that as such she did not need to pay for the dolls. All turned out well for Claudette, but could she afford to be supplying the entire royal court of France with dolls with only vague promises of payment and—

"Of course, we have not yet resolved the price for the dolls, and since I will be leaving England soon, it would be best if I paid you in full now, yes?"

So the deal was struck, and Claudette was left with the most important commission she had ever had. How proud Papa would be.

She later received a note from Count Fersen that Marie Antoinette had been delighted with her dolls, claiming them better quality than anything else in her collection. She had Fersen place more orders. Soon thereafter Claudette began receiving orders from a select few members of the queen's court, those that did not think the dolls foolish. These orders were accompanied by notes saying that the customer found her dolls to be "quaint," or lovely "conversation starters." No one other than the queen seemed to value them for their inherent artistic excellence.

Once the English aristocrats realized that the French were interested in Claudette's *grandes Pandores* as well, their own fascination trebled. Orders were now placed with instructions to make them "more stylish than what goes to the frogs."

How do I follow such an instruction? Claudette wondered.

She started making the French export dolls just a tad shorter as a way to establish the English ones as "better" without offending her French clientele.

And so her personal coffers grew. Another trip to Mr. Benjamin resulted in an additional investment, this time in a sugar plantation in Barbados, a faraway place she had never heard of, but which Mr. Benjamin told her would give her lucrative returns. She also opened an account for Béatrice and deposited a substantial sum for her faithful and hardworking friend. How far they had come from their arrival on the London docks with Marguerite and Lizbit Preston.

Claudette was soon presented with another unusual investment. Mrs. Jenkins desired to retire to the ground floor of her building, as she was getting a bit gouty and the work of landlording was too much for her. Would Claudette like to purchase the town house? There was only one other tenant left in the building, who planned to move out soon, and it was his rooms Mrs. Jenkins wished to occupy.

"What do you think?" Claudette asked Béatrice over supper at the Fox and Hounds, a nearby tavern. She explained Mrs. Jenkins's offer over their spit-roasted ham with Madeira sauce and root vegetables.

"Doesn't it sound like an enormous risk?" Béatrice asked.

"Not especially. I think Mrs. Jenkins is offering a fair price, and I don't have to pay her all at once. Just think, we could renovate the entire first floor into two flats, one for each of us, perhaps decorated in the Adams style. Or whatever style you wish!"

"What about Mr. Greycliffe?"

"Mr. Greycliffe? What of him?"

"What if he should divorce his wife and ask you to marry him?"

"Béatrice, where do you get such fanciful ideas? I, for one, entertain no thoughts whatsoever of the man and you shouldn't either. He is arrogant and selfish and more beast than man."

"But he saved you from that vicious bird. I think he loves you. He's very dashing."

"I won't hear another word about him. All I want to hear is that you'd like me to buy the town house."

"Of course! I can hardly wait to begin sewing draperies."

"Then I'll see Mr. Benjamin in the morning."

In short order Mrs. Jenkins had transferred ownership of the town house to Claudette and moved to the recently vacated ground floor. An architect and workmen were hired to redesign and renovate the four first-floor rooms into two flats, with a common sitting room between them at the top of the stairs leading up from the front entrance.

The ensuing dust and mess exacerbated Béatrice's delicate constitution, making her more prone to coughing paroxysms and sneezing. For several months, her eyes wept a thin mucous. Claudette suggested a visit by a physician, but Béatrice demurred.

"It's just a reaction to the excitement, is all," she said.

The architect recommended a cabinetmaker, who provided them with beds, tables, and other necessary furnishings. Claudette even splurged on a fancy tall-case clock for the sitting room. Her father had never had such an extravagant tribute to his success, and Claudette considered the purchase her mark of respect for her esteemed papa.

How she wished he knew that his cherished daughter had thrived against all probability of her doing so.

❧ 17 ❧

Paris, 1787. The trial over the wretched diamond necklace had taken place in May 1786. As further humiliation for the queen, her brother, the Archduke Ferdinand, had arrived for a visit in the middle of the situation. Not only was it discomforting for her to be embroiled in an infamous legal battle upon his arrival, but the archduke himself was a bit embarrassing, thinking it grand to arrive in Paris "incognito" and devise all manner of schemes to travel about in disguises. Her discomfort was increased by the fact that she was heavily pregnant again. What should have been joy at the prospect of another possible son was clouded by her perpetual troubles.

She could not take comfort in Alex, who had run off to England for a visit, and was, according to reports, being fêted everywhere he went. Even the king had left her side, traveling to Cherbourg and other seaports on an eight-day tour.

When Louis returned, the queen was sufficiently excited by his homecoming to greet him on the balcony of the palace with her three children: the Madame Royale, now aged six; the Dauphin, who was five years old; and Louis Charles, the Duc de Normandie, a mere fifteen months old. The entire family wore their finest court attire but with no hint of jewelry, a statement that Marie Antoinette was still the country's majestic queen, but that she was also sensitive to the suffering in it. The king's seaport visit had been a great success, and witnesses to the family reunion cheered the royals.

The next day, Louis returned to his normal monotonous routine of hunting, which had been interrupted by his coastal tour. Marie Antoinette was still alone.

Ten days later, she felt unwell. Refusing to believe that she was having labor pains, she continued with her own routine. By late afternoon, she realized that, indeed, her confinement time had arrived early. Servants hastily put together the dreaded, airless confinement room, with its tightly sealed, covered windows and utter lack of privacy. At seven-thirty on the evening of July 9, the queen gave birth to Sophie Hélène Béatrice before a noisy gaggle of courtiers crowding around to watch.

The king was ecstatic, although many others thought it a pity that it was not a third son. In any case, the infant did not flourish. Combined with the Dauphin's continued illnesses and overall weakness, plus the disgusting outcome of the diamond necklace trial, a pall was cast over Versailles.

On June 19, 1787, just a few weeks shy of her first birthday, the baby Sophie died, having never developed much at all. The queen was bereft. A family portrait in progress by the artist Elisabeth-Louise Vigée Lebrun had to have Sophie painted out of it. Instead, it was replaced by Louis Joseph's finger pointing toward an empty cradle. The painting depressed the queen further, but not as much as the knowledge that Jeanne de la Motte had escaped La Salpêtrière prison a few days before Sophie's death, and had made her way to England, where she was now venomously penning her "autobiography." These supposed memoirs, which detailed a Sapphic relationship with the queen, were enthusiastically received by an English public who loved gossip, particularly if it concerned the hated French.

London, January 1788. The boy picked his way into the C. Laurent Fashion Doll Shop the way his grandfather had shown him. His hands were shaking badly, and he considered it only very good luck that he had not been seen. He had nearly lost his nerve and run back to his grandfather's own shop. It was the thought that such an action would probably result in a beating that kept him firmly perched behind an empty vegetable stand across the street in the freezing cold, blowing on hands protected only by fingerless wool gloves and watching until all of the shop's employees were gone for the evening.

He darted across to the front door with his tools hidden by a folded sack under his arm. Retrieving a couple of implements from the bag, he manipulated the lock until it gave way for him, then slithered in and shut the door quickly behind him.

Here he was, actually standing in the shop belonging to that witch. Grandfather always cuffed him on the ear when he called her that, saying that witches don't exist anymore, but that Miss Laurent was simply too stiff-rumped to be abided and had to be taught a lesson.

But the boy wasn't sure. He had seen Miss Laurent on the street and although Grandfather was right, she did carry herself proudly, the boy thought that her natural beauty and ability to acquire so many wealthy customers must be the result of supernatural doings. He hadn't seen any witch's marks, but they could have been hidden under her clothing. Maybe she was out right now buying potions and secret herbs to use on an unsuspecting lout. He shuddered and hoped he wouldn't come across any implements of torture in the shop.

Before anyone passing on the street could see him in the waning hours of daylight, he scurried through the shop seeking his goal. He opened cabinet doors and drawers, careful not to disturb anything that might make the witch—er, Miss Laurent—suspicious later.

Where was it all? He nipped to the back of the shop, opening doors. A small worker's bedroom, a closet . . . Ah! This must be it. He stopped in wonder at how neat this workshop was, everything tidied up and placed in bins along the wall. Grandfather's shop didn't look like this. The boy would have to tell him about it. This was proof of witchcraft, now wasn't it? What mortal being could keep a shop this orderly?

He saw the things he was after and began scooping them into his bag, apprehensive that the witch might have a familiar lurking about, watching him and ready to fly off and report to its mistress. What if she turned him into something terrible, like a pig or a calf? The butcher would get hold of him and cut his throat. Then Grandfather would be furious with him.

The sound of the front door creaking split his already fragile wits apart. He banged into a box of tools sitting on the floor before diving headfirst under the counter-high worktable sitting perpendicular to the doorway.

"Béatrice, you don't look well. I think it's time to return to the shop."

The two women stood on a busy London street in frosty twilight. They had gone out late that afternoon to deposit money with Mr. Benjamin, then hired a carriage to take them to the Giffords to pick up some specially ordered bolts of fabric. Normally Claudette would send Joseph out to run such an errand, but these were expensive silks for use in a set of ten fashion dolls for an earl's daughter, who wanted them to match her wedding trousseau. Aristocracy could be fussy, and the minutest mark on a hidden section of a dress might cause the earl to return the entire set, so Claudette preferred to handle the bolts personally. While at the Giffords, they also selected a few fabrics to have turned into serviceable day dresses for themselves and Marguerite.

Béatrice coughed lightly against a handkerchief. "It's just the cold. My gloves aren't warm enough. I keep meaning to purchase another pair."

Claudette hired a hackney coach for their return trip. Really, she should just purchase her own. There was enough money to buy a small carriage and horse. Perhaps a landaulet? Maybe one day soon she would talk to Jack about what local auction she should attend. Of course, she would then have to hire someone to drive it and keep the horses stabled, groomed, and fed. And then there was the actual storage of the carriage itself. No, she thought. It would be an imprudent purchase, and she had not come this far to end up doing something foolish.

After unloading their bundles in front of the shop and paying the driver, Claudette inserted her key into the front door lock while a gentle snow began floating around them. It was dark inside, as Agnes or Roger must have closed up at least an hour ago and escorted Marguerite to Mrs. Jenkins. As she pushed the door open fully it creaked, and a muffled thump from somewhere in the workshop startled both women, resulting in a small squeak from Béatrice.

They stood paralyzed at the open door, snow gathering lightly at their feet and on their cloaks, and drifting inside.

"Something must have fallen. I hope we haven't lost any dolls," Claudette said with more confidence than she felt. Béatrice responded by shivering.

"Come, let's go clean up before we catch our death standing outside." They hauled the bolts just inside and Claudette shut the door, groping about on the front counter for an oil lamp and lighting it before leading the way to the workshop with Béatrice trailing right behind her.

At the workshop entrance she held up the lamp but could not see anything unusual amid all of the neat rows of supplies lining the walls. They must have dreamed they heard a noise. Only, two awake people cannot have the same dream at the same time, can they?

Béatrice grabbed her elbow and pointed to a place under the large worktable. Part of a man's worn leather shoe peeped out.

"Who's there? Why are you hiding in here?" Claudette tried to keep the tremor out of her voice.

A young man, a boy really, with cropped hair so blond it was nearly white, burst out from under the table carrying a large sack and darted toward the women with one hand shot straight out to act as a battering ram.

The boy clipped Béatrice, who fell against a *grande Pandore* in progress. Both she and the frame went clattering to the floor. Claudette reached wildly for a weapon, and her hand closed around a broom leaning against the wall behind her. With the broom in one hand and the lamp in the other, she was on the boy's heels. He stumbled with his heavy load, and Claudette used the instant to drop the lamp and begin pummeling him with the broom. Amid his howls of protest, she relentlessly smacked him on the head, at his knees, and on his stomach, circling him like a bird of prey closing in on a rodent.

The boy went to his knees and dropped the sack. All manner of incomplete dolls and their parts spilled out.

Why would anyone steal unfinished dolls? They had no value whatsoever. Why wasn't he lifting one of the creations from the display shelves?

"Stop, miss, stop! I'm sorry, I am. It had to be done." The boy was blocking his face with his hands. "Please, I don't want to be someone's supper!"

By this time, Claudette was exhausted from her exertion, and Béatrice had rejoined her, rubbing her side in pain from her collision with the iron doll frame.

Still holding the broom threateningly over the boy, Claudette asked, "What's your name? What in heaven's name are you doing?"

"I'm Ralph Pierotti, miss. My grandfather owns the Pierotti Fashion Doll Works. He made me do it, I swear to you." The boy's pleading eyes rested in a face full of straw scratches. Gray broom dander rose from his head in wispy columns.

"I know of the Pierotti shop. It's very successful. Why would your grandfather need to steal supplies from me?"

"We're not so successful as of late. Your shop is taking a lot of his trade with the upper class, miss. He says it's because you're uppity. I told him it's because—" The boy stopped, his eyes darting around the room.

"And so he sends in a child to steal parts from my workroom? Whatever for?"

"To figure out how you do it. What's so special about your dolls, why is your experimentation with wax so much better than his? He wanted some samples he could examine and copy from, but didn't want me to disturb your finished pieces. He said that wouldn't be right."

Claudette lowered the broom and burst into laughter, throwing

Ralph into confusion. Even Béatrice was puzzled by her amusement.

"So, Ralph, stealing my expensive supplies was perfectly acceptable to your grandfather, but lifting a completed doll, well, that
was beyond the bounds of propriety. Oh dear." She shook her
head, still smiling.

She made a sudden movement with the broom, which sent Ralph
scrabbling away from her, but she motioned for him not to be
afraid. Instead, she opened the sack on the floor, swept all of the
scattered doll parts back in, and handed it to Ralph.

"Here, Ralph. Give this to Henry Pierotti with my compliments.
Tell him that I would be delighted to discuss my doll manufacture
with him, and that he doesn't need to impress his relatives into
criminal activity."

Still terrified, the boy grabbed the sack from her and ran out the
door into the frigid night air, the door banging shut behind him.

"Well, my friend"—Claudette yawned contentedly—"I thought
we had made our mark when we got Queen Charlotte's notice.
Now I know we are truly famous because we have inspired a great
heist. I say we toast our good fortune with Mrs. Jenkins before retiring tonight."

London, April 1788. Claudette and Béatrice had just finished
having soup together in Claudette's flat one evening when they
heard a carriage come to a stop outside their building and someone
knock on the front door. Béatrice went to the window.

"Oh," she breathed.

"What is it?"

Before Béatrice could respond, they heard a sharp rap on the
door of Claudette's flat, followed by Mrs. Jenkins's voice.

"Miss Laurent? You have a gentleman caller."

Claudette looked at Béatrice quizzically, but the other woman
turned back to the window.

Realizing that Béatrice was avoiding her, and quickly thinking
that it simply could not be *him* coming to see her, not again, she
opened the door, and her heart quit beating for an instant before
leaping into her throat and making her speechless.

"Miss Laurent, this is Mr. William Greycliffe here to see you." Mrs. Jenkins was glowing as she gazed up at the handsome gentleman standing next to her.

"Yes, so it would seem," was all she could articulate.

When Mrs. Jenkins made no move to leave the doorway, William turned to her. "Madam, thank you for your assistance. You have been most kind."

"Oh my, yes, well, certainly, Mr. Greycliffe, you need only knock should you need anything." She scurried off downstairs back to her flat.

Claudette and William stared at each other steadily, each waiting for the other to break the silence. Finally, with her wits back in place, Claudette said, "Mr. Greycliffe, to what do I owe this rather unexpected pleasure? I require no dance lessons, I have not been under avian attack as of late, nor do I keep dollmaking supplies here just in case a customer should follow me home."

Behind her, she could hear Béatrice move quietly into her own quarters, shutting the door behind her.

"Miss Laurent, I am not here to do battle with you. I merely wish to have a civil conversation. After you hear what I have to say, you may decide whether you wish to maintain acquaintance with me. However, I do ask for some indulgence."

He looked toward the door through which Béatrice had passed and offered his arm to Claudette.

"Might I suggest a quick supper nearby? The roasted pork is excellent at the King's Head Inn."

She contemplated him for several moments more and said, "I suppose I might spare you a short amount of time."

They walked several blocks to the inn, and were shown to a table in a back room. A roaring fire in one corner took the chill out of the early spring evening as they sat together and sipped claret while waiting for their meals. They spoke of innocuous things— the long-lasting winter, the troubles with France, the increasing trade with the Americans, Mr. Pitt's latest policies. Claudette's thoughts bubbled and roiled. She had not lain eyes on him in so long, and believed she had relegated him to an untouchable part of her mind. Why did he affect her so much, even after a protracted absence?

Best to maintain a cool composure.

After their meal had been devoured, gooseberry pie eaten, and glasses of after-dinner digestifs served, William turned serious.

"Now, Miss Laurent, I have something serious to talk to you about. I wish to discuss my marriage."

"Oh." Claudette's voice was light, although she was trembling inside. "You needn't do so. I have already heard the gossips go on about your various marital tragedies."

"Perhaps, although undoubtedly you have not heard the truth. Or at least not the entire truth."

Claudette started to push her chair back to leave the table. She couldn't bear to listen to this. William reached out and put his left hand over hers. He wore no ring. She slowly sat back down.

"You must listen to me for once. I've been trying to explain this to you for nigh on to five years."

She sat still, her hand still covered by his. As he began to talk, he took her hand inside his, and began stroking her palm.

"Lenora and I were friends as young children. Her parents met mine when they purchased a neighboring residence as a summer home to get away from the London heat. Lenora and I were of an age, and our parents had always hoped for a match between us when we were old enough, though neither of us was particularly interested. The Radleys gave her a season in London, and because no one suited her fancy, they assumed it was because she had her heart set on me. We had been young playmates, and were certainly friends, but Lenora found me too serious, and in return I thought she had an unsuitable wild streak.

"Our fathers entered a partnership to purchase some shares in a trading company, becoming the major stockholders together. Part of their unspoken contract was that we would become engaged to marry, which they thought would delight the two of us. It was during the time of that negotiation that I first met you at the obnoxious Mrs. Ashby's. Her husband was offering his services as broker for the trading company deal. Our parents thought it might be a good idea if we attend some social events together, even at the Ashbys', as a sort of pre-betrothal coming-out. I was on the verge of telling my parents that there was to be no betrothal, when Lenora came to me secretly in a panic.

"The wild streak I had suspected lay under the surface had taken control of her. She had been dallying with not only a local married apothecary who had been providing her mother with medicine for her headaches, but she had also discovered a smuggler operating out of a local inn, and the thrill of that was too much for her. She got entangled with him as well, and ended up with child. Only she wasn't sure if it belonged to him or the apothecary, not that it mattered. Either one meant complete disgrace for her.

"She begged me to go through with our betrothal and wedding, to save her from ruinous shame, and, fool that I am, I agreed. She was a friend, and I thought that the marriage would at least be polite and agreeable, given our long familiarity. My sense of duty to her overrode everything. I also didn't realize that my entire being would become consumed with desire for an insufferable little dollmaker on Oxford Street.

"The marriage was initially polite, and platonic in its entirety. Within a couple of months, though, Lenora miscarried the child. She was inconsolable, and soon found fault with everything either I or any of the household staff did. She was not above throwing china and books about, and cuffing the maids on the ears for minor infractions.

"It became worse. Not only was she becoming cruel toward everyone around her, but she began having blatant affairs with any men that would cross her path, from delivery boys to aristocrats. I became known as the Kent Cuckold. Still I did not wish to expose her, and let others think that it was my inattention to my wife that led her astray.

"I had no idea how to appease Lenora, who was clearly losing her hold on reality. She was no longer able to hostess parties in our home, as she would drink excessively and try to lure women's husbands into guest bedrooms right under their wives' noses. Hevington was becoming an intolerable place to live.

"I purchased a house in London and intended to bring her here to stay for a short time, to rest and recover her reason. Before I could escort her here, she abandoned me, running off with one of my footmen. Poor lad. They set up house together with his parents, with my blessing, and Lenora was soon pregnant again. Her own parents were apoplectic over the situation.

"I would have happily granted her a divorce, if she thought she could find happiness with someone else, but she didn't want it. Instead, she continued insulting me from afar, sending me cruel letters and 'accidentally' running into me at church or in the town square, each time using it as an opportunity to embarrass me."

Claudette interrupted, "Did Lenora know that you rescued me from the bird at Leadenhall?"

"No, my feelings for you were my own secret, although I did think that perhaps *you* understood them." William looked at her, the question in his eyes palpable.

Claudette bit her lip. "Yes, I did know. I ignored it."

He barked a short laugh. "Indeed you did. If only Lenora could have ignored me half as successfully.

"When her time came, she went into labor for a very long time. The midwife sent for a doctor, and he determined that the baby was breech. Both Lenora and her baby daughter died, the baby's cord wrapped around its neck, and her mother from uncontrollable blood loss."

"Oh, I see." Claudette's voice was tiny.

Briskly he concluded the tale. "Her parents had them both buried in the family crypt, and my footman ran away, not even telling his parents where he was going.

"I have waited through the recognized period of mourning for my late wife, and I will wait no longer. Claudette Laurent, I would like permission to pay you court. Properly and openly."

Did he mean this? Truly? To court a tradeswoman, which surely could only end in his own disgrace. His family had become important in society. His friends were undoubtedly all aristocrats and would shun her from their company. Eventually he would be pressured into marrying another proper English lady, like Lenora Radley. Why bother being courted by a man who needed to make a *proper* marriage? Her heart would end up broken by this man with his strong hands and deep, abiding constancy. Wasn't one heartbreak by Jean-Philippe enough? *Do I dare risk this when I have finally made my life comfortable and secure?*

"Miss Laurent, what are you thinking?"

"I'm thinking I need air."

He pushed his chair back and helped her out of her own. Quickly settling the bill with the manager, he escorted her outside.

"Are you all right? Do you need a doctor?" he asked. His eyes were worried and intense.

"No, I just wanted the fresh night air, to clear my head."

They began walking slowly back toward Claudette's flat. For the first time, she reached out first to tuck her hand in his arm. She could see a smile flit across his face in the moonlight. She stopped and turned to him.

"Mr. Greycliffe, I agree to your offer of courtship, but under certain conditions. First, you must realize that my doll shop is of utmost importance to me. I shall never give it up. Second, your friends and associates will never accept me, and therefore I will not place myself in their company under any circumstances."

"Does that constitute the entirety of your demands?"

"Why, I suppose so. Are you not angry? Do you not want to cast me aside?"

He laughed as they continued walking to her building. She could see that Béatrice had left a candle burning in the window for her. William pulled her to him as they approached the ground floor door.

"Miss Laurent, I accept your terms of surrender. Although I think you may eventually find my friends to be a little less vile than you currently do, provided you give them an opportunity to prove it. Now, however, there is the matter of sealing our agreement."

He brought his smooth-shaven face down to hers for a kiss. It was soft and undemanding, yet spoke of hidden longing and desire. She could smell his masculine scent enveloping her, protecting her from the rest of the world. *Claudette Laurent,* said a voice at the back of her mind. *The earth has stopped rotating again.*

1 JULY 1788
QUEEN MARIE ANTOINETTE OF FRANCE
REQUESTS YOUR PRESENCE AT VERSAILLES. THIS
HONOR IS BESTOWED UPON YOU, AS THE QUEEN HAS
BEEN MUCH PLEASED WITH THE DOLLS FROM THE
C. LAURENT FASHION DOLL SHOP AND WISHES TO
MEET THEIR MAKER. YOU MAY BE PRESENTED TO THE
QUEEN ON 14 JULY AT VERSAILLES. YOUR ESCORT AT
THE PALACE ENTRANCE WILL BE J. P. RENAUD. THE
ENCLOSED LETTER OF INVITATION WILL PROVIDE
YOU WITH ENTRY TO THE PALACE GROUNDS.

Claudette read the invitation and its accompanying letter in disbelief. She, presented to the Queen of France? If only Papa could see this. More importantly, who was J. P. Renaud? Could it be . . .

❧ 18 ❧

London, July 12, 1788. "What in heaven's name does one wear when being presented to the queen of France?" Claudette was busy finishing her packing for her visit across the Channel. Her bedchamber was strewn with gowns, shoes, and undergarments. She wore an unfastened dress for travel, and was shoeless.

Standing in the doorway and shaking his head at Claudette's state of disarray, William observed, "My love, I presume this is just a visit, and that you are not actually moving to Versailles?"

"This is no laughing matter, William. The queen is reputed to be the most fashionable of women. I simply cannot go there looking like a slattern."

"Claudette, I hardly think that you will be called a slattern in this." He picked up an emerald gown and handed it to her. "You are a beautiful woman and wear everything with grace."

"William, I adore your confidence in me, but this is serious. I want to impress the queen, and bring more respect to the doll shop. Do you realize that a good reputation with Marie Antoinette could mean orders from the entire French court? Perhaps I could even move back to France, if I thought the commerce would justify it."

"What? You haven't mentioned this before. Claudette, you would seriously contemplate leaving me? Leaving England and the life you have built here? But I have not yet—" He stopped.

She added the gown William had handed her to the trunk she

was packing, keeping her head down to avoid his gaze. "I don't know. Paris was my home my entire childhood."

"But you yourself admit that after the fire, there was nothing left there for you."

"Yes, but—"

"What are you not telling me?"

She busied herself in closing the trunk and securing its leather straps before rising to meet William's hard stare. "I must go to Paris to see if it stirs in me a desire to return. I cannot explain my feelings to you now. Please understand that this has nothing to do with you, or the life I have here in England."

"I understand nothing." He looked at her expectantly.

Receiving no response, he stiffened. "Very well, Claudette. I'll return in three hours to see you to your ship." He turned abruptly and left the room. Moments later, she could hear the door to the front of the building slamming shut, and from her window could see him giving sharp orders to his driver before the carriage rattled off with a lurch.

Not unexpectedly, Béatrice came scurrying into her rooms. "Claudette, why has William left in such a hurry? I thought he was going to spend time with you today and then escort you to your ship?"

"I told him I might possibly move back to France, if I thought my business might benefit from it."

Béatrice's eyes became round globes of horror. She parroted William almost word for word. "You mean you would leave here? Leave England? What of your workers? What of Marguerite and me? Claudette, no!"

Claudette immediately regretting telling her nervous friend what had transpired between her and William just moments ago. Béatrice's anxious nature would probably result in a mental breakdown while she was in Paris.

"Béatrice, don't worry about this. I'm sure I am just experiencing nervous feelings at returning to our homeland, and I have no idea what I am saying."

Béatrice contemplated her friend for a long moment. "It's that Jean-Philippe, isn't it? The betrothal you told me about when we came over on that horrible passage from France. You want to try to find him again." Claudette's silence gave her away. Béatrice's eyes grew large again. "Oh, poor William. Did you tell him this? No, I can see you spared him the truth. Oh, Claudette, nothing good can come from this."

Claudette was defiant. "Don't be foolish. I am going to Paris to meet Marie Antoinette, Queen of France, to hopefully convince her to purchase more of my dolls, and to leave a good impression at court so that all of the nobility will want to send orders to me. I would be most happy if you would help me arrange my traveling clothes, and forget this nonsense about my childhood betrothal." She turned and presented her back to Béatrice, to avoid looking into her face.

Béatrice's shaking fingers fastened the laces of the back of the dress. Silently, she pushed Claudette down into a sitting position on the bed, and, rummaging through the heaps of garments, found the shoes that her friend typically wore with the dress. She kneeled down and placed them on her friend's feet, then looked up soulfully into Claudette's face.

Guilt pierced through Claudette. Why was life so confusing? First she had tamped down her emotions about Jean-Philippe, and then she had refused to let William occupy her thoughts. But William reentered her life dramatically, and she had allowed herself to be swept away by his integrity, his steadfastness, and most of all by her own intoxicated senses that overpowered her whenever he came near.

Now Jean-Philippe might be reappearing, and, like an autumn leaf blowing about with no control over its destiny, she was going to ride the winds to France to see what happened.

Was she about to destroy this new and fragile bond she had with William to chase a phantom?

Am I still an idiot?

Unexpectedly, Claudette's eyes moistened. "Oh, Béatrice, you are my dearest friend in the world and I would do nothing to hurt you. I promise I'll return. After all, what is the C. Laurent Fashion Doll Shop without Béatrice du Georges?" She threw her arms around Béatrice's shoulders, and the two women clutched each other.

"Please, Claudette, don't do anything imprudent while you are there. William loves you so much. And so do Marguerite and I."

"Silly Béatrice. Let's go back to the shop. I want to make sure all the workers are aware of my instructions while I'm gone, and that they understand you are in charge in my absence."

William returned later with his coach and driver. The driver hauled out Claudette's luggage, while William silently escorted her into the carriage, nodding to Béatrice on the landing as they went down the stairs.

"To the *Lady of York,*" William instructed as he rapped on the ceiling of the carriage. They began traversing London's busy streets on their way to the docks. The coach's two passengers sat silently, Claudette staring out the window, and William shifting his morose gaze from the floor to Claudette and back to the floor again.

Finally she said, "William, I promised Béatrice that I would return, and I make the same promise to you."

"I'm relieved to hear that, but not if you have somehow found some powerful reason to stay in France."

Uncomfortable once again under his penetrating stare, she looked down at her hands in her lap. "No," she whispered. "I'm sure there is nothing left there for me."

As they pulled into the harbor and began the final approach to the ship, William moved across the coach to sit next to Claudette. He gently cupped her face and turned it to him, planting a soft kiss on her forehead.

"I love you, Claudette Renée Laurent. I will count the hours until you return to me." Claudette was shaken to find herself inwardly trembling at the thought of leaving him, even temporarily. Still holding her face in both hands, and staring into her eyes as if willing her to reveal the hidden part of her heart, he lowered his head down for a kiss on her mouth. It lasted mere seconds, but conveyed his pain and worry and even the great passion she knew he kept hidden below the surface.

"We're here, sir. I'll take Miss Laurent's luggage aboard, then return to the coach to wait for you."

"Very well, thank you." William gently helped Claudette from the coach and they strolled to the gangplank. The docks were as busy with travelers, merchants, and dockworkers, as she remembered from her frightful arrival seven years earlier. It was also just as dirty: carcasses of fish and other sea animals lying about, and stray dogs eagerly sniffing these potential feasts. The stench was nauseating, and she put a handkerchief to her nose. She was grateful to note that there was no apparent prostitution going on, at least none that she could see. But perhaps the latest shipment of unsuspecting girls had not arrived yet. She shuddered at the memory, which she had recently revived during one of the habitual coffeehouse chats she and William had established while getting to know one another.

Sensing her distress, William said gaily, "Here we are, my love. It's finally time to embark on your great adventure to visit the queen of France." He gave her a final, swift kiss. "I will be waiting for you."

Claudette's eyes welled up, then she turned and nearly ran up the gangplank to avoid making a foolish scene of sentimentality in front of him.

The voyage across the Channel was uneventful. Upon arrival in Calais, she found a fellow female passenger also planning to continue on to Paris, and together they paid fare on a coach to complete the journey.

Her new traveling partner, a middle-aged, exceedingly obese and plainly-dressed woman named Madame Junesiere, was impressed that Claudette had obtained an audience with the queen. "*Chérie*, tell me again what it is you have done that has captured the notice of Marie Antoinette?"

"I'm a dollmaker. The queen has several of my creations already."

Madame Junesiere's hand flew to her throat. "You are involved in business activity? How wretched for you. Your husband allows this?"

"I am not married."

"Very well, then, your parents allow it?"

"My parents were killed in a fire several years ago. My father was a dollmaker and taught me his craft. After my parents' death, I went to England, and established my shop there."

Claudette's companion shook her head in disapproval. "*Chérie*, it is not fitting for a beautiful young woman to be dirtying her hands in the trades. You should find a husband, preferably a nice Frenchman, and settle down to the business of having children."

Claudette smiled ruefully and reflected inwardly on how close to home this stranger was hitting. What if she found Jean-Philippe? Was he married now? If not, would he still love her? Would she move her doll shop to France, or would she abandon all to become her long-lost love's wife, and mother to his children? Her memory began reforming his face in her mind. She could almost remember the feel of his arms about her in the small alleyways near their homes. Her racing mind shifted to thoughts of William. She felt guilty at the thought of her dishonesty. *But I must not think of him,* she decided. *I must concentrate on my visit with the queen, and whether or not Jean-Philippe is still alive.*

Madame Junesiere broke into her thoughts. "We're approaching a town. This coach is the worst excuse for a conveyance I have ever seen. My bones threaten to break over every pebble we cross in the road. Why don't we stop at an inn for the night, and hire a private coach in the morning?"

Claudette agreed, and the two women spent an evening in companionable silence before retiring to bed and rising in the morning to secure more comfortable transportation and continue the journey. Upon arrival in Paris, the coach first dropped off Madame Junesiere at her daughter's home, where she was visiting to await the birth of her first grandchild.

"*Au revoir,* Mademoiselle Laurent, and remember my advice to you. Forget your pretend babies and have real ones."

"*Merci,* Madame Juensiere. I have enjoyed our journey together."

Finally alone with her thoughts for the first time since leaving the ship, Claudette allowed herself to forget her troubles with men, and to give herself over to the excitement of meeting the queen. How her father would have been proud to see this day! She, little Claudette Laurent, permitted formal presentation to the most important personage of all the royalty in Europe. With the exception of King Louis XVI, of course.

The coach was now running alongside the front of the Palace of Versailles. Claudette gasped at its beauty and immense proportions. The driver stopped for traffic at the Avenue de Paris, giving his passenger a view to the front of the palace. A tall, wrought iron gate running along the front of the estate obscured some of that view, but she could see the entry to the magnificent three-story structure. All three levels were filled with tall windows. Palladian arches topped those on the first and second stories. The second story had groups of eight columns spaced at regular intervals. Even from a distance she could see the statuary lining the third floor above the second story columns. The palace did not appear to be a single building, but a main house with multiple wings, both attached and detached. The stone of the palace was actually beige, but it dazzled in the sunlight, making it look gold to the eye. This was undoubtedly part of Louis XIV's plan when he reconstructed what had been a hunting lodge into this glorious monument to himself and the power of France. No wonder he was called the Sun King, she thought. Many coaches were stopped in the circular courtyard in front of the palace. Claudette could hardly believe that she was going to join them the following day.

With a start, the coach began moving again, then turned a corner, and the palace disappeared from view. Claudette leaned back against the seat and closed her eyes, imagining the thrill of being presented to the queen at Versailles. Traveling several more blocks, the coach finally arrived at the Hôtel du Grand Maître, where the driver assured her many visitors to Versailles stayed. She paid him, waited to be sure her luggage was delivered, then immediately requested a bath be brought to her room.

Inside her beautifully appointed room, Claudette unpinned her hair while waiting for her bath to arrive. The bed had several feather mattresses on it, and was topped with a coverlet of blue and gold. A vanity and mirror also served as a nightstand. The writing desk contained exquisite linen papers in one of its many drawers. The walls were covered in blue and white damask wallpaper, and Aubusson rugs graced the floor. She felt as though she was already beginning to taste the life of royalty. She would have to write to William and Béatrice right away to describe how beautiful the hotel was. A knock on the door alerted her that her requested bath had arrived.

After the tub had been set up and the servants had departed, Claudette stripped off her dusty traveling clothes, and settled down into the warm, soapy water for a long soak.

The following morning she awoke early to sunlight streaming through the tall, multi-paned windows. She arose, and, putting a robe around her, opened the windows to lean out and enjoy the sunshine. The cacophony from the street assailed her. She marveled that even outside Paris the distinct sounds of the city—the rumbling of carriages traveling along rough roads, the shouting of street sellers, and the barking, braying, and wailing of animals—could still overwhelm the senses. But what matter, today she would be presented to the queen! And, just possibly, she might meet Jean-Philippe again.

A light rap on the door brought her out of her reverie. Outside, a small chambermaid was holding a tray of food. "Madame, I have brought your breakfast," she said shyly, holding it up for inspection. The girl could not have been more than fifteen. She had dark hair cut at odd angles, as though hacked at without benefit of a mirror, and her gray eyes stood out like giant watery spheres in her pale, thin face. Claudette had the impression that a lost kitten had just wandered into her room.

"*Merci.* Please place it on the writing table. What is your name, little one?"

"I am called Jolie."

"Very well, Jolie. Are you the innkeeper's daughter?"

"No, madame, I am an orphan. My parents both died of the fever. My uncle Bernard is the proprietor here."

Claudette felt a pang of compassion for the girl, a child really, who had also lost her parents tragically. "How old are you?"

"I am eighteen."

Eighteen! Only five years younger than Claudette. She was ob-

THE QUEEN'S DOLLMAKER   167

viously not very well nourished here at the inn. "Well, Jolie, would you like to earn some extra money?"

The gray eyes managed to do the impossible and grow even wider in the kitten's face. "Yes, madame! How may I be of assistance to you?"

"Jolie, I am Claudette Laurent, a dollmaker. Today I am to be presented to the queen, but I have no attendant to help me dress and do my toilette. Can you help me?"

"Oh, yes, madame. The queen, do you say? Oh my, yes, I shall make you beautiful." Realizing her mistake, she quickly covered. "Oh, but you are already very pretty. I but meant that I will help you emphasize your every pretty feature."

Claudette smiled. "Be at rest, Jolie. I am not offended in the least. Finish your other duties quickly and return to help me. I must leave in two hours."

Jolie scampered out of the room, and Claudette sat down to her hearty breakfast of an omelette, rolls, cheese, and coffee. By the time she was finished, Jolie was outside the door again. Looking at her new attendant, who was now carrying a bag filled with supplies, Claudette wondered briefly if this poor lost kitten, with her disheveled hair poking out under her cap, could actually help her create a successful toilette. She was quickly assured that asking Jolie was the right thing to do. The girl practically attacked Claudette's trunks, pulling out gowns, tsk-tsking that they had been left in a crumpled state too long, and why were they not separated by tissue paper? In response to Claudette's inquisitive gaze, she said, "For several months, I was a maid to a duchesse staying at her chateau near the town where I lived with my parents. When her husband died, she sold the chateau and returned to her family in Avignon, and I returned home. But I promise you that I learned enough to help Madame Claudette rival all of the beauties of the court."

"That is an insurmountable task, I fear, Jolie, but nevertheless let's set out to make me at least presentable."

After seating Claudette in the chair in front of the vanity, Jolie pulled from Claudette's luggage a box containing perfumes and cosmetics. With a skill that surprised her subject, Jolie expertly applied rouge, eye color, and lip color. Next, she opened a small jar and scooped out a sticky substance that she fingered through Claudette's hair before teasing it out and up until Claudette was certain her head would not fit through a doorway.

"Jolie, what is that smell?"

"Ah, I do not have the pomade necessary for the powder to attach, so I had to make do with some substitution from the kitchen. I added scent, madame, to mask any unpleasantness."

Inserting a small pad on top of Claudette's head, Jolie swept up her hair and then gathered it to a point around the pad, tying it together with wires. After fastening it all firmly, Jolie rummaged through her bag of supplies. Various items, obviously confiscated from the kitchen and other parts of the inn, were now being twisted together and formed almost into a landscape in her hair. She could see a large spool of thread, the top of an infant's christening gown, a pair of glasses, and the handles from a pair of scissors, all miraculously woven together and seemingly nestled into her mountain of hair, although the items were actually pinned at various points to the pad base.

"I don't understand, Jolie, what this hairdressing means."

"It is the fashion of Queen Marie Antoinette's to create a depiction in the coiffure. You are a dollmaker, therefore you have the representation of your trade here for all to see."

"But I'm worried that when I stand up, I may fall over from this concoction on my head. You will have to be here when I return to bring my hair back to normal."

"I will, madame, I will. No, no, do not get up yet, I must finish your toilette. Here, I will use this puff to powder your hair." She handed Claudette a mask and draped a cloth around her shoulders. "Hold this over your face, madame, while I begin."

From behind the mask Claudette heard Jolie coughing from the dust. Being fashionable must be the utmost chore at court, Claudette realized.

"*Voilà*, madame, your toilette is complete."

Claudette removed the mask and looked at herself in the mirror. She was a completely different woman. The cosmetics lent her an air of sophistication she did not think she actually possessed, and her newly powdered hair, white as snow except for the implements woven into it, well, the hair was something William would probably pay money to see.

"Well, now what shall I wear?"

"Oh, madame, I have selected your dark blue gown with the lace-ruffled sleeves. However, I would like to use the pink underskirt from this other gown with the blue. If I apply some of this rouge to your satin shoes, I can make them a close match to the underskirt. These stockings are not silk, but if you do not lift your skirt too much when curtsying, the queen will not notice. I will remove the bow from your nightdress, and with just a few stitches apply it to the front of your gown."

Claudette nodded her assent to all of Jolie's suggestions, and patiently stood while her young attendant fussed over her and dressed her. Claudette was certain that she would not be able to walk, much less curtsy to the queen, under the weight of Jolie's handiwork.

"You are a fairy tale, madame. The queen will be most impressed."

"Well, first let's see if I am even able to get to the queen." Claudette rose slowly. "Stay there, Jolie, and I shall practice my curtsy to you." Attempting to keep her head erect, Claudette swept down to the ground, taking care not to expose more than her shoe when grabbing her skirts.

"Madame, I am certain that was perfect!" Jolie clapped her hands together. Jolie had never actually witnessed a presentation to the queen and had no notion of a proper curtsy, but wanted to please Claudette.

"We can but hope so. Now for your final task, Jolie, find someone to hire me a carriage to go to the palace."

Surely the carriages of the court must be taller than this, Claudette thought as she found herself sitting nearly on the floor to ensure that her head remained upright and her coiffure untouched by the carriage's ceiling. Her discomfort was forgotten, though, as the carriage went rumbling down the Avenue de Paris, toward the enchanting Palace of Versailles. They also passed other coaches, clearly belonging to nobility, on their way to Versailles. Some of them had intricately carved, gilded wheel spokes and fanciful scenes painted on their sides. One coach was even topped with a gilded statue of a prancing horse. Claudette had never seen such magnificence in a conveyance since her meeting with the Dauphine those many years ago, but then she had never been invited to Versailles before, either.

At the iron gate leading into the marble courtyard in front of the palace, Claudette's coach was stopped by a palace guard. She listened to the conversation that ensued between the driver and the guard.

"What is your business here?"

"My passenger says she has an appointment with the queen."

"Does she? How interesting. Who is she?"

"How do I know? I do not interview my passengers, *mon ami*, I merely ensure they have enough for their fare."

A sharp rap on the door of the carriage. "Your papers, please."

Claudette opened the door to the guard, who was elaborately dressed in an embroidered red coat and matching breeches. Like her, his hair was powdered white. He looked down his long nose at Claudette crouching on the floor to protect her hair, and shook his head. Really, these women were ridiculous.

"Here, monsieur, is my letter of invitation from the queen."

He looked over the invitation with the suspicion of a man used to miscreants attempting to falsify documents in order to reach the royal couple.

"Hmm, everything seems satisfactory. However, you will not be permitted to enter through this courtyard; it is for nobility only." Shutting the carriage door and turning back to the driver, he said, "Follow along the front of the palace until you come to the next guard gate. There you will be shown to a side entrance."

At the side entrance, another guard checked her invitation again. This time Claudette produced the J. P. Renaud letter. "Please, can you tell me where I can find Monsieur Renaud? He is to be my escort and I believe he might be a lost friend of mine."

Claudette could sense that this guard was just as skeptical as the first one. He sighed, then walked over to another guard, and apparently began issuing instructions.

"Please, madame, step over here." Claudette paid the driver and followed the queen's man into the guard house, walking gingerly across the gravel path leading up to it to avoid kicking up dust on her skirts. He indicated that she should wait, then walked back out to his duties. Left alone for several minutes, Claudette began pacing back and forth in the room, to the extent that her wobbling hairdressing allowed her to pace. Was she foolish to have requested to meet Monsieur Renaud? It probably was not Jean-Philippe. Why couldn't she be satisfied with just a visit to meet the grandest queen in all of Europe?

Suddenly, the door was flung open, and Claudette suffocated from shock. He was older, and looked tired, but, oh yes, it was Jean-Philippe.

Before she could say anything, he rushed to his knees before her and grabbed both her hands in his, kissing them. "My darling little dove, I had hardly thought it was possible that it was you who was the dollmaker coming to visit the queen, but it is true. Unless my eyes are deceiving me?"

Claudette drank in the sight of him. His dark, wavy hair already had just a hint of gray in it. He was just slightly older than her, yet there was a bit of weariness around his eyes. Neither the gray nor his apparent fatigue detracted at all from his handsomeness. She wondered what had happened to him in the intervening years.

She laughed lightly. "No, Jean-Philippe, your eyes are quite sharp. I wondered as well if it was you who sent me the letter with instructions for my visit."

"I knew that if it was you that you would ask for me upon your arrival. Oh, Claudette, how happy I am to see you. I will escort you to the queen personally. Incidentally, I believe your coiffure bests that of many ladies here at court."

She reached up and self-consciously patted the concoction on her head. "I know nothing of court styles, but my new maid, Jolie, insists that this is most fashionable at the court of Marie Antoinette."

He walked completely around her, pausing once to place a

quick kiss on the back of her neck, which sent an old but familiar warmth radiating through her. "She is generally correct, but today the queen is at her Hameau. Come, let us proceed."

Without an explanation as to what the Hamlet was or how its existence affected Claudette's fashion, he led her out of the guard house, and into one of the fancy, gilded coaches she had seen on her journey to Versailles. She was astonished by the luxury inside the coach, which equaled its fancy exterior. Far larger than any coach she had ridden in before, the upholstered seats were of red velvet, and on the ceiling was a fanciful painting of two lovers in a garden. Claudette's enormous hair fit easily into the coach. Jean-Philippe climbed in behind her.

The coach traveled down a gravel path behind the palace and alongside a canal. The canal was punctuated with spraying dolphins and marble maidens at regular intervals.

"This is extraordinary," Claudette marveled.

"Royalty is interesting, is it not, Claudette?"

"More than that, it's breathtaking. Between the palace, this coach, and sitting across from you, I feel I'm in a dream."

He flashed a set of beautiful white teeth at her. "Let's continue the dream. You wear no wedding ring. Are you married, little dove?"

"No, not yet, although there is someone whom I believe wants my hand. And you?"

"No. For a long time, I considered myself still betrothed to you. But I had no way of knowing if you were still alive, and I gradually lost hope. Several ladies of the court have given me indication of their interest, but they are such simpletons that I cannot think of them as any more than sport. There is still time for us, then. I insist that you allow me to escort you to dinner and on a drive around Paris after your visit to the queen."

"I would like that."

The coach was now stopping. Jean-Philippe jumped out of the carriage and helped her out once more. Claudette nearly gasped aloud at the scene before her. They had traveled past the magnificent Palace of Versailles itself, and were at the entry of some magical little town on the edge of a lake.

"Jean-Philippe, where are we?"

"This is the queen's Hameau. She had it built specifically for her own enjoyment, and it was just completed three years ago. You can count that there are twelve buildings, all built to resemble village structures. But don't let the exteriors of the buildings fool you. The interiors are meticulously decorated. See the two buildings over there, connected by a wooden gallery? That is known as the Queen's House, and from there she watches her hired servants perform farm chores."

Claudette saw that the buildings were of rough-hewn stone, with thatched roofs and wooden porches, and there appeared to be a nearby working farm. Barnyard animals walked freely about, many with bejeweled ribbons around their necks. Ivy climbed in earnest on the buildings, covering windows and railings with bursts of showy leaves. In great contrast to the simple buildings were the fashionable people strolling about the Hamlet. Although they were dressed modestly, they carried themselves like the elite of French society. Seated on a plush crimson stool in the center of activity was the queen. She was plainly dressed in a muslin gown with an unadorned white cap on her head, but no jewels or other accoutrements of state, yet the others were buzzing about her like bees to a flower, waiting for recognition and attention.

"Come, I will present you now. You are fortunate to have come today, since the queen is much less formal when she is at the Hameau."

Claudette took Jean-Philippe's arm, and let him lead her to the busy hive.

"Your Majesty, may I introduce you to Claudette Laurent, a French émigré to England, and a dollmaker of remarkable skill." He stepped away and melted in with the other onlookers.

The queen looked at her, and in the depths of the royal blue eyes Claudette immediately realized her great mistake. This hair was appropriate for a gathering at Versailles, but not here, where Marie Antoinette was obviously pretending to live a simple life. Even Claudette's gown was far too sumptuous for the pastoral surroundings the queen had created. Other female attendants of the queen turned to pay attention to Claudette, and she could hear titters behind hands covering mouths. Before the queen could see her face, now burning with shame, Claudette swept down into the curtsy she had practiced with Jolie just hours ago, ensuring she did not show her inferior stockings.

She arose when the queen said, "We welcome you, Mademoiselle Laurent, to our humble village. We would have you know that we live modestly here, despite what you may hear about us in England. On future visits we would have you not take such great care with your appearance."

Claudette looked up to see that the queen's blue eyes were twinkling with kindness in her peaches and cream face, which was fuller than it was when she first glimpsed the queen on the road to St. Denis, and she immediately felt relief. One of the ladies nearby whispered loudly, "I wonder if the little toy maker thinks she is a grand duchesse now?" More tittering.

"Silence! We will not have our guest mocked. There, come here, my dear. Sit next to me and tell me of your work with dolls. Madame Victoire, you and your rude mouth may go and ask Mesdames Bertin and Grosholtz to join us. The rest of you may go about your activities."

Claudette saw that the group dispersed except for two people, a man and a woman, both of whom stayed at the queen's side. The woman was one of the most beautiful creatures Claudette had ever seen in her life. She had large, soulful eyes, giving her an air of complete purity. Her gown of ruffled lace around the bodice, and her country hat trimmed in roses, added to the impression of an innocent young girl.

The man was her male counterpart, being extremely handsome, although Claudette had an intuition that he was quite worldly and experienced. He looked directly at her, and his good looks, with large flashing eyes, a high forehead, and roguish smile, caused her to gasp. She knew this man. It was the count, the one who had come to her shop and placed the initial order for dolls for the queen. He winked conspiratorially at her.

The queen introduced the woman in the country hat as her dear friend, the Princesse de Lamballe. Born Marie-Thérèse-Louise de Savoie-Carignan, she was half Italian and half German, her mother having been a German princess. She had been widowed at the age of eighteen by the early death of her dissolute young husband, the only son of the famously charitable Duc de Penthièvre, and she now concentrated on acting the devoted daughter-in-law to the bereaved duc. The duc was a grandson of Louis XIV, his father having been a royal bastard legitimized by the king. The queen first met the princesse during her bridal party journey to France.

"Your Majesty, that was the first time you met me, as well."

"Indeed, Mademoiselle Laurent, how might that be so?"

Claudette described how she and Jean-Philippe had been the cause of stopping the bridal train years ago. Marie Antoinette proclaimed her delight to be reunited with one of her first friends in France, and feigned dismay that Jean-Philippe had not told her the story.

"And this is my very special friend, Count Axel Fersen." The queen looked up at Fersen, and Claudette saw her covertly reach a hand over to squeeze his arm.

"I believe Mademoiselle Laurent and I have made acquaintance before, Your Majesty, in the commission of your first doll from mademoiselle's shop." Much was conveyed in the words "Your Majesty." He spoke them like a caress.

"Tell us, Mademoiselle Laurent, of your background. Prior to our fortuitous meeting, of course. Monsieur Renaud tells us that your father was a dollmaker of some repute during the reign of the previous king. Why do you no longer live in France?"

Claudette described for the queen and her friends the fire that devastated her neighborhood and took the lives of her parents, and her subsequent flight to England to begin anew. The Princesse de Lamballe sighed softly in sympathy, leading the queen to press Claudette for more details. She then described her brush with prostitution upon landing in England, her employment with the Ashby family, and the eventual building of her dollmaking business. She omitted any mention of William.

As Claudette's story concluded, the queen signaled to a member of her retinue, who scurried off to do her bidding. A look passed between her and Fersen, one of intimacy and understanding, and for several minutes the queen's attention was diverted from Claudette to Fersen, who periodically touched the queen's hair, or her shoulder, in a personal way that, to Claudette, was unseemly. But what did a dollmaker know of court etiquette?

Claudette used the opportunity to look around her. She couldn't see Jean-Philippe, but the queen's ladies and courtiers were milling about nearby. Some looked at her with pity, some with amusement, but most regarded her with disdain. One gentleman, dressed in the oddest shade of green and reminding Claudette of an old turtle shell, looked directly at her with a frown, then out toward the queen's pasture and back at her, this time with meaning.

She looked out toward the pasture and saw what she hadn't before. A scattering of shepherds and dairy maids, dressed in the finest servant uniforms Claudette had ever seen, were working in the fields. So that was the intent of the courtier's look. He thought Claudette belonged out there, not with his peers, and certainly not with the queen. She sighed. Her life perpetually repeated itself. She wasn't really welcome anywhere.

"Ah, Mademoiselle Laurent, here are two of my attendants who will be most interested in hearing about your dollmaking. You must meet Madame Rose Bertin. She is my dressmaker, and I would have her involved in clothing my next doll. I wish to have made"—she looked lovingly at the princesse—"a replica of my dearest friend in all the world."

The princesse's hand fluttered to her throat, and she curtsied deeply at the honor being shown her. But Claudette had no time to digest the important sale she had just unknowingly made, as Madame Bertin was tapping her foot impatiently.

The woman standing before her was full-faced and florid, and she looked imperiously down at the young woman whom she clearly disdained for being working class. Would the queen have much choice in what she wore, with such a harridan for a dressmaker? Claudette attempted to curtsy to Rose Bertin, but Marie Antoinette stopped her. "That is not necessary, my dear," she said in her kind voice. "And this is Madame Marie Grosholtz. She is art tutor to Madame Elisabeth, my sister-in-law. She is fascinated by the composition of your dolls, how you create them. La, I just like to hold the finished creations. Please, tell Mesdames Bertin and Grosholtz more about your work."

Marie Antoinette turned back to Axel Fersen, and Claudette realized that her audience with the queen was over. With Jean-
Philippe back at her side, she joined Rose Bertin and Marie
Grosholtz to discuss plans for a future royal doll. Rose immediately
stated that she would handle all details of the doll's dress, to be in
the style of the queen's most elegant gown, and that certainly the
queen would wish her to import more of the blue silk she had just
found. And there was no need for Claudette to be involved with
the gown. Certainly she, Rose Bertin, dressmaker to the finest court
in Europe, was capable of making a dress for—of all things—a doll,
a child's plaything. Fortunately, Madame Bertin stalked off shortly
thereafter, muttering about silly toys and royal whims, and why
was the queen's dressmaker's time wasted with such frivolities.
Claudette was then able to talk more with Marie Grosholtz.

Marie was a short woman of slight build, with a hooked nose and
wide-set, blinking eyes. She reminded Claudette most of a bird,
darting its head back and forth and looking inquisitively at whomever
held her attention for the moment. Claudette felt affection for the
young woman, who must only have been just a few years older
than Claudette herself.

Marie explained to Claudette that she had been brought to
France several years ago, having come to the attention of Madame
Elisabeth, the king's sister, and now had her own apartment at the
splendid Palace of Versailles to assist with Madame Elisabeth's
artistic education. Marie was actually a gifted wax sculptress, and
in her native city of Strasbourg had studied under Dr. Philippe
Curtius. Together they had made wax sculptures of such famous
personages as Voltaire and the American Benjamin Franklin, and
the public was intrigued enough to spend good money to see rep-
resentations of famous people they would never likely see in person. Marie's love was in sculpting, not painting, and she was
fascinated by Claudette's dollmaking, as the two skills were so
closely related.

Claudette described for Marie, at first in general terms, then—
as the large eyes blinked at her rapidly in understanding—in more
depth, about her doll designs and compositions. Marie interrupted
frequently with questions. "What if you do not have lamb's wool

for hair? What other animal hair works? Where do you get your carving tools? Do you make doll clothing yourself?" Claudette intercepted and answered the questions as rapidly as she could, and through the conversation grew to like the other woman's deep intelligence.

Marie talked animatedly about her own work at court. Not of aristocratic birth, she had been fortunate indeed to be selected to serve as the royal art tutor. However, she hoped to return to sculpting.

The queen's exclamations interrupted their discussion. They looked up to see a woman leading a young, hunchbacked child, who was clearly unhappy with being outside, toward Marie Antoinette. The queen rushed over to the boy and hugged him. She made a motion to the woman, who walked over to Marie and Claudette.

"*Pardon*, you are the dollmaker, *oui?*"

"Yes." Claudette was confused. The woman was well dressed, but the queen treated her as a servant.

"Her Majesty wishes that you meet her son."

Claudette followed the woman, with Marie on her heels. Jean-Philippe retreated to a shady location under a tree to wait. Marie whispered, "That's the Marquise de Tourzel. She is one of the queen's attendants, but she is devoted to the Dauphin and spends much of her time in the nursery. She should have been named governess instead of the Duchesse de Polignac."

All of these names were confusing Claudette. How could she ever keep them in order?

The queen was playing a clapping game with her son, whose facial expression oozed the physical pain he was in. "Ah, Mademoiselle Laurent, you must meet my darling son, Louis Joseph."

The boy attempted a smile to please his mother. "*Bonjour*, mademoiselle." Turning back he said, "Mama, may I go back to my rooms now?"

"Of course. Madame Tourzel, will you please take the Dauphin to his apartment? Please be sure that he is given his palliative." The queen watched his retreating figure lovingly.

"Is he not a most handsome boy? He is not well lately, but I am sure he is just overtired and needs rest."

Claudette agreed that the queen's son was very fine-looking, though secretly she thought him exceedingly unwell. She and Marie Grosholtz resumed their discussions.

Several hours later, the two women were walking arm in arm around the Hameau, flowers they had picked wound through their hair, now that Marie had brought Claudette's tresses down to a more modest style. They deliberated intensely over the design of what they were already referring to as the de Lamballe doll. Marie had inks and paper brought from the palace, and the two women sketched one design after another, alternately laughing in delight and grimacing in disgust at their creations.

It was Jean-Philippe's tug at her arm that made Claudette realize how much time had passed. It was nearly twilight, and the Hameau had been lit with torches strategically placed at intervals to best illuminate the thatched house, the lake, and the grazing sheep which had not yet been taken into barns. Claudette gasped anew at the outrageously expensive simplicity of it all. Such a peasant's setting, but how much did it cost the taxpayers to maintain flocks of sheep—wearing ruby-studded ribbons around their necks—for no reason other than to decorate the landscape?

Jean-Philippe held Claudette's arm and gently guided her back to the queen. She curtsied again, praising the queen for her lovely Hameau, and assuring her that the doll would be made with all speed possible. She backed away curtsying, as demanded by a court etiquette that could not be wholly forgotten even at the Hameau.

Jean-Philippe escorted her back to their carriage, one hand covering hers as it rested tucked in his elbow. "Jean-Philippe, I saw very elegantly dressed workers in the pasture, but they did not seem to be doing much."

"Those are the servants I told you the queen hires so she can watch them do farm chores on days that she is at the Hameau. They are hired to be present when the queen chooses to visit her cottage, but she doesn't want them actually getting dirty, which would destroy the perfection of the queen's vista."

"Then how are the animals actually cared for?" The queen of France was proving to be perplexing.

"Once she returns to the main palace, the real farm workers will come and collect the animals to take care of feeding and stabling them."

"I see." But she really didn't. Nevertheless, the queen had been very kind to her, certainly more benevolent than most people of far lesser stature had ever been to her.

Stepping back into the carriage, she lay back against the head cushion, closing her eyes and sighing contentedly. She opened her eyes presently to find Jean-Philippe gazing adoringly at her.

"Claudette, I have so much to show you while you're here, to show you how much I still love you. Your time here in Paris will be unforgettable."

William was finishing breakfast when Dobry presented him with a silver tray containing mail. William flipped through it quickly, looking for a letter from Claudette. Not seeing one, he set aside everything but *Le Journal de Paris,* the first of the French dailies. The news was sometimes weeks old, but it gave him an opportunity to stay in touch with activities on the Continent, and also to practice his French. Claudette avoided talking in her native tongue because she had been so poorly treated in some quarters for her nationality, so he never practiced with her. He shook his head, smiling. As though anyone could hear that charming accent and not know exactly where her homeland was.

He scanned the leaflet for social announcements. Turning the page, he spotted a headline for royal engagements at Versailles. Tracing his finger down the listings, he found it near the end.

> Mademoiselle Claudette Laurent, formerly of Paris and now residing in London, presented to the queen on the morning of fourteenth July, accompanied by Monsieur Jean-Philippe Renaud.

He furrowed his brow. Who was this Renaud fellow? Probably one of the queen's courtiers, escorting a woman alone to be introduced to the most famous woman in Europe. He forgot about it in the press of his day as he had to mediate a dispute between the local saddle-maker and one of his grooms, who claimed that a recently delivered harness was inferior and unacceptable.

Several days later the mail contained the much-anticipated envelope from Claudette. She recorded her visit with the queen, and described in detail the gardens of Versailles, the latest Parisian clothing styles, and the gastronomic delights she had forgotten about during her years in England.

> *. . . and now I am meeting with Mesdames Grosholtz*
> *and Bertin, art tutor and dressmaker to the queen, and*
> *making plans for the queen's newest doll. I have attended*
> *several soirées and am quite frankly fascinated by the*
> *manic social whirl. The wealthy live almost as if*
> *tomorrow will never come.*

She went on to give him specifics of the ship on which she was planning to return. With her letter she enclosed a sprig of jasmine she had surreptitiously plucked at the palace.

Attending soirées? With whom? Surely she was not cavorting about France alone. Was someone else dancing the *contredanse allemande* with her?

William grunted in his displeasure and went to his study to pen a reply. He kept it brief, giving her news about one of his mares in foal at Hevington and wishing her a safe sea journey on her return. He signed it "Her waiting servant, William." It would do no good to caution her on her associations with the lecherous French. The woman was damnably stubborn when she wanted to be.

He would not sleep well until she was home again.

❧ 19 ❧

Jean-Philippe arrived at her hotel early the following morning, and every morning for a week, to escort Claudette to a new amusement or entertainment. They strolled about the public gardens at Versailles during the day, watched street performers at dusk, and went to the opera at night. Jean-Philippe constantly surprised her with gifts. A carriage full of flowers, a string of pearls brought with dessert in an elegant restaurant, a porcelain box adorned with cherubs waiting in her hotel room. She never knew what wondrous present would be awaiting her as she traveled around.

Each day they chattered about events that had occurred during their separation. Jean-Philippe had completed his interminable apprenticeship under Monsieur Gamain, who had taken his family in temporarily after the fire. Gamain wanted him to work as a locksmith for him, but Jean-Philippe was interested in Gamain only as a source of knowledge, not caring a whit about the detailed work with the metal mechanisms. Much to his father's dismay, Jean-Philippe convinced Gamain to help him get a placement at court through his position as Louis XVI's locksmith, so that he could personally witness all of the extravagances he had been hearing about throughout his apprenticeship.

Claudette asked about this. "And what do you think? Versailles is of course glorious, but do you think the queen is all the people accuse her of, an avaricious spendthrift? She seemed very kind and unpretentious to me."

"Well, for certain the king is an *imbécile*. He would have been happier as Gamain's apprentice than as ruler of France. Every day he either hunts or plays with mechanical things. So long as he does not have to deal with his cabinet and make sound decisions.

"As for the queen, I dislike her Austrian ways, although I suppose she is not unkind. She is as profligate as any of her courtiers, which I think is a disgrace in a queen at the helm of a nation full of starving people. They say she is having affairs with the Duchesse de Polignac and the Princesse de Lamballe."

"The princesse!" Claudette was taken aback. "But that's not who the queen is—" She stopped. How did she, a mere London dollmaker, know whether the queen was involved with Count Fersen?

"But that doesn't seem like something the queen would do," she finished lamely. Jean-Philippe didn't notice.

Claudette told him of her desperate search for him and her subsequent flight to England, her employment with the Ashbys, and the establishment of her doll shop. She made no mention of William Greycliffe. Jean-Philippe laughed uproariously at her final altercation with Mrs. Ashby.

"Oh, my love, you are truly an independent spirit with an innate understanding of the rights of man."

While sipping cordials one afternoon at an outdoor café, Jean-Philippe presented Claudette with his latest offering: a box of candied flowers, each dusted with a different color of sugar. He leaned forward eagerly to be heard over the street noise of carriages rumbling down the dusty street and their bawling drivers jockeying for position in traffic. Claudette was not sure if passage was worse in London or Paris. Both cities were full of bullying carriage drivers.

"Claudette, finding you has been remarkable. Could you have imagined that we would find each other again? You will want to move back to Paris right away so we can be married."

She hesitated. "Jean-Philippe, I have obligations in London. My shop . . ."

He waved a hand. "You can create your dolls here. After all, the queen is your biggest customer. You belong here with me."

"This is all very sudden."

"Surely you cannot mean that you have any uncertainty about this? Claudette, we are still betrothed. Look." From his pocket he pulled two small jewel boxes. He opened one. Inside was the locket she had given him.

"Do you still have your ring?" he asked.

She reached into her reticule and pulled at some stitching she had done in the lining. Tucked in a secret compartment was the ring, which she pulled out and silently showed him.

"You carry it but do not wear it? When did you stop wearing it?"

"Once I realized how difficult life was going to remain for me at the Ashbys, I became worried that one of the housemaids might steal it. So I sewed it in here to keep it safe. I suppose once I left there I did not think it wise to wear while in the workroom."

"What you mean to say is that you forgot about it. And me."

"That is not true! Jean-Philippe, I was heartsick for ages over you."

"And at some point you ceased to be. Nothing has changed for me, Claudette, but perhaps it has for you. I can see that I have to work more arduously to convince you to become my wife." He sat back and stuffed both of the tiny boxes back into his pocket without showing her the contents of the second one.

Claudette returned to her hotel that night with her thoughts muddled. Where *did* she belong? Was she still French or was she now English? Had all of her feelings for Jean-Philippe indeed vanished? And there was William's curt and impersonal letter delivered to her room today. Had she offended him more than she knew by coming to France? Would he welcome her home? Where *was* home?

When Jolie came to undress her and comb her hair, she remarked that madame was unusually quiet. Claudette smiled wanly and assured the maid she had simply had a busy day. The girl shook her head but made no comment.

*   *   *

Notes had been delivered each day to Claudette's hotel, expressing Jean-Philippe's utter and unfailing devotion to her. The following morning's missive grew more passionate.

> *My Dearest Dove,*
> *Do you remember that I used to call you that when we were teenagers? I still think of you as my precious little bird, who needs me to feed and care for her. Once you return to Paris permanently you will see what a good husband I will be to you. I will eventually leave the servitude of the court to establish my own trade. You would not always have to toil away on the little dolls. When I am successful, you would have the luxury of raising all of our children while I provide us with a comfortable home. It is what we both want, Claudette. When can we set our marriage date?*
> *Yours unto death,*
> *Jean-Philippe*

Is this what I want? she wondered. She mentally compared her life in England with what it might be in France again. Oh, to live in her home country, speaking her native language and enjoying custom with the Bourbon court. But William's face loomed up before her, and the thought of his kisses and masculine ways threatened to undo her.

Claudette made her toilette as usual that morning with the assistance of Jolie, who was quickly becoming indispensable to her. She scrawled out notes to Rose Bertin and Marie Grosholtz containing her thoughts on the doll commission and seeking a time to meet with them both. Jolie took the letters and promised to give them to a messenger. After a quick breakfast with other travelers in the dining room, she was greeted by Jean-Philippe in the lobby.

"I have a surprise for you today, Claudette." As always, he carried a small, fragrant bouquet of flowers for her.

Each day brought something new, so she was hardly bowled over to hear this. "Again, Jean-Philippe? Could there possibly be anything new in France that you have not yet shown me?"

"This is not entirely new, but I think it will please you greatly."

He escorted her to another of the palace carriages, this one painted pink, with gilded wheels and a hunting scene painted on the door. She was quickly becoming accustomed to this luxury and indulgence, and knew she would need to return to England soon before she became so heady from the magnificence of the French court and the joy of being home again that she would be unable to leave.

"Jean-Philippe, are we going to Versailles again?" she asked, as they were pulling up to the palace gates.

"*Oui,* but to a place you have not seen." He signaled to the guard to let them pass. The carriage continued on its way along the Grand Canal. It seemed from Claudette's perspective to go on forever, and she said so aloud.

"Yes," Jean-Philippe replied. "The Sun King had it designed so that it gets wider the farther away one is from the main palace, so that when viewing its length from close to the palace, it seems to have the same perspective of width all the way to its end. It was really quite clever, I must admit."

They continued in companionable silence. Jean-Philippe reached over and placed his hand over Claudette's, and she did not resist its warmth.

They pulled up in front of a square marble building, three stories high and diminutive in comparison with the main palace, but far grander than most French citizens could ever imagine. Shrubbery in enormous planters lined the first-floor windows.

"Where are we?" she asked.

"This is the Petit Trianon. In addition to her Hameau, this is the other project on which the queen wastes vast quantities of money repainting, redecorating, and refinishing." He shook his head wryly. "I obtained special permission for you to come and see her personal doll collection. Even the king has to ask consent to set foot inside this home of the queen's. It is for her and her friends only."

"Oh!" Claudette nearly squealed in delight. She impulsively kissed his cheek. Embarrassed, she jumped down from the carriage without waiting for him to help her.

"Is the queen here?"

"No. She is receiving official visitors today from Austria. No one is here except for a few groundskeepers."

Inside the Petit Trianon, which was just as elaborately furnished as Louis XIV's grand palace at the top of the Grand Canal, Jean-Philippe escorted Claudette through the rooms, each decorated with thick, detailed carpets; rich draperies in blues and golds; hand-painted wallpaper; intricately carved, gilded furniture; and the finest of porcelain and other ornamentation.

"Louis XV built this for his mistress, Madame du Pompadour," Jean-Philippe explained. "She died before it was completed, so he gave it to his next mistress, Madame du Barry, whom the current queen still despises even though she left the palace as soon as the old king was dead. Our current Louis gave it to Marie Antoinette when he ascended the throne. She was nineteen years old when she came in possession of it."

In one salon, Claudette noticed that some of the floorboards had been pulled up, leaving a large gaping hole in the parquet flooring. She asked about it.

"Oh, the queen is having mechanical devices built so that servants can load the tables with food from within the cellar and then the tables can be lifted up to this room for her specially invited guests. Then the tables will be cranked back down again, and the flooring laid back down in large planks after each meal."

Claudette was astonished. "But why?"

"So that the room can be used for other things, instead of being blocked by a large dining table. And also so the servants do not have to be seen."

Again Claudette saw there was great irony in the French queen. She could be endlessly kind and sincere to a mere commoner such as herself, yet she had a great sense of her own importance and was careless about spending great sums of peasant taxes on her own pleasure. It was as though she didn't understand that maintaining her "simple" lifestyle was onerous on the royal purse.

They finally ended up in one of the queen's private chambers containing her doll collection. There were dolls everywhere, lining the walls from floor to ceiling on specially constructed shelving.

The dolls seemed to reach the sky, and indeed the ceiling of the twenty-foot-tall room was painted with puffy clouds, birds, and pink-faced cherubs looking down on visitors from the corners of the ceiling. Each doll had its own rounded ledge that protruded from the wall on a support. The ledges were gilded and ornamented to match twenty chest-high pedestals placed around the room. Each of these pedestals held what were obviously the queen's favorites in her collection. One pedestal in the center of the room was conspicuously devoid of an exhibit.

"Why is there no doll here?" she asked.

"I believe it is waiting for the Princesse de Lamballe doll you are creating. Undoubtedly the queen and her friends will have some extravagant party to celebrate its arrival."

"Well, it is an honor for me and my shop to be recognized by the queen of France."

Jean-Philippe scowled but did not protest.

From this room, they went outside to stroll about the set of gardens attached to the Petit Trianon. In contrast to the formal French style, the architect had developed a landscape of meandering paths, hills, and streams. Flowering shrubs were deliberately planted according to size and color against backdrops of trees with gracefully arching limbs, with the intent of pleasing the eye in an eruption of complementary colors.

The whole look was one of cultivated wilderness. From atop one of these hills, Claudette could see that the grounds connected to the Hameau, the queen's little farming village.

Standing next to her and also looking out at the Hameau, Jean-Philippe said, "Some people call the Petit Trianon 'Little Vienna.' They think the queen is trying to establish a foreign court here."

"Do you believe this to be true? I don't. I think the queen is every inch the Frenchwoman. Remember how coarse her pronunciation was when we met her carriage all those years ago? All traces of her Austrian accent are gone. She seems very devoted to her family and friends here."

He shrugged.

They finished their evening together over coffee and pastries,

Jean-Philippe clearly amused that Claudette had developed a taste for the bitter drink.

In response to Claudette's note, Marie Grosholtz arranged a sitting with Claudette, Madame Bertin, the Princesse de Lamballe, and herself. When the queen heard of their impending appointment, she insisted that they come to the Petit Trianon to spend the day with her. Claudette was privileged to see Marie Antoinette even more relaxed that day. She dressed simply but elegantly, in a dark blue dress with a white apron over it, and a relatively basic poufed hat with just a single feather as adornment. A choker set with a single sapphire outlined in diamonds gleamed on her neck as her only piece of jewelry.

When Claudette mustered up the courage to compliment the queen on her simple but striking necklace, Marie Antoinette's hand fluttered to her throat as she said, "Thank you, Mademoiselle Laurent. It was a gift from a dear friend." The queen's cheeks pinked and she changed the subject by asking about the doll's progress.

She watched with interest as Claudette spent about an hour taking the princesse's measurements and noting the tiniest details of her hair, eye color, and the shape of her fingers, documenting it all in a small notebook. In response to Marie Antoinette's questions, Claudette told her that the measurements would help her build a doll that would be completely accurate and to scale, even down to the size of her hands.

"Why, Thérèse," the queen exclaimed. "The doll will be an absolute miniature of you!" She clapped spontaneously at the thought.

The queen had picnic baskets delivered for their lunch, which they had at the Temple of Love, a rounded gazebo set high atop steps in the landscape of the Petit Trianon. The baskets were gorged with foodstuffs, and Claudette tasted from dishes she had never even heard of before. Stuffed partridges in aspic, eel with truffles, roasted larks in pastry, trout with tomato and garlic sauce, braised goose, and a salad of pike fillets with oysters were presented by liveried servants.

Claudette sampled everything except the eel, which was too

richly sauced for her liking. The women finished off their food with a fine Bordeaux.

She thought the meal was over, but the servants merely removed their dishes in order to present desserts of petit fours, peaches with cream sauce, almond cheesecake, and custard.

Claudette was certain the boning in her bodice would snap under pressure. She was duly surprised when the queen, now sitting contentedly on layers of down-stuffed coverlets, commented on the simplicity of the meal.

"What a relief not to be encumbered with *service à la française*," she sighed, patting her stomach. "I wish every meal was this unpretentious."

At Claudette's confused expression, Marie Grosholtz leaned over and whispered, "The court serves in three courses: the entrées, followed by the afters, and then the pastry cook's creations. Each course may have up to thirty dishes and it takes hours to serve it all."

Claudette shook her head in disbelief. No wonder the queen had become so stout since the time she traveled to France as a young bride.

As the women digested their food, they laughed together and talked idly until Madame Bertin became weary of "the foolish chatter" and asked for leave to return to her own shop.

The remaining four women continued chattering, mostly gossip about people and events Claudette was unfamiliar with, but it was gratifying just to be there, so she closed her eyes and leaned back against a pillar of the gazebo to listen to the pleasant voices. *How had an orphaned little dollmaker ended up having a picnic luncheon with the most famous queen in Europe?*

She sat up with a start. Yes, she had been orphaned, but it was only back in France that she felt that way again. England had become her refuge, her place of success and friendship. And love. It was time to declare where home was.

Home was England.

As she bid good-bye, Claudette promised to begin work on the de Lamballe doll straightaway upon her return to London. The queen responded that she was most eager to receive the doll and have it placed in the Petit Trianon.

As for Claudette, she was just as eager to return to London. Her time in France had been a bucolic retreat, but she realized now that it was neither what she wanted nor what she needed.

She needed William.

Back at her hotel, Claudette prepared for her sailing, scheduled three days hence. Jolie showed up at her room that evening with a fresh vase of cut flowers for the bureau, and saw her recent bene-factress struggling to pack all of the gifts that the dark-haired man had given her.

"May I be of assistance to you?"

Claudette stood up from what she was doing and surveyed the chaos around her. "Indeed, Jolie, I am in great need of help."

In her indomitable way, Jolie set to work repacking Claudette's pile of belongings. Claudette smiled as Jolie tsk-tsked and shook her head while methodically organizing the great mountain of be-longings that now needed to find their way back to London.

On impulse, Claudette asked, "Jolie, what keeps you here in Paris?"

"*Pardon?*" The girl looked up from where she was wrapping a bone-handled mirror and matching brush.

"Do you think your uncle would greatly miss you if you left? Would you like to return to England and live with me as my lady's maid?"

The great orbs expanded. "Madame," she breathed. "I should be your most devoted servant. You will be the most elegantly dressed lady in London. I will—"

Claudette laughed. "Jolie, I know I can rely on you. Now, I shall pay you a fair wage, and you will have a comfortable bed, and you need never, ever worry that I would lift my hand to you. You will be a welcome member of my household."

Claudette found that Jolie's uncle was not quite as enthusiastic about the idea as young Jolie was, since he would be losing his free domestic help. Ultimately, it came down to a cash payment for releasing the girl, which Claudette agreed to gladly. He hardly noticed Jolie's departure, so intent was he on counting money and bragging of it to his wife.

Claudette's final task before leaving was to write a very difficult letter, for which she paid a courier handsomely to deliver at once.

> *Dearest Jean-Philippe,*
>
> *It grieves me terribly to write this letter to you. I know that it is your desire that I return "home" as you say, so that we can resume our relationship as we left it when we were sixteen, and be married and have children together.*
>
> *However, I have decided to return to England, permanently. Prior to my journey back to Paris, I was not sure what my feelings were concerning my birth country, but now I am convinced that England is where I belong, with my doll shop and the friends I have made there.*
>
> *You will always occupy that portion of my heart that longs for a time of innocence and carefree days. I shall never forget what we meant to each other, and hope that I can rely upon your understanding.*
>
> *In everlasting friendship,*
> *Claudette*

William's most recent letter had been even more distant than the first one detailing his mare's confinement. Perhaps she had become too sure of his devoted pursuit of her. Any thought of a pleasurable reconciliation with Jean-Philippe paled in comparison to the terrifying notion of William's possible desertion. Her only concern now was to return home.

To her surprise, Jean-Philippe was waiting outside the hotel to escort them all the way to Calais. Jolie was round-eyed and dazed by Jean-Philippe's handsome looks and impeccable French manners. Realizing the girl's awe of him, he went out of his way to be considerate of the new servant, whom Claudette seemed to hold in high regard. The interminable carriage ride was one of uncomfortable silence, with Jolie staring incessantly at Jean-Philippe, and Claudette avoiding his gaze entirely.

Jean-Philippe sent Jolie ahead onto the ship, saying he knew he could count on her to ensure the luggage was delivered aboard properly. The girl obeyed him without question. As soon as she was out of earshot, Jean-Philippe unfolded a piece of paper from his vest and held it out to Claudette, beseechingly.

"Surely you do not mean this?" he asked.

Her lips trembled. "I do. I do mean to return to England for good."

"This is impossible. Claudette, you belong to me, to France. I understand that you went to England in desperation, but that is a country of nothing but sots and sheep farmers. They have no art, no culture, no manners. How could you possibly wish to spend your life there, away from me?"

She looked down. The guilt was unbearable. "I . . . I have responsibilities there. Not only to the shop, but to other people—friends."

"What friends are these?"

"You remember that I mentioned Béatrice, whom I met on the ship to England? She and her daughter live with me, and I help support them."

"What of it? Either they can come back here with you, or they can find another benefactress in England."

She met his gaze and kept her voice steady. "I would not ask it of her. In any case, I do not find that I miss France as much now that I have returned for a visit."

Jean-Philippe blinked at her in disbelief. "What are you saying? That now that you have spent time with me, your betrothed, you find that you are anxious to return to that bleak isle across the Channel?"

"No, I—"

"Is it that English pig you say wants to marry you? No matter, I'll tear him to shreds with my own hands for daring to lay claim to you. Just say the word, my love."

"Jean-Philippe, it's not—"

He grabbed her around the waist with one arm, and, cupping her head with his other arm, pulled her toward him for a violent kiss. Unlike the Jean-Philippe of years ago, his kiss did not thrill her young senses. Instead, it terrified her. He forced her lips apart with his tongue, a battering ram intended to break down her reserves by force. In mere moments he was moaning wildly.

Taken unawares, Claudette did not at first struggle until she realized he did not mean to be gentle with her. She pushed against him but he did not release her, so she kicked him in the shin, which startled him into letting go.

"Claudette," he whispered from deep in his throat. "I'm sorry. I lost my head."

"It's nothing. The whistle is blowing; I have to go."

"Darling, please, stay here with me. Do not end it this way."

She turned her back on him and walked toward the gangplank, wiping the back of her hand across her mouth to erase what had just happened.

"Claudette, I do not accept your refusal. You will come back to me one day. We are destined for one another. We will—"

She lost the sound of his voice as she boarded the ship that waited to take her back to England and William.

❧ 20 ❧

Claudette enmeshed herself in a new endeavor to clear her mind of what had transpired in France: developing a stamp for her dolls. Her father never put his mark on his merchandise, feeling that his goods were recognizable by their quality and design. Claudette, however, wanted customers to know her fine dolls by an easily-identifiable marking. The silversmiths used these marks—why not a dollmaker?

She browsed through dozens of shops, surreptitiously turning over goods and looking for their marks with a small, bone-handled magnifying glass she purchased expressly for this purpose. She acquired several articles that had interesting maker's marks, including a silver wick trimmer, a brass candlestick, and an ornate wooden table clock. She spread them out on the writing desk in her refurbished flat to examine them all more closely, and added to them the small pewter betrothal ring Jean-Philippe had given her, which she discovered also had a small marking on it.

After scrutinizing her samples at length, she began sketching her own designs for a mark, finally deciding upon one that was in the shape of a square with rounded corners. The square was divided into quarters, with a "C" and an "L" in the top left and right quadrants, an "FD" in the bottom left section for Fashion Dolls, and a tiny face to the bottom right.

She gave the design to Roger for experimentation in both wax and wood. When both were accomplished to her satisfaction, she instructed all the employees that no doll was to leave the shop without her special identifying mark. Her sample items remained on her writing desk, except for Jean-Philippe's ring, which she sewed into another small reticule she did not use often, and hid in an armoire.

Secreting the ring away once more was her way of trying to bury the past. William's greeting when she disembarked from the ship had been cool, and the lips that brushed hers were not enthusiastic to have found their loving mates. He had thawed over the course of a few weeks, as Claudette's bubbling enthusiasm for her shop and the most important commission she had ever had melted the reserve he had built up during her absence.

The ring had to stay buried. She must never give William reason to doubt her again.

Her mind cleared and, confident that remaining in England with Béatrice and William was the proper course of action, she was now ready to begin work on the de Lamballe doll.

Letters, sketches, and supplies shot back and forth across the Channel, as Claudette, Marie Grosholtz, and Rose Bertin continued on their collaboration. Marie painted a detailed miniature of the Princesse de Lamballe, so that Béatrice had a model from which she could mix paints for the doll's face exactly. Forgetting Madame Bertin's earlier command about how the doll should be dressed, Claudette suggested that the couturier select a flattering gown from the princesse's wardrobe and send it to her for replication. A stern rebuke quickly arrived from the dressmaker.

> *Mademoiselle Laurent:*
> *I regret that I must inform you that under no*
> *circumstances will a dress that has been worn in Her*
> *Majesty's presence more than once be engaged as the model*
> *for the de Lamballe doll. As the queen's trusted advisor, I*
> *am relied upon to ensure that offensive materials do not*
> *pass before her eyes. A used dress, particularly one that*

was not created and assembled under my expert eye, is a
completely unsuitable solution for the doll's garment.
  I shall design an appropriate gown, one that is flattering
to the princesse, and in colors that the queen prefers. Once
the princesse's gown is complete, I shall request that
Mademoiselle Grosholtz paint the princesse in the dress,
and send it to you with sufficient quantities of fabric, laces,
and trims for the smaller version. Kindly use only the
materials I send you, and make no substitutions of inferior
quality, English cloth.
  Yours, etc.
  Rose Bertin

Claudette raised an eyebrow over Madame Bertin's imperious
missive.

"Do you think the queen knows that her minister of fashion has
deemed herself 'a trusted agent'?" Claudette asked aloud of no
one in particular as she folded the letter to lock it away in her desk
with the other documents pertaining to the commission. Rose Bertin's
notoriety had become well-known in England as well as France,
and some ladies now sought to have her gowns imported from Paris.
If the Englishwomen only knew that custom with Madame Bertin
entailed hiring a tyrant, they might reconsider.

The most important decision to be made for the doll regarded
the overall building material. Wood or wax? A wax doll would be
finer to the touch, and more easily resemble human skin, but it was
still a relatively new material in dollmaking and its durability was
left wanting. Some of the dolls in the queen's collection at the
Petit Trianon already had melted and gouged areas on them. Wood
was resilient, but tended to look stiff and its carved faces inexpres-
sive. This doll must be perfect, a flawless example of her craft. After
consulting with Roger, she decided that the doll would be made of
wood. Since it would be larger than most, they would expend extra
effort in the carving to make it just as beautiful as a wax doll.

Eschewing the oak block from which she would typically make

a doll, Claudette decided upon a high-grade maple, for its particularly creamy-white look and also because it was nearly impervious to rot and insects, yet easy to handle. This species cost her double what even French oak did, but this was no time for cost considerations.

Roger Hatfield had developed into a master carver, and to him Claudette entrusted the blocks of rough wood to be honed by hand, seasoned indoors for several weeks, then sanded to a fine finish. In a typical doll composition, only the head, arms, and legs would be constructed of wood, and the torso comprised of a linen sack stuffed with sawdust shavings or straw. For the de Lamballe doll, Claudette insisted that the entire body be carved of wood. Roger spent two weeks carving the doll to exacting specifications, ensuring that the miniature princesse was replicated in precise proportions to the real model. The resulting doll was more than two feet tall.

During Roger's hibernation with the maple block, Claudette wanted him to be left alone to do his carving in private, and relegated him to a small space near a window to work. She herself only checked on his progress every three or four days. On one of her checks, she found twelve-year-old Marguerite at Roger's feet, peppering the man with questions.

"What will happen to the wood shavings? What if you make a mistake? What color eyes will the doll have? Can I see her hands when you're done with them?"

Patient soul that he was, Roger tried to answer her questions without losing his own concentration.

"Marguerite!" Claudette said. "Mr. Hatfield cannot concentrate with you pestering him to death. Leave him be."

"But Aunt Claudette," the girl protested as she was led from the room. "I just want to *know*."

She had taken to referring to Claudette as her aunt as a way of expanding her family circle beyond her mother. An orphan herself, Claudette enjoyed the sound of it. It was impossible to stay angry with Marguerite. She had her mother's beautiful, fragile looks, but she was made of iron. Like Claudette, she had experienced too much tragedy too young, yet had grown independent and self-confident as a result. Béatrice sometimes jested that it was fate that they had met, because Marguerite could have clearly been Claudette's child, not her own.

And now Marguerite wanted to know about dollmaking. Maybe it was time to think about apprenticing the girl.

"If you'd really like to know, I'll let you watch and help with the rest of the Princesse de Lamballe doll, but you must promise to leave Roger Hatfield alone."

Marguerite kissed her cheek. "I promise, I promise, Aunt Claudette."

So Claudette began to carefully explain every step of how she was making decisions about the manufacture of the doll, and what went into each step of the process. Marguerite's interest far surpassed that of her mother, who saw dollmaking primarily as income. She clung to every word Claudette said, and her constant questioning transported Claudette back into her own childhood, when she interrogated her father in much the same way. Marguerite was becoming a kindred soul.

In creating the doll's eyes, Claudette requested, and received quickly from a royal courier, two identical stones of sapphire from the queen's personal collection. Roger carved out small sockets for the orbs, just large enough in which to tuck the stones under the wax in a depression in the wood. Each jeweled eye was secured in its socket with horsehair glue. Another package delivery revealed a velvet box with a handwritten note from the queen herself, requesting that the enclosed diamond earrings be used on the doll, as they were duplicates of a gift she had given the princesse the previous year.

Béatrice hand-mixed the pigments and thinner for painting the doll's face, lips, eyebrows, and fingernails. Claudette fretted audibly over the doll's skin tone, lip color, and cheek blush until in frustration Béatrice finally barred everyone except Marguerite from the workroom until it was finished. The results were exactly what Claudette had hoped for: delicate coloring that accurately reflected the princesse's own shades.

To the top of the doll's head Claudette applied the hair, which was cut from her own head, powdered by Marguerite, and sewn to a linen cap before being glued down.

A small trunk arrived two months after Rose Bertin's letter. The trunk contained a hand-stitched book, inside which were several thick pages, each one titled "Bodice," "Sleeves," "Petticoat," and so on, with fabric and trim samples in shades of pink and cream pinned to each page. Also in the trunk, layered in tissue, were the promised materials for making the doll's dress. At the bottom of the trunk was Marie's painting of the princesse in her new gown, done in oil on a rolled-up piece of canvas. Agnes put aside all other doll clothing she was designing to prepare the de Lamballe trousseau. Each evening she would cover her work with muslin sheets to prevent any specks of dust from landing on her exquisite work until it was finished. Once the gown and undergarments were complete, shoes and gloves were cut from kid and sewn firmly onto the doll. As an added touch, Agnes created a tiny lace-edged handkerchief embroidered with the letters "MA" and attached it via a loop to the doll's wrist. The final activity was to carve Claudette's mark on the back of the doll's neck.

The results were breathtaking. The twenty-seven-inch doll, nestled in a splintwood box lined with deep blue velvet, was amazingly lifelike. Claudette, Béatrice, Marguerite, the three shop workers, and little Joseph Cummings stood around the box, admiring their joint creation. The wooden head was topped with a fashionable French hat of pink satin and accented by a band of pale blue with a young-ostrich feather inserted in the band. Claudette's curly blond hair, now powdered white, was swept up and secured under the hat. The jeweled eyes sparkled mischievously at the group, and the painted lips smiled their approval. Even the diamond earrings seemed happy to be forever resting in their new location.

The de Lamballe doll's gown, consisting of a pink and cream satin stripe overlay riding on a cream embroidered damask underskirt, was accented everywhere with ribbons and lace—at the neckline, the elbows, and around the bottom of the overlay. Tiny seed pearls had been sewn onto the kid gloves and heeled shoes in a fleur-de-lis pattern.

Claudette tucked into the doll's box a note to the queen:

Your Most Gracious Majesty,
Enclosed please find the replica of your dearest friend,
the princesse. I have endeavored to create a doll of such
accuracy and beauty that it is worthy of your presence. It
has been my greatest pleasure to execute this commission
for you.
   Your most humble servant,
   Claudette Laurent

The box was tied with a deep blue velvet ribbon to match its lining, and given to a royal courier for delivery directly to Versailles.

❧ 21 ❧

London, July 1789. Béatrice stepped into the sitting room, lightly patting her face with a handkerchief. Claudette would have sworn she seemed feverish, if not for the fact that it was an unusually hot day.

"It is so warm outside today. I believe I'll sit and rest awhile before continuing my errands—Marguerite, my love, yes, we will go to purchase more hair ribbons as I promised—oh, Claudette, here is your mail. Marguerite, come sit and read to me while I lie quietly." Still chattering in an exhausted but happy way, Béatrice disappeared into her own apartment.

Claudette quickly scanned the letters that had arrived, and a square envelope with a vaguely familiar slanted scrawl leapt out at her. She tossed aside the other correspondence and opened that one.

> *Curtius House*
> *Paris*
> *July 10, 1789*

> *My Dearest Claudette,*
> *I do hope this letter finds its way to you safely. Paris*
> *has become an unsettled city and we try to stay indoors as*
> *much as possible. I have found a trustworthy courier to*

*bring this to you—at an outrageous price, but that is the
state of France these days—and he is presently waiting for
me to finish.*

*The de Lamballe doll's arrival was well-timed, as the
palace has been cloaked in grief as of late. The queen's
precious son, Louis Joseph, died last month at the tender
age of seven. The poor boy was so misshapen and sickly
that we all knew he could never make adulthood, but we
did not expect his death so soon. She and the king were
nearly inconsolable in their anguish. Her Majesty locked
herself in her apartment for days, admitting only the
princesse. Even the count was not permitted to be in her
presence. When your package arrived and she was prodded
gently to open it, I knew that we finally had something to
breach the wall built around her heart. She actually
laughed when she lifted the doll from its velvet confines,
and hugged it to her as though it were an infant. I think
the princesse is almost embarrassed by what an incredible
likeness it is to her. The queen has named the doll
Josephina after her poor boy, and carries it with her
everywhere, even in public, causing the more libelous
newspapers over here to note that it is proof positive that
the queen is having an unnatural relationship with the
princesse. The queen, of course, turns her nose up at the
press, but in truth, these ongoing public attacks continue to
wound her. The new doll is a much-needed distraction
from her troubles.*

*She has slowly started to take an interest in life once
again, and is allowing small trays of food to be occasionally
sent to her. The king, while in misery over his son and for
other reasons, rejoices in Her Majesty's recovery. Particularly
since hers is the only advice he takes, and even that is very
infrequent.*

*As I have said, France is in turmoil. In addition to the
large debts accumulated over the last century of wars, we
have had a run of poor harvests. You know that I am not
political by nature, but I hear the court gossips twittering*

about, and they say that His Majesty has largely excluded the middle class from political influence. They and the peasantry, depressed from our declining economy, are resentful of the aristocracy. They see the revolution of the English colonies as an example for them to follow, heaven forbid.

Earlier this year, the king assessed taxes on the nobility in an effort to overcome the country's financial crisis. Their protests forced him to summon the Estates-General to Versailles for the first time since 1614. When they met in May, a quarrel broke out over whether the Three Estates should debate and vote by order—giving the aristocracy and clergy a permanent majority over the bourgeoisie—or as a single body. The matter was settled when the Third Estate, at its own separate meeting (on a tennis court of all places) declared itself a National Assembly. They took an oath not to disband until they had given France a new constitution. The king has given in and ordered the other estates to join the new National Assembly.

But still it is not enough. The Three Estates agree on nothing. There has been rioting in the streets for days.

So you see, His Majesty is attacked from all sides. The peasantry, middle class, clergy, and aristocracy all despise him. How ever did such a kind man deserve such animosity? I fear that something dreadful will happen, but I maintain a good humor and trust that all will go well. In the meantime, I am content that the queen has found joy in the miracle of wood, cloth, and paint you have created.

I pray to see you again soon when this trouble is all over. In the meantime, I shall see if Her Majesty would be willing to sit for a portrait with the doll, and I shall create an additional miniature of it to send you.

Your faithful friend,
Marie Grosholtz

Claudette folded the letter slowly. The poor queen, suffering so terribly, self-exiled in her apartments. And the king! What a terrible state the country was in. How could his own subjects be so filled with rage, with hate? Was he responsible for France's woes, or just himself swept up in the political climate? And Marie, always so practical, so focused on her work, was now weeping on paper over her royal patrons.

She shared the letter with William. He nodded gravely. "Yes, the situation in France deteriorates daily. I know how much you love the queen, but you must face the fact that she and King Louis may eventually be dethroned—"

"William, no!"

"And will probably be exiled. The populace has gone mad over there. Claudette . . ." He put an arm around her and kissed the top of her head. "Things may not end well for them. Do you realize that?"

"I cannot believe that. They are the king and queen! Duly anointed sovereigns, ordained by God. It's impossible that they would be cast out of their country like common criminals."

Another kiss, this time to her forehead. "My love, there may come a time when they are indeed treated like common criminals."

❧ 22 ❧

London, July 25, 1789. They were sitting companionably at a part-
ners desk in William's London town house study, Claudette bent
over her accounts and William sifting through an accumulation
of mail.

"I've received an invitation to Knole." William tapped an envelope whose red wax seal had been broken. "Dorset is having a dinner party to celebrate his return home from his posting as British
Ambassador to the court of Louis XVI. Claudette, I would like you
to accompany me."

She looked up sharply from her work. "William, no. Your friends
despise me for being French and for not having their social standing. I could not bear it."

"They think they despise you because they don't know you as I
do. This is an opportunity to correct their bad impressions."

She returned to her ledger. "I will not do it."

William chuckled from the back of his throat. "The first thing
they will learn about you is your enduring stubbornness."

Several days later, the pair walked about Hevington after William
had invited Claudette to see a new lake he was having installed in
the rear of the property. They paused together on a stone bridge
spanning one of several streams on the property. The stream was

to be rerouted as a feeder for the lake. William leaned over with his elbows on the ledge, looking out at the landscape. Claudette tucked her arm through his and leaned against his shoulder, closing her eyes to fully enjoy his warmth and the sound of the flowing water beneath them. She could hear the soft whinnies and snuffles of the estate's mares in the distance.

William broke into her peaceful silence. "I want you to do this for me."

"Mmm, do what?"

"I want you to come with me to Knole. You may see whatever dressmaker you wish, and have the bill sent to me."

His request shocked her out of complacence. "William, I can't. I'm just a tradesperson. They will mock me incessantly. I remember vividly how one particular rising aristocrat used to do so." She tried to cover her emerging panic by playfully swatting his arm.

"If they mock you, it is only to hide their great admiration of you. As one particular rising aristocrat used to do."

She cast her eyes down. "I can't," she whispered. "It will be a thousand Maude Ashbys."

"Claudette, look at me. You handled Maude Ashby skillfully with no concern for her estimation of you. The queen of France even invited you to a private picnic luncheon. I want you to show Dorset's guests your delightful charm and intelligence, while wordlessly telling them they can go to hell with their opinions."

"Do you really think I can do this?"

"Foolish girl." He brought his lips down to hers. "You did it to me."

Knole House, Kent, August 1789. The English were observing international affairs with an interested diffidence. Although protesting that the French were, as usual, behaving like boorish heathens, London society still found fascination with all things French— fashion, food, wine, and manners. The storming of the Bastille prison on July 14 had astounded Europe. The Bastille, which housed a handful of prisoners, none of them political, had become a hated symbol of authoritarian rule. A populace frustrated with ever-climbing bread prices and the king's refusal to accommodate the people's demands exploded that summer day in a march on the Bastille.

Guests sat rapturously at the dinner table as the third Duke of Dorset, his scandalous Italian mistress at his side, told tales of revolutionary France. His escape from Paris had been so sudden that he had turned back an English cricket team that had assembled in Dover en route to a match the duke himself had arranged in Paris.

Stroking the smooth and glossy hair of his beloved Giovanna Baccelli, a beautiful but unconventional woman whom the duke had met when she was a noted ballerina, he opined, "The French have no sensibilities whatsoever. Common fishwives are stamping about with pitchforks and torches, threatening their betters. There is no sense of order and tradition in that vile country, and I'll be happy not to ever visit it again."

"But, my lord," asked a guest. "Isn't it true that many of our countrymen are traveling to Paris just to witness events?"

"Yes, unfortunately. It seems as though there is a mad dash to the Continent to find a piece of souvenir rubble from the Bastille to bring home, and now the grand tour is not complete without a stay near Versailles to catch a glimpse of the idiot King Louis and his whore. We may call our king Old Satan, but he and his queen have dutifully produced a bevy of royal heirs and marriageable princesses, and they know how to behave properly in the eyes of the world."

A general murmur of agreement passed over the long mahogany table, which was covered in countless salvers of food, sterling candlesticks, and profusions of floral arrangements and candied sweetmeats.

"D'you know, that strange sculptress Marie Antoinette employs—Marie Gershon, Groton, or some such thing—was forced to make a death mask of the Bastille's governor, Monsieur de Launay, after the mob killed him? Only the French could behave so abominably."

Claudette breathed sharply inward and her trembling hand spilled some wine from its goblet onto her plate. Poor Marie! She caught long glances from guests, some in sympathy, some in disgust. She heard one gentleman lean over to another to say, "Imagine! William Greycliffe with a Parisian on his arm. After all he has been through with that Radley woman, now this. And if he marries the common little trollop and she begins dropping brats, the entire English countryside will be overrun with fanatical revolutionaries. I, for one, will not have it." The hearer nodded sagely in agreement. Claudette's cheeks were burning. William gently squeezed her arm and imperceptibly shook his head, "No." Claudette clamped her jaws together and continued to steam.

The duke resumed. "The National Assembly has now been recognized, and has adopted the Declaration of the Rights of Man and the Citizen. Meaning it has declared the 'nation' sovereign, instead of God. Sounds like a nation of fools to me." The guests laughed heartily at French expense.

Later, the men retired to the duke's heavily paneled library, while the women gathered in the great hall to play cards and drink sherry from diminutive crystal stemware. It was the largest room Claudette had ever seen in her life. The soaring twenty-foot ceilings were covered in an elaborate plaster frieze, and the walls were paneled in dark oak halfway up to the ceiling. One end of the hall was layered in wood carvings and panels so intricate—including rams' heads, lions, coats of arms, and lattice work—that Claudette could not help but gawk just like one of her own customers. A fireplace engulfed one side wall, its fire screen taller than any of the women in the room. The interior of it was surely as large as Claudette's room at the Ashbys'. She had thought William's country home to be extravagant, but realized now that he lived simply in comparison to his neighbors and others in his class. Unlike how the "common trollops" might live. She narrowed her eyes again, remembering.

As she stood there, taking in the magnificence of the room, the other women were sitting down at card tables around the room. None had acknowledged her presence, and no one invited Claudette to her table. Seeing her discomfort in a room full of society ladies, Giovanna rushed over and took her hands. "My dearest Signorina Laurent, have I told you how simply lovely your dress is? It sets off those luminous blue eyes of yours. I really am most envious."

Giovanna dropped her lilting voice to a theatrical whisper. "You mustn't be intimidated by these women. Most of them live under their husbands' strict rules of obedience, and can barely leave the house without permission. They are not like you and I, yes?" Giovanna smiled as Claudette bristled at the implication that they were both mistresses.

"My dear, no, I mean that society finds us outrageous for no reason other than our birth. Do you know that they call me The Baccelli? It makes me sound like a statue, not a person, doesn't it? I met the duke when I was dancing at the King's Theatre in Haymarket. I was not seeking an entanglement with some stuffed poppycock. I had my own money, my own house, and complete freedom. But who can predict what the heart will demand, yes? And so—" The Baccelli clasped her hands together, then threw them wide, as if on stage. "And so now I live here at Knole, with my dearest love, and our son John Frederick. Society accepts me now because they know he will never marry me. Eventually he will have to marry to get legitimate heirs, and I suppose I will be pensioned off to some distant estate." The hands came back together as Giovanna shrugged dramatically. "But I will have achieved much for a lowly Italian ballerina, yes? You, however, Signorina Laurent, are outrageous too, in your own way. A dollmaker of some repute in London, yes? A woman of her own means, not inherited, is simply not possible in English society. Especially in someone who has the stink of France upon her! They do not hate you; they are jealous. Use this to your advantage, Signorina Laurent. Help the women look beyond their prison walls made of their marriages to see their possibilities."

Giovanna gave Claudette a quick kiss on the cheek and guided her to one of the larger tables of women, directing her comments to the one who was clearly the most dominant in the group. "Lady Bewley, have you been formally introduced to Signorina Laurent, beloved of our Signor Greycliffe?"

Lady Bewley stiffened but knew her manners. "I do not believe I have had the, er, pleasure, of your acquaintance, Miss Laurent." She nodded her head very slightly at Claudette, as though any more would indicate an actual pleasure.

With an encouraging glance from Giovanna, Claudette replied, "Lady Bewley, I am honored to be here. With you. This evening." Laughter broke out in the room at her stilted language. Really, this was just like being at Mrs. Ashby's, except now she could not run and hide in the library.

A small silence ensued, then Giovanna piped up brightly, "Signorina Laurent has had many adventures. Please, my dear, tell us about your harrowing escape from Paris to London." How did Giovanna know so much?

Omitting information about Jean-Philippe, Claudette once again told the story of the fire, and her near-miss with prostitution on the London docks. The women at her table gasped. Her story was inconceivable. Everyone knew that women fell into prostitution as a result of bad breeding; they were not *forced* into it. Claudette now had the attention of this table and all the other women in the room. She told of her household employment as a servant, and the browbeating she took from her social-climbing employer, including her forced pantomime of a lady's maid before Mrs. Emily Harrison. Caught up in her own story, Claudette acted out and mimicked much about her employment. Soon the women were laughing uproariously, causing the men to send in a servant to find out if anything was amiss.

"Stop," said Lady Bewley, gasping. "You must tell me right now who this harridan was."

With hesitation, Claudette stated that it was Maude Ashby, née Carter. Lady Bewley clapped her gloved hands together in glee. "Yes, I thought that was whom you might be referring to. Maude Ashby has been trying to enter London society for years. The woman is absolute poison. We always ignore her invitations. I am amazed that you slipped through her clutches. I have no idea why Mr. Greycliffe frequents her parties. Well, I suppose he did meet his Miss Laurent there, didn't he?" She cocked her head to one side, but she no longer seemed as antagonistic as before. "You are certainly nothing like Lenora Radley. I see warmth in you. Perhaps you'd care to join us for a game of whist?"

The conversation turned to talk of revolutionary activities in France. The women, having heard little but what their husbands had told them and what they read in society newspapers, were convinced that Marie Antoinette was an immoral harlot, and the cause of all of France's problems. Gently, Claudette told them of her meeting with the queen the previous year, and her conviction that the queen had been much maligned by the populace. She may not have convinced the women of Marie Antoinette's innocence, but they were duly impressed that she had been presented to the queen of France. By the time the men came to collect their companions at midnight, Claudette had lost terribly at cards, but collected no less than three invitations to tea, a promise that Lady Whittington would call upon her doll shop, and an order from Lady Bewley for "one of those famous *grandes Pandores* I am always hearing about."

At Claudette's departure, Giovanna kissed her cheek and whispered delicately in her ear, "Do you see, my dear? Now they see in you a heroine, and they will persuade their husbands that you can be one of them. Marry this William Greycliffe—he loves you deeply—and be as happy as me, without the threat of dismissal. I am certain he will let you continue with your dolls."

In the carriage ride back to Hevington, Claudette was quiet and thoughtful. When William escorted her to her guest quarters and bowed over her hand, she responded by wordlessly pulling his face to hers in a deep kiss. As he walked back down the hallway, he continued to turn back and look at her, puzzled. She gave him a contented smile. Perhaps Giovanna was right. Maybe it was time to stop fighting against a life with William.

Curtius House
Paris
September 8, 1789

Dear Claudette,
Paris teems with madness. One can hardly take a carriage ride a city block without some mob marching in one direction or another, screaming for vengeance against an unknown perpetrator, or terrorizing shop owners by

*smashing windows, stealing goods, and threatening to
defile their wives and daughters.*

*You have perhaps heard by now of the mob that
stormed the Bastille two months ago. They marched up
with pitchforks and torches, demanding that all of the
prisoners be released. Prisoners! Just a couple of lunatics
in residence, but for the mob it was a glorious defiance of
the regime. Governor de Launay tried bravely to dissuade
the mob from its actions, and found himself ripped to
pieces. The rabble then brought him to me—to me!—and
forced me to make a death mask of the poor governor.*

*I find myself starting at the slightest creak of the floors,
and my hand seems always to tremble now when I write. I
leave my rooms only when absolutely necessary. Perhaps I
am becoming mad, as well?*

*Dearest Claudette, I would find comfort in a letter from
you. I've not lived at Versailles for some time, but reside
with my uncle, Philippe Curtius. He insisted that I leave
the services of Madame Elisabeth, which I did with regret.
I now live and work at his studio, which is presumably
safer than Versailles. It may not be long, however, before I,
like the long list of émigrés before me, will have to leave
France for whereabouts unknown.*

*Your friend,
Marie*

Despite the troubles in France, Claudette still received orders
from Marie Antoinette for dolls, but the orders were for simpler,
less expensive versions. Still, the same care was taken with these
orders, and each of the French queen's dolls was ensconced in a
velvet-lined box with a matching velvet bow around the outside of it.

❧ 23 ❧

October 2, 1789, Versailles. Louis entered the queen's apartments, roughly dismissing all but her closest attendants.

"Have you seen what that devil says now?" he asked, flourishing a newspaper before her as she sat at a beautifully gilded and painted desk.

By now used to journalistic diatribes, the queen waved him away without putting down her pen. The king insisted that she read it, and sat down across from her where she was in the midst of writing a letter to a creditor. He put the paper on top of her stationery, and stared at her insistently with his bulging eyes.

Not Marat again. She touched this latest edition of *L'Ami du Peuple* with distaste. As usual, he had twisted the previous evening's events into something repulsive.

> In the course of an orgy at the home of Madame Deficit last evening, the tricolor cockade—that symbol of our nation's emerging freedom and self-sovereignty—has been trampled underfoot. Is it not the aristocrats, the king and queen chief among them, who are responsible for our bread shortages? Do we riot for food, or do we riot in our despair against the hypocrisy of a failing monarchy?

While we starve in the streets, the bloated
pig and his wife encourage their friends and
coconspirators to insult us and show us
their utter disdain. We should—

Marie Antoinette put down the paper. "Can they not leave us
alone? Last night I thought perhaps we were regaining the affections of the people."

The previous evening they had hosted a banquet in the theater
of the palace for the Flanders regiment, brought from Douai to
Versailles. Many others were in attendance, including Count
Fersen. With the king by her side, she could do little but greet
Alex formally, but her eyes followed him everywhere.

She was tightly corseted in her favorite color of pale blue, a vo-
luminous gown with ropes of pea-sized pearls overlapping the
bodice, and matching ropes twirled through her hair, which she
wore modestly high for the occasion. The gown's neckline was
edged with a thin line of ermine, and the elbows dripped with layers of fine lace. The gown was cut low, to show off to advantage the
stunning turquoise necklace adorning her translucent skin. She dared
wear this latest gift under the king's nose as he tended to be oblivious to her personal furnishings. Fersen's gaze was appreciative as
he looked up from bowing before her, and she could see the hint
of a wink as he moved on to let another guest pay homage to the
royals.

Later in the evening, the king and queen presented young
Louis Charles, now the Dauphin since the death of his older brother
in June, to the crowd of diners. The entire royal family stood together, clothed in blue and fine laces. Amid cheers and toasts, the
band struck up a royalist air. In their enthusiasm for the royal family, the guests threw the new tricolor cockade of Paris on the floor
and stamped on it as a mark of loyalty to their king and his consort.
Even the musicians were so captivated by the show of patriotism
and fervor that many of their wigs slipped or fell off in their zeal-
ous renditions of tunes praising the monarchs.

It had been so long since she had been cheered that it was all
the queen could do not to break into grateful tears. In the early

hours of the following morning, as she lay in Fersen's arms in his secret but comfortable lodgings at the palace, she recounted to him her joy and gratitude at the acclamation of the banquet's guests. He stroked her hair and let her chatter on happily, until finally the sun's position outside told her that she needed to slip back to her own apartments before her ladies came to wake her.

The evening had been an outstanding success, a welcome relief from recent events. In September, a baker was half-hanged for allegedly giving his richer customers better loaves of bread than his more common patrons. The anger of the people was bewildering to the king and queen, who were isolated at Versailles, and relied on scheming and conniving ministers for much of their information. Fersen was a source of reliable information, but he was not always available. The king seemed to accept Fersen as a close friend of the family, without inquiring too deeply as to his relationship with the queen, and in turn Fersen stayed as reserved and inconspicuous as possible.

Despite the king's acceptance of the count and his trustworthy reports, he could not bring himself to take advice from the Swede. Or from the queen. Or from any of his ministers, for that matter. Louis's stubbornness was renowned at court, leading even his faithful ministers to despair. Regularly Marie Antoinette would plead with her husband to make concessions with the National Assembly, anything to keep peace, but he resolutely refused, considering his position one by divine right and not answerable to any government body. So the quarrel between king and government maintained itself in perfect form.

For one evening, though, they had recaptured the glory of the early years of their reign. It would last mere hours, then the newspapers would once again pick up their poisoned pens, and more bread riots would follow.

On October 5, a crowd of women collected at the National Assembly after once again finding no bread on the bakers' shelves.

"Why is it that banquets can be held at Versailles, while we go hungry?" they asked, echoing Marat's demand.

The government could offer them no help, so the infuriated

women broke into the Assembly hall, stealing several muskets and some of the city funds, then in an amazing moment of audacity, headed off en masse to Versailles, to "see what the king could do." They collected fresh groups of marchers as they passed through the city, some joining to support their cause, some just curious, and others intrigued with the idea of profiting from the day's adventure.

"Bring back the baker, the baker's wife, and the baker's boy!" they chanted, an analogy to their conviction that the king controlled the bread supply. "To Paris! To Paris!" As the crowd increased, it became more volatile and even began forcing onlookers to join them. As commandant of the National Guard, the Marquis de Lafayette needed to stop the march, but, ever concerned with his vanity over all else, he was afraid for his popularity if he were to use force against a horde of women. Eventually his own men insisted that they hurry to Versailles to protect its citizens and to bring the king back to Paris, primarily for his own protection.

At the palace, the king was out on one of his usual hunts, and Marie Antoinette was spending the day at Petit Trianon with Axel, playing cards, dining in her private salon, and walking through the manicured gardens which were quietly losing their summer blooms. They were admiring her new boudoir mirrors, which contained remarkable moving mechanisms, when a servant from the main palace ran up breathlessly.

"Your Majesty," he bowed, red-faced from exertion. "Quickly, you must return to the palace. There is a mob headed here from Paris, and they mean to do you and the king harm."

"What do you mean, do us harm?"

"Er, the fishwives are angry, and they say that they will . . . that they are going to . . ." The man stumbled for words.

"Fishwives! Fishwives have marched here from Paris? Truly?" Marie Antoinette was intrigued more than shocked.

"Yes, madame, and I've heard say they intend to . . . to . . . to cut off your head, Your Majesty."

This startled the queen into action. After a quick argument with Alex—he insisted he would stay to protect her; she commanded that he leave the premises to remain safe himself—she instructed the servant to have a carriage brought around to take Fersen back to his rented lodgings in town. She picked up her skirts and dashed along the Grand Canal back to the main chateau building. The inside of the palace was in disarray, with servants scurrying up and down staircases in a panic, and some of her women weeping piteously in corners.

"Where is the king? And my children?" she demanded.

The Marquise de Tourzel entered the hall where the queen stood alone, hardly noticed by the rushing palace workers. "Your Majesty! *Mon Dieu*, you have returned. His Majesty is also on his way back from his hunt."

"What about the Dauphin and the Princesse Royale?"

"They are in your apartment."

The two women ran up the stairs into the *grand appartement de la reine*, passing through the queen's guard room, the antechamber, the peers' salon, and finally into the queen's bedchamber. The children were huddled together on the queen's enormous silk-draped poster bed, which was crowned with a mass of peacock feathers. They looked like quivering little mice, so small and scared were they in the middle of her vast sleeping chamber. Marie Antoinette scooped both children into her arms with hugs and reassurances that all would be well.

The king arrived back at the palace by three o'clock in the afternoon, sweaty and reeking of horse. Tense discussions ensued as to how to handle the impending invasion. The royal family was urged to flee the palace, but Louis, ever vacillating and deeply reluctant to become a fugitive, was unable to make up his mind. Several advisors recommended that at least the queen and children be removed to the palace of Rambouillet for safety, but this Marie Antoinette refused. Her place, she insisted, was with the king. The stalemate resulted in no action taken prior to the mob's arrival.

A heavy downpour now soaking the marchers had not diminished their resolve at all. Their cries became more furious. "We're going to put the queen's head on a sword! We're going to make cockades out of her entrails!"

Soon the women stood before the gates of Versailles, dripping wet and shouting epithets at the royal family members they knew were hidden inside. Any original notion of asking the king what he could do about the bread shortage had been completely supplanted by a plan to take him bodily back to Paris.

The royal family went to bed uneasily that night, with Lafayette's National Guard standing watch. As always, observing court customs, the king and queen each slept in their own apartments, the king's above hers. Their individual lodgings were connected by a hidden staircase Louis had had installed years earlier to make his conjugal visits more private. The mob remained outside the gates, burning torches and brandishing whatever weapons they had— stolen muskets, pikes, broomsticks, and an occasional pistol and gun carriage. At four o'clock in the morning on October 6, the sleepers were rudely awakened by a din in the palace.

"What is happening?" asked the queen, disheveled from an uneven night of sleep. She sat up in bed and arranged her nightgown around her. One of her ladies, a Madame Auguié, ran quickly to the hallway to investigate and returned minutes later in a panic.

"Your Majesty! It is some of the market women. They have entered the palace through an unlocked gate and are looking for you. Quickly, you must get dressed."

Getting dressed swiftly was nearly impossible in the French court, and no monarch could possibly dress herself, even if she wished to do so. Dressing entailed hours of preparation, with dozens of buttons to be secured and laces to be tied, not to mention corsets, petticoats, hosiery, and other garments to be put on. The queen's nervous ladies fumbled with her attire while trying to clothe themselves at the same time. They could hear voices coming up the staircase to the apartment and within moments there was pounding and shouting at the door of the guard room. Madame Auguié now ran out to the outermost room to bar the door for as long as possible. The queen and the rest of her entourage slipped through a secret door next to her canopied bed and fled up the staircase behind the wall to the king's apartment, the queen's petticoat only partially tied and various fastenings undone.

The secret door had barely closed when the mob of women stampeded into the queen's private bedroom. They had already killed two royal bodyguards, and now howled in rage that they could not find the primary object of their hatred. In a fury, they drove their pikes into the queen's luxurious bed, claiming they wanted to make sure she was not hiding in it. The de Lamballe doll had been on a slipper chair next to the bed, and tumbled unharmed onto the floor under the immense mattress, while the women carried out their vicious task. After destroying the bed, they hacked away at the walls' gilt panels, and splintered whatever doors they could find. With their violent energy expended on the queen's room, they made their way back outside to join the rest of the mob, which was now assembled in the courtyard outside the balcony leading to the king's apartment.

Inside the king's rooms, Marie Antoinette found her children already gathered with their father and Lafayette. The king was, for once, behaving with remarkable clarity and purpose, and they had a rapid discussion as to what to do next. Louis had been awakened in the night and requested to meet a deputation of the women. To mollify this group of angry Parisians gathered around him, he agreed that he would consider returning to Paris to reign from there. They had been satisfied—even pleased—by the king's commitment, but the rest of the mob, still thirsty for revenge, had continued on its rant through the palace.

Marie Antoinette was horrified to hear that her husband had acquiesced to the women's demand that he go to Paris, insisting that it was unsafe to leave Versailles under any circumstances. In the meantime, they needed to deal with the crowd outside.

By agreement, first the king went out to the balcony to greet the people, and from inside the queen could hear them cheering. *"Vive le roi!"* they shouted. Feeling a little more confident, she took her children by the hands and went to join her husband, but the furious crowd shouted, "No children! No children!"

Louis Charles and Marie-Thérèse, already terrified from their ordeal thus far, were quickly taken away by servants. Marie Antoinette, though pale and very frightened of assassination, stood steadfastly next to her husband and even made a pretty curtsy to the throng. Lafayette, ever popular with the people, came out and kissed the queen's hand as a symbol of his dedication to her and to demonstrate that she was under his personal protection. It was all to no avail. The people were determined now to bring the baker's family back to their capital city.

"To Paris! To Paris!" they began clamoring once more. Murderous insults to the queen could be heard, interspersed with their demands for the king to leave Versailles. Marie Antoinette turned to her husband and gave him a silent nod, her assent that they now had no choice but to do as the crowd wished. To Paris they would go, to be installed at the Tuileries, a palace that had not housed a monarch in more than a century.

They were given leave to quickly pack. The queen's ladies and servants scrambled through her tattered apartment, tossing as many clothes, jewels, and personal belongings into trunks as they could in a short time. One quick-thinking attendant looked under the sliced-up bed for anything of value, and scooped up the de Lamballe doll. The royal family was escorted to a waiting carriage that was driven slowly back to Paris in the middle of the rabble marching back on foot. At the end of this bizarre cortège, the heads of the bodyguards killed inside the palace were carried on pikes, a symbol of the mob's great victory this day.

Axel Fersen stared in dismay at the letter that had been secretly couriered to him from the queen, who was now living at the Tuileries Palace. She and the king were virtual prisoners inside their new home, a residence that had not been used by the royal family since Louis XIV abandoned it in the late seventeenth century. Surely it was not fit for his captivating and exquisite Antonia. Soon he would have to do something to save her. But what?

The fall of 1789 continued to be chaotic in France. In October, the National Assembly split itself into three groups. The first group, the "Patriots," was also known as the Center because they sat in the center of the Assembly hall. Their leading figure was Lafayette. Sitting on the right side of the hall were the Royalists, who wanted to see the government returned to what it was under the king. To the left of the hall resided the extreme revolutionaries, or Jacobins, led by Maximilien Robespierre. This group was not afraid to use violence to accomplish its radical goals of equality for all men.

November was a new month, and the burgeoning new government was busy developing new plans for running the country. On November 2, the National Assembly took matters into its own hands to begin solving France's financial problems by taking over church lands and issuing *assignats*. These bonds pledged an interest rate of five percent, and the public could buy them to exchange for the land the government had seized. The move outraged the clergy and initiated more howling from disgruntled groups.

Soon after, the Civil Constitution of the Clergy was enacted. As a follow-up to its earlier confiscation of church property, the Assembly decreed that the selection of priests would be conducted by district electoral assemblies. Bishops and clergy would be paid from the government purse, and, as a final sword thrust at the church, it abolished all papal jurisdiction in France.

Chaos and outrage continued throughout the remainder of the year.

Hevington, December 25, 1790. Claudette closed the shop during the week of Christmas to give her grateful workers time with their families. She and Béatrice accepted William's invitation to spend Christmas at Hevington, and rode there with Marguerite in his finest carriage, sent up to London to fetch them. Hevington was ablaze with lights, and coaches were scattered all over the drive. William greeted them warmly, and introduced Claudette to face after face of his neighbors and associates. The Bewleys were there, but the Duke of Dorset and the delightful Giovanna were absent. William told her quietly that Dorset had finally put The Baccelli aside under pressure from his family, and had recently married a young heiress whom he detested. Much to the duke's dismay, Giovanna had run off in protest with the Earl of Pembroke, a family friend. The duke no longer visited socially and instead stayed cooped up morosely at Knole.

"Poor Giovanna!" said Claudette. "She loved the duke so much and she was of so much help to me. I must write to her when I return to London."

After a joyous and boisterous dinner of roasted goose, vegetable pies, pudding with brandy sauce, sugared fruits, and other dishes from estate-grown livestock and vegetation, finished off with aged bottles of claret from the cellar, they moved into the music room where Lady Something-or-other sat down to play the pianoforte. This time, Claudette slid easily into William's arms as they danced the minuet together. For once, she felt completely at ease in his lifestyle.

Béatrice retired early, suffering an upset digestion from the rich dinner. Marguerite stayed with the party, in complete rapture over being in attendance at this adult event. She practiced dancing off to one side, stepping backward and forward and twirling by herself, until one of the male guests noticed her and squired her onto the floor.

The festivities went on into the wee hours of the morning. When the door closed behind the last guest, and Marguerite had sleepily wandered off to find her room, William asked Claudette to accompany him to the north wing of the house, as he wanted her opinion on something there. Puzzled, she took his proffered hand and followed him to a room she had not been in before. He opened the door, and she was startled by what she saw in the glow of dozens of candles placed on tables around the small room and reflecting off a mirror hanging over the room's fireplace. Next to the crackling fire was a chair, but not just any chair. It was gilded in the French style, and its lushly padded seat covered in cerulean blue brocade. Scattered around the chair was a profusion of loose stems of roses and lilies, their fragrance enveloping Claudette in wonder.

She stood there, dumbstruck, until William urged her into the room and guided her over to the chair. She sat down, and he took his place on one knee at her feet.

"Claudette, have you been happy here tonight?"

"Of course. Why ever should I not be?"

He did not answer her question but returned with another of his own. "And my friends? Are you comfortable with them now? Do you realize that you are their equal and more?"

"I believe I do. Giovanna helped me to realize that. But what—"

He picked up a single red rose and a snow white lily from the floor and brought them both up to her. She took them and inhaled deeply.

He smiled. "They are good together, are they not, the rose of England and the lily of France?"

She nodded, still puzzled.

William wrapped his hands around both of hers, which still held the blooms. "Sweetheart, darling, I would like you to be my lily here at Hevington forever. Please marry me."

"Oh," she breathed. "Oh. Oh my, yes, William. Yes, a thousand times yes!" She leaned forward against him and he lost his balance, sending them both tumbling into the mass of flowers. They laughed together as they saw stems and petals crushed into each other's hair and clothing. Claudette picked up an unharmed lily, and, propped up on one arm, batted William on the nose with it.

"You realize that I am a wild-grown lily, and not the greenhouse variety?" she teased.

He laughed again. "As though I could be happy with any other kind." He pulled her down for a long kiss. They continued to lie there together among the floral debris, with the fire slowly crackling down to embers.

As the early morning light began encroaching into the room, Claudette sat up.

"William, I must make a request of you."

"Of course, anything," he mumbled, overcome by the warmth of the room and his own sleepy contentment.

"I would like our betrothal to be a secret between us for now."

This snapped William awake and into an upright position. "Why? I thought we might be married immediately."

"I would like nothing more than that. But I'm worried about Béatrice. You know she is utterly dependent on me, and we even have adjoining flats. I think she would be devastated if I left her suddenly like this. It would be preferable if I could bring her along a little further in managing the doll shop, maybe even turn over daily management to her, so that when we are married, she can feel confident staying there and being on her own. Marguerite is showing some interest in the shop as well, and I would like to train her a bit."

"Are you saying you plan to give up the doll shop?"

"Mmm. Not initially. But I suppose when I have a flock of Greycliffe sons to look after, I'll have to rely on someone else to manage the shop on a daily basis." She smiled at him, and he stood, offering her his arm as assistance up from the floor.

"Well, my future Lady Greycliffe, I agree to your terms. We had better get some breakfast now, to begin fortifying ourselves for the time that I start getting sons on you."

Tuileries Palace, January 1791. An urgent rap on Count Axel Fersen's door was immediately followed by a desperate cry and rattling of the knob. Fersen opened the door and admitted the queen, who immediately threw herself in his arms. He quickly kicked the door shut before any curious palace servants or guards could see them together. His new accommodations at the Tuileries had been prepared with the greatest secrecy, and few people on the outside knew that he spent as much time here as in his rented lodgings in town.

"Antonia, what is wrong?"

"Oh, Axel. It just isn't fair. Everyone is leaving me! What am I to do?" The queen sobbed against his shoulder. Her wig was in disarray and her rouge was wearing off onto Fersen's jacket.

"Antonia, you must tell me what has happened." He led her to a cream silk-covered settee, which matched one in the queen's apartment. Gently offering her a handkerchief, he waited for her to stop trembling.

"Axel, she's going away."

"Who is going away?"

"It's Madame Bertin, my dressmaker. She said she cannot remain in France, in this palace, another moment. She is leaving, and will not even tell me where. I begged her to stay, but it seems that being the queen of France no longer means anything. I pleaded with her, promised her more money, but she wouldn't listen. She said that all the francs in the treasury could not keep her here, and that she did not think that we have any control over the treasury anyway. Axel, Axel, are you my only friend in the world?"

He pulled her close again. "Antonia, Madame Bertin is a faithless friend to you, something that you know I shall never be. But what of it? She's just a seamstress."

"Axel! She is the royal dressmaker. She selects all of my clothes for me and I am greatly reliant on her. Who has her talent and skill when it comes to fashion? Besides, I thought she cared for me, despite her temper."

"Come, stop these tears. You have me here, and I will always stand by you, no matter what. Here, take a new handkerchief. That's my sweet love." He cupped her face in his right hand. "Antonia, it's time to be serious about your situation. Your life, the king's, that of the children; I fear you are in danger again."

"But Axel—"

He continued over her protest. "We must do something to prepare for any eventuality. You need to leave France." Her eyes flew open. "I know we have tried to convince the king of this before. But we must try again. Just temporarily. Just until we can bring Austrian troops in to regain control. We need to begin planning."

"Axel, I could not even begin to think of this. How disappointed my mother would be if she were still alive. To see what has become of her favorite daughter, her great hope of an alliance between Austria and France." Drops spilled down her cheeks again. "I am so weary of being hated."

"I'll take care of this," he soothed her. "I will ensure your safety and that of the entire royal family. Don't worry, Antonia. Leave everything to me." He lifted her chin. "Let's meet tomorrow. We will walk in the gardens and talk, far away from prying eyes. Say yes."

The reputedly haughty queen of France wiped a moist eye with Fersen's handkerchief. "Yes, tomorrow."

"Will there be anything else, my lord?" Fersen's valet was tired, but maintained his customary correctness, never letting his master know when he was exhausted from unending service in support of the count's career—the constant rounds of dances, masques, dinners, hunts, and other previous court entertainments, now replaced with furtive meetings, hallway whispers, and secret messages. He knew that the queen had been alone with Fersen this afternoon for nearly an hour in his room, and his master had been pensive and withdrawn ever since, barely touching his supper tray. Lucien's curiosity had been short-lived, though. Years of living with the vagaries of the aristocracy had taught him never to be astonished by anything they did.

"No, I am fine for the evening. Please just have some wine brought to me. And I shall not need you until at least eleven o'clock tomorrow morning."

Lucien inwardly heaved a sigh of relief. He could spend a long night sleeping, even if he did have to share a room with three other servants. He shut the door behind him gracefully, permitting only the tiniest click of the lock to intrude into the room.

Fersen sat down at the writing desk, surveying the small apartment he had been given, located behind a disguised panel under one of the palace's many sweeping staircases. The queen had managed to provide him these secret lodgings at her own personal risk, and he made sure to depart and arrive back to his quarters as unobtrusively as possible. His personal valet was hardly noticed in the crush of all the other servants at the Tuileries. Although tiny in comparison with rooms he had rented on his own nearby, the room was still as elegant as anything to which Antonia touched her hand. The ceiling was skillfully painted with cherubs darting in and out of clouds, and the wall panels were trimmed in gold leaf. Silk curtains of pale blue—the queen's favorite color—adorned the windows, and the finest wool carpets on the marble floors provided a soft cushion for his feet.

He could probably slip unnoticed to her apartment later, but he would not visit her, not tonight. He needed time to think. He sat perfectly still behind the writing desk, his gaze lodged on a portrait of old Louis XI across the room. "The Spider King" he had been called during his fifteenth-century rule, partially because of his paunchy body set on spindly legs, but also because of his constant and tireless work in rebuilding France after a series of revolts started under his father.

How would you fix France now, Your Majesty?

As if the old king were calling to him from across the room and across the centuries, a tiny seed of an idea was dropped into Axel's mind. He drained the decanter of wine brought to his room before pulling quill and paper from inside the desk, and beginning the first of several letters that would set his newly-germinated plan in motion.

Marie Antoinette was sufficiently recovered when she met Fersen the next day in a section of the Tuileries gardens that contained tall hedges. Her gowns were becoming slightly shabby, although her toilette was still impeccable. He recognized this particular dress as one that had been a favorite of hers to wear at her Hameau, but the fichu had tears in it. Her wardrobe was not being taken care of properly. Why had he not noticed this before?

They walked about the grounds of the Tuileries. The landscaping had been quickly refurbished for the royal couple to some level of grandeur so that passersby would not think that the revolutionaries were keeping them in a cruel state. Unfortunately, the interior of the palace was not yet back to its full glory and probably never would be. So the gardens had become a place of serenity and peace for Marie Antoinette, but not today. Fersen was trying to distract her with comments on the white Bourbon lilies that were attempting to poke themselves out of the ground. She responded that the flowers had more freedom of movement than she did, so he dropped that line of conversation and simply walked companionably with her until they reached a large fountain containing three large dolphins in its center, each poised animal spraying water enthusiastically into the air. They sat together on the fountain's outer ledge to talk, so that the noise of the jetting water would ensure their conversation was not overheard.

"I believe I know how to get you out of the country and into Austria, but you will need to convince the king."

"Axel, you know he doesn't listen to anyone, now least of all me. Besides, we no longer have control of the treasury, so how can we possibly do anything?"

"I can get access to some considerable sums of money."

She looked at him quizzically. "How is this?"

"Antonia, you have only to trust me. What is important is that you persuade the king to do as I suggest, which is to prepare the family to leave the palace in secret. Pack only necessary personal belong-

ings, and sew any valuables into your clothes. I will arrange new iden-
tities for all of you. How would you like to pose as a governess?"

Marie Antoinette, who had never in her life known a single moment when she was not either an archduchess or the Dauphine or
the queen, laughed.

"You must be prepared to depart swiftly at my prearranged signal. I will ensure that you are accompanied by various trusted agents
throughout the trip to the border, and you will be handed over to
Austrian officials once you arrive."

The queen felt a small glimmer of hope. Perhaps they could get
out of danger, and who could she trust more than Count Fersen,
the handsomest, most loyal man ever to grace her court.

They stood up together to begin walking back toward the palace.
They had been gone long enough, and the queen needed to make
an appearance inside before her absence became noteworthy.

"I'm ready to do as you say, but it is ever so ridiculous that a
reigning king and queen must sneak out of their country in the
middle of the night like common thieves. Were ever two monarchs
so plagued by misfortune?"

"Soon it will be over, and I'll meet you in Vienna. From there
we can plan how you and the king can regain control of the government once troops have been sent in to quell the rioting."

Almost as if in response to his statement, a thinly-clad, unshaven
man loitering outside the grounds peered through the hedges and
saw the pair walking. Recognizing the queen, he began jeering at
her and shouting, "Austrian whore! Baker's wife! See what we
think of you here?" The man proceeded to urinate openly against
the shrubbery.

Marie Antoinette ignored the man entirely, but Fersen could
see that her lips had gone white. He escorted her quickly to the
nearest entrance to the palace, which was hidden from public view
by a small portico. Before releasing her to the guarded fortress she
now called home, he folded her into his arms and gave her a lingering kiss.

"*Au revoir* for now, Antonia."

Tears shined in her eyes. "*Au revoir*, my love. I hope it is not a
permanent good-bye."

* * *

Tuileries Palace, June 1791. Louis had been waffling and hesitating for months as to what to do, despite the queen's pleading and begging that he agree to flee the country. She had earlier even attempted to declare war on Austria, knowing it would compel Austria to respond in force against France, thereby providing the royal family an opportunity for exile in Austria. Unfortunately, such an act by the queen was tantamount to treason and only worsened their living conditions. Servants now looked askance at them, and were slow to obey the simplest orders. Marie Antoinette might be kept waiting for an hour for her breakfast tray, and she had no power to gainsay their behavior. She maintained a quiet, dignified composure to cover her mounting anxiety.

It was Axel Fersen who finally convinced the king to attempt escape. He told Louis that he had been able to secure significant funds from émigrés now residing in England. Louis's persistent questioning as to how much money was available and how Fersen was able to get the money into France was met with evasiveness. Marie Antoinette, ignorant herself on that score, joined with Fersen in cajoling the king that there was little time left to leave the country. The king finally agreed, but the plan was doomed.

Using his cache of money, Fersen secured a carriage that would spirit the royal family and their closest attendants, disguised as simple travelers, out of the Tuileries and on a secure routing to Austria. Fersen would escort them outside Paris and then the party would make various connections with loyal citizens throughout the journey until they were finally able to make it over the border.

They departed secretly around midnight on June 20, 1791, with the party panicking when the queen did not show up on time at the designated meeting location, a rarely-used palace entrance. She arrived fifteen minutes late, first because she could not get rid of all of her attendant ladies quickly enough, then she had almost reached the exit when she realized she had left her de Lamballe doll on a settee, and went back to retrieve it. Axel chastised her quietly for her impetuosity then herded the royal family into the massive coach, which kept up a steady pace of six to seven miles per hour. A series of mishaps, including a broken harness, the abandoning of his post by the Duc de Choiseul—who was to wait for them at Somme-Vesle and provide them a military escort to Austria—and recognition of the disguised king by someone at a rest stop, led to eventual disaster. Unfortunately, too, the carriage was magnificent, as befitting a royal family and not a family of little means, and stood out as a spectacle as they traveled farther into the countryside.

The party was apprehended by revolutionaries just forty miles from the Austrian border in a small town called Varennes. They were escorted slowly back to Paris, with citizens jeering at the passing carriage during the entire miserable trip.

The king was quickly portrayed in the press as a helpless pig, concerned only with eating. The queen, never popular and now held responsible for the king's flight, was caricatured as a harpy, thirsting for the blood of the people.

London, September 1791. A carriage bearing the House of Hanover coat of arms pulled up to the shop one day, and a thin, fussily-dressed, bewigged and bespectacled man exited its interior. Claudette welcomed him into the shop, sweeping the curtsy she had practiced in France.

"Ahem, yes," the man began. "I come from Windsor Castle. I have a commission for you from Her Majesty Queen Charlotte. The queen is aware of your—what do you call them—great panniers—and wishes to have one made."

"Pardon me, sir—a what?"

"I do not know the exact name. One of the adult figures."

"Yes, of course. We would be most pleased to do this for Her Majesty. What type of personage does she wish?"

The man hesitated. "Er, well, it's not exactly for the queen. She wants it for the king. Yes. Hmm, this is most awkward." He sighed. "Well, I suppose most of England knows by now of His Majesty's . . . eccentricities. Talking to trees and such. The good queen thinks that one of these dolls might provide, er, companionship for His Majesty when he is having an episode."

"I see. Perhaps a *grand Pandore* that resembles Mr. Pitt?"

The man's face brightened considerably. "Yes, that would please the queen greatly, I am sure."

232 Christine Trent

Claudette wrote out an order for the doll and gave it to the man. He agreed to send someone to retrieve it in two months' time.

Marguerite proved very helpful in this commission, suggesting that Claudette write to Marie Grosholtz for advice on creating a more realistic wax head that would trick the king's mind into thinking he had his friend and confidant, Mr. Pitt, with him during those periods when he was rather out of touch with his surroundings.

As with the de Lamballe design, letters flew back and forth between the two women, with Marie advising Claudette on every step of the wax modeling portion of the doll. Marguerite enthusiastically dove into experimenting with molding wax, but her inexperienced fingers caused many a re-melted blob. Nevertheless, she cheerfully tried again under her aunt Claudette's supervision. Béatrice was happy to see her daughter finding a place in the doll shop and encouraged her work.

Even William was intrigued by the requisition of a *grand Pandore* for the king's amusement, and would come to watch progress on it.

The finished doll was draped in heavy black material so that it could not be seen by the king's subjects passing by on the street, for surely some of them would make out what was being done if they saw Mr. Pitt's face on the figure. As an added precaution, royal servants arrived in the predawn hours upon its completion to load the shrouded *grand Pandore* onto a special cart and take it to its new home. No one was the wiser.

Shortly following the royal commission, Claudette was astonished to receive a royal warrant for providing "unrivaled quality in dollmaking." She was given permission to display the Hanover coat of arms prominently in her shop's window.

"It won't be long now," William told her one evening as they ate a late supper at the King's Head Inn. "Not everyone can display the Hanoverian seal. Soon your trade will be secure enough that you can turn it over to Béatrice and we can be married."

She put down her fork. "About that," she began.

"Oh no, Miss Laurent, you won't put me off again. I'll carry you to Reverend Daniels over my shoulder if need be."

She smiled. "That won't be necessary. I just mean that I'm

thinking that Marguerite has shown such interest in the shop that maybe it is to her I should turn over the workings."

"But what about Béatrice? She has been your ally in the enterprise since the beginning."

Claudette picked up her fork and shifted around the remains of her round of veal in cream. "True. And I had always intended to put Béatrice in charge. But now I suspect that she doesn't care much to run the shop, and might in fact welcome her daughter doing so one day. So what I'm saying is that I need just a little more time to be sure I am making the right decision about the shop before we marry."

"Very well. Just a little more time is all I'm willing to grant you. I'm growing anxious to have you with me at Hevington. And those Greycliffe sons won't come about on their own, you know."

Claudette blushed at his words spoken in public. "I may have to continue spending time in London for a while until Béatrice and Marguerite are comfortable without me."

The royal warrant increased sales five-fold, since everyone wanted to shop at establishments that serviced the royal household. She was finally succeeding at her father's dream, she was secure in William's love, and she was surrounded by her friends.

Nothing could go wrong now.

Axel Fersen entered his dark apartments and shifted the bundle under his arm so he could bolt the door. It wouldn't do to have an accidental interruption from his valet.

He placed the twine-wrapped parcel on his desk and lit the oil lamp, the only object on the exquisitely-painted but otherwise bare piece of furniture.

The package was lumpy and misshapen, with twine knotted in several spots. He would need to chastise the handler for such sloppy wrapping. The contents required a crate. He worked patiently to unwork the knots, and was rewarded when he finally loosened all of the twine to find that the shipment had arrived entirely intact. Thank God. He had taken a big risk on this. He spread his perfectly manicured hands across his prize, and his sense of triumph soared.

This was going to work. The queen would be safe.

❧ 24 ❧

Paris, April 15, 1792. The interior of the customs barrier was busy, bustling, and frenetic with activity as agents inspected packages and shipments arriving in Paris from faraway places. The work was haphazard. Although ostensibly to determine what taxes could be assessed on these incoming goods, the end result was a corrupt system where agents stole goods they desired, or accepted bribes from importers to overlook their shipments.

Inspector Séverin did not perform his job on the main floor, however. His position was a special one. Secreted in a spacious room away from the noise and chaos, Séverin's work was very specific and very focused: He searched through boxes and packages slated for delivery to any of the royal residences. The work was tedious, examining individual boxes and parcels for any suspicious smells, bulges, or sounds. If anything seemed of interest—and he had little guidance as to what, exactly, would be of interest—he was to report it immediately to his superior, who would then notify Robespierre. So far, he had found little other than some enormous bundles of silks and velvets, miles of lace, and containers of fresh fruit that the average citizen could not afford on a year's worth of wages. Inspector Séverin periodically pinched a few things that he thought would go unnoticed—a porcelain trinket for his carping wife, a wooden toy for his dour son. Lengths of fancy fabrics and trimmings he saved for his mistress, Camille.

The inspector was not a particular devotee of Robespierre, leader of the Jacobins and a rising member of the Assembly, nor did he have allegiance to the now imprisoned king and queen, and even less did he care what the politics of France were. He was a bureaucrat, seeking simply to rise in his station, and willing to go whichever way the prevailing winds might carry him. For the moment, it seemed as though Robespierre's faction would take the day, so hopefully his work in the customs barrier on behalf of the Assembly would be financially gratifying. Then he could afford to buy his grousing wife—who never ceased to remind him of how unsatisfactorily his career had advanced—a larger house in town, perhaps on the Rue Saint-Louis en l'Ile. Séverin chuckled to himself, thinking of how he would install Camille in his current home near the customs barrier, so that he could visit easily and discreetly, as often as he wished, with his wife none the wiser.

Although he had profited personally thus far in his work, the inspector was disappointed by his inability to find anything substantial to report to Robespierre. An approval from Robespierre might mean a promotion, higher wages, a better position. But for now, he continued plodding through his days of sniffing, rattling, and poking. With a sigh, he pulled yet another bundle toward him.

More frivolous gifts for the queen no doubt, from her equally frivolous émigré friends who had fled the country at the first sign of trouble. The package was from London, and was heavy for its size. He shook it slightly. The package rattled oddly. Best to examine this one more closely.

Inside was a long box wrapped in a velvet bow. Untying the box, he found the object of his pursuit. Just another of those infernal dolls for which the queen had such a penchant. It was dressed in a fancy gown, and Séverin thought it was material that Camille would call "stylish." Perhaps she would like to have it. As he turned the doll over to scrutinize it further, it slipped from his hands to the floor. The wooden head separated from the body and a glittering assortment of rubies, sapphires, diamonds, and English coins came tumbling out of the torso's hollow cavity. What was this? It must be thousands of livres' worth of valuables. His first instinct was to scoop up the jewels and money and stow it away for himself. But as he stared down at the cluster of gleaming valuables in his hands, he reconsidered. How could he ever sell the jewels without raising eyebrows in Paris? The current Legislative Assembly was very sensitive to unusual movements that might indicate illegal activities. Perhaps he could benefit from this in a much better way. Finally, here was something that would be very interesting to Robespierre.

Maximilien Robespierre stood behind a desk overlooking the north garden of the Tuileries, his glasses perched low on his sharp nose set in a narrow, bony face. The green eyes behind the glasses were chilly and blank, devastating in their insensitivity. The writing desk was one specially made for Marie Antoinette. It was covered in gold leaf and exquisitely painted with brightly colored birds on tree branches. He looked incongruous situated at the desk, reviewing a packet of incriminating documents that had just been delivered to him. He had eschewed the ornate chair that matched the desk, preferring to stand when working. Robespierre, previously an attorney from Arras known as "The Incorruptible" because of his unswerving honesty and rigid standards, could work for long stretches without sleep. He was frequently seen traveling back and forth at all hours through the Tuileries, which had been appropriated by the evolving republican government even though the king and queen still occupied a section of it. From here he conducted the business of the Assembly. Robespierre had been influenced by the idealistic works of Rousseau, and saw the implementation of Virtue as his singular goal, to be accomplished at all costs, preferably through the spilling of blood to wipe out evil. He had yet to learn that the French people wanted food and security, not a program of morality and self-denial.

Robespierre separated each of the documents out on Marie Antoinette's desk. A disgruntled royal locksmith named Gamain had passed along word that an iron chest "of interest" was in the royal apartments at the Tuileries. Gamain had made this chest at the request of Louis XVI, and he knew with certainty that the chest was crammed with the king's secret papers, many of which would incriminate him for leading a counterrevolution by attempting to flee France to gather troops in Austria. Robespierre had created a diversion for the entire royal family and their attendants, allowing them to host a dinner party among themselves, with no expenses spared. While they dined, officers broke into the king's study and found the chest. The letters, documents, and maps proved Gamain's information to be correct.

The knowledge did not particularly surprise Robespierre. What did raise an eyebrow was a cryptic letter in the chest from an unknown source, stating that funds for the escape would be made available to the king and queen via special transport. Combined with Inspector Séverin's discovery at the customs barrier—well, even Robespierre, a man who prided himself on utter imperturbability, was astonished by the sheer audacity of how money and valuables were being smuggled in to the royals.

He barked "Enter!" in response to a sharp rap on the door. One of his new confidants entered. "Citizen Robespierre, you wished to see me?" the man asked, standing directly across the desk.

"Yes, I have an interesting assignment for you. I need you to track down an enemy of France." He explained what had been discovered and what he wanted done. His confidant was slightly startled by the information, but gladly accepted Robespierre's instructions. *"Liberté! Égalité! Fraternité!"* the man called out as he left the highly-ornamented room.

⮷ 25 ⮶

London, June 30, 1792. Lizbit was a more frequent guest now at Claudette's flat and in the shop. With Béatrice and sometimes Marguerite, the women would frequently shop and dine together. Lizbit always served as the center of attention, regaling the others with stories about her travels to the Continent. Still her concerns revolved around marriage.

"And why is this precious one not married off to a rich earl yet, Claudette? Doesn't your gentleman have any good connections?" Lizbit patted Marguerite's reddening face one day as they parted ways in front of the shop.

"Lizbit! She's only fifteen."

"She's old enough. You can never begin the search too early."

As cowed as she usually was by Lizbit's forceful personality, even Béatrice intervened.

"Claudette and I both made love matches, and that's what I want for my daughter."

"Oh, piffle. The child is practically a woman and is already devastatingly beautiful with those auburn locks. Best to find her a husband who can help keep you in comfort in your old age, Béatrice."

"My old—" Béatrice gasped, which led to a coughing fit.

"Thank you, Miss Lizbit, but I don't plan to marry. I'm going to be a great dollmaker like my aunt Claudette and I don't need a husband for it."

Claudette suppressed a smile in seeing her own mulishness in Marguerite's folded arms and lifted chin.

"No husband at all?" Lizbit said. "Well, well, aren't you just the old Queen Bess? Never mind then. I don't want it said that I poked my nose in where it didn't belong."

Claudette invited Lizbit to join her and William to see a performance of Sheridan's *School for Scandal* at the Theatre Royal in Drury Lane. She hadn't told anyone yet of her secret engagement to William, but was considering doing so tonight. Sipping glasses of cherry cordial in their box seats while waiting for the play to begin, Claudette witnessed her friend flirt outrageously with William. Normally the gallant gentleman, William firmly rebuffed her. Lizbit fanned herself furiously to cover her embarrassment, and, recovering her composure, smiled sweetly at Claudette.

"La, *chérie*, your man is a bit tedious, isn't he?"

Claudette hid a smile behind her glass. Maybe she should wait to announce her engagement. Lizbit chattered on about a new millinery shop she had discovered, run by a Polish immigrant of all things, until the curtain rose.

Lizbit swept into the doll shop several days later wearing a pale blue hat perched fashionably to one side of her dark-tressed head, a small bunch of lavender tied to it with a cream-colored ribbon. The aroma clung to her like a velvet blanket. In her hand she held a small package.

"Claudette, I just intercepted this."

She took the parcel from Lizbit's hand. Inside were two letters, one with a familiar royal seal on it, the other with her name written across the front in Jean-Philippe's handwriting. She opened the letter she knew must be from the queen. It was more personal than the first one, and asked if the dear dollmaker could come to France to visit a monarch seeking some joy. It would please the queen greatly if Mademoiselle Laurent would accept an offer of an apartment and a workshop at the Tuileries for a short time to make some dolls representing the remaining ladies of her court.

"Is the queen still living at the Tuileries?" she asked.

Lizbit was reading over her shoulder. "I'm sure she is. Are you going to do this, Claudette? It seems very dangerous. What will William say when he returns?"

William was away looking over some Welsh cob studs for his stables at Hevington, and would not return for another week.

"I'll send him a note to let him know that I've gone. He'll understand."

"If you say so." Lizbit seemed unconvinced. "What about your other letter?"

"I think I'll read it later."

Later ended up being many hours afterward, once she had returned to her town house. Lizbit departed the shop with her usual flair, then customers streamed in and out in a constant flow until she finally locked the door after seven o'clock in the evening. She and Béatrice had dinner together quietly in the parlor, then she quickly went to her own rooms and shut the door to read Jean-Philippe's letter.

> *Dearest Claudette,*
> *I pray you are in good health. As you will see from the queen's letter enclosed, she is in need of friends now and wishes to see the best dollmaker in Europe. I know you may have heard that France is experiencing some disorder at the moment, but this is not for your worry. I would like to escort you back to France personally, to serve as your guide and protector during your trip.*
> *You no longer love me, you have made that perfectly clear. Perhaps, though, you will allow me this small kindness to show that I am ever your friend?*

The letter went on to give details about his planned date of arrival to escort her to France. How presumptuous, she thought. Yet she was strangely thrilled. Jean-Philippe was making it plain that he would be her escort only so that she could feel safe, through the tumult of France, and have the opportunity to meet again with that gracious monarch. His letter closed with continued assurances of his intentions of friendship with her.

"I'll do it," she said aloud.

❧ 26 ❧

July 15, 1792. The coach rumbled to a stop at the docks on an over-cast but warm afternoon. Stepping down from it, Claudette was as-sailed by the stench—the seawater, the rotting offal, and the odor of unwashed men—that reminded her once again of her flight to England from Paris.

Jolie had once again proven herself to be a treasure. In her haste, she had sworn the girl to secrecy to prevent Béatrice from finding out before she left and begging her not to go. Giving her mistress only a quick frown, Jolie had agreed and set about helping her pack. The girl was a wonder at it. Inside a small valise and two small trunks were enough to set Claudette up for an extended visit far beyond what she anticipated it to be.

Claudette gave the girl letters for William and Béatrice, and made her promise not to have them delivered until the day after her departure, when Claudette would be safely in France.

"Madame, will you be seeing Monsieur Renaud while you're there?"

"Hush, Jolie, don't think about such things. I'm just going back to visit the queen. Our queen of France, remember?"

Jolie's owl eyes regarded her thoughtfully. "What should I tell Monsieur Greycliffe? He will surely ask me more than what your letter says."

"You haven't read my letter."

"No, madame, but I'm sure that he will want to know more than whatever you've told him."

Impudent girl! Yet Claudette's face flamed with embarrassment.

"Tell him what you know, which is that the queen seeks my company, and I've gone to France to give it to her and will explain everything when I return." She turned away so those owl eyes could not probe the depths of her own.

Now, though, she was eager to be on her way back to France. Scanning the crowded wooden dock near the *Maiden's Glory*, Claudette spied Jean-Philippe talking to the ship's captain.

"Jean-Philippe! Here I am," Claudette cried excitedly, waving.

"Ah, Claudette, it is indeed a pleasure to see you again." Jean-Philippe approached, his mouth curved in a grin. "Assuredly, I will take care of you on this trip and return you unharmed and as lovely as ever." He reached over and took her bag and offered his arm to her, sauntering with her to the waiting vessel.

On board the ship, Jean-Philippe had already made cabin arrangements. "I spent time with Captain Peterson on the way over to England, letting him beat me at several rounds of card games, so that I could ensure the best quarters for you, Claudette. Your other luggage has already been taken down, but let's not worry about that yet. Would you like to stroll around the ship before it departs?"

"Oh, yes, this is a much bigger ship than what I have traveled on during any of my other journeys." In a move reminiscent of their past, Jean-Philippe tucked her hand in his right elbow, keeping his left hand curled protectively around the top of hers. They strolled about peacefully. The breeze from this high on the deck blew away the unpleasant smells that clung so heavily to the docks.

"Jean-Philippe, the wind appears to be getting stronger."

"Mmm, yes, it does seem to be blowing a bit harder. Do not worry, my little dove, this is a big ship and can handle inclement weather."

Claudette started slightly at his use of his old nickname for her, but decided that he had used it unthinkingly.

Unfortunately, the winds had changed across the Channel, and an unexpectedly large storm was sweeping up the coast, forcing the captain to postpone departure for a day. Walking along the deck where the two stood talking, Captain James Peterson approached them and said, "*Pardon*, monsieur, I would like to advise you and Madame Renaud that we will remain at shore probably until to-morrow while a storm passes through. I recommend that you re-main on or very close to the ship, as we will pull out quickly after the storm passes." Giving a knowing wink to Jean-Philippe, he continued on to relay the news to other passengers.

Greatly dismayed at the thought of remaining on the ship for an extra day, but even more perplexed by the captain's turn of phrase, Claudette asked, "Jean-Philippe, why did Captain Peterson refer to me as your wife?"

"Ah, Claudette, to get the two best cabins on the ship, I had to assure him that you were my beloved bride returning with me from England to France. Losing a few sous at the card table will ensure that we eat at the captain's table as well, instead of with the other passengers. Please do not be angry. I did this so you would have a comfortable journey to and from France. You only have to pretend in front of our shipmates that you are my wife, that is all. We have separate cabins."

Claudette was disturbed, but could see no reason not to do as he asked.

Their next few hours were spent strolling the deck, chatting with other passengers, and watching another ship pull in to expel passengers and mail. At the dinner hour, the captain invited them to his own dining table, as Jean-Philippe had predicted. During dinner, as he shared the captain's finest Bordeaux, Jean-Philippe regaled Claudette and the other diners, mostly crew members, with stories of the French court.

"The king had so many attendants who had to have the privi-lege of waiting upon him that sometimes he was left freezing naked in his bedroom, while dozens of courtiers handled his night-shirt before it was placed over his head. And these people were all being paid out of the treasury. It was criminal."

Claudette hid a smile behind her hand, remembering what a shy, retiring nature the king had, and understanding how he would allow such a thing to happen to him, rather than allow a member of the court to be insulted. Jean-Philippe held up his glass to signal for a refill.

"Louis's great-great-grandfather, Le Roi Soleil, began some of these ridiculous practices. He instituted feasts with hundreds of dishes, each to be served by someone different, while most citizens were lucky to have a loaf and mutton grease to be sopped up.

"Men were not to be men. He gave his courtiers—many of them granted high posts—nothing to do but write letters, give speeches, fence, and dance. Is it any wonder the government fell into such deplorable condition?"

Tipping his glass back to catch every ruby-red drop of wine, he called out, "More wine here, *s'il vous plaît*." Hungrily eyeing a newly arrived bottle of wine, Jean-Philippe poured a copious amount into both his and Claudette's glasses. Claudette began to feel a small prickle of discomfort at the back of her neck.

"You must fortify yourself, Madame Renaud, for the sailing to France may be strenuous," he said, once again gulping more wine, but this time more clumsily, spattering some of the liquid on his shirt.

"Jean-Philippe, you were telling such amusing stories. Perhaps you have had enough to drink, but please do continue your storytelling."

Leaning close enough for her to smell the drink on his breath and to see the glitter now formed in his eyes, Jean-Philippe whispered harshly, "Madame, it is not for you to decide for Jean-Philippe Renaud. Here I am the master of your future, not you of mine."

Gasping audibly, Claudette quickly recovered herself. "Of course, *mon cher*, as you wish." Her stomach was now overcome with nausea. What was happening to Jean-Philippe? Why was he drinking so much? Where were his impeccable manners?

Jean-Philippe continued his tales, only now in a more sinister vein. "The queen—bah, that Austrian whore. She is pulling the strings of Louis Capet, that paunchy puppet. And all the while she has her lovers of all types, including the de Lamballe. Everyone knows that they are much more than innocent friends. Probably the king watches them together." Jean-Philippe chuckled at his own cleverness. "Yes, he watches the queen with her ladies-in-waiting, then returns to his room to tinker with his locks and toys, because the queen does not desire him—oh no, her tastes run in a different direction."

Claudette's entire body was now rigid. What sort of filth was Jean-Philippe spreading? Who had convinced him of these lies? Jean-Philippe had been a trusted member of the royal household and was handsomely rewarded for his services. Why was he betraying the royal family?

Eyeing Claudette's full glass, Jean-Philippe nodded to her. "Madame, are you not thirsty?" She shook her head silently. "Very well. I shall enjoy myself from your glass as well." Again, seeming to enjoy his own private joke, he grabbed her glass and downed its contents in two long swallows. Wiping his mouth with the back of his hand, he stood up unsteadily. "Madame Renaud, it is time to retire to our quarters."

Paralyzed by fear, Claudette looked around at the other faces at the table. No one else seemed to notice Jean-Philippe's odd behavior. Probably many of them had spent evenings immersed in bottles. She stood up as unsteadily as Jean-Philippe, but out of dread instead of drink. Desperately, she called over to the captain. "If you do not think we will be departing soon, may we stay the night in town?" She hoped that if she could get Jean-Philippe off the ship, she could sober him up.

Throwing her a lewd look, the captain replied, "The winds have calmed; we will be leaving before dawn." Sensing Claudette's tenseness, he said, "Now, now, madame, you have no fear of your new husband's prowess, now, do you?" The table exploded in laughter. Encouraged, he continued, "Monsieur assured me that a cabin as far below deck as possible would prevent your cries of pleasure from keeping us all awake and jealous." More laughter.

Claudette's mind raced. A cabin as far down as possible? What was the meaning of this? She knew from her first journey across the Channel that the cabins farther down in the ship were more cramped, noisier, and dirtier. She should have insisted that Jean-Philippe show her to her cabin when they first came aboard, to see the accommodations.

Jerking her out of her thoughts, Jean-Philippe grabbed her arm and doffed his hat to the table. "Gentlemen, we take our leave of you and will join you tomorrow for a very large breakfast, as I am sure we will both be ravenous."

He pulled Claudette out of the captain's dining hall and into the passageway. She squirmed out of his grasp and demanded, "Jean-Philippe, tell me instantly what is the meaning of this. Why is my cabin buried below deck? Why have you degraded me before the captain and his company? And why do you slander the king and queen?"

He stood and watched her thoughtfully, as she trembled angrily. She was obviously terrified, but it was tempered with indignation, and he felt a small rush of desire. She had become a very beautiful woman in the years since that childish betrothal. He almost regretted what he would now do. Seizing her arm once again, he began to drag her down the passageway to the stairwell that would lead them below decks. Claudette cried out, "Stop! I insist that you stop!" She struggled to get out of his grasp.

He slapped her hard across the face with his free hand to silence her. She was stunned for an instant, long enough for him to clap his hand over her mouth and begin dragging her again toward the stairwell. He then made his way down the narrow circular staircase. By now, Claudette had dropped to the ground behind him. Instead of helping her up, he simply dragged her down the stairs, much like mates aboard the ship had probably dragged sacks of flour down the stairs to the galley. She was quickly becoming entangled in her skirts, and she knew that the bump of each stair would be leaving behind a painful bruise.

Claudette begged, "Jean-Philippe, please, let me up. Please."

At the bottom of the first stairwell he stopped, breathing hard. "You must remain utterly silent, or I will have you thrown off this ship into the Thames. If I give him enough money, the captain will turn his back while I do whatever I wish. Do you understand, my *little dove?*"

She winced. "Yes," she whispered, barely audible.

They marched another two levels into the ship together, Claudette subdued at Jean-Philippe's side.

He escorted her down a dank passageway. Several doors stood open, and she could see that most were storage rooms. At the end of the passage, he stopped abruptly, inserted a key into the last door on the left of the passageway, flung it open, and pushed Claudette inside. He followed her in, pulling the door shut behind him.

She could not believe her surroundings. Surely this could not be happening. A straw-filled mattress was suspended from the ceiling along one wall. The linens looked serviceable, but based on the location of the room, she questioned how long it had been since they had been changed. A second wall held a small chest of drawers, and the opposite wall held a rickety chair, with a *commode* next to it. The chest of drawers held a candlestick, a Bible, a small cracked mirror, and a small washbasin. The dust was thick enough to obscure the lettering on the Bible.

"How is this, Madame Renaud? This is what all royal-lovers of your ilk receive."

"Jean-Philippe, whatever are you talking about?"

"You know. You have been conspiring with the Austrian whore and her husband for years now, have you not? You thought you were very ingenious, did you not, with all of your plotting and planning? Well, I will tell you that I am honored to be the one to prevent you from working against the good of France. You are discovered, Claudette, and you will be brought to justice!"

Feeling weak and confused, Claudette stumbled over to the chair and sat down in a layer of dust.

"Jean-Philippe, you must have me confused with someone else. I am a loyal adherent to both the king and queen and to France." Tears of frustration welled up in her eyes. "What exactly are you accusing me of? What have I done? Why are you treating me so roughly? We are friends, yet you treat me as a common criminal." The tears began rolling down her cheeks. "I am beginning to think you are mad, or perhaps I am."

Erratically changing course, Jean-Philippe threw himself to his knees, and wrapped his arms around her legs, then dropped his head into her lap.

"Oh, my little dove, I am so sorry. I have so loved you since we were children and cannot bear to lose you. I gladly accepted this assignment from Citizen Robespierre so that I could see you again. *Ma chére,* promise to return to me, become my betrothed again, and I will forgive all and see that you come to no harm."

Dropping her hand onto his dark head, Claudette said quietly, "Harm from what? Jean-Philippe, you know that my life is in England now."

"No! The English are swine. You only became one of them because you thought I was dead. Your future is with me. Let me show you my love."

Getting up, he swept Claudette into his arms and carried her to the swaying hammock. He gently put her down then climbed in with her, one leg crossing both of hers, his body leaning against her.

"Little dove, little dove, kiss me."

Wrenching her head away from him, Claudette whispered, "No, Jean-Philippe, remove yourself. What are you doing? I do not understand you."

He grabbed her face and turned it to him. "You do not realize the trouble you are in. I am the only one who can help you. You will become mine now, and I will give you my name in marriage when we arrive in France." His eyes became glazed. "I will convince Robespierre that you are innocent. Or perhaps I will find a prostitute and send her in your place. Together, Claudette, we will have many children. You will be my beloved wife." He placed a gentle kiss on her neck.

"No, Jean-Philippe, no." Trying to wrestle her way from him, she threatened, "I shall tell the queen, and she will be very angered by this."

He laughed throatily. "The Austrian whore? Who cares what she thinks? She is nothing, as you are nothing without me. *Mon Dieu,* you are achingly desirable."

He covered her mouth with his, forcing her lips open and sweeping her mouth with his tongue. He moved to rest his body on top of her completely. Claudette was pinned, and unable to breathe. The alcohol on his breath permeated the room. She could feel his passion welling up against her right leg, as he began groaning against her mouth. She knew that this far into the ship, no one would hear her cries for help. Even if they did, the captain would ensure that no one bothered monsieur as he availed himself of madame on their "wedding night."

She struggled beneath him, but it just seemed to increase his excitement.

"Jean-Philippe, please, in the name of our friendship, let me go."

"Ah, Claudette, would that I could. I am crazy for you." He was now panting. He grabbed her *chemisier* and began fumbling to remove it. In frustration, he ripped the cloth, exposing her shift beneath the material. Now seeing her exposed form beneath the thin material of her shift, he seemed to be infused with a passion beyond all reason. He moved to bring his mouth down to one of her breasts, and began to nibble on it through her shift. His action gave Claudette enough mobility to push him from her, and she leaped up from the hammock in an attempt to run from the room. He grabbed her around the waist just as she was about to touch the door latch. He turned her around to him, and pressed her against the swelling protruding from his midsection.

"My little dove, we are destined for one another. Do not fight me." He sank to his knees, his arms clutching her tightly about the waist as he once more concentrated his attentions on her breasts. Her arms free, Claudette looked wildly around the room for a way out of her hopeless situation. She spied the dusty candlestick on the dresser. Could she reach it? No, it was too far away. Thinking quickly, she put her hands on either side of his face and murmured, "Oh, Jean-Philippe, you are right. We belong together. Take me to bed."

Smiling in triumph and lust, he released her momentarily so that he could stand up. She stepped backward out of his grasp toward the dresser, and grabbed the candlestick. Swinging wildly with all of her strength, she connected the brass stick with the side of his skull. Howling in pain, he lunged for the candlestick. Claudette quickly threw it under the bed, hoping he would not attempt to reach for it. He once again slapped her across the face. Putting his face near hers, and grabbing the neck he was lovingly kissing just moments ago, he growled, "You filthy little bitch. You are deluded in your importance, just like Madame Capet. Very well. You will get what is coming to you. You will stay in this room for the rest of the journey." He then shoved her toward the hammock. She slipped and fell to the floor. She sat up, only to see Jean-Philippe slamming the door behind him, and to hear him turning the key in the lock.

❧ 27 ❧

July 30, 1792. Claudette awoke slowly, pain making itself known slowly from her hips up to her face. She could taste blood. Ah, Jean-Philippe's handiwork. She opened her eyes. The cabin was dark. She was still on the floor where he had left her. She reached up to her face and felt the side of her mouth. Her cheek was swollen, and blood was crusted on her lips, but she did not seem to have any broken teeth or other permanent damage.

Reaching in the air for the hammock, she lifted herself to a sitting position. Definite bruises had formed on her legs and hips from Jean-Philippe's careless dragging of her body down through the ship. *I must think,* she mused. *Why am I confined like this? Why was Jean-Philippe accusing me of conspiring with the king and queen? Conspiring to do what? How could the royal family be conspiring to do anything? Perhaps he is simply mad. But he seemed perfectly sane before we boarded the ship. What shall I do?*

She crawled in the blackness to the door of the cabin, got on her knees, and tried to call out to any passersby. "Hello? Hello? Please, I need help." Silence, except for the distant raucous laughter of the ship's crew and passengers. "Please, please, I'm trapped in my cabin. Help me!" She began banging on the door, becoming more hysterical as she tried to raise her voice over that of everyone else. She knew it was futile. They were too far away. She sank back to the floor, resting her head on the doorframe, tears quietly streaming down her face.

She woke with a start. There was a clamor coming from above. Had they arrived in France? Perhaps Jean-Philippe would be returning soon. She crawled back over to the hammock, and began feeling around for the candlestick she had thrown under it. She would need protection from her captor, whose intentions had proven to be despicable. She patted around the filthy floor. Oh, please, where was it? She crawled farther under the hammock. Finally, her hand closed around her brass savior.

A rattling noise, then the door was thrown open with a loud crash. She winced at the sudden light from the lantern Jean-Philippe was carrying.

"So, Madame Renaud, I trust that you are well rested. We will be docking soon, and I came to tell you exactly how you will conduct yourself on our arrival. Are you listening?" He crouched down and held the lantern near her face. "*Mon Dieu*, but you are grimy. It hardly matters, but here, take this." He offered her a cloth square from his breeches pocket. Shaking, she reached out her free hand to take the cloth, and feebly attempted to wipe some of the blood and dirt from her face.

"Quickly, then. No need to primp, madame. Where you are going your appearance will certainly not count. Stand up."

"No." Barely audible.

"You will get up immediately."

Claudette clenched the candlestick in her right hand behind her back. She would not easily be able to rise while concealing the heavy brass piece. Taking her unawares, Jean-Philippe reached out and grasped her under her right shoulder and yanked her to her feet. In her surprise, she lost the candlestick, which hit the floor with a dull thud. Both of them stared silently at the floor where the weapon lay.

"So, I see you were planning a surprise for Jean-Philippe, you filthy little whore." He reached down and picked up the candlestick, placing it on the dresser. "No matter." He grabbed her chin in his hand and turned it to expose the right side of her face, and once again held up the lantern to look at her. "I believe we can convince the captain that our games got a bit rough last night." Squeezing her face a bit harder, he said, "Now listen to me. We are going to go back up to the captain's dining quarters, where I will allow you to eat some breakfast. If Captain Peterson or anyone else addresses you, you will say that you are tired from your husband's arduous attentions, and would like to be left alone. If you make a signal to anyone, I will bring you down here and finish what I started last night. Is that clear?" She nodded numbly, her face still in his hand. He released her and stepped back.

"We will then go out on deck, and stroll about like a couple in love. When we dock, you will put your hand in my arm, and we will disembark together. Not a soul shall think that you are anything other than my adoring wife. Am I understood, Claudette?"

Trembling once again with a mixture of rage and fear, she replied, "Yes, Jean-Philippe, I understand."

"Very well, you may step out of the cabin."

She arranged her torn dress as best she could to maintain her modesty, and they walked side by side down the hallway, back to the foot of the circular stairway, which intersected their hallway with a cross passageway. She paused, unwilling to make the treacherous return on the stairs. "Take my hand, madame, and I will lead you up." She remained still. Noise from the intersecting passageway indicated that someone was coming. "Do not try it. Take my hand and come up the stairs. Now." Realizing her futile position, Claudette gave him her hand, and allowed him to lead her back up to the dining room.

Entering the captain's dining galley once again, Claudette and Jean-Philippe were met with cheers and catcalls. Claudette lowered her head so that no one could see her burning cheeks. Jean-Philippe quickly led her to an unoccupied table at the back of the room, then walked back to the center of the room where most of the occupants were.

"Eh, Monsieur Renaud, your wife is looking a bit tired now, ain't she?"

Another wag joined in. "Good thing we're docking. I bet she'll be eating the rest of our provisions."

Jean-Philippe smiled indulgently and approached the men with an exaggerated wink. Raising his voice he said, "Now, now, I will not have my tired bride mocked." Lowering his voice so that Claudette could not hear, he added, "Tired *and* just a bit sore, yes?" Claudette could only hear rollicking laughter near Jean-Philippe, and cringed as she imagined what he was saying.

A mate brought her a wooden platter heaped with salted fish, dried fruit, and cheese, accompanied by a tankard of watered-down ale. Claudette pushed the food around some, nibbled on the cheese, and downed the ale in nearly a single gulp. *Perhaps this will give me strength*, she hoped.

After leaving her alone for several minutes, Jean-Philippe walked back over to her, again using a loud voice. "My darling, are you full? You have hardly touched your plate. I know that you are used to fancier dishes, but I think you should have shown your appreciation for Captain Peterson's hospitality better than this." More laughter from the dining room.

Hissing under her breath she replied, "Jean-Philippe, enough. Take me out of here."

Still keeping his voice raised, he put a hand to her elbow to help her up from the table and said, "Yes, my dear, let's go up to the deck for some fresh air."

Claudette rose, and Jean-Philippe smoothly tucked her hand in his arm. He nodded to the crew and passengers as they left the galley. Claudette kept her face lowered, unable to face her audience, until Jean-Philippe subtly squeezed her hand against his side, letting her know that she was not playing her part properly. She looked up, and gave a wan smile to the room, and prayed that she could make it to the exit without fainting.

Outside of the galley, they continued their walk to the deck. Jean-Philippe said under his breath, "Not too bad, my little dove, but our journey is not quite over." The air on deck was bracingly fresh. After the musty smell of the cabin and the smoke-filled atmosphere of the galley, Claudette felt relief at being in the open air. They were pulling into port. A frenetic level of activity began, as the ship's mates began yelling instructions to one another to see the ship safely into port. Claudette looked around in desperation, but no one took any notice of Jean-Philippe Renaud's quiet bride.

Finally, they were ready to disembark. "Monsieur Renaud! Monsieur Renaud!" Captain Peterson was puffing his way up to them. "I take it you found your journey, er, to your liking?"

"Yes, Captain. Madame Renaud and I were delighted with our journey. Is that not so, dear?"

Claudette gritted her teeth and nodded. She saw Jean-Philippe pass a small pouch to the captain, which he took greedily. The bag jingled. She wondered ironically what price her humiliation had been worth to her captor.

"Why, now, monsieur, it almost pains me to take this, seeing as you and your wife have been made so happy on my humble little ship."

Jean-Philippe's eyes were twinkling. "Nevertheless, I will insist that you keep it as a token of our gratitude. Now, Captain, may we be among the first passengers to leave?"

"Of course, of course. Lucas, over here, boy. Help this fine couple off the ship. Make sure their bags are brought down. Right away. Stop gaping, you idiot." The young boy, who could not have been more than twelve, scampered off to do his master's bidding.

Again ensuring a tight grip on Claudette, Jean-Philippe descended the gangplank with her. At the bottom of the causeway, they paused to wait for their bags. Claudette wondered bleakly where they would be going from here. Soon, Lucas appeared with another boy, both of them dragging down luggage to the waiting couple. Jean-Philippe thanked them. "There's a sou for each of you to bring our luggage to that coach waiting over there."

Claudette's eyes followed his pointing finger. A carriage stood apart from the other conveyances waiting to take away arriving passengers. The boys began eagerly lugging Claudette's belongings to the carriage. "Is the coach yours, Jean-Philippe?"

"Yes. Come along, wife."

"Please, no more pretenses now that we are off the ship."

"As you wish." Jean-Philippe walked her very casually over to the coach. He flipped each boy a shiny coin, and they ran off, whooping. He then nodded to the driver, as though giving him a silent instruction, and helped Claudette into the coach. The interior of the coach was clean and comfortable, much to Claudette's surprise after her vile lodgings on the ship.

"You look surprised. Do not let it be said that the French cannot be hospitable, even to traitors." The coach began to move.

"Jean-Philippe, where are we going? I demand that you take me to the queen. You have much to answer for!"

Chuckling and shaking his head, he said, "*Au contraire,* in fact it is you who have much to answer for. The queen will not be seeing you today, as she no longer sees anyone. That filthy whore and her husband are being kept as, hmm, as guests of the new government."

"Jean-Philippe! Are you saying that the king and queen have been made prisoners? For what reason?"

"The people have suffered under Madame Deficit and her husband long enough. Soon we will have a government in place that is of the citizens of France, and royalty will be a thing of the past. *Liberté, Égalité, Fraternité!*" His eyes had a gleam that was wild. Claudette shivered inwardly.

"And you, my little dove, will be interrogated as to your part in the plot to whisk the Capets out of the country. Have no doubt, what you have done will be considered treason. And you know what happens to traitors." The words hung thickly in the air.

"A traitor? But, Jean-Philippe, I have been living quietly in England for years, except for one visit back to France to be introduced to the queen. Why am I accused of treason?"

"Enough. You'll not trick me into saying something that you can use against the government." He looked at her speculatively. "However, I might be willing to forgive you your rough treatment of me aboard the ship, and do what I can to protect you from those who now rule France."

No, not again. "I refuse you." She turned her head to stare out the window of the coach. They were rumbling down along the Seine, past the familiar sights of the Tuileries and the Palais Royal.

"You? You, a traitor, refuse me? You have become a haughty bitch living in London. You showed me that on the ship. You could have had a very pleasurable crossing to France, but made it difficult for yourself instead. I've a mind to show you what it means to have manners. It is unseemly for you to have a business. It has muddled your head with fancy ideas about your own grandness. But I will show you that Jean-Philippe is master here."

He moved forward suddenly, grabbing both her elbows and pulling her to his side of the coach and onto his lap. "My mistress enjoys a periodic romp in the coach. She thinks it wickedly delicious, knowing that someone might see us."

"Your mistress is obviously a whore."

He threw back his head and laughed. "I guess you are probably right, but she would not like to hear you say that. She's actually quite rich, you know, and a supporter of our cause. Now, give us a kiss."

Claudette struggled against him, but was powerless in the confined space. He brought his head down to hers, and covered her lips with his. Realizing that her struggle was futile, she became still. Mistaking her calm for acquiescence, he slid a hand under her dress and began moving her skirts out of the way. With her one free hand, she began to beat wildly against his chest to stop him, but it only served to inflame him more.

She whimpered, completely frustrated and helpless. All of a sudden the coach crashed to a halt, tumbling them both over. Swearing under his breath, Jean-Philippe opened the door to yell at the driver.

"What has happened?"

"We are here, monsieur."

"Take us around the block once more!"

"Monsieur Renaud, the Rue St. Honoré is crowded. I will not be able to pick up your other guest on time if I do not leave now."

Grumbling, Jean-Philippe lowered himself back to his seat. Claudette had recovered her skirts and was now sitting primly on her seat, staring toward the ceiling.

"We are thwarted again, little dove. Perhaps again someday—"

"Never!"

Without a response, he stepped out of the coach, and pulled her out behind him. She looked up at the imposing building in front of them, of gray stone and narrow slits for windows. Iron bars graced the slits.

"Where are we?"

"See for yourself."

She looked at the sign on the building. "*Maison de La Force.* What? *Mon Dieu*, Jean-Philippe, no! Do not bring me here. I am guilty of nothing! I swear! Please, I will become your lover if that is what you wish, but do not take me in there, in the name of our parents and all that has passed between us, please do not do this."

"Come. Your promises matter nothing to me now." He pushed her toward the entry of the forbidding building, as the driver blended back into the crowded street to pick up Jean-Philippe's mysterious guest. To gain control of Claudette's struggling, Jean-Philippe grabbed her from behind, wrapped an arm under her breasts, and began dragging her to the entrance. At the doorway, he rapped imperiously. A viewing slot was pulled aside, and a single eye appraised the visitors. The sound of bolts being pulled back reached them, and the door opened into the dark, yawning mouth of La Force prison.

"I have another traitor for you, Lieutenant Napier. Believe it or not, this citizeness masterminded the jewel smuggling for the Capets. Send a message to Robespierre. He might be interested in interrogating Citizeness Laurent himself."

A man emerged from the shadows. Of average height and weight, he had stringy brown hair and a pockmarked face. His loose shirt and striped trousers were dirty and marked him as one of the sans cullotte radicals. He looked at Claudette. "Quite a tasty little morsel, this traitor is, Citizen Renaud. The usual uniform for her?" His breath was sour against her face.

Napier snapped his fingers, his eyes never leaving Claudette's face. Another prison worker, a middle-aged woman, came scurrying up carrying clothing. Napier threw it at Claudette. Grinning to show a gaping hole where his two front teeth once were, he turned his attention back to Jean-Philippe.

"Shall I escort her down myself?" His arousal was almost palpable, and Claudette wondered how many young women had become his victims in this place.

"No, I shall conclude her journey myself. A key, please?"

From a large ring hooked to his trousers, Napier extracted an iron key. "As you wish, Citizen." Napier looked regretfully at Claudette as Jean-Philippe led her down the hallway, into the bowels of the prison. Calling after them, he said, "Perhaps later, Citizeness, we shall have the pleasure of getting to know one another." Claudette could hear his chuckling in her head after they passed out of earshot.

The hallway was made of stone. Moisture oozed from various spots, making the air chilly and damp, and creating long streaks of green and rust on the walls. Iron lanterns that hung from the walls offered only enough light for them to make their way in without stumbling. They proceeded about a hundred feet, then Jean-Philippe turned her to the left, down an intersecting hallway. She began to hear noises, the bleatings and pleadings of miserably incarcerated people. Now she was to become one of them. The hallway was lined on both sides with cells at various intervals. Some cells had solid doors, with only a sliding opening for food at the bottom, whereas others were no more than large cages with iron bars. The walls of each cell were the same cold, dank stone of the hallway, preventing prisoners from seeing each other, especially since no cell was directly across from another. The wailing of prisoners was louder now, as they were in the middle of the row of cells. Was she to be deposited here?

Jean-Philippe continued to guide her down the hallway. An old crone in an iron-barred cage reached a claw out to grab Claudette's skirt. "Eh, mademoiselle, would you be my daughter come to get me?" Claudette wrenched herself away. Farther down, she saw a young man sitting on the floor of his cell, his eyes weeping yellow and green pus from an infection that was being allowed to fester. All along the hallway, prisoners called out, either leeringly or begging for help. Claudette's head was filled with their piteous cries, and she attempted to run to escape the noise somehow. Jean-Philippe, however, kept a tight grip on her elbow.

"This way." He led her to the right, down another hallway. Did this cursed place ever end? She noticed, however, that this group of cells was far less populated than on the previous hallway. As if reading her thoughts, Jean-Philiipe said, "Better here, is it not? I selected the luxury suite especially for you."

He stopped in front of a nondescript cell, inserted the key in the lock and pulled the iron-barred door open. He pushed Claudette inside, and slammed the gate shut. Claudette stood numbly, staring at her new surroundings. She could see why it was a luxury suite. There was actually a washbasin in the room. Would it ever actually be filled with fresh water? She doubted it. A chamber pot stood in the corner. Would it ever be emptied? A straw mattress lay on an iron cot, approximately six inches off the ground. Perhaps this would save her from being gnawed on too much by rats. The thin sheet on top of it would certainly not protect her from the cold of this place. How cold would it be at nightfall? How would she even know when it was nightfall? The only other articles in the cell were a rickety chair and table. Having seen the other cells, though, their only furnishings straw pallets, Claudette knew that this was, indeed, the luxury suite.

Breaking her out of her reverie, Jean-Philippe told her, "It is time to change into your uniform."

She had forgotten the cloth bundle in her hand. She shook it out and held it up to the dim light at the front of the cell. It was a simple shift of muslin. The dress was filthy and smelled of an unwashed body. What had happened to the last woman who wore this dress? she wondered.

"What are you waiting for? Get into your uniform."

"I will change into it when I am in private."

"You will change into it now, or I will come in and change you myself."

Biting her lip at this further humiliation, Claudette began loosening the torn, lace-fringed blouse at the top of her once-beautiful dress. Grimly she thought that the prison gown was probably not much filthier than her own clothes had become. She turned away from Jean-Philippe to at least provide herself with some sort of modesty.

"No, Claudette, you will face me as you change."

She turned around. "Can you not leave me with a little bit of dignity, Jean-Philippe? I am an innocent woman being imprisoned on some trumped-up charge. You have been taking advantage of me since we left England. Please, leave me be."

"Take your clothes off."

This was even more degrading than his attack on her in the coach, since she was at least not exposed completely to him during his groping. What if that horrible Napier were to come down while she was changing?

"Immediately, Claudette. You know that I am a bit temperamental when I do not get my way."

Helpless, Claudette continued removing her clothes. She bent down and unbuttoned her fashionable kid boots and removed them. She then slowly unrolled her stockings, one at a time, delicately, as though she must save them in case she might be able to escape her desperate situation. She unbuttoned her gown overlay and let it fall to the ground. The lavender color was now just a dingy gray. She finished untying the blouse, and pushed that off her shoulders, as well. She untied the underlying brown skirt, and let it drop to the ground. She stood shivering in her shift. She looked with distaste at the prison gown awaiting her on the chair.

"I do not have all day. My guest will be waiting for me at my home. Finish changing."

"Your whore, perhaps?"

He laughed. "Indeed. I need to hurry home so she does not become too impatient waiting for me. The minx has scratched me before when I have angered her."

Claudette was appalled. What manner of man had he become?

"Claudette, I shall not ask again."

Slowly, she lifted her chemise over her head and tossed it to the chair, quickly grabbing at the prison garb and slipping it over her head, thinking she would change back into at least her chemise when Jean-Philippe had gone.

"Give me your clothes, Claudette." She looked at him in horror. "You did not think you would be allowed to keep them, did you? Hand them to me."

Shaking, she gathered up the garments, still warm from her body, and wordlessly crossed the cell to hand them to him. Jean-Philippe put the clothing up to his face and inhaled deeply. He then tucked them under his arm and turned to go. After a couple of steps, he turned back and said, "Enjoy your new home, Claudette. You won't live to enjoy it much longer."

❧ 28 ❧

Hevington, Kent, August 10, 1792. William slouched moodily in front of a blazing fire, drumming his fingers on one heavily carved arm of the chair. Why had Claudette not written to him since arriving in France? It was most unusual. And she had been damned secretive running off like that.

A manservant entered the room to offer him the latest newspapers and a decanter of port. William growled his acceptance of both, and the servant scurried out quickly, not used to his master in such an ill-tempered state.

William put aside the *London Times*, and quickly plunged into *L'Ami du Peuple,* The Friend of the People. He had picked up this wretched daily paper as a means of staying informed on the radical perspective of the rapidly disintegrating state of affairs in France. As always, Marat was naming his own "enemies of the people." Jean-Paul Marat, as vitriolic an editor as could be found, was perpetually condemning people and reporting their alleged disloyalties. The paper could only be termed a rag, but it provided fascinating insights into revolutionary thought. William scanned the typical deleterious headlines about France's woes, searching for any royal social commentaries that might mention Claudette's name. Nothing. Drat it all, she had been in Paris nearly two weeks and not a single mention of her. His eye roved over other articles. What was this? The king and queen had been removed to the Temple. Had

Claudette seen them before this happened? Things were becoming exceedingly dangerous in Paris. Was Claudette safe?

He crumpled the paper angrily and threw it in the fire with a grunt. Eyeing the port decanter, he whisked it off its tray and smashed it into the fireplace as well. He felt no comfort.

Several nights later, William attended a soirée at the Earl of Pembroke's London home. He had planned on sending his regrets, but his young cousin Arabella, who was currently visiting his parents and had already been making the social rounds in Kent, had pleaded very prettily to go in Claudette's stead. Arabella had a fascination for Charles Durham, whose family had invested profitably in the East India Company, and that young man was to be in attendance at the party, so William acquiesced and escorted his relative to London.

It cheered him to find Giovanna Baccelli there. She had been the Earl of Pembroke's paramour since her dismissal from Knole and the Duke of Dorset's life almost three years earlier. The pair had moved to London from his Wiltshire estate, after Pembroke's estranged but outraged wife insisted that she was moving back into the family home.

Giovanna was as lovely as ever, even if she seemed a little faded.

After dinner, as the group moved into the ballroom for dancing, William drew The Baccelli aside to a window in the earl's study, and explained to her his concerns about Claudette's recent trip to France.

"Giovanna, share with me your womanly intuition. Am I just being foolish about this?"

The earl's mistress carefully considered William, furrowing her brow. She dropped her usual theatrical whispering to speak in low tones.

"You say she only left you a note before she departed? How very curious. Well, what I know of Signorina Laurent tells me that she would never do anything to betray you, if that's what worries you." Only a margin of relief showed in William's face. "However, it is troubling that she would agree to go to France knowing how unsafe it has become."

"She is very devoted to the queen there. Not only because she has custom with Her Majesty, but also because she believes the Bourbon royal family to be overly vilified and friendless. I suppose I am not surprised that she wanted to go, only that she would be so silent."

Giovanna took one of his hands in both of her own. "Signore Greycliffe, it would be a tragedy for us both if we lost the little dollmaker. I believe you must investigate her whereabouts, to set both our minds at ease."

William smiled for the first time that evening. "Yes, I must take action," he said. He kissed The Baccelli's hand, and returned to the ballroom to impatiently wait for Arabella to conclude an evening's flirtation with Mr. Durham. Arabella chattered the entire way back to Hevington, but William didn't hear a word. He left her in the care of his housekeeper, and vaulted up the stairs to his bedchamber to begin making plans.

❧ 29 ❧

Paris, August 13, 1792. The royal family's imprisonment within the walls of the Tuileries still did not satisfy the revolutionaries. The *assignats* were devaluing rapidly, with an accompanying rise in food prices. To multiply the country's problems, hoarders were keeping grain from a good harvest off the market while merchants were exporting it for greater profits. Riots still occurred regularly.

The Assembly had become dominated by another group, the Girondists, who had been born out of the Jacobins. The Girondists—so named because many members were deputies from the Gironde department, which represented the provinces of Guyenne and Gascogne—tended to be idealists and dreamers, incapable of making realistic and achievable plans. Consequently, it was difficult for them to squarely face troublesome issues. Into their hands went the fate of the king and his family.

The Girondists' unbelievable solution to the country's problems was to seek another country to attack, believing that by spreading the new French method of achieving democracy, the French populace itself would be distracted from the country's internal woes. Louis, with what little power he had left, vetoed every measure put to him that furthered this plan.

An ultimatum was sent to the Assembly that unless the king was deposed by August 9, the palace would be attacked and the monarchy overthrown by force. Supporters of the king gathered inside the Tuileries that day to repel any invasion. In the early morning hours of August 10, alarm bells from church steeples began to peal and rebellious subjects went on the march to the palace. Realizing that all hope was gone, Louis gathered up his family from their quarters and retreated to the National Assembly building, located on another part of the palace's grounds.

From inside the Assembly, they heard shots being fired and the clash of pikes and other weaponry, accompanied by shouts and screams, as the mob broke through the National and Swiss Guards into the palace itself. The mob raged through the Tuileries, smashing windows and hurling furniture through the broken frames in their destructive fury.

Under pressure, the Assembly formally deposed Louis XVI, King of the French, and ordered the royal family to be housed in the grim and gloomy Temple, one-time headquarters of the Knights Templar. The Princesse de Lamballe and other close friends chose to accompany them.

❧ 30 ❧

William's first act was to engage a constable-for-hire to look into Claudette's whereabouts. The man wanted an outrageous sum to perform any work having to do with the destabilized situation in France, but William agreed to his asking price without question. The man left Hevington knowing he should have doubled his quoted price, since this customer was not only rich, he looked desperate.

A week later, no word was yet forthcoming from the constable-for-hire. William returned to the house from a long ride through the Kentish countryside to work off his tension, and saw a fresh batch of newspapers on the table in the entryway. Giving the housekeeper orders that no one was to disturb him, he tucked the papers under his arm and headed into the library.

William snapped open the *L'Ami du Peuple* newspaper, as he had now done dozens of times. Marat was particularly malicious on the front page, relishing his broadcasts of all the "traitors, scoundrels, and thieves" that were being brought to justice now that the people were being allowed to determine their own fates. William wondered if Claudette was aware of all this lunacy. He returned his attention to the newspaper, scanning all of the usual headlines, and found a column of names on one side of the page. He ran his finger down the list, and swore.

> Claudette Renée Laurent, formerly of
> England, has been arrested for conspiring
> to give aid to the most undesirable ele-
> ments in the nation of France, and is now
> imprisoned in La Force. It is this paper's
> most fervent wish that she be executed as
> soon as possible, as an example to all other
> would-be schemers against the freedoms
> demanded by the people.

William's heart stopped beating as his body became encased in icy rage. *Damnation! Who has manufactured false evidence against her? And why? How did she get mired in this? I must find her myself.*

William barked out a series of instructions to his servants regarding care of Hevington during his absence, and hurriedly scratched out two notes. One he ordered taken quickly to Béatrice to let her know of Claudette's predicament and his planned action; and a second note to immediately disengage the ineffective constable-for-hire. Dobry threw together essentials into a valise for William, who was galloping toward Dover within two hours of seeing Claudette's imprisonment notice.

❧ 31 ❧

La Force Prison, Paris, August 14, 1792. Claudette's captivity had
stretched from the first miserable day and night, into an everlasting
sequence of endless days and nights. Initially, Claudette was certain that Lieutenant Napier, who had leered at her so lecherously
upon arrival at the prison, would be imminently visiting her cell,
but she had never seen him again.

The pervasive low lighting of the prison's hallways made an actual determination of day and night impossible. The weeping and
howling of the inmates, punctuated by periodic sounds of sharp
slaps and beatings from jailers who grew tired of the noises, were
Claudette's primary source of company. A wooden bowl of thin,
watery soup, sometimes accompanied by hard bread, would periodically appear at her cell, but not with any consistency that would
have allowed her to track the cycles of the days.

Her food was almost always delivered by the woman who had
provided the prison garb that now attired Claudette. After several
visits by her female jailer, who barely acknowledged Claudette
when delivering food or an occasional change of shift to something
as equally malodorous as what her prisoner already wore, Claudette
attempted to get some information.

"Please, can you tell me how long I am to be kept here?"

"Not for me to say."

"Do you mean you do not know or you cannot tell me?"

"Do not know, do not care." Claudette's bowl was set down on the stone floor with a smart rap, causing some of the fluid to slosh out of it. The woman turned on her heel and left.

When she returned to pick up the empty bowl, Claudette tried again.

"Can you tell me what day this is?"

"Saturday."

"Is it morning or nighttime?"

"You just ate supper. It's around seven o'clock in the evening."

"Thank you." Claudette decided it was best not to push further on her first tiny success. The information gleaned was not much, given that there was really no way to track time from this point forward. And how long had she been in this filthy cell? A week? A month? Longer? Surely William was trying to find her. Was she to be formally charged with a crime, or just left here to die?

At the next meal interval, Claudette again forged ahead with conversation with her captor.

"Please, what time is it now?"

"What time is it? What day is it?" the woman mimicked. "What kind of idiot are you? You eat at seven o'clock in the morning and seven o'clock in the evening, on days that you are fed. It never changes, so why do you ask?"

Ignoring the jibe, Claudette took another step. "My name is Claudette Laurent. What is your name?"

The woman said, "I am Emeline," then seemed startled that she had actually responded to Claudette with this personal piece of information. She turned on her heel to leave the cell area. Claudette leapt to her feet from her cot.

"Wait! Please, let me ask you one more question."

Emeline turned back. "Let me guess," she sneered. "You want a message taken to your sweetheart, do you not? Or perhaps you want to tell me you are related to someone most influential who will reward me handsomely for freeing you? I am no simpleton to be tricked, I can tell you. Better folk than you have tried to play me for a fool."

Swallowing her impatience, Claudette said, "I would just like to know if I am to be formally charged and brought to trial, and if so, when?"

"Hah! That's what everyone wants to know. I stay out of details, Citizeness. Trials and inquiries are handled by my superiors. I don't want to know what happens to anyone in here."

The days continued to pass. Claudette could not be sure, but it seemed as though about four weeks were gone. She received another meal visit from Emeline, but this time her life was to change a bit.

"You're being moved, Citizeness Claudette. Come with me." The door was unlocked and Emeline stepped into the cell.

"Where am I being taken?"

"Just another cell. Be grateful. You'll have friends now."

Friends? Claudette no longer knew what the word meant. Emeline led her down the passageway, in the opposite direction from where she had entered when first jailed. She was eventually brought to a large communal cell, at least fourteen feet wide, where several women were seated about on chairs, embroidering or playing cards, while one of them read aloud to the group. All of them looked up as their cell was opened and Claudette entered by way of Emeline's shove. A plump, older woman, with deep lines furrowed in her forehead and a deck of cards in her hand, stood.

"My dear, welcome to our little troop of woeful captives. Gossip actually travels quickly within these damp walls. We heard that you were here and that you were the maker of those exquisite dolls the queen kept at the Trianon. We were anxious to meet you, and bribed Lieutenant Napier to relocate you with us. I hope you will find these quarters, and our company, adequate."

"I am most grateful to be moved out of my cell."

"Well, then, we welcome you to our humble circumstances." The woman introduced herself as Madame D'Aubigne, and explained that she was remotely related to the Bourbons through her marriage to a bastard descendant of Louis XIV's. Her husband had been killed in a hunting accident two years ago, but Madame D'Aubigne had continued in comfort thanks to her husband's careful preservation of the monies that the former king had provided from the royal purse for his upbringing. The revolutionaries had, in her opinion, eyed her fortune avariciously and made some excuse that she was interested in promoting the future of the Bourbon monarchy so that she could maintain her status. Her fortune was confiscated and she was promptly delivered to La Force.

Madame D'Aubigne introduced Claudette to the other five women in the cell. All were either members of the nobility, or distant relatives against whom charges had been trumped up. None of them were exactly sure what their crimes were, other than being born aristocrats.

"But that is what happened to me!" cried Claudette. She told them that she was accused of treason involving assistance to the royal family, but she was not sure exactly what she had done.

"I would never commit a treasonous act, although had I known the king and queen needed help, I would have done so willingly."

"Hush, my dear, do not speak so loudly. We are in much danger here, and such statements overheard by our jailers can do us no good. Now, I think the first thing we must do is make you more comfortable."

The women went over to some shabby trunks in the corner of the cell and began pulling out hairbrushes, cosmetics, and clothing. Obviously, these women were given more privilege than a pitiful dollmaker was. They fluttered about her, tsk-tsking about her emaciated state, rubbing cream on her face, applying rouge and lipstick, brushing out the snarls and tangles from her hair, and stripping her filthy shift from her and replacing it with an ill-fitting, yet reasonably clean dress. It was missing buttons and ribbons and was a bit large, but was a relief from the tatters she had been wearing.

Madame D'Aubigne gave a helpless shrug. "My dear, I'm sorry. We had to use some of the accoutrements on that dress to mend our own clothing. None of us was given much time to pack to come here, and we have limited access to our friends and relatives."

Claudette, however, was nearly teary-eyed in appreciation. "Madame D'Aubigne, in all the time I have been here, and I'm not sure how long it has been, no one has shown me the least kindness until now."

"Those in our, er, reduced positions, must take care of each other, must we not? We have some small ability here to purchase goods that we need, although our captors are quite sure to line their own pockets well in the process. When was the last time you had something to eat?"

Claudette pondered. "I don't know. I do not believe I am on a regular meal schedule, although I have been assured that I usually eat twice each day."

"Bring some of the Cantal cheese for Mademoiselle Claudette." She motioned to one of the other cell mates. "We shall also open a bottle of wine to celebrate the new addition to our living quarters. May we all survive these difficult times."

Claudette fell upon the proffered food and drink. The fragrant wedges of hard, tangy cheese, so unlike the moldy breads and watery soups she had become accustomed to, spent mere seconds in her mouth before being swallowed. She followed the cheese with great gulps of the rich red nectar from the bottle, dribbling some down the front of her borrowed dress. She was embarrassed by her display of greed, but Madame D'Aubigne, clearly the leader of this group, smiled indulgently.

"I believe you have come to us just in time, Mademoiselle Laurent."

Claudette spent the next several days getting to know her fellow captives, grateful to spend time with other human beings who did not show up simply to throw different dirty shifts into her cell, or to pass inedible food to her. She learned the basics of fine embroidery, but did not play cards, as she had no money to wager with. She also split reading duties with one of the other ladies in the cell, who was happy to be able to share that task.

Considering her previous quarters, Claudette was reasonably content, even sometimes forgetting that the threat of Madame Guillotine hung over her head. She received no further visits from Jean-Philippe.

Surely William was searching for her, but how would he ever find her here? All he could possibly know is that she had come to visit the distressed queen and he'd be no wiser as to what had really happened to her. What a fool she had been to trust Jean-Philippe! Why hadn't she simply married William and settled down to raise a brood of children, instead of obsessing about her doll shop and its clientele? Even if William had searched for her, perhaps at this point he would have given up.

Béatrice would be running the shop, which meant that it was probably close to disaster. Maybe Marguerite was helping her. Poor Béatrice. A small smile flitted briefly across Claudette's face at the thought. No point in contemplating the fate of the doll shop. She would never see it, nor William, nor Béatrice, nor anything outside these walls, ever again.

August 19, 1792. A commotion in the hallway disturbed the relative calm of the group. Abnormal shouting and pleading could be heard above the normal din of the prison. They quickly realized that more prisoners were being led toward their cell. Claudette was the first to jump up from repairing a torn undergarment in recognition of the new prisoners.

"Princesse! Madame Tourzel! Why are you here?"

The Princesse de Lamballe was wild-eyed and disheveled. At first she did not recognize Claudette, then fell into her arms weeping. Loud, convulsive sobs exploded from the delicate princesse, and she clung to Claudette ferociously. The other cell mates looked on with interest, but without surprise. Hadn't they each had the same reaction to being tossed into La Force?

The princesse related how they had come to be in this despicable prison. The Commissioners of the Commune announced that the queen's remaining attendants were to be removed for interrogation. This instruction resulted from a new order by the Commune, which set up a special tribunal to try royalists for crimes allegedly committed during the overthrow of the monarchy. The queen had tried desperately to keep the princesse with her, on the grounds that she was a relative, sensing rightly that the Temple was a safer place than a regular prison. It was a futile effort, and both the princesse and Madame de Tourzel were whisked away.

Madame de Tourzel, who was also accompanied by her daughter,

Pauline, added, "The queen urged me to look after the princesse, and I will try to do so. But I have no idea what is to happen to us or how I can help her."

The princesse focused her attention on Claudette. "But how did you come to be in this wretched place?"

"I was deceived by my childhood love."

This actually piqued the princesse's interest enough to forget her own troubles for a moment. "What do you mean?"

"Do you remember the day I was presented to Her Majesty, and the gentleman who was with me?"

"Yes, I believe I do."

Claudette explained her early betrothal to Jean-Philippe, her separation from him in the fire, and her reconnection with him years later. "I was a fool, Princesse, because I had once thought I might leave England to come back to France, make dolls here and marry Jean-Philippe. I did not know that he was being slowly indoctrinated into the madness of the Revolution. He has now somehow decided that I have committed a treasonous act involving the king and queen and tricked me into returning to France so that he could incarcerate me. It is simply preposterous. What is worst for me, though, is that I left behind in England the man who truly loves me and to whom I should be married now if I weren't such a self-centered addle pate. William could not possibly know what has happened to me, yet I continue to survive, thinking that maybe one day I will see him again. I am a fool, am I not?"

"Perhaps there is hope for us both, Mademoiselle Claudette. Perhaps one day we will both have rescuers to free us from this horrible dungeon. I pray the queen and her family do not meet our fate."

The princesse settled into the same tedious routine as Claudette and her cell mates. Cards, sewing, and reading were punctuated by a periodic delivery of special food or household goods, depending on the effectiveness of a bribe. Tedious days stretched into one another. One cell mate tried to scratch a line in the wall to mark each passing day, but either lost interest or was unable to keep track. At least one could always while away a few hours of time by sleeping.

As long as no other prisoners were screaming or moaning to disturb the sleeper, that is.

A guard, one Claudette had never seen before, came to their cell. He pointed to several of them, including Claudette, Madame D'Aubigne, the princesse, Madame Tourzel, and her daughter Pauline. They were taken to a questioning room near a side entrance of the prison. The women could hear raised voices and periodic shouting floating in from outside.

Claudette was the first to be questioned, by a short, self-important official. He had a red, white, and blue cockade in his cap, a welcome distraction from his mouth, which not only contained uneven, yellowed teeth, but whose oily smile emphasized that one of his front teeth was much shorter than the other. The longer tooth had a tendency to extend over his lower lip exaggeratedly when he spoke, giving the impression of a lisping beaver. He pulled several papers toward him.

"State your name, Citizeness."

"Claudette Renée Laurent."

"Resident of Paris?" His tooth did not permit his lips to close completely on the word "Paris," making it sound like "Fairy."

"Originally. I have lived for several years in London."

"Are you aware of the charges brought against you?"

"Yes, but I am not—"

"You are accused of treason against the new Republic of France. You have been involved in plotting to send valuables to Louis Capet and his wife so that they could flee justice. What have you to say?"

Finally, Claudette's opportunity to clear her name.

"I am innocent of these charges, monsieur. I have a doll shop in London, and apparently someone was smuggling money or other valuables, without my knowledge, into France, with shipments of doll orders to the queen—I mean, Citizeness Capet." Claudette's hands were clasped together in front of her in earnestness.

"Without your knowledge?" A raised eyebrow pointed toward the cockade.

"Yes, monsieur. I think that someone working in my shop was responsible for this."

"And who is this individual?"

"I don't know. I have hired many workers over the last year as my orders have increased."

"You are the proprietress of a shop, and have no knowledge of valuables being smuggled out of the shop, nor of which of your workers was doing so." Sarcasm dripped out of his rodent-like mouth.

"Yes, monsieur, that is so."

He began shuffling through the papers, and selected one. "I see you were brought here by Citizen Renaud. He affirms here that he witnessed your criminal actions." He held up a document with Jean-Philippe's signature boldly scrawled on it.

"But it is not true! Jean-Philippe was angry with me for not marrying him. I have committed no crime, against France or anyone else." Claudette felt someone touch her elbow, and looked back to see the princesse give her a warning look.

The inquisitor saw the princesse step forward, and lost interest in Claudette.

"You may be seated. I wish to interrogate *you*, Citizeness."

The princesse guided Claudette back to a chair at the edge of the room, then went back to face questioning. From Claudette's vantage point, it was disjointed yet vicious, the questions fired at the princesse with no logical direction.

"Your name?"

"Marie-Thérèse-Louise de Savoie Bourbon Lamballe."

"What do you know of the events which occurred on the tenth of August?"

"Nothing."

"Where did you pass that day?"

"I followed the king to the National Assembly."

"At what hour did the king go to the National Assembly?"

"Seven."

"Did he not, before he went, review the troops? Do you know the oath he made them swear?"

"I never heard of any oath."

"Have you any knowledge of cannon being mounted and pointed in the Tuileries apartments?"

"No."

"Do you know the secret doors of the Tuileries?"

"I know of no such doors."

"Have you not, since you have been in the Temple, received and written letters, which you sought to send away secretly?"

"I have never received or written any letters, excepting such as have been delivered to the municipal officer."

"Do you know anything of an article of furniture being made for Madame Elisabeth?"

"No."

"What are the books which you have at the Temple?"

"I have none."

"Do you know anything of a barred staircase?"

"No."

And so on. After listening to an hour of this questioning, Claudette was removed from the room and taken back to her cell. She was joined later by Madame D'Aubigne, Madame de Tourzel and Pauline. The princesse returned what seemed like ages later.

She had been interrogated for thirteen hours, under the malevolent gaze of her captors. At length, it was decreed that she be detained till further orders, but she was given the choice of prisons, La Force or La Salpêtrière. She immediately decided on the former. At first, it was determined that she should be separated from Madame de Tourzel, but her captors were apparently humane enough to permit the solace of that woman's company, and of her other fellow cell mates.

Time continued to drag on, although Claudette and the queen's friends found consolation in talking together about the royal family, wishing for their safety and wandering back in time to more joyful moments each had experienced as royal intimates. Day followed day, with the inmates no closer to freedom or sentencing than they had been upon incarceration.

❧ 32 ❧

September 2, 1792. "Why another interrogation?" fretted Madame de Tourzel, pacing back and forth across the hard floor, her own dress now tattered and filthy along the edges. "What do they think they will learn from the princesse that they did not know before?"

Claudette tried to comfort her. "Perhaps there is some news that exonerates her, and she is being released."

"Released! Ha! They had no evidence to put her here to start with. Why should there be anything that exonerates her from imaginary crimes?"

Her retort pierced Claudette in the stomach. Why should there be a reprieve from a trumped-up charge, indeed?

Soon Madame de Tourzel was summoned for questioning again, as well. She and Claudette clung to each other briefly before the older woman left the cell.

"Please tell the princesse to be of good cheer," she whispered to Madame de Tourzel. "And you will be brave under examination, I know." Claudette smiled encouragingly at the woman.

In a moment, Madame de Tourzel was gone, and there were only eight bedraggled prisoners left in the cell, including a highly-distraught Pauline.

Claudette and the other women waited anxiously for their cell mates' return, but for hours they heard nothing. Finally, Madame de Tourzel was brought back down, having been miraculously acquitted of all charges, but desiring to return to her new friends to report that the princesse had bravely told her interrogators, "I have nothing to reply. Dying a little earlier or a little later is a matter of indifference to me. I am prepared to make the sacrifice of my life."

However, she had been directed to the exit leading to Abbaye Prison, and Madame de Tourzel hoped that she had been spirited away there safely, and that perhaps it was a sojourn on the way to her release.

Madame de Tourzel and her daughter were soon released from the prison, and kissed each of them good-bye, promising to try to work for their release. It was a lovely gesture, but everyone knew it was impossible for them to have any influence whatsoever. The prisoners quickly returned to their mind-numbing routine of sewing, reading, and cards.

A loaf of stale bread and a cracked tureen of thin broth was brought to the cell. By employing some of the spices they had secreted away, the meal was made palatable and the cell mates fell upon it. A different guard came to collect the tureen, and lingered about the cell, grinning slyly as though he was in possession of a large secret. Wiping her mouth with the back of her hand, Claudette looked at him. "Monsieur, you seem to have something to say."

"Your friend, she isn't here anymore."

"What, do you mean Madame de Tourzel? Of course she is not here. She has been released."

"Not her, the other one."

"The princesse?"

"There's no such thing as a princesse anymore. New government says so."

Claudette sighed. "Very well. Do you mean Citizeness de Lamballe?"

"That's her."

"What of her? She was transferred to Abbaye Prison. She will be released soon."

"No, she won't."

Claudette's neck prickled. "What are you saying? Was she placed in a different prison?"

" 'Abbaye Prison' is just code."

"Code? Code for what?"

"Code for going out the other door."

"Monsieur, this is trying. What other door? Where did the princesse—Citizeness de Lamballe– go?"

The guard described with relish the princesse's fate. She was sent out into a courtyard of the prison, where a mob, notified of her impending departure, was waiting for her. They fell upon the unsuspecting woman in a frenzy, killing her and hacking her body to pieces. The last anyone had seen, the mob had put her head on one pike, her entrails on another, and some unrecognizable body part on a third. They had marched off with their trophies, singing lustily and laughing, as though out on a spirited boys' prank.

The prisoners were numb. If the Princesse de Lamballe could not be saved from such a brutal fate, what hope was there for any of them?

Claudette took the princesse's death the hardest, and remained curled up on the stone floor in the farthest corner of the cell. She swatted halfheartedly at a large cockroach that came near to inspect whether or not she was food. She wondered idly if she would be tasty enough for a cockroach. Or for one of the rats that periodically passed through the cells on its way toward the foulest stenches in the prison that indicated a recent prisoner's demise, and therefore a succulent dinner. What did it matter anyway? She was forgotten here, left to die a wretched mess. *William, William, where are you? I could endure this if I thought you were looking for me.*

A few hours later—or was it years?—she heard a familiar noise in the passageway that indicated someone was coming. She lifted her head to listen, but the effort was too much and she fell back, closing her eyes once again. She felt someone shaking her.

"Mademoiselle Claudette, you have a visitor." Madame D'Aubigne was tugging on her shift. Claudette looked up. Jean-Philippe was at the cell door. She elevated herself on one arm.

"Jean-Philippe, go away. Have you not tortured me enough?"

"Citizeness Laurent, you will rise and come forward."

"Leave me be."

"You will come forward to hear what I have to say."

Madame D'Aubigne was still standing next to her, and placed an arm under Claudette's waist to lift her up, whispering in her ear, "Mademoiselle, please, it will be better for all of us here if you obey him."

Claudette moved to the front of the cell, hardly caring what Jean-Philippe had to say. She looked at him blankly. "What is it?"

He unfolded an official looking document. Claudette could see a signature and a seal on it. He cleared his throat.

"Citizeness Laurent, for crimes against the nation of France, including espionage and treason, you are hereby sentenced to death by beheading under the guillotine, to be conducted at the Place du Carrousel tomorrow morning at eleven o'clock." He folded the paper again. "Consider yourself fortunate. You will have the luxury of traveling alone in a tumbrel. Most prisoners are loaded in groups onto carts. For reasons of efficiency. You will be attended to this evening to have your hair shorn in preparation." He turned on his heel and departed the way he came, the tapping of his heels receding in the distance.

Claudette turned to face the others in her cell. Without exception, they all looked at her in horror and disbelief. Madame D'Aubigne, still standing where Claudette had been curled up on the floor, rushed forward to take Claudette in her arms.

"Dear child, how could this be happening? You are too young for this dreadfulness that has been inflicted on the rest of us. Please believe we are in grief for you."

Claudette buried her face in the woman's shoulder, but no tears would come. She was empty and devoid of feeling, save one thought: *William, darling, I love you. I wish I could tell you one more time. I wish I was to die your wife.*

A female prison worker she had never seen before showed up later to see Claudette. She entered the cell, unceremoniously twisted Claudette's long and once luxuriously curly hair up in the air, and hacked at it with a knife until the bundle fell loose in her hand. The woman, who had not bothered to introduce herself, tossed Claudette a mobcap, instructing her to put it on when the guards came for her in the morning. She also placed a small clock on the cell's lone table, ordinarily a precious treat, but now just a mocking reminder of what was to come. Claudette stared at the cotton cap, her hand trembling violently. She looked up to see the woman walking up the corridor, Claudette's tresses dangling from her hand. Claudette momentarily thought of how many doll wigs she could make with that much hair, then shook her head to clear her mind of such a trivial reminder of her old life. There was nothing before her now but death.

❧ 33 ❧

The Temple, September 1792. The Temple's medieval structure was bleak and forbidding, and now served as a virtual prison for the royal family. Held under "protection" now were the king, Marie Antoinette, the king's sister Madame Elisabeth, the Dauphin Louis Charles, and his sister, Princesse Marie-Thérèse. They were little more than a band of criminals held at the nation's pleasure.

However, their daily routine, if one forgot about the circumstances under which they were being held, was unremarkable in its domesticity. The royal couple began to fulfill the roles of mother-nurse and father-teacher to the utmost. Breakfast was eaten at nine o'clock. Afterward, Louis gave Louis Charles his school lessons, while Marie Antoinette taught her daughter. Madame Elisabeth took responsibility for teaching both children mathematics. Afterward they took some exercise as a family in the garden. Their rooms were usually searched while they were outside.

Dinner was at two o'clock, and games or cards would follow. Louis typically fell into a deep slumber during the late afternoon, snoring loudly while the women watched. Prior to bedtime and prayers, which the queen conducted with the children, there might be more lessons and play for Louis Charles, or the king might read aloud to the family. After supper was more reading or quiet time, then they went to bed around eleven o'clock.

The only interruption to the daily domestic scene occurred at about seven o'clock each evening, when criers would appear outside the Temple to relay the latest news. Otherwise, each day was much the same as another for the royal family. In an ironic way, the queen had achieved her wish to lead a simple, unfettered life, as she had attempted to do at her Hameau.

On September 2, their lives were disrupted again, this time in a horrifying way for the queen personally.

The king and queen were playing backgammon in an upstairs room when shouts could be heard from outside. Recognizing the noise as the approach of some rabble, a couple of the few servants they had had assigned to them peered out a window to see what the trouble was. With an inward gasp, one attendant slammed and shuttered all of the windows and ran from the room, calling for assistance.

The king looked up, unconcerned. "Another demonstration for man's rights again?" he asked.

Now they heard the sound of frenzied laughter coming from beneath one of their windows. The king summoned one of the officers on duty, asking what the commotion was.

"If you must know, monsieur, they are trying to show you the head of Madame de Lamballe." Other members of the household rushed in to confirm this.

Marie Antoinette stood up from the game table, staring at the closed window, unblinking. For several moments she stood there, frozen with horror, and even the least sympathetic of the royal jailers was struck numb with the vileness of the act.

Without uttering a word, the queen fainted away, crumpling to the floor. She did not respond at first to repeated taps on her hands and feet, or the sound of her name being called. Her daughter stayed huddled over her, offering pale words of comfort, and refused to let anyone else near.

But there was still more to be borne. The mob started piling up pieces of rubble from around the Temple's environs, and were building a small mound on which to climb with their precious trophies. The occupants of the Temple heard a tapping on one of the windows.

"Hey, Antoinette, come and see your friend! Kiss, kiss, we will not leave until you give her a kiss, kiss." Uproarious laughter followed. From inside the room, it sounded as though the rabble might be able to break in.

"If you do not give her a kiss, perhaps we will add your head to hers, eh? Come out and see what happens to those who deny the will of the people, you Austrian bitch!" More taunts and mockery followed.

"Savages," muttered Commissioner Daujon, who was in charge of the Temple and had entered the room to investigate the tumult. He disliked the king and queen as much as any good French citizen, but this was too much even for him.

He strode down to the Temple's entrance, and had it blocked. He told the jeering crowd outside, "The head of Antoinette does not belong to you." Instead, he said, they could march around the Temple grounds with their distasteful pikes, which they did gleefully until about five o'clock the following morning, when their stores of righteous anger and wine were depleted.

The queen never saw the grisly trophies. She was finally roused and put gently to bed. She went without protest, crying out only once from her room to have her Josephina doll brought to her. From outside the queen's chamber, the remaining household could hear her, alternating between piteous sobbing and rational conversation with the doll as though it were actually her late friend.

Two days later it was reported to the king privately that the Duc de Penthièvre, the princesse's old father-in-law, had managed to have her head and body buried together in his family plot.

Louis responded, "It was her conduct in the course of our misfortunes that amply justifies the queen's choice of the late princesse as a true and dedicated friend, both to her personally and to our entire wretched circle."

❧ 34 ❧

La Force Prison, September 3, 1792. By dawn, Claudette was resolute about her execution. She would go silently and without protest. *Mama, Papa,* she prayed. *I will be with you soon. Please don't be disappointed in me.*

With all condolences exhausted, her cell group sat silently, watching the inexorable movement of the clock's hands. Six o'clock. Only five hours to live, perhaps a few minutes longer, depending on travel time in a cart to the execution spot. *Will anyone attend my execution?* Much worse than dying would be dying without a soul around who was interested in your death.

Does the blade hurt? When the English Queen Anne Boleyn learned that she was to be beheaded by an expert French swordsman, she reportedly laughed delightedly at her good fate in avoiding the clumsy ax, saying, "I heard say the executioner was very good, and I have a little neck."

Claudette had not heard of the guillotine ever failing in its job and only partially severing a head, so if she could be brave until she got to the platform, all would go quickly and painlessly.

Promptly at eleven o'clock by the clock's reckoning, she heard several sets of footsteps approaching the cell. Claudette remained motionless on her cot. Three men in uniform she had not seen before unlocked the chamber. She laughed mirthlessly. "Does it require so many of you to remove my head this morning?"

Madame D'Aubigne gasped audibly. The men were momentarily nonplussed, but the shortest of the three, who was apparently their leader, stated in an imperious voice, "Citizeness Laurent, you are to be removed immediately to the Place de Carrousel for your execution."

She saw now that one of the other men had two pieces of rope in his hand. He bound her hands together behind her, while Madame D'Aubigne tut-tutted in outrage. He saw that Claudette was staring at the remaining piece of rope in his hand and said, "It's for later. For your feet. So you don't fall off the board."

Claudette breathed deeply and banished the thought of being tied to a board and slid under the blade. It would be over soon enough anyway.

She didn't look back at her cell mates as she was escorted out and through the prison's dank hallways, for fear of losing her calm resolve. They reached a side entrance and the door was thrown wide open. Claudette was temporarily blinded by the brilliant, warm sunshine. She stood still, blinking rapidly for several moments to become accustomed to the light. It must have been a common occurrence, for the men indulged her this preciously brief time to take in her surroundings.

From the doorway she was led to a tumbrel, a small wooden conveyance big enough for just a single passenger to sit on its rough bench. It rode low to the ground, such that the occupant was at the same height as anyone walking past. It had clunky wooden wheels and looked altogether uncomfortable for one's last moments. The cart was connected in front to a small floorboard, on which a driver stood holding the reins to a horse. This particular horse had probably seen better days, but why would a quality animal be used to haul around the doomed? The driver's back was already to her, but she could see lanky, greasy hair trailing out from under his head covering, the ubiquitous tricolor cockade pinned to it. She wondered if she could convince him to collect her body and send it back to England, but realized she had nothing with which to bribe him, and bribes were what improved any prisoner's lot.

The man who had bound Claudette tossed the second piece of rope to the driver, with an instruction to give it to whomever was waiting at the steps of the platform when they arrived. The driver snapped back that he was not an *imbécile,* and knew perfectly well how to conduct his business.

Claudette was seated in the tumbrel facing the rear, an additional insult to the condemned. With a huge lurch, her final journey started. The wheels rotated slowly and made a deafening noise as they pounded on the cobblestones. As they turned onto the Rue Pavée, several young boys noticed her and ran up to the cart, following its slow progress. They recognized the mobcap covering shorn hair and her bound hands as sure signs that an execution was about to take place.

"Are you a murderess? Did you do in your husband?" they asked. She remained silent, resolutely fixing her gaze into space. Other citizens took note as well and began following the cart. A public execution was always much more interesting than working or household chores. It made no difference what the crime was; one execution was as good as another and made for great street entertainment.

The throng around the cart began growing. Claudette felt a sharp stinging on the side of her face. Wiping her cheek on her shoulder, she saw a red smear left behind. A small stone lay at her feet. Almost immediately another projectile slammed into the side of the cart. It reeked of horse dung. The swelling crowd, full of bodies that smelled as unwashed as her own, began impeding the already torturously slow movement of the cart.

Now the crowd began jeering at her, hurling insults and spitting at her. Their great desire was to anger her and provoke a heated response, which only increased the excitement of the occasion. She inadvertently cried out as a rotten piece of fruit hit her in the chest, momentarily taking her breath away. The crowd cheered, whether from her cry or the accuracy of the hit, Claudette was not sure. To her great surprise, the cart driver shouted at the thrower, and, cracking his whip loudly, began moving quickly through traffic. Claudette became alarmed as the cart started bouncing off the uneven stones. She was bound and had no means for keeping herself from being thrown onto the street and into the hands of the mob. Was she to meet the princesse's fate?

The cart's followers kept up with its increased pace, determined to witness the spectacular event. She saw people pointing and shouting gleefully about something in front of them. Looking back over her shoulder, she could see what was stirring them. They were hurtling toward the Place du Carrousel, and Claudette could see the giant guillotine looming on the platform, which was raised roughly six feet off the ground. She didn't think her legs would be able to carry her so far up the steps. Atop the platform stood various men milling about. It was difficult to tell if a condemned man or woman was on the platform as well. In any case, the guillotine, a much larger contraption than she had imagined, consumed Claudette's attention. The blade was pulled all the way to the top, poised and waiting for its next victim. On the platform beneath the blade was the grooved neck piece where in moments she would be placing her head, after her bound body was tied to a board and positioned properly under the chopping mechanism. A basket awaited her head on the other side of the neck piece. Panic bubbled into her throat, resulting in a small cry of anguish.

The driver suddenly veered the tumbrel to the left, down a side street, just before reaching the execution area. Claudette pitched forward to the floor of the cart, grateful that she had not tumbled out of it. The driver was reckless, yelling at pedestrians, conveyances, and street sellers who impeded his progress for even a moment. The mob had dispersed when the cart had changed course, since it was now easier to wait at the guillotine to see if another hapless prisoner might be coming along, rather than try to see where this one, lone criminal was being taken.

Claudette remained crouched at the bottom of the cart, unable to get up without her hands for balance. She could feel the cart swerving into various streets and alleyways, and soon she could look up and tell that they were leaving the center of the city, as trees replaced city buildings in her line of sight. Was the driver insane? Did he intend to do worse to her than the guillotine?

They slowed down after about a half hour of swift progress, and even from her disadvantaged position Claudette could hear the bedraggled horse protesting the hard ride with snorts and snuffles. At this reduced pace she was able to struggle her way back up on the bench. The sun's position told her they were heading west down what appeared to be a small village lane. The horse was guided into the drive of an abandoned cottage. Now what was to happen to her? *Please, God, help me,* she breathed.

She braced herself as she heard the driver dismount from the floorboard and smack the horse on the rump with a word of praise. She knew she was powerless, constrained as she was by the rope digging into her wrists. Her arms ached from their awkward positioning behind her back. She shut her eyes. She felt the mobcap snatched from her head and flinched, expecting a blow.

Instead, the man cupped what remained of her hacked hair in his hands. "Look at me," he demanded.

Instead, summoning what energy she had remaining, Claudette shot up from the seat, ramming her head into the man's chin and sending him sprawling backward onto the ground. She kept up her forward motion, jumping off the tumbrel and running down the lane away from the cottage. Her bound hands made her gait clumsy and stilted. She was only fifty yards past the cottage and already gasping for breath when she heard her captor, recovering his wits, roar in anger and come after her. In moments he was behind her and grabbing her around the waist.

"Claudette!" the man commanded, spinning her around.

She stared at him, uncomprehending. His hat and greasy, dark, matted hair were both askew on his head, and he looked more ghastly than she did. Was he an escapee from La Force?

"You don't know me." His voice was flat. Claudette stood frozen, staring into the stranger's eyes. There was a familiar glint in them.

"William?" she asked tremulously. "Can it be? How did you find me?"

He swept off his hat and bowed. His false hair was messily glued inside the cap, and now his blond hair framed his face, making her realize that it truly was William.

Tossing both of the now unneeded caps aside, he gently untied the ropes from behind her back, and rubbed her arms to bring circulation back to them. Seeing color return to her arms and face, he picked her up in his arms, astonished at her emaciated state, and carried her to the cottage, kicking open the loosely jointed door. He set her gently on a stuffed mattress next to a fireplace that had probably not seen a flame in ten years or more. After she assured him that she was not particularly ill or injured beyond a serious case of heartache, hunger, and fright, he gave her a swift kiss and promised to return shortly. True to his word, he was back within an hour with kindling, firewood, and some food he had purchased from a nearby farmer.

While he started the fire, Claudette pounced on the crate of food, exclaiming over each item. "Eggs! I have not seen a fresh egg since I have been in prison. I should like to kiss the chicken that produced it. Oh, William, is this actually fresh bread? It must have cost a fortune."

"The farmer took the horse and cart in payment. He seemed quite happy with the trade." William also produced a sack of cast-off clothing he was able to purchase from the man. Claudette found a serviceable dress in the sack and discarded her prison garb into the flames, where it joined her cotton cap and William's makeshift wig and hat.

With the fire crackling comfortably, the pair hurriedly prepared a meal from the ingredients he had purchased, and washed it down with a small bottle of wine the farmer had sold him at twice its value. They sat together contentedly on the mattress, talking as it grew dark outside.

William told her of seeing her name on the La Force imprisonment list in Marat's newspaper and his subsequent rush to France. Once in Paris, he had continually observed the prison to figure out a way to get in. After discovering that she was to be imminently executed, he knew he had to act without delay.

"But how did you ever take possession of the tumbrel?"

"I made friends with one of the guards in La Force, someone originally from Suffolk who married a French lass and is now making his home here. I convinced him to help me."

"Convinced him? I never met a single worker in La Force who could be reasoned with!"

"Every man has his motivator. In Mr. Roger Wickham's case, he had launched a dairy business and failed, and now needed the financial resources to move him and his wife Simone back to England. I provided him with a tidy sum for what amounted to just a few minutes of work on his part, which was to make sure I was the driver of your cart."

In her turn, Claudette told him that she must have been sent a fabricated letter from the queen, that in actuality she had been made a prisoner upon boarding the ship in England. With some difficulty, she told him about her childhood betrothal with Jean-Philippe, her time spent with him during her first visit to the queen, and his subsequent treachery on this voyage. She omitted details of Jean-Philippe's attempted abuse of her, despising the memory and knowing William would immediately seek to avenge her honor.

William grew very quiet after this. Resting next to a blazing fire with her stomach full of her first true meal in nearly two months, she fell into a dreamless sleep.

Bright sunshine woke her in the morning. William was already putting the cottage back as they had found it. He silently offered her what remained of the food, then showed her a well in back of the cottage, where she was able to draw water to bathe herself of all the grime and stench of La Force.

Back inside the cottage, William had completely tamped out the fire. He sat her down on one of the two rickety chairs that comprised the sum total of furniture in the dwelling. He looked at her seriously.

"Do you still love him?" he asked without preamble.

"No." She returned his gaze just as steadily. "I thought I did when I was a child, and I was a little confused about it when I saw him during my trip to see the queen, but I knew even before I left there that my life belonged with you. What I was not sure of was whether or not I could become a proper Englishwoman for you."

"A proper Englishwoman? You?" William laughed. "I will not hear of it. You are like no woman I have ever met in England. I admire your courage and pluck. I still remember how angry you got at me at the Ashbys' when you assumed I didn't think you could read."

Claudette laughed at the memory, as well, but it reminded her of more serious issues. "But this is what I mean. I am like no high-born Englishwoman. I am in a trade. I am a foreigner. Until I met

The Baccelli at Knole, I did not think I could truly move into your social set. Giovanna helped me to see that maybe I could."

"Indeed, The Baccelli is unconventional as well as a good friend. She should have an honored place at our wedding."

Claudette looked at him in surprise. "Do you still mean to marry me? After all that has happened? And my pitiful state?"

"I am enchanted by your pitiful state, and more determined than ever that this never happen again to Mistress Greycliffe. But for now, we need to find our way back to England. By now there will be search parties looking for us, and at some point the farmer I visited will hear of a female escapee and her driver and probably be able to put together that I was that driver, given that I sold him a horse and cart belonging to La Force."

In her painfully thin condition, Claudette could pass for a young boy. They found trousers and a loose shirt for her to wear, and covered her butchered hair with a farmer's cap. If anyone questioned them, they would say they were brothers heading to a nearby market to buy some sheep on behalf of their father. They headed toward the sun, always keeping to narrow paths and slipping into the forest when possible to avoid all contact with other people. At the end of the first day of walking, Claudette remembered her old friend Jacques, who said he was joining relatives in the town of Versailles after the fire. Upon her suggestion, they shifted direction slightly to head there for rest, more food, and assistance in getting passage back to England.

❧ 35 ❧

Paris, September 21, 1792. The daily criers were still the royal family's only source of news, other than occasionally smuggled messages, but most materials for note writing had been taken from them, and even such essentials as sewing scissors and shaving soap had been removed from their rooms. In contrast, they were still served elegant meals on silver salvers, and given fine wines to drink, of which only the king partook.

On September 21, the criers announced something incredible in a year full of inconceivable events. Not only was the king deposed, but the monarchy itself was hereby abolished. To give further weight to this declaration, the calendar was officially overhauled, making September 22 the first day of the year, and the names of the months were reconfigured to be named after seasons and nature, such as "Fructidor" (fruit) and "Thermidor" (heat). The new year of the French Republic began with the month of "Vendémiaire," meaning vintage.

This new year resulted in fresh attacks and dissent among the various factions in the Assembly. Robespierre began gaining prominence as the head of the Mountain, a new group that had taken over the Jacobin Club, and so named because they sat on the highest benches in the Assembly. They wanted a strong central government based on the Parisian point of view, and their central leaders were Robespierre, Danton, Saint-Just, and the followers of

Marat and Hébert, who were known as *enragés*, or maniacs. The Mountain concluded that the republic could not move forward unless the previous monarch was eliminated, for good.

Thundering from inside the Assembly, Saint-Just stated that "Louis cannot be judged, he is already judged. He is condemned, for if he is not, the sovereignty of the Republic is not absolute."

Robespierre added convincingly that Louis had already condemned himself, not for what he had done, but for what he was.

The Assembly did not require convincing. A trial would be held for Louis XVI.

❧ 36 ❧

Kent, October 1792. Claudette and William were married on the sweeping lawns of Hevington on a perfect autumn day, attended only by the local rector, William's parents, Béatrice, Marguerite, Jolie, the doll shop workers, and the Earl of Pembroke and his highly-prized mistress. Giovanna had insisted upon providing Claudette's wedding gown, a flowing concoction of pink silk dupion with ivory-laced sleeve flounces trimmed in pearls. A matching veil fluttered down the length of the dress. Giovanna had helped her dress inside the country house and exclaimed, "Sweet signorina, you have done it! You have achieved the matrimonial state. Ah." Her eyes rolled back. "Now if only you would have some children to play with my John Frederick."

The teenage Marguerite found much to entertain her at Hevington in the form of one of William's young grooms. While he was preparing the horses and carriage for the newlywed couple's honeymoon trip, Marguerite, who was completely uninterested in horsemanship, was apparently enthralled by every word he had to say on the subject. She reappeared in the wedding party only when cake and punch were to be served.

The gift table, laden with presents from well-wishers, was dominated by a crate so large it had to be placed on the floor next to it. Inside, the couple found a spectacular wax replica of Claudette sculpting a doll, an unexpectedly generous gift from Marie Grosholtz.

Marie had also managed to get a secret message to the queen regarding the nuptials, so even Marie Antoinette had sent a letter of congratulations, though the letter was tinged with her regrets that Claudette suffered because of her association with the queen. Accompanying the letter was a scented lace handkerchief, a fleur-de-lis design embroidered around the edges in gold thread, the best gift the queen could provide under her reduced circumstances. Claudette later told William it was her most treasured wedding gift.

While William spent time with the earl and Giovanna, Claudette used the opportunity to talk with Béatrice. Her friend's red-rimmed eyes spoke of her deep happiness intermingled with heartbreak over Claudette's marriage, which would necessitate her move from their town house.

Claudette kissed Béatrice's cheek. "All will be well, my dearest friend. Here, I have a wedding gift for you. Take it."

"A wedding gift for *me?*" Béatrice took the proffered document, which was folded and sealed. Opening it, she found it to be a legal document, granting her the lease of the town house for £1 per annum for the remainder of her life.

Béatrice's puffy eyes flowed accordingly. Amid protestations and snuffles of thanks, she declared her devotion to her "friend unto death."

After a round of good wishes, lengthy good-byes, and admonitions to produce many Greycliffe children, the couple was escorted to their carriage. More tearful declarations of affection, accompanied by frantic waving, escorted them down the long drive of the home.

William and Claudette spent time traveling along the coast of Cornwall, enjoying the exhilarating spray of water along its rocky shoreline, savoring each other's company, and relishing Claudette's newly found freedom.

She had regained her figure and some of her hair's length and fullness following her flight from prison. She never again spoke of Jean-Philippe and his mistreatment of her at La Force, and William did not press for details.

After two weeks together in Cornwall, William wanted to return to Hevington for an extended honeymoon, but Claudette insisted that they go back to London. They returned to check on the shop, Claudette assuring herself that things were being well run. The newlywed couple then purchased a spacious, comfortable town home in Vauxhall Lane and sold William's other London residence, which had been intended for Lenora's convalescence. They spent much of their time in supervising renovations to their new home: replacing wallpaper, hanging new drapes, reconstructing fireplaces in the popular Georgian style, and making general repairs.

Claudette went to the doll shop periodically to oversee operations and to encourage Béatrice to be more assertive in her handling of the shop. At the same time, Marguerite's skill as a carver and designer was increasing with astonishing speed.

One early morning, Claudette opened the shop to find a note under the door.

> *Mistress Greycliffe,*
> *Im verry sorry about what I did to you to make you be in gaol in Perris. i dint mean to get you in trubble, but lord Fershun set me and me mam up in nice lodgings just to make secret compartmints in the dolls going to the queen in france. He then sent me pakages to stuff in the dolls, but I dint see whot were in them. He swore it werent nuthin, and that it was just a joke he were playing on you and the queen. I culdn't see no harm in it. He even gave me two shillings extra-like for each doll i fixxed up for him.*
> *Mam dyed of the flux last week, so I dunt need them big lodgings anymore, and plus he quit sending money once you got over to Perris and then i hurd you was in gaol.*
> *Mistress, I hope you fergive me for my sins, and I won't be any more trubble to you and yours.*
> *Signed from yer servent,*
> *Joseph Cummings*

Claudette sighed. So that was how it happened. Whatever Count Fersen had been sending to the queen had been discovered by Jean-Philippe and was deemed a threat to the new government.

And Jean-Philippe would have recognized the dolls as being from her shop, particularly with their special insignias engraved on them.

Poor Joseph, he didn't need to run away; he was just a child caught up in a dangerous game. As soon as someone else arrived at the shop to take care of customers, she would go out and look for the boy and offer him back his job as her apprentice.

Roger Hatfield arrived at the shop, breathless, a few minutes later. "Miss Claudette, er, I mean, Mrs. Greycliffe . . . is it Lady Greycliffe?" He scratched his curly-haired head.

Claudette smiled. "Roger, let's just keep it Miss Claudette between us, shall we? What's your news?"

"Bad news, I'm afraid. Remember little Joseph Cummings? He was just found washed up under Battersea Bridge. Looks like he took his own life. His mother died last week. Must have sent him off his head. Poor mite. Good little worker, too."

No, Claudette thought. *Not another life sacrificed to the insatiable beast of the Revolution.* She closed her mind to the thought of the young boy afloat in the murky Thames River. "Does he have any family left in the area? If so, we need to help them. And we need to give him a proper burial, too."

Under Claudette's guidance, Béatrice was eventually able to handle the store properly on her own, although she frequently called on her daughter for assistance. Marguerite now spent many hours helping her mother with the administration side of the business, but the young woman enjoyed dollmaking best. Béatrice's only child had long ago lost any French accent she had had, and with her pert nose and auburn hair arranged fashionably around her face, she looked like any young woman descended from good English stock. When she was comfortable with some of the more mundane management tasks, Claudette easily convinced Béatrice that her teenage daughter should be brought to the front of the store to interact with customers. Her winsome smile only added to her charming exchanges with patrons.

Marguerite's engaging personality meant that she heard gossip, most of it tales of the House of Hanover—King George's episodes of madness, the prince's extravagant spending on his foppish friends and mistresses, and Queen Charlotte's stifling management of her daughters. But occasionally the gossip had to do with other dollmakers. Some customers would drop hints about other shops as a way to try to elicit discounts.

One woman alluded to better deals to be found elsewhere. "I'm sure I could get this much less expensively at Dunstan and Hegman's shop. They've gotten into trouble with creditors and now all of their merchandise is at discount."

Claudette responded with a firm "We do not price our goods based on the misfortunes of others, madam," and ushered her out of the shop.

Other regular patrons were genuinely fascinated by the French dollmaker, and if they dropped information, it was because they had seen another doll or puppet shop elsewhere, and wanted to be sure to let the proprietress of C. Laurent Fashion Dolls know of the competition.

One dollmaking rival, the infamous Pierotti family who had once tried to rob her, did give Claudette some concern. Mr. Henry Pierotti had inherited the business from his father, Domenico, who had brought his family and doll business to London from Northern Italy in 1770. She heard from other customers that this family was also making wax dolls that were of such high quality that they felt like they had real skin. Had the sack of parts she had sent back to them actually been enough for them to not only copy, but improve upon? From beneath a wide country hat that concealed her face, Claudette surreptitiously visited the shop without mentioning it to Béatrice. She surveyed the dolls, which were indeed realistic to the touch. However, the dark beeswax being used made the dolls look stained and streaky. Satisfied that her own techniques were superior, and in any case her clothing was far more exquisite, Claudette returned to her own shop, relieved, but knowing she would have to constantly stay alert for new techniques and fashions in dolls.

❧ 37 ❧

Paris, December 1792. The King of France, now just simply Louis Capet, citizen of France, was brought before the Convention on December 11 to be tried. The National Convention was comprised of the Constitutional and Legislative assemblies and now held executive power in France.

For three hours, Louis sat bravely and answered his accusers' questions without flinching. His only emotional response was to the accusation that he had caused the blood of Frenchmen to be spilled.

"No, sir!" he cried. "I have never shed the blood of Frenchmen." He was led away, tears coursing down his face.

The king's defense was presented on December 26. Few attorneys were willing to serve the disgraced sovereign, but, at last, a seventy-year-old retired attorney named Malesherbes, and a young lawyer named de Sèze, stepped forward courageously. They were given only ten days to examine the documents from the iron chest, which Robespierre had intentionally jumbled into total disarray before handing them over, to ensure the lawyers would have a very difficult time mounting a defense. Ultimately, their defense was pinned on the hope that the Convention could not try the king at all, since it was not a recognized judicial body.

Their strategy failed, since the Mountain had predetermined to offer the king as a sacrifice to the Revolution. The king's fate was debated for twenty-four days. Those who had assumed the king would be deported were to be appalled by his sentence. An overwhelming majority found Louis Capet guilty. By a hairsbreadth vote, he was condemned to die.

Louis received the news calmly on January 20, 1793. He asked for three days to prepare himself, but was refused this courtesy. He was allowed a visit from an Irish priest, the Abbé Edgeworth, and also permitted a visit with his family. He talked frankly with his wife, whom he had grown to cherish in their shared troubles, despite her transferred affections, which he was aware of but chose to ignore.

"It was inevitable, madame. They are determined to eradicate any vestiges of a king in this country. And what more of a reminder than the king himself?"

It was no use reminding Louis what might have been done by a less stubborn, more decisive king. Besides, in her own way, Marie Antoinette had grown very fond of her husband as well while in captivity.

"Your family will be bereft without you. This is the worst thing that could happen, to us and to France. Oh, why must we be so cursed?" Abandoning all display of royalty, she threw herself into her husband's arms.

Louis patted her awkwardly as both of their children looked on. "There, there, madame, courage! We are sons and daughters of the royal houses of Bourbon and Hapsburg. You must be both father and mother now, and make sure that the Dauphin successfully makes it back to the throne someday. He must make the Bourbon dynasty great again, to undo what I have wrought."

She looked up at him through teary eyes. Throughout her marriage, she had learned many things about Louis XVI: his shyness, his abnormal fascination with mechanical things, his irrational obstinacy, and his general slow-wittedness. But this was something new, this calm in the face of death. Dare she say she had never seen her husband so brave?

"Dear husband, I am sorry for anything that has ever been wrong between us." She put her face to his expansive chest.

"I know. Think nothing of it. You have always been an elegant queen, more than I could have asked for. I have never been displeased with anything you have done, nor with any of your choices of friends."

The children were becoming distraught watching the unusually tender interchange between their parents. Young Louis Charles burst into tears, with the princesse royale close on his heels. Marie Antoinette wiped her face with her hands, no longer having dainty, lace-edged linens to use, and addressed them both.

"Children, we have a great hardship to endure. Your papa is to be taken away from us permanently. But he will come back to say good-bye once more in the morning, will you not, monsieur?" She looked at Louis, using the name of respect for him that she had throughout her marriage.

"Yes, yes, of course I will return tomorrow morning." He signaled to the guard that he was ready to leave and turned to the queen one more time.

"Remember to do everything you can to protect our children and to return Louis Charles to the throne one day. Hopefully they will have accomplished all they want by taking me. They will not hurt you, you are just the queen. You must be valiant and endure." He stepped over to the dressing table and picked something out of the heap of writing papers, clothing, and books strewn upon it.

"Here. Remember this? The little *poupée* of your cherished friend, the Princesse de Lamballe? You must hold her to you like you did that dreadful night. It was a source of comfort to you, wasn't it?"

Marie Antoinette nodded dumbly. It was, but how was it that she needed that comfort again so soon?

"Sleep well, madame, and I will return in the morning."

But Louis did not return in the morning. He declined a final visit to his family to spare them yet another parting. Instead, he had eaten a hearty dinner the previous evening, spent time in prayer, slept well with a clean conscience, and in the early hours of January 21, prepared himself as though planning to hold an audience with his advisors.

He was escorted to the scaffold, where he calmly attempted a speech before a stilled crowd. "My people, I die innocent . . ." he began, but at a prearranged signal a group of drummers sprang to life and drowned him out in their thunder. Moments later, the former king's head was held up with the cry, "The king is dead; long live the Republic!"

The queen heard the cheers from inside her rooms in the Temple. What did this really mean for the rest of the royal family?

London, January 1793. Claudette and William pored over the newspaper articles announcing the king's death and all of the details associated with it. She gripped his hand tightly as he read from the latest account of the execution. Always rivals with the French anyway, English newspapers were unanimously outraged at France's actions against its sovereign.

London Times
January 25, 1793

The REPUBLICAN TYRANTS OF FRANCE have now carried their bloody purposes to the uttermost diabolical stretch of savage cruelty. They have murdered their King without even the shadow of justice, and of course they cannot expect friendship nor intercourse with any civilized part of the world. The vengeance of Europe will now rapidly fall on them; and, in process of time, make them the veriest wretches on the face of the earth. The name of Frenchman will be considered as the appellation of savage, and their presence shunned as a poison, deadly destructive to the peace and happiness of Mankind. It appears evident that the majority of the National Convention, and the Executive

Government of that truly despotic country,
are comprised of the most execrable vil-
lains upon the face of the earth.

William shook his head as he finished the article. "At the bottom of the page is a statement from King George condemning the
murder of a reigning monarch. The French have no more regard
for their sovereign than they do putting down a lame horse. But
what will they do now? They have no real plan for a system of government. They're just a bunch of vultures trying to pick each
other off. There is no rule of law, citizens are beheaded indiscrim-
inately for trifles. It is plain anarchy."

"But the queen, William, the poor queen. What will happen to
her? Do you think she still stands a chance of being exiled?"

"I don't know. The revolutionaries' thirst for blood may not be
slaked so easily. They seem to have a taste for it, as you well know."

Claudette was unsettled for weeks, wishing there were some
way she could comfort the queen of France. But that dear lady was
swept into events beyond anyone's control. Claudette resolved not
to look at any more newspapers and would not even let William
read to her from them. Yet still she spent her days in troubled thought.

"Aunt Claudette, we are completely out of gesso. Wasn't more
ordered?" Marguerite's eyes reflected her concern. At Claudette's
insistence, the doll workroom was always fully stocked with supplies to prevent delayed deliveries.

"Hmm?" Claudette had pulled Joseph Cummings's letter out of
a drawer where she had locked it up after initially reading it. She
was lost in contemplation about the poor boy's senseless death. Just
last week his headstone had been erected at St. George the Martyr's: JOSEPH CUMMINGS, 1780–1792, BELOVED SON AND APPRENTICE.
Claudette purchased very expensive pink marble for the stone,
and oversaw its placement herself. She thought to herself that
death was really a very exhausting business.

"Claudette, did you hear me? Last month we ran out of wax and
now there is no gesso. Is Roger not ordering supplies?"

Claudette forced herself back to the present. "What? Oh, Marguerite. No, your mother took over ordering from Roger. She felt it was something she had a better aptitude for."

"Where is Mama?"

"I don't know. I have not seen her yet this morning. Did she leave your lodgings ahead of you?"

"I thought she had, but I did not check. Since we took over your flat as well, we keep our own separate spaces for privacy."

Leaving the shop in Roger's capable hands, Claudette and Marguerite walked rapidly to the lodging house still run by Mrs. Jenkins. All was quiet in Béatrice's side of the flat. They peeked into her bedchamber, and saw her moving restlessly under the blankets. Marguerite rushed to her side.

"Mama, what's wrong? Are you ill?"

Claudette approached the bed and could see that Béatrice was ill, indeed. Her face was in high color and she was shivering violently beneath the blanket.

Béatrice smiled up weakly at her daughter. "It's nothing, darling. I'm just a bit tired."

"Tired? Mama! You're burning up with fever!"

Marguerite turned wild eyes to Claudette. "Did you know about this?"

"Certainly not. Your mother has never complained of anything to me."

"Ohhhh," Béatrice moaned in pain, rolling to one side.

"Mama, what is it?"

"Just a little pain in my side. It only hurts when I breathe deeply. I am sure it's just a little tightening of my muscles." Béatrice's teeth began to chatter.

Claudette ran down a flight of steps. "Mrs. Jenkins! Please, we need a doctor right away. Mrs. du Georges is very ill."

A physician appeared shortly, with Mrs. Jenkins on his heels. While the doctor examined Béatrice, Mrs. Jenkins fussed over her, fluffing pillows and giving her sips of water. The doctor came out of the bedchamber after an hour, shaking his head gravely, and delivered the bad news: an advanced state of pleurisy. He recommended a bleeding, as large a one as the patient could tolerate.

After that, she should be made to rest and to drink warmed barley-water with a little honey or jelly of currants mixed with it. This was done with expediency, but with no improvement in her condition. In fact, she seemed weaker.

Claudette hired a watcher to sit with Béatrice during the day while she was at the shop, then she and Marguerite took turns at the bedside each night. Claudette caught the woman pilfering through Béatrice's belongings and fired her on the spot. Another watcher she employed showed up dead drunk most mornings. Mrs. Jenkins volunteered to sit with Béatrice after that, and did so sacrificially, becoming pale and wan herself as the days dragged on and she disregarded her own basic needs to serve her patient.

William had his own family physician visit Béatrice, but the verdict was worse: no chance for recovery. Béatrice began quickly slipping away, sleeping most hours of the day and waking because of thirst. One evening she sat up in bed, more alert and responsive than on any other day since they had found her. She called Claudette and Marguerite to her side.

"Dearest Claudette, you have been such a friend to me these past years. After Alexandre died, I did not think I could survive, but you have been my savior." She clutched her friend's hand inside her own hot and dry one. Claudette, uncomfortable with the direction of the conversation, demurred.

"No, you must listen to me. Claudette, I love you second only to Marguerite. I would die a happy woman if I thought that she would go into your keeping. Swear to me that you will treat her as your own. Bring her into the doll shop as you brought me." Béatrice's eyes were becoming glazed. She gripped Claudette's hand tightly. "Swear it!"

"Dear friend, you need have no worries on that score. Marguerite is like a daughter to me, and she will have everything you might have ever wished for her. In fact, I shall make her the inheritress of the shop." Claudette brushed back the hair from Béatrice's face and kissed her forehead. "Now rest and get well, so that we need have no more of this talk."

Béatrice closed her eyes to sleep, a peaceful smile on her face and the lines of worry erased from around her eyes. She awoke only two more times over the next few days, once in a delirium in which she asked for more soap to finish the laundry, and then once more, crying out for Alexandre. She passed away quietly on April 10, 1793.

Béatrice was buried on an achingly beautiful day, in a grave next to Joseph Cummings. Blinking into the sunshine as Reverend Daniels droned on at the grave site, Claudette thought that it was just the sort of day Béatrice might twitter on about—the warmth of the sun, the smell of honeysuckle wafting in the air, the happiness of children playing in the parks. How Claudette would miss that irritating twittering. William felt her shudder, and pulled her close.

Next to her, Marguerite stared dully into space, hearing and seeing nothing. She would not allow Claudette to touch her, and took little food, having remained secluded in the room Claudette and William gave her in their town home. Mrs. Jenkins, also present at the funeral, along with all of the doll shop employees, was in the process of packing Béatrice and Marguerite's belongings so they could be brought to her new home.

Jolie had thrown up her hands in frustration. "Madame, she will not allow me to dress her, or even comb her hair."

"She will come around. She has just lost her beloved mother. Have patience, Jolie."

Marguerite emerged from her room only to go to the funeral. Her drawn face was devoid of cosmetics or color, and her dark hair lay limply around her face. She wore a gray dress that looked like a sack around her frame, which hinted of emaciation. *In a few more days,* Claudette thought, *I will have to force her to eat something nourishing.*

Claudette tried to return her attention to the minister, who was talking about God's infallible grace. She saw a movement just outside her range of vision and turned her head. Standing inside a copse of trees nearby was Nicholas Ashby. He didn't realize Claudette had seen him. His gaze was intent on Marguerite. What was he doing here? How had he heard about Béatrice? She nudged Marguerite slightly, and nodded in Nicholas's direction. The girl frowned and shook her head angrily, as though resentful of an intrusion into her misery.

Following the funeral, William, Claudette, and Marguerite returned home and retired to the rear portico to sit in the warm sunshine. Claudette urged Marguerite to take some tea, which the girl did, and the three of them reminisced about Béatrice. An hour later, a house servant appeared to announce a guest, Mr. Nicholas Ashby.

Marguerite bristled again at the sight of him. He joined the threesome for tea, and added his own remembrances of Béatrice to the conversation. He confessed his crush on the former Ashby house servant. His mother had sarcastically mentioned the passing of "the half-wit servant," which she had heard about from Emily Harrison, who had it from the Radleys, whose housekeeper was a second cousin to one of the Greycliffes' servants.

When quick-traveling word had reached Nicholas, he made it his business to find out the details of the funeral so he could come and pay his respects.

"Well, we welcome you with pleasure," said William.

Nicholas blushed at the older man's acceptance.

Claudette could see Marguerite softening slightly at Nicholas's admiration of Béatrice.

"So you were in love with my mother?" she asked.

"Well, that was years ago, when I was just a boy. But I have always remembered her fondly."

Claudette added, "Nicholas was always our ally in the Ashby household. In fact, he was the one who made sure you had medicine when you had that fever."

"He did? I hardly remember being sick at all. I just remember the Mr. and Mrs. Ashby dolls you gave me afterward." She actually emitted a small giggle. Claudette threw William an optimistic look.

"I remember those dolls, as well, although I'm afraid I was much more focused on your mother at the time," said Nicholas. "Do you still have them?"

"I do. Our landlady is packing everything up"—Marguerite's face darkened momentarily—"to be moved here. I will be dividing my time between here and Hevington."

"Perhaps I can return here next week to see them?" His voice was hopeful.

"All right." Marguerite was noncommittal, but she self-consciously brushed her hair from her face.

Nicholas returned exactly a week later, his vest and breeches crisply pressed. From a second-story window, William and Claudette watched him hand his horse's reins to the groom and bound up to the entrance of the house.

"He's very well-groomed for a visit to play with dolls, isn't he?" Claudette laughed from behind the curtain where she was concealing herself.

"Well, I suppose he will have an easier time of things than I did with you, you stubborn wench." William caught her about the waist and nuzzled her neck.

Claudette pretended outrage. "Whatever do you mean, sir? I have ever been a proper lady."

"Indeed," he said drily. "A veritable paragon of womanly acquiescence."

Nicholas continued visiting regularly over the next several months, making his interest and intentions toward Marguerite clear. His attentions brought Marguerite's spirits quickly out of their black depths. She soon spoke of her mother in fond terms rather than in self-pity, and her eyes regained their sparkle.

᭰ 38 ᭰

Marie Antoinette lived in a suspended state after the death of her husband. Rumors floated to her that she would be exiled, or sent back to her native Austria, but sitting in her cold quarters, she knew the truth: She would never be leaving Paris, and she would never be freed.

On July 3, her son was taken from her, despite her bitter protestations. According to her jailers, he needed his own quarters so that he could be trained as a man instead of lodging with a bunch of silly women. But night after night she could hear him crying in some distant part of the fortress. No one would tell her anything about him. So she pined away for her lost country, her husband, and her son. She had not seen Alex since the botched flight from the Tuileries, and she hoped he would not foolishly attempt to see her, since her friends tended to meet with ghastly demises. Perhaps he had already returned to Sweden permanently. His safety was more important than her own anymore.

Her hair went completely white, but there was no one but the princesse royale, Madame Elisabeth, and disrespectful jailers to notice anyway. Her days were spent staring vacantly through a window at a walled courtyard below.

Marie Antoinette knew that it was just a matter of time before she was brought to an illegal trial with a predetermined outcome, just like her husband.

* * *

The inevitable occurred on August 2. Representatives from the Assembly came to escort her to her third home in under four years: the Conciergerie, a women's prison on the Ile de la Cité. She was to be housed there to await her trial date, while her daughter and Madame Elisabeth were to remain in the Temple.

"Of what am I accused?" she demanded of her captors, a small flicker of her old spirit emerging and dying quickly like a match.

"Treason. Instigating food shortages. Unseemly acts with other women. Take your pick, Widow Capet." Since Louis's death, she had become known by this moniker, which referred to Hugh Capet, the first king of France. She shrugged it off as she had had to shrug off every insult and slander heaped upon her.

She was transferred to the prison without complaint, even when they showed her to one of the worst cells in the prison, located in the basement, with only one small, filthy window so high up on the wall it was impossible to see out of and provided little light. The room contained a cot, a small writing table and chair, and a dressing screen. Behind this screen the queen placed the single valise of personal belongings she had been allowed to bring. She was permitted an attendant by the name of Rosalie Lamorlière, who quickly became devoted to the sad but sweet dethroned monarch.

"Thank you, my dear," said the queen graciously when Rosalie first appeared. "But as you can see, my living circumstances really preclude my need for assistance."

Still Rosalie chose to tend to her, trying vainly to get the queen to eat hot food, which was mostly rejected, and protecting her modesty from prying eyes. The guards were allowing people to come in and, for a small fee, stare at the jailed monarch as though she were a caged animal. In addition, some of the guards took their instructions to "keep an eye on the Widow Capet at all times" to an extreme, not allowing her privacy to change her soiled personal linens. The dressing screen provided little privacy. Her polite requests for time alone were met with derision.

At night she had her only solitary peace. The gawking spectators were gone, Rosalie would return to her parents' home, and the guard on duty would fall asleep at his post.

The queen sighed as she sat at her rickety, unpainted table, nicked and gouged from years of frustrated prisoners etching names and words of grief in the wood. She was permitted one tallow candle at a time, and she savored the light as she unwrapped some writing paper and dipped her pen in ink to begin writing letters to whatever friends and family she had left. Propped on the table next to her was her de Lamballe doll, which had been a source of comfort to her since the royal family's confinement had started in the Tuileries. Twice now the doll had nearly been forgotten or left behind, but fortunately she had not lost it. The doll, some writing materials, a change of clothes, and a few trinkets of memorabilia were all she had been able to pack to bring with her to the Conciergerie. Rosalie asked about it.

"Madame, why do you have the little *poupée* with you here?"

"No reason at all, I suppose. It merely reminds me of what was, and is no more."

The young girl, unaware of much of what had happened to the queen, looked puzzled, but said nothing else. She seemed to realize, though, that the doll was important to the queen, and ensured that the guards never saw it, lest they deem it a subversive item and take it from her. The queen pulled the doll from her small trunk each night and either propped it up on the table as she wrote letters, or hugged it close to her on her uncomfortable cot each night, putting it away each dawn as a small trickle of sunlight tried to force its way into the room, and prior to the guards and onlookers beginning anew their mental torture of the dethroned queen.

Paris
December 15, 1793

My Dearest Claudette,
I am so sorry to hear of your dear friend's illness and subsequent passing. It is always grievous to lose someone you cherish. She had a daughter, did she not? Although presumably she is nearly an adult by now.
Since I last wrote you, France has passed into what can only be described as terror. In fact, I think the newly

installed government intends it to be so. The last year has been so horrifying that probably you will think I have lost my reason when I tell you of it.

The royal family was removed to the Temple, located near the Tuileries Palace. The queen always hated the Temple, with its imposing walls and rounded turrets. Yet here she was unceremoniously discarded with her family.

You know that the dear Princesse de Lamballe was executed—should I say brutally murdered—at the hands of the mob while you were both imprisoned at La Force. What you may not know is that that same mob brought her head to me to be dressed. I protested fiercely, but they threatened my life if I did not clean her face and arrange her hair. I was also required to make a wax model of her head. It was far worse than when this happened with the governor of the Bastille. My hands shook so badly that I continuously dropped my tools, and the urge to be sick was overwhelming. I had no idea they were carrying the princess to the Temple. If I had, I might have preferred death at their hands than to know the anxiety it was to cause the poor queen. But it all matters not anymore.

By now you have learned that the king was put on trial for treason against the nation of France. A more ridiculous charge could not have been made, as Louis XVI cared only for the people, however ineffectual he may have been. He went to the guillotine resolutely and confidently. One would think the madness, the craving for blood, would have stopped there, but no.

They put our dearest friend the queen on trial as well, on October 14. They accused her of the most vile acts, including indecent acts with other women, and, worst of all, with her son. When she stood there, stunned, and did not immediately respond to the charge, she was pressed for a response.

"Nature itself shudders at such an accusation made to a mother. I appeal to all mothers who may be present!"

Even the market-women in the courtroom, who have

been so vehement in their hate toward our queen, were filled with sympathy. What a heinous lot of beasts to make such an accusation.

The rest of the trial, which lasted until eleven o'clock on the first evening with only one short break, and all of the next day, produced nothing. The brave queen resolutely refuted anything that was put to her, and, of course, they had no proof of anything.

She was questioned regarding everything from the flight attempt from the Tuileries to whose locks of hair she had brought to the Conciergerie in little packets. They were from her husband and children. It was a pathetic attempt at defaming an innocent mother and wife who had already been brought so low.

It was also a disgrace of a trial in that the public learned later that the monster Hébert had already given the Convention a command: "I must have the head of Antoinette."

In the early morning hours of October 16, she was declared guilty of a variety of crimes against the nation and sentenced to death. You have probably already read in the English papers of her calm reception of the news, and subsequent bravery before the guillotine. I still weep over the unjust treatment of that poor lady.

And so now the Convention acts with impunity. If a monarch can be executed with flimsy evidence, what chance does anyone else who goes against their wishes have? You only experienced the beginning of their madness, dear girl. People are now brought to the execution platform in droves, for real crimes or those imagined. What will happen to France?

Under separate cover I have sent you the de Lamballe doll that you made for the queen. She had her prison attendant take it away with a letter to the princesse royale prior to her execution, asking her daughter to keep the doll safe. The doll was one of the only items the queen took with her in her imprisonment. The princesse came to me with it,

318   *Christine Trent*

*and I advised her that the rightful owner of the doll now
was you. Please keep it dear to your heart, as a
remembrance of our tragic friend and queen.*
>   *Ever your friend,*
>   *Marie Grosholtz*

Several days later, the package arrived. The doll's gown was in disarray, dirty in spots and torn a bit along the hem. The diamond earrings and other valuable trimmings had been hastily torn off. She was missing a shoe and her hair needed to be arranged, but Claudette could put most of the damage aright.

Little Josephina, what stories could you tell me about your mistress? she wondered.

❧ 39 ❧

London, October 1794. Marguerite was now accompanying Claudette on buying trips for doll supplies. Claudette enjoyed the young girl's enthusiasm and verve, and her natural eye for color. Béatrice's daughter also had a gregarious nature that her mother had never possessed, and she easily learned how to charm vendors and negotiate the best deals possible. They, in turn, loved her engaging personality, and frequently confused her as being Claudette's sister.

Claudette was gradually focusing solely on designing custom dolls for a limited number of select clients, and allowing Marguerite to take care of more of the overall operations. Roger was her trusted man in the shop, supervising the daily work schedule.

No one was surprised when Nicholas proposed marriage to Marguerite, first asking for William's permission, which was gladly granted. No one, that is, other than Maude Ashby, whose rage reached all the way to Hevington. She sent a letter to Claudette demanding to see her. Claudette courteously invited her to tea at Hevington.

Maude entered the house and, despite herself, was impressed by its grace and beauty. Remembering her mission, she sat down in the drawing room and opened the discussion.

"As you must realize, Claudette—"

"Lady Greycliffe. The king has granted William the rank of baron."

Mrs. Ashby reddened. "Lady Greycliffe, then. I am in a *most* difficult position. Mr. Ashby and I are naturally very pleased that Nicholas should be marrying the ward of so fine a gentleman as William Greycliffe. However, her unfortunate mother's *history* suggests that she may not be quite suitable. Plus the girl is involved in such a common trade. That and the fact that William—Lord Greycliffe—has married, well, quite frankly, a bit beneath him. Really, the scandal of it has been quite the talk of society."

Claudette smiled slowly. "Mrs. Ashby, the only talk in society is of what a beautiful bride Marguerite will be. We are delighted to welcome Nicholas into our family, despite his harridan of a mother, and we expect that you will welcome Marguerite into yours. Of course, we are looking forward to having the lovely couple at our home for our society events, and since you are so displeased with the marriage arrangement, we will make certain to leave you off the guest lists to avoid offending your sensibilities." She stood to indicate that the conversation was finished. She could see the other woman making furious mental calculations.

Maude sputtered, "Well, now, just a moment, I did not think about . . . certainly I would never wish to . . . Lady Greycliffe, I am sure Mr. Ashby and I would be honored to be guests at any of your fine soirées."

"Indeed, I am sure you would. Good day, Mrs. Ashby." Claudette left the room, and the housekeeper escorted her guest out. That evening, she and William sent word offering Nicholas the use of their Vauxhall town house as his residence until the wedding, which he gratefully accepted.

Marguerite strove to learn everything she could about dollmaking. Roger showed her the different types of wood, and how to apply varying levels of carving pressure, depending upon wood softness and the depth of impression to be left.

Claudette gave her instruction in how to make doll molds, and how to pour wax into them at just the right temperature, leaving them to set until just the right moment to break the mold apart. Working with wax was an ongoing struggle for Marguerite, but a process she was determined to master.

Together, Claudette and the shop's seamstress, Agnes, showed her the procedure for clothing design, with Claudette giving over her store of sketches for future reference and Agnes teaching her how to make miniature patterns. Marguerite had already become an expert seamstress under her mother's tutelage.

Claudette and the young woman were soon working side by side in the shop, designing new *grandes Pandores*. Together they would work far into the night together on one of their new creations to be custom built for one of London's elite.

In time, Claudette began spending less time working, sometimes feeling almost unneeded, so well run was the shop now. On one occasion, she entered the shop to have Marguerite look up and say, "Why, Aunt Claudette, I didn't know you were coming today. Honestly, I'm not sure what there is for you to do."

She shook her head ruefully, knowing that she had wanted to extricate herself from the daily operations of the shop, but missing the regular thrill of holding up a finished creation and having its recipient gasp with pleasure. How life changes, she thought, in ways we can never expect.

❧ 40 ❧

September 1795. Marguerite had gone on a shopping trip for her trousseau, and Claudette had eagerly returned to run the shop for several days. At the end of one day, she closed the door behind the final customer, and threw the bolt to lock it, breathing deeply. Two elderly women, rich and demanding, had tested Claudette's nerves to the breaking point earlier. They were completely unsatisfied with any samples she showed them, nor could she entice them with rough sketches contained in the shop's portfolio. The women were sisters, and their great-niece, little Bonnie or Betty or whatever the tiresome child's name was, simply must have the nicest, most elegant, frankly my dear, the most *expensive* doll to celebrate reaching her eleventh birthday. Shaking her head at the memory, Claudette finished tidying up the shop.

As she was stacking up all of the drawings she had hauled out in her attempt to satisfy the aunts, she heard a scratching at the door followed by a loud thump. Knowing that she was alone in the shop, Claudette hesitated, then approached the window next to the door. Huddled outside was what appeared to be an old vagrant woman, her hair long, matted, and dull brown streaked with white. She was wearing a dress that may have once been a mauve silk, but was now filthy, tattered, and entirely too large for the woman's emaciated frame. Beneath a stained and dirty headscarf, she was shaking violently and attempting to stand up. The effort was too much, and she collapsed back into a heap.

Claudette unlocked the door's bolt and cautiously opened the door. The old woman slowly looked up at her, her eyes vacant with near blindness.

"Claudette? Is that you?" whispered the quivering wraith. Claudette bent down to help the woman up. She was nearly weightless. She brought the old woman into the shop and made her comfortable in a chair. Claudette hurriedly made tea, and brought it, along with biscuits, to her sickly guest, gently putting the cup to her lips, and pressing the food into her hand. The woman ate and drank greedily for a moment, then pushed Claudette away.

"No, please, stop. I must t-t-talk to you." The woman looked directly into Claudette's eyes and offered a familiar, lopsided grin, showing a mouthful of rotting teeth and reddened gums. Beneath her lower lip was an oozing sore caked with dried pus and blood. Claudette drew back at the sudden realization of who this bedraggled, ancient creature was. Lizbit.

"I loved him, Claudette, truly. But it was no use. He never loved me, and I know it now.

"I met Jean-Philippe during one of my visits to see my aunt, before she died. I first saw him making a speech at Luxembourg Gardens. He was a man beyond all others: passionate about his beliefs, passionate in love, strikingly handsome. But you know this. I swear, at first I did not know that he was your betrothed from childhood. But when we realized we had you in common, it was too late. He possessed my soul. I, of course, possessed my aunt's fortune to help in his cause, and he convinced me that the cause of the revolutionaries was true and just, that the time for monarchs was finished, and that he needed my help. Help him? I would have slit the queen's throat personally for him.

"We lived together in his apartment. His landlord frowned upon us as an unmarried couple, but what did I care? I loved him so much, and I knew he was going to be a great man in the new government. I would have done anything—*anything*—to make sure he achieved his goals.

"Jean-Philippe became a close confidant of Robespierre. He believed everything Robespierre had to say about his concept of Virtue, and that elimination of the monarchy had to be accomplished through blood and fire. I got swept away with the idea, too. When Jean-Philippe told me you were trying to help Louis and Marie Antoinette get out of the country, I was more than willing to believe it was true."

Lizbit paused, wiping her grimy face with her grimier sleeve. Claudette offered a handkerchief, but it only resulted in moving dirt around on her face. Lizbit resumed her story, twisting the handkerchief in her fingers.

"Oh, Claudette, what kind of friend was I? How could I think for a moment that you would do such a thing? Even if you had, how demented had I become that I would permit—no, aid—your arrest and imprisonment?

"But that is what I did. I delivered Jean-Philippe's forged letter from the queen to you. At the time, I was quite ecstatic that you were being punished. Much to my shame, Claudette, please believe me. I cannot dwell on it for long periods—my guilt and anguish are such that I get blinding headaches when I think much about what I have done to you."

Lizbit brought the knotted handkerchief to her nose and blew, which sparked a coughing fit. The coughing opened the wound beneath her lip, and it seeped a trail of vile liquid while she talked.

"I met Jean-Philippe at our apartment right after you were dragged off to La Force. He was fiery that night. I had never seen him so zealously self-righteous. I thought our relationship was becoming even more passionate. I never equated it to his concealed obsession for you." Drops of blood followed behind pus, lightly falling onto Lizbit's lap.

"Jean-Philippe grew in Robespierre's esteem. Soon, Robespierre had him doing private investigations into suspected enemies of the nation. Jean-Philippe had his own staff of soldiers to do his bidding. His position as a former attendant on the queen's staff gave him much knowledge of who was doing what, and which people were royalist sympathizers. At night, he would show me his secret lists of names, and I could always count on seeing them on the newspapers' condemned lists within a few short days. Robespierre forever praised Jean-Philippe's thorough work at identifying traitors, and I knew that Jean-Philippe would be at Robespierre's side when that man took total control of the government. Jean-Philippe would always whisper to me deep in the night of the exalted place I would hold as his partner. He never did make reference to me as his wife, but I overlooked it, so in love with him that I couldn't imagine that he didn't intend to marry me. I didn't understand that he was just exacting his revenge on you with me.

"But things went wrong. Robespierre became obsessed with his idea of Virtue, and began eliminating anyone in his way. His enemies began plotting against him, eventually denouncing him and his followers at the Assembly. Some unknown deputy even demanded Robespierre's arrest.

"Jean-Philippe's end came with Robespierre's. They were seized together last July when Robespierre was at the mayor's house after having delivered one of his speeches to the Convention. There were others grabbed, as well, including that angel of death Saint-Just, and they were imprisoned in the Tuileries. By the time I realized what had happened and could make my way there the following morning, they had both been hauled away to the guillotine. I ran as fast as I could, and got there as they were dragging my beloved up to the platform. He tried to move forward to make a speech to the gathered spectators, but he was quickly drowned out by the shouting and roaring of the crowd. They didn't care about him; they wanted to see Robespierre. Jean-Philippe was yanked back before he could say his last words, and they put him under that damned, infernal blade. I cannot forget the sound of the blade traveling in the channel as it made its way to its target. It is like a carriage rumbling behind horses, the wheels squeaking and protesting, until it stops with a great 'whump.' And then you find that your beloved's head is detached and his body is spewing blood everywhere, and the crowd enjoys it—no, relishes it. They *cheered*, Claudette, to see his head cut off." Lizbit was now sobbing. Claudette thought grimly back to her own near execution, and shuddered.

"Jean-Philippe's body was thrown to the side, and they dragged Robespierre up. Did you know that they don't clean anything before executing the next prisoner? His head is simply placed on the same stinking, bloodied neckhole that the previous victim was on just moments before. Robespierre's jaw was bound up and he was screaming. Someone told me later that he had been shot in the face, but I don't know if he had been shot by guards or had done it to himself. The blade was used as mercilessly on him as it was on my Jean-Philippe just moments before. His body was also tossed aside, as there were more executions to be completed. Spectators ran forward to dip their handkerchiefs in Robespierre's blood dripping from the platform. I asked for Jean-Philippe's body later and arranged for a burial. Some ruffians had dragged his head behind a cart, for blocks. I could not bear to look, and paid a gravedigger to retrieve it and bury it with his body.

"I did not think things could get any worse, but my sins run deep, Claudette, and I realize they must be paid with great misery on my part. I returned to our apartment to grieve. For days I just sat there, curtains pulled tight to prevent any light or life from entering. Eventually I decided that it was time to leave Paris and that existence behind, and went through my things—our things—in preparation to come back to England.

"Imagine my surprise," Lizbit said, her old eyes bunched up in pain, "to find among his possessions a large doll whose head had been broken off. Inside the doll I found a locket with your picture in it, several old letters from you, and a small box containing a ring set with a large emerald surrounded by pearls." She laughed hollowly. "An emerald—green, the people's color. A symbol of all he intended for the future. And this ring was for *you*, Claudette, not me. Never me. All of his talk about having me at his side when the citizens would rule was just his consideration for my feelings. Always he had memories of you tucked away nearby. How often do you imagine he thought of you, Claudette? His true love who had forsaken him? He put you in jail, all the while telling me he hated you for your role in serving the queen and not the people. I wonder how he even slept at night while you were rotting away in La

Force. And I! Well, what a fine friend I was. A liar, a betrayer, and a fraud."

Claudette interrupted. "Lizbit, please, it is over and done with. It doesn't matter to me. Don't—"

Lizbit pretended not to hear her protestations. "I left Paris and came back to London, where I began my repentance in earnest. Since I had given all my money to Jean-Philippe, I was nearly penniless. I found myself engaged in service with Simon Briggs. You remember him, don't you? Now I was also a whore. He placed me first in one of the city's finer brothels, but the customers didn't like me. I was pretty enough, but I talked back too much and wouldn't do anything too perverse. Soon the madam threw me out, and Simon had to move me to a lower-class section of town, where the customers didn't hesitate to clop me across the head if I talked much beyond 'Aren't you a handsome one?' and 'That'll be three quid.' I lost my looks. My hair seemed to go gray overnight, my teeth soon followed, and I'm pretty sure I contracted the French pox somewhere along the way. I took to drink, the only refuge from my slatternly existence. Simon refused to keep up my wardrobe since I did not earn as much as the other sluts, and I was eventually left with just this dress." She held up the hem. "This was once a fine gown, even if it was just a dress that a customer gave me because his wife didn't want it anymore.

"When I finally wasn't even able to attract more than a few customers each week, down on the docks where they aren't too picky, Simon hauled me to his rooms one day, enjoyed me, then beat me within an inch of my life and pushed me through his bedroom window to the ground below. I still have glass embedded in my arms and legs, and my lip has never healed from the infection I received from the ground glass that got in my mouth. I prayed that God would let me die there, but He must have had other plans for me, because I continued to live. That was when I knew I had to come to you, Claudette, and seek your forgiveness.

"I wandered about for several days, hungry and crazed from lack of wine. I could not remember where you were in the city. I found a convent. The nuns there took me in, and I tried to get better. It was no use; I'm too ill. I left there, and found my way to you here today."

Lizbit reached out and gripped Claudette's hand in her own feverish one. "Claudette, Claudette, please forgive me. Forgive me for being so selfish and faithless." Her eyes, though almost sightless, were becoming bright.

Claudette patted Lizbit's clutching hand with her free one. "Lizbit, all is well. I forgive you. Please don't let it trouble you further. What we need to do now is make you better." She led Lizbit through the workshop to a small room set up for workers who periodically needed to stay overnight. Tucking Lizbit under the quilt, she told her friend, "We don't need to talk of this again. Promise me you will try to get better. Tomorrow I will send for a doctor."

Lizbit looked at her again with sightless eyes and pawed at Claudette's dress. Grabbing hold, she whispered, "It is too late. Too late. What I have done is unforgivable. I have to pay my penance with my life. Here—" Lizbit reached into the folds of her dress and pulled out a small wrapped parcel which she pushed into Claudette's hand. "This is for you. My sin offering."

Claudette put the parcel on the nightstand and bent down to wipe Lizbit's face with a damp cloth. "Lizbit, just sleep now. In the morning things will seem much better. When you're well, we will go shopping and buy you ten new dresses and satin slippers to match." She sat and held Lizbit's hand until her breathing settled into that of the sleeping. From the bed Claudette reached over and unwrapped the parcel.

Inside were the locket and emerald ring.

Early the next morning, Claudette checked in on her once sharp and witty friend. Lizbit was dead.

EPILOGUE

Hevington became home to a thriving family. Edward was born in 1797, followed by Rebecca in 1798, and finally Elizabeth, nicknamed Little Bitty, at the turn of the new century. William and Claudette had one of their rare disagreements when naming Little Bitty. Claudette insisted that Lizbit be honored by it, and William was just as insistent that she not be. Little Bitty, though, quickly became her father's darling, demonstrating none of the tragic flaws of her namesake.

Marguerite and Nicholas married, and rented the Greycliffes' London residence until they saved enough money to purchase their own home. Marguerite happily accepted Nicholas's faithful and constant nature, and she returned it in kind. Even strangers on the street were struck by how devoted the young Ashby couple was, walking arm in arm everywhere they went. Maude Ashby, crushed in her game of social ascension, had finally yielded to the fact of their marriage and had even taken some interest in helping them decorate their new home.

Marguerite gradually took over much of the day-to-day operations of the doll shop. Frequently, she and Claudette could be seen together in the Hevington drawing room or in the Greycliffes' London home, heads bent over a new doll design, or sorting through a trunk of the latest wildly tinted fabrics from Paris. As much as Claudette Greycliffe loved being a mother and wife, she still felt a thrill when Marguerite arrived at the door with a bundle of rolled drawings in her arms.

Upon Claudette's advice, Marguerite expanded the business to include the sale of baby houses and their accessories. To fund this expansion, Claudette sold the town house she had purchased from Mrs. Jenkins, whose health had forced her to move in with relatives on the balmy, developing shores of Brighton.

Sales of the baby houses also led to the creation of families of dolls to fill them, all of them made from wood and jointed just like the larger fashion dolls. The wealthy women who ordered these dolls' houses would ask for a set of dolls made to resemble their own families. A purchase of a single dollhouse could represent many sales for the C. Laurent Fashion Doll Shop, in terms of miniature furniture, carpets, silver pieces, linens, and now doll families.

Jack Smythe, as clever as always, had invested most of the money he had made through his association with Claudette's doll-making business. When he had saved enough money, he left the Ashby household in the middle of the night, and opened his own tavern. He met and married a girl from Northumberland, and they ran the tavern and its attached inn together quite successfully. Together they raised six boisterous young boys.

Marie Grosholtz remained a good friend, visiting mostly through correspondence. She married François Tussaud in 1795 after her own stint in a prison as a guest of the French revolutionaries. Together they had two boys, Joseph and Francis. By the tone of her letters, it was obvious that the marriage was not a happy one. However, Marie continued her work with wax sculpting, and had in fact developed a traveling show in 1802, which saw her wax figures being shown all over England, Ireland, and Scotland. Marie's letters were always peppered with amusing stories of People of Quality who would visit her showcase, gawping open-mouthed in astonishment.

William and Claudette took a trip to London once to visit Madame Tussaud at her waxworks exhibition, which had made a stop in England's capital. They were intrigued by the realistic work she was doing with the life-sized figures. Most fascinating was a figure of a woman that lay on a reclining couch, her arm across her forehead in repose. Upon closer examination, they could see that the woman appeared to be breathing. Claudette uttered a spontaneous "Oh my!" and Marie laughed in her sharp, bird-like way.

"Do you like it? This is Madame du Barry, favorite of King Louis XV. She may have met her end at the blade like so many others—oh, sorry, my dear—but she lives on here in wax."

Marie offered to do a wax model of Claudette, promising to add it to her special exhibit on the Revolution, which already contained the death masks of Louis XVI, Marie Antoinette, Jean-Paul Marat, and Robespierre. Claudette politely declined. She had enough unspeakable memories of that interlude without a permanent reminder of her horror set up as a public spectacle.

They had no communication from anyone else surrounding the Revolutionary period except for Roger Wickham, the La Force guard that had helped William save Claudette. As a gesture of respect toward his patron, Roger and his wife Simone settled in Kent near the town of Sittingbourne, and each Christmastide he would send the Greycliffes containers of high-grade cream.

Claudette kept the de Lamballe doll in the room at Hevington where William had proposed to her. She had a special locking case made for it to keep light and dust off it. She rarely went into the room.

For Claudette, life became an endless series of joyful and contented moments. Only when she was seated alone in Hevington's gazebo with a book or a piece of embroidery in hand would she allow the memories of Jean-Philippe, La Force, and poor Queen Marie Antoinette to seep into her consciousness. How quickly her body became rigid, reliving that period of death and destruction. She would just as quickly forget the past when one of her children came to show Mama what interesting trick the pet spaniel had just learned, or when her beloved William came looking for her, always seeking a kiss and a gentle caress of her cheek. Life for the orphaned little French dollmaker had turned out gratifyingly well.

AFTERWORD

Although most of the characters in this novel are of my own creation, quite a few are also historical personages. I have attempted to place them in my story in ways that are believable, and within the context of true historical events, but to my knowledge there was never an actual plot to get Louis XVI and Marie Antoinette out of France by means of a doll conspiracy!

Marie Grosholtz, later Madame Tussaud, was a protégé of Dr. Philippe Curtius, a doctor skilled at modeling wax to create anatomical figures. These subjects led to portraiture, which soon became more lucrative than his medical career. Dr. Curtius taught Marie the techniques of wax sculpting from an early age, and she became so proficient in wax portraiture that she was soon making figures of many of the prominent people of the era, such as the writer Voltaire and the U.S. statesman Benjamin Franklin. In those days, wax portrait figures were rather like the movies and TV of today—people knew the names of the famous and infamous people of the time, but didn't know how they looked, so were intrigued enough to pay to see their wax portrait figures. Soon Dr. Curtius had a traveling exhibition.

It wasn't long before Marie's skills came to the attention of Louis XVI's sister, Madame Elisabeth, and Marie was invited to live at Versailles to help in Madame Elisabeth's artistic education. Marie spent nine years at court and while there she created figures of Louis XVI and his family.

Marie was in fact forced to dress the newly piked head of the Princesse de Lamballe, and to create death masks for Marie Antoinette and Louis XVI. She also made death masks for Robespierre, Jean-Paul Marat and other prominent figures, including the Bastille's governor, de Launay. Like so many others, Marie spent time in prison during the Revolution, but was released just before her scheduled execution. Dr. Curtius died shortly after the Revolution, and she took over the exhibition they had established.

After marrying François Tussaud, she took her exhibition on tour for thirty years across Great Britain, eventually settling her growing wax collection in a spot near where it is presently located. You can still see the death masks for King Louis XVI, Queen Marie Antoinette, and Robespierre at the Madame Tussaud's exhibition on Marylebone Road in London. The oldest piece in the collection is an animatronic of Jeanne du Barry, a favorite mistress of France's King Louis XV. Really, it is well worth a trip to London just to go to this museum.

Count Axel Fersen was indeed a special friend of Marie Antoinette's. Were they actual lovers? Many historians think so, but I am not certain Marie Antoinette was of a temperament to engage in an actual illicit affair. She was well aware of her position in life as mother to the heir of the throne. However, it is certainly possible that an affair occurred, and there are incriminating letters left behind that suggest it was a physical relationship. Fersen did travel to England during the time I placed him, and he was goggled at by the smart English, who nicknamed him "The Picture" for his handsome looks. In 1810, seventeen years after the death of the queen, Fersen was torn to bits by a mob. The count had incurred the wrath of the Swedish crowd at the funeral procession of Christian, heir to the throne of Denmark. The mob was incited to believe that he had poisoned Christian. It was a fate he had often predicted for Marie Antoinette.

The Princesse de Lamballe was one of the queen's dearest friends, and most certainly was not her lover, much as the harsh royal critics of the time wanted to portray her as such. I consider her one of the most tragic figures of the time, because she truly was without guile, and her devotion and loyalty to her king and queen are unquestioned. Her fate with the mob at La Force prison was as described in the story. On the day of her death, there were general massacres in prisons across Paris. Around 1,300 prisoners were killed, not including similar killings that went on at Versailles and Rheims.

Marie-Jeanne Rose Bertin was Marie Antoinette's chief dressmaker, and became the first celebrated French fashion designer. Under the queen's generous patronage, Bertin was able to charge very high prices for her fashions: her gowns and headdresses would easily cost twenty times what a skilled worker of the time earned in a year. During the French Revolution, with many of her noble customers fleeing abroad, Bertin moved her business to London. She eventually returned to France, where Josephine de Beauharnais became a customer, but there was little demand for Bertin's excessive fashions of the *ancien régime*. She died in 1813.

As opposed to many others in the Revolution, who sought rebellion for their own personal gain, **Maximilien Robespierre** was a true believer in the cause. He saw the Terror impersonally, as a method of implementing "Virtue." In an ironic moment of justice, he experienced the same fate as so many he had condemned. He was dragged to the guillotine in July 1794, in a drunken stupor and in acute pain from a shattered jaw resulting from an apparently self-inflicted gunshot wound. It was he who wrote into law "Any individual who usurps the nation's sovereignty shall be immediately put to death by free men," and it was on this basis that he was executed.

Cordelier leader **Jean-Paul Marat** was a vicious journalist who used his extremist newspaper, *L'Ami du Peuple*, to fan the flames of hatred against anyone he deemed to hold too much power, whether they be royalists, the courts, or Girondists. He was stabbed to death in July 1793 by Charlotte Corday, a Girondist sympathizer.

The locksmith **François Gamain, Governor de Launay, Madame de Tourzel,** her daughter **Pauline, Jeanne de la Motte, Cardinal Rohan,** the jewelers **Boehmer and Bassenge,** and the dollmaker **Pierotti** were also real persons. **John Sackville, the third Duke of Dorset,** his mistress, **Giovanna Baccelli,** and her subsequent protector, **Henry Herbert, the tenth Earl of Pembroke,** were quite the scandal of late-eighteenth-century Kent.

The guillotine was first proposed as a preferred execution device by Dr. Joseph-Ignace Guillotin. A physician and humanitarian, he was disturbed by the vulgarity of public executions and petitioned for a single method of capital punishment to be used for all crimes demanding the death sentence. The device was viewed as dispatching its victims with "swiftness and decency." It wasn't until after 1792 that it was adopted and nicknamed "Madame

Guillotine" for its sponsor. During the Terror, it is estimated that an astonishing 40,000 people were killed: 17,000 with trial, 12,000 without a trial, and thousands more perished in prisons. The guillotine was used until 1981, when France abolished capital punishment.

The Terror came quickly to a close with Robespierre's death. Riots in the spring of 1795 were now easily crushed by the National Guard, which gained control of the Convention. A new constitution was drafted, which placed the executive in the hands of a directory of five men. Before the directory was even in place, thousands of royalists marched on the Tuileries Palace to protest the new constitution. The regular army was called in for protection, and a young Corsican artillery captain named Napoleon Bonaparte was summoned to lead them. Bonaparte's quick handling of the rebellion would propel him into the limelight, and begin yet another chapter of French and English history.

SELECTED BIBLIOGRAPHY

I am indebted to a great number of historical references I have read over the years pertaining to Marie Antoinette and the era spanning her reign and that of the Terror. Listed below are the books that became permanent fixtures on my desk while writing this book.

Dobson, Austin. *Four Frenchwomen*. London: Chatto and Windus, 1890.

Editors. *Horizon Magazine. The French Revolution*. New York: Harper and Row, 1965.

Fraser, Antonia. *Marie Antoinette: The Journey*. New York: Doubleday, 2001.

Genet, Jeanne Louise Henriette (Madame Campan). *Memoirs of Marie Antoinette*. New York: P. F. Collier and Son, 1910.

Hearsey, John E. N. *Marie Antoinette*. New York: E. P. Dutton and Co., 1973.

Hyde, Catherine (Ed.). *Secret Memoirs of Princesse Lamballe: Her Confidential Relations with Marie Antoinette*. 1901.

Loomis, Stanley. *The Fatal Friendship*. New York: Doubleday, 1972.

Pilkington, Iain D. B. *Queen of the Trianon*. London: Jarrolds; Akron: St. Dunstan Society, 1955.

Schama, Simon. *Citizens*. New York: Alfred A. Knopf, 1989.

THE QUEEN'S DOLLMAKER

Christine Trent

ABOUT THIS GUIDE

The suggested questions are included
to enhance your group's reading
of Christine Trent's
The Queen's Dollmaker.

DISCUSSION QUESTIONS

1. What were your assumptions about the use and manufacture of dolls during the book's time period? What surprised you about dollmaking in the eighteenth century?

2. Do you think Claudette made a bad decision to go back to Paris for a second time to visit Marie Antoinette? What positive outcomes were there as a result of this visit?

3. Why was Jean-Philippe willing to imprison—and even approve of a death sentence for—his long-lost love, Claudette? Were his motives pure? In other words, did he believe in what he was doing, or was he merely angry at Claudette for rejecting him? Did you feel sympathy for Jean-Philippe? Would he have been less inclined to join the revolutionaries had Claudette returned to Paris and married him?

4. What factors in England and France during the time period of the novel made it difficult for women to learn a trade and become successful entrepreneurs? Where did tradesmen fit into the social hierarchy of English society? How did those social factors affect Claudette's ability to start, maintain, and grow her business?

5. For centuries the English appear to have had a love-hate relationship with the French, mistrusting them on the one hand, and following their fashions and their trends on the other. This was apparently at play when Mrs. Ashby wanted to impress her guests with a French maid. What skills (besides dollmaking) and personality traits did Claudette possess that helped her maintain her "elevated" position while in the employ of the Ashby family? How did those skills and traits help her in the growth of her doll business, and then through her ordeal in a French prison?

6. Was Count Fersen acting maliciously toward Claudette when he concocted the idea to use her dolls to smuggle valuables to the king and queen of France? Why did he think this was a good plan for helping the monarchs?

7. How do you think Marie Grosholtz's experiences in the days leading up to the Revolution affected her future plans for a wax museum?

8. Compare and contrast William and Jean-Philippe. In what ways did they make poor decisions regarding Claudette? What was each man's greatest show of love for her?

9. Did William's position as someone favored by the king— but not yet made part of the peerage—make it more socially acceptable for him to fall in love with a tradeswoman? Would Claudette's trade itself, dollmaking, have been more acceptable to the upper ranks than, say, that of household servant, actress, or dressmaker?

10. What were Lizbit's real motives for everything she did to Claudette? Do you think her suffering at the end of the novel provided redemption for her activities?

11. What was the socioeconomic environment in France that caused the French Revolution? Could a convergence of such circumstances cause a similar political reaction in today's world, or does the election system of a democratic society such as that of the U.S.'s give the populace enough voice to preclude such an upheaval?

12. Why do you think the revolutionaries were determined to execute their king and queen? Was it a personal vendetta against them, or did they represent something undesirable? Or was there another reason?